THE MEDAL SUPER EDITION
RIDE THE PANTHER

PACER WOLF McQUEEN—As unpredictable as a summer cloudburst, as quick and violent as a panther, the red-haired Choctaw Kid had a woman to look after, a shame to live down, and a battle to fight.

JESSE REDBOW McQUEEN—He was appointed Territorial Ranger to hold the Indian Territories together in the face of war. But a "friend" with a traitor's heart wants to see Jesse's mission fail—and the McQueen men dead, by fair fight or by treachery.

RAVEN McQUEEN—She was a medicine woman, a healer. Now she must try to heal the rift between brothers, the grandsons she had raised to honor the legacy of the medal.

LORELEI—Lithe, beautiful, and hard-bitten, she was used to using men to gain what she wanted. But when she was saved by Pacer from a brutal lover, she would learn what the McQueen name meant—and the power of courage and commitment.

CAP FEATHERSTONE—Ben McQueen had ridden and fought by his side and would trust the big man with his life. But Featherstone had interests he'd never revealed to Ben, which wouldn't be served by peace in the Indian Territories—or by the peacemaking efforts of the McQueens. . . .

Bantam Books by Kerry Newcomb
Ask your bookseller for the books you have missed

GUNS OF LIBERTY
SWORD OF VENGEANCE
ONLY THE GALLANT
WARRIORS OF THE NIGHT
RIDE THE PANTHER
MORNING STAR
SACRED IS THE WIND
IN THE SEASON OF THE SUN
SCALPDANCERS

★ **THE MEDAL** ★
Book 5

RIDE THE PANTHER

Kerry Newcomb

BANTAM BOOKS
NEW YORK • TORONTO • LONDON • SYDNEY • AUCKLAND

RIDE THE PANTHER

A Bantam Domain Book / October 1992

DOMAIN and the portrayal of a boxed "d" are trademarks of Bantam Books, a division of Bantam Doubleday Dell Publishing Group, Inc.

All rights reserved.
Copyright © 1992 by Kerry Newcomb.
Cover art copyright © 1992 by Louis Glanzman.
No part of this book may be reproduced or transmitted in any form or by any means, electronic or mechanical, including photocopying, recording, or by any information storage and retrieval system, without permission in writing from the publisher.
For information address: Bantam Books.

If you purchased this book without a cover you should be aware that this book is stolen property. It was reported as "unsold and destroyed" to the publisher and neither the author nor the publisher has received any payment for this "stripped book."

ISBN 0-553-29445-8

Published simultaneously in the United States and Canada

Bantam Books are published by Bantam Books, a division of Bantam Doubleday Dell Publishing Group, Inc. Its trademark, consisting of the words "Bantam Books" and the portrayal of a rooster, is Registered in U.S. Patent and Trademark Office and in other countries. Marca Registrada. Bantam Books, 666 Fifth Avenue, New York, New York 10103.

PRINTED IN THE UNITED STATES OF AMERICA

RAD   0 9 8 7 6 5 4 3 2 1

*"For Patty, Amy Rose, P. J.,
and Emily Anabel"*

"He who chooses to ride the panther can never dismount"

—RAVEN MCQUEEN

PART ONE

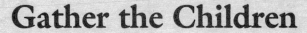

Gather the Children

Chapter One

Ben McQueen crouched low behind a barrel of nails, tore a strip from his shirt, and wadded the piece of cloth into the bullet hole in his tricep. His wounded left arm hurt like hell. It had left a trail of blood leading directly to his hiding place in this corner of the warehouse. Gritting his teeth, Ben probed the wound. The pistol ball had almost passed through the underside of his arm. He could feel the slug beneath his skin. He fished in his coat and found a pocketknife, then slit the skin with the blade's keen edge and flipped the bloody slug out into the palm of his hand. Ben wrapped his upper arm in the torn sleeve of his shirt. He had to hurry his doctoring. After all, two men were trying to kill him. It was the night of August sixteenth, 1863. Ben wondered if he'd live to see the seventeenth dawn.

At six feet two inches, Ben McQueen had offered a big target for his would-be assassins. It was a testament to their poor marksmanship and his surprisingly quick reflexes that he was still alive. His hat was gone; his red hair trimmed close to his skull was matted with sweat. Salt stung his pain-filled green eyes. He hurt. But he was alive and wanted to stay that way.

Who was trying to kill him? The message to come alone and at night to the warehouse had been a ruse to trap him. He'd expected as much, but he had come anyway, risking his life on the slim chance the note had been for real.

Well now, Ben McQueen, he thought, *you've joined the game and must play the cards you're dealt.*

Ben slipped a hand inside his coat and drew a .36 caliber Navy Colt from his waistband. An extra cylinder, fully loaded, was a reassuring weight in his side pocket. Slow as molasses in winter, he eased up and to the side, keeping to the shadow cast by another couple of nail barrels stacked one atop the other. From this vantage point he could study the entire warehouse.

It was a dark, spacious building with its back to the Missouri River and front door opening onto River Street, bold and brash and sinful; home to some of Kansas City's more notorious denizens. The warehouse was nearly filled with neatly arranged stacks of barrels and crates and fifty-pound sacks of grain that formed islands of merchandise between intersecting aisles wide enough to accommodate loading carts.

Ben was hunkered near the back wall. He'd been caught in the middle of the building and had run a gauntlet of gunfire to reach the nail kegs where he'd gained a few moments of respite. The wounded man searched the gloomy interior for some sign of his attackers. He inhaled slowly, measuring every breath. And he listened for the telltale creak of timber, the misplaced step, anything, no matter how subtle. He glanced toward the back door and figured it opened onto a pier. While calculating his chances of reaching the door without being shot, Ben caught a glimpse of a stoop-shouldered, bearded man in a wool cap. He darted through a patch of moonlight that streamed through an unshuttered window just beyond the back door.

That's one, Ben silently counted. A gunshot sounded to his left and a bullet fanned his cheek before exploding a fist-sized chunk out of a nail keg. He caught a faceful of woody debris and dropped to the floor. *That's two.*

"I got him, Seth!" a voice bellowed. Heavy steps thudded on the wooden floor. Fabric ripped as this second attacker tore his shirt on the splintery corner of a crate.

"Be careful, Justin," Seth, the stoop-shouldered man nearest the pier door, shouted out.

"Careful, sheet-it. You just want first claim on his boots. Well, you're too late. I shot him plumb dead. Right through the brisket. I seen him fall."

"It's too damn dark to see," Seth replied, unwilling to leave the safety of the shadows he had found. He lacked the confidence of his associate. And he'd heard stories of Ben McQueen.

"C'mon, Yankee, you're dead, ain't cha?" This assassin was not a patient man. Despite his companion's words of warning, Justin hurried down the dusty aisle between the stored goods until he reached the rear wall of the warehouse.

Ben crouched like a big cat and edged soundlessly past the kegs. His cheek bore a pattern of crimson streaks where wood splinters had stung his flesh like so many angry bees. Working his way in the dark, he brushed his crudely bandaged left arm against the corner of a workbench and had to bite his lip to keep from crying out as pain seared the length of his left side from his toes to his neck. His knees trembled, his stomach did flipflops, and he would have doubled over right then except it might have cost him his life. So Ben resisted the temptation and inhaled slowly and rode the waves of nausea and hurt. Pinpricks of light exploded on the periphery of his vision like fireworks, but he remained conscious and in control of his faculties.

Ben studied the tabletop he'd brushed against. Some worker had abandoned an assortment of wooden pulleys and other hoisting equipment, even a couple of coils of rope. Ben chose a heavy metal pulley with an iron hook at one end and two free-spinning wheels encased by a worn wooden frame. He knelt and laid his Navy Colt on the floor, hefted the pulley in his strong right hand, and hurled it toward the center of the warehouse. The man called Seth was a cool one and not about to fire blind. Justin was another story entirely. A pair of guns opened fire. The twin muzzle flashes revealed a grizzled-looking individual with stringy brown hair and close-set eyes. He was dressed in a ragged frock coat a size or two too big for him and drab blue dungarees. Unarmed, he would have presented no threat, but his booming Colts were the measure of this man.

The assassin fired four quick shots in the direction of the pulley, then, as if suspecting a ruse, charged the nail kegs. He filled them full of holes, and when he reached the back wall, he shifted his aim yet a third time and squeezed off several rounds at an array of farm implements. One slug shattered a broom handle, another a hoe, and he shot a pick axe to slivers. The noise of his guns was deafening in the confines of the rear passageway. Black smoke clouded the confines and blinded him further. He sensed motion to his right and tried to shift his stance, but Ben fired as the man turned. The gunman dropped one gun and clutched at his throat. He staggered off toward the center of the warehouse, tripped over a whiskey bottle, and bounced off a stack of fifty-pound bags of oats— and all the while he made the most horrid sound, a kind of strangled scream like a man drowning, a man come face to face with death and wholly unprepared, a man in agony and desperate for one . . . precious . . . minute . . . more . . . of . . . life.

Justin toppled back against the bags of oats. Dying, he fired a final round that blew a hole in a burlap bag. Dried oats cascaded over the man's head and shoulders as he slid to the hardwood floor. His upper torso was soon buried in the dusty white grain.

Silence. The gunshots would alert no one. Along Kansas City's riverfront at night, trouble was a way of life. Flesh was bought and sold. Raw whiskey flowed like sweat. Men minded their own business here. And women minded the men.

Fortunately Ben McQueen was not the kind to wait around for help. He intended to walk out of this warehouse alive and kicking, and if that meant through a haze of powder smoke, so be it. Someone had set him up. He intended to find out who. He figured he already knew why. Ben McQueen had been an ardent and vocal supporter of the Northern cause since Fort Sumter, a stand that had placed him in the gunsights of Confederate sympathizers. He winced and adjusted the makeshift bandage on his arm. But for uncommon swiftness and pure dumb luck, he would have been worm food.

"Justin?" The voice sounded near the rear door. Ben continued to crouch near the worktable. Barrels of salt pork and wooden crates whose contents were unknown separated him from the bearded assailant called Seth.

"Justin? Damn it."

Ben shifted his stance, eased underneath the worktable, and positioned himself behind a long row of pork barrels stacked three high. Ben wrinkled his nose at the strong smell.

"Is the bastard dead?"

"Not hardly," Ben said. A shot rang out. He ducked instinctively. The bullet thudded into an empty coffin set upright in a far corner at the end of the rear aisle. Two more gunshots followed the first. Ben heard the rasp of a wooden bolt sliding back. The sound galvanized him into action. He stepped out from hiding. Seth stood by the rear door. The bearded man was outlined against a shaft of moonlight filling the window behind him.

Ben fired. Seth answered. Gun blasts illuminated the darkness. The stoop-shouldered man shoved the door open and vanished outside. A bullet from McQueen chased him through the doorway. Ben trotted down the aisle and peered past the doorsill and saw his attacker stumble out onto the pier stretching out from the dock that ran the length of the warehouse.

Ben wasted no time in following the man into the night, then stood motionless while the warm evening air washed over him. Smoke trailed from the barrel of his Navy Colt, but the breeze bore only a faint trace of the gunpowder's acrid residue. He heard the distant tinny melody of a piano drifting on the wings of the wind. The river seemed ablaze, reflecting the glare from brightly lit saloons, brothels, and gambling dens lining the waterfront. Ben abandoned the safety of the doorway and started after the man who had tried to kill him. There was no place to run. A pier ran straight out from the doorway into the black expanse of the Missouri River.

Up ahead, the bearded man stumbled the remaining twenty yards, then dropped to his knees a few feet from pier's end.

Ben took his time, his left arm cradled stiff against his side. The wooden planking creaked and groaned beneath his weight.

Seth heard the big man approach, and extended his right arm, dropping the Dragoon Colt in plain sight. The heavy weapon clattered onto the weathered planks.

"Enough. You've done me," the bearded man

groaned. With his left hand clamped to his gut he bowed forward, his breath coming in ragged gasps. "I'm all . . . cut up inside. Your last bullet caught me in the . . . "

Ben slowed but continued to warily close in on the man who had tried to kill him. He lowered his Navy Colt, but was ready to bring the weapon to bear at the first threatening move from Seth. Across the river, twinkling lantern lights dotted the opposite shore where buffalo hunters had made a camp and were awaiting a ferry to take them across come morning. Ben stood alongside his attacker and nudged the Dragoon Colt out of its owner's reach.

A pool of blood had begun to form beneath the kneeling man. The left side of his shirt was soaked. Suddenly, gunfire erupted on the opposite bank as two quarrelers settled their differences in the court of Judge Colt. Seth grimly chuckled as he watched those distant guns blossom flame. "Looks like I'll have company with the devil."

Ben McQueen shook his head in disgust. He took no pleasure in this. "I don't even know you."

"Don't matter. I ain't nobody. Just tryin' to earn a few dollars." From downriver came a menacing hiss as someone bled the steam pressure from the boiler of a riverboat, the *Missouri Queen*. Ben glanced around at the sound and then down at the gun in his hand. He'd thumbed the hammer back and was ready to shoot. The attack in the warehouse had left him as skittish as a yearling. He returned his attention to the man at his feet.

"Who sent you?" Ben asked.

The wounded man, kneeling at the end of the pier, eased over on his backside to better face McQueen. "Never seen a big man move so quick." Indeed, Ben towered over him as Seth lay with his legs splayed out and struggled to stay alive. Seth gasped and his bearded features drew tight against the bones of his face. "See that I'm laid out proper. And I want a coach with six black horses to carry me to the buryin' ground. And someone to read words over me. You promise and I'll tell you."

"I promise. It will be as you say." Ben took a step closer. "Now, who paid you to kill me?"

A lurid grin split the assassin's ugly features as he raised a hand and pointed past McQueen. "Him," said Seth.

Ben heard the groan of weathered wood behind him. He stiffened. A gunshot rang in his ears. Something kicked him in the back and he stumbled forward, arms outstretched, reaching into space. He felt pain, numbness, a curious mixture of both and a loss of breath and black waters rushed to engulf him as he toppled from the pier and broke the cold black surface of the river.

"Got him. Got him dead to rights," Seth called out, then coughed and clenched his fist at the pain. "That damn mixed-blood sure put me in a bad way. But if you can get me to a sawbones . . . " Seth's voice trailed off. "Oh no. Please. We had a deal—"

A second shot took the top of his head off and slammed him backward, left him dangling over the end of the pier. The weight of Seth's upper torso gradually dragged him over the edge and into the Missouri where, like Ben McQueen, he disappeared without a trace.

Chapter Two

Ordinarily, Captain Jesse Redbow McQueen would have cut his losses and folded his hand. But he had glimpsed something in the gambler seated across the table from him. The game had lasted most of the night and run the sun up without a break. It had begun with five men seated round the table. Now two of them were enjoying a delayed breakfast of country ham, biscuits and gravy, black coffee, and corn dodgers dipped in wild honey.

The men were gathered in the saloon on the hurricane deck of the *Westward Belle;* it was a cheerfully appointed, wood-paneled room that sported oil-lamp chandeliers hung from the generously high ceiling. A gleaming walnut bar offered just about any libation known to man. Often drinks were concocted on the spot. The *Belle*'s captain, Nicodemus Stockwood, was famous for his ability to imbibe copious quantities of spirits and maintain a level head. Jesse had expressed concern to the riverboat captain and suggested the man might curtail his proclivity for drink, to which Stockwood promptly responded with accounts of his only two accidents, both of which occurred when he was stone-cold sober.

The *Belle* was three days out from St. Louis and loaded with blue-clad troops camped amid crates and barrels on the lower deck. Rooms on the hurricane deck were reserved for merchants bound for points west and Union officers posted to the border states. Jesse wore the garb of a cavalry officer, a dark blue coat with yellow shoulder bars adorned with the two gold bars that indicated his rank and pale blue pants tucked into knee-high black boots. His coat was unbuttoned to reveal a loose-fitting white cotton shirt and the shiny brass buckle of his gunbelt.

"The raise is fifty dollars to you," Enos Clem announced for the second time. And again he licked his lips. It was an almost imperceptible gesture, just a tiny pink flick of tongue. But Jesse had noticed. Clem was beginning to tire. Clem had been a shrewd player, taking his winnings a little at a time, riding his luck, increasing his wagers the more he came to know the other men in the game. But he had become overconfident, and he'd begun to take risks.

Throughout the night Jesse had played cautiously and conservatively, only staying in the game when he had a chance at winning the pot. Now Enos Clem figured he had the officer pegged. As the other men folded and Jesse remained, Clem had thrown caution to the wind. Now suddenly the stakes had gotten out of hand and there were six hundred and thirty dollars in gold and greenbacks on the table.

Jesse examined the cards he held: the deuce and four of diamonds, a jack of clubs, the seven and ten of hearts. It was a bust hand in any book, as bad a hand as he'd been dealt since sitting down at the table. Jesse glanced at the man on his left, a stocky good-natured lawyer who could not seem to stop yawning.

"Let's make this interesting. According to Stockwood, we'll be in Kansas City within the hour. I need a shave before we dock," Jesse said, and promptly took the assortment of coins and currency in front of him and added them to the pot.

"I'll see your fifty and bump it up another two hundred and fifty." Jesse placed his five cards face-down on the table in front of him, like a gauntlet hurled down in invitation to a duel. The raise took the gambler by surprise. He wiped a hand across his mouth, then rubbed his eyes, and studied his opponent.

The eldest son of Ben McQueen was a handsome young officer who at the age of twenty-two had earned his captain's rank. His eyes were dark, the color of old leaves become black with decay. His black hair was an unruly forest of curls. In his boots he stood no taller than five foot ten, but size had little to do with his presence. Even in repose, he possessed a catlike grace, relaxed in his chair yet ready to spring. He'd grown a black mustache since the Vicksburg campaign, throughout which he'd played an integral part as both Union spy and officer assigned to General Sherman's staff. But those months of danger and bloodshed lay behind him. As for what lay ahead, only time and a certain Major Peter Abbot awaiting him in Kansas City would tell. Jesse glanced at the two men who remained in the game. His features were as flat and expressionless as an unmarked grave. The ability to disguise his intentions had saved his life on more than one occasion.

"A man would be a damn fool to cross that bridge," the lawyer said, and tucked what remained of his cash inside his coat pocket. He rose from the table, nodded to the dozen or so spectators circling the table at a respectful distance. Clem had taken a healthy share of their money over the past three days. More than one man wanted to see the gambler get his comeuppance.

Enos Clem ran his long fingers through his brown

hair and rubbed the back of his neck. He studied the officer across the table from him and then lowered his gaze to the money on the table. Sweat ran a trail along the side of his pasty white features. Tiny veins, like spiderwebs across his cheeks, reddened.

"You're running a bluff, Captain McQueen," the gambler muttered, sliding his thumb over the three eights he held. He had tried to draw to a full house and failed. He had expected the lawyer to fold, but the Yankee captain was proving far more stubborn. For the past hour, Clem had sensed "lady luck" was turning her back on him. He should have quit hours ago but, damn it, the lure of easy money had bound him to the table as if he had been chained to his chair. As for McQueen's cards, Clem wasn't nearly as confident as he sounded. The more he considered it, the less likely it seemed the officer was bluffing. No, the Yankee's hand would just about clean the gambler out. And if he lost, then he was down to stake money, the few bills he kept tucked away inside his boot. He had figured to buy the last pot, but the tables had turned and he didn't like it. The snickering among the spectators didn't help matters. Sure, they'd like to see him lose it all, to throw away every last dollar. Well, Enos Clem knew when to fold, and he was not about to give his fellow passengers the satisfaction of watching him leave with empty pockets.

The steam whistle sounded three blasts to alert the passengers that Kansas City was in sight. Belowdecks the reassuring rumble of the steam engines and the throbbing revolution of the paddle wheel at the stern of the boat plunged the *Western Belle* upriver to its destination.

"The hell with it," Clem said, and tossed his cards onto the money in the center of the table.

A cheer rose up from the merchants and McQueen's fellow officers that filled the shipboard saloon. Enos Clem glowered and a twitch developed around his left eye. Had he been bluffed? Pride demanded he learn the truth. He slid his chair back, stood, and, leaning across the table, attempted to flip over the five cards Jesse had placed facedown. Jesse caught the gambler's wrist.

"I'll see those cards," Clem said.

"You didn't pay for the privilege," the officer reminded him. Tension suddenly filled the room and men, despite their curiosity, began to give ground and find excuses to put themselves out of harm's way.

Enos Clem, wearing a black frock coat, string tie, and baleful expression, could have passed for an undertaker appraising a prospective client. Jesse knew little of the gambler's history, other than the fact he was an Easterner headed for the gold fields of California and traveling on the winnings he acquired along the way. But Jesse McQueen was no stranger to violence and he could see trouble coming like a thunderhead on the horizon of the gambler's eyes.

Clem dropped a hand toward the gun butt protruding from the waistband of his trousers. It was a Starr revolver, caliber .44, with a sawed-off barrel to enable the weapon to ride comfortably against the gambler's belly. He'd kept the Starr concealed beneath his vest, until now.

Enos Clem was no slouch. He moved fast, fueled by his pride and his anger. But Jesse McQueen was faster. Survival spurred him. He overturned the table and stepped forward. His right hand was a blur as he caught Clem's gun hand in middraw and shoved the Starr .44 back in the gambler's waistband. Clem grunted and winced in pain as the muzzle of the revolver dug into his groin.

Jesse held the gambler's hand in an iron grip, thumbing the hammer back on the Starr and forcing his finger through the trigger guard. An ounce more of pressure and Clem would shoot himself in the testicles.

"You've finished one game. Better not start another," Jesse said in a quietly ominous tone of voice. He glanced down at the revolver bulging the front of the man's pants. "You're not in Boston now, pilgrim. And this is one game I don't think you'll have the balls to finish."

A silver dollar rolled off a nearby table, landed on the wood, rolled a few feet, then spun and settled flat against the floor. A dropped pin would have been heard just as clearly. Jesse never took his eyes from the gambler. The fire cooled in Enos Clem's veins. It was time to cut his losses before they became—he glanced down at his crotch—unacceptable. Jesse read the surrender in the man's lowered gaze.

The steam whistle sounded again and the boat shuddered and slowed as it approached the river town. Jesse removed his hand from the gambler's belly gun. Clem took care to pat the wrinkles from his coat, then sniffed indignantly and, mustering the last of his pride, walked stiffly from the saloon.

The crowd of Union officers and merchants collectively sighed, relieved there hadn't been gunplay. The quarters were too close and no one in his right mind wanted to risk a stray bullet. Jesse knelt to pick up his winnings off the floor. He was more than six hundred dollars to the good.

"Welcome to Kansas City," someone said dryly, breaking the tension.

It would do.

Chapter Three

"Captain Jesse McQueen. Your presence
in Kansas City is urgently required. Come
with all due haste. I will be staying at the
home of Doctor Milburn Curtis.

Major Peter Abbot"

Jesse absently reread the dispatch that had found
him in Vicksburg, then folded the missive and tucked
it away in his pocket. He glanced around the dock.
The waterfront was crowded with townspeople and
soldiers, buckskinners, rivermen, and freed slaves
who had escaped bondage in the South and found
work as common laborers in this Union-controlled
town. Glistening black muscles unloaded goods from
the *Westward Belle* and carried crates and barrels
aboard. A couple of young lads in faded canvas pants
and loose-fitting shirts drove a herd of goats up the
pier and into a makeshift pen on the lower deck of the
Belle, toward the bow.

Jesse noticed Enos Clem disembarking from the
riverboat. The frock-coated gambler paused just a
step off the gangplank and lit a cigar. Smoke curled

beneath the broad white brim of his flat-crowned hat. He gestured to a young mulatto, a lad of eleven or twelve, who clambered down off a barrel and for the promise of a few cents took up the gambler's carpetbag and followed the man down the pier and along the dock. No doubt Clem intended to visit the saloons along the waterfront and restore to health the contents of his much-depleted purse.

Jesse shrugged, and slung his own saddlebags over his shoulder and headed out onto River Street. No doubt the town marshal would help him locate Doc Curtis. Jesse wasn't worried.

Peter Abbot was like a member of the family. He had served with Jesse's father in the Mexican War and had become an unofficial uncle to the children of Ben McQueen. At the outbreak of war, it was to Peter Abbot that Jesse had come with a request to serve under the major's command. Abbot had been only too happy to oblige. The major's dispatches, however, were always cut and dried—"Report here" and "Go there" and "Wait until contacted." Jesse never knew what to expect. However, one thing was certain: no matter where the major's orders sent Jesse McQueen, the captain could always count on finding trouble at the end of the line.

The marshal of Kansas City was home tending his wife and helping as best he could in the birth of his second child, but his deputy, a laconic young man by the name of Hiram Hays, managed to bestir himself from the marshal's chair long enough to refill a blue tin cup with coffee from the stove back near the jail cells at the rear of the building. Hiram took his time, enjoying his authority and posturing with all the gravity of a man wise beyond his years.

Jesse waited patiently, allowing the deputy his moment of glory. Come tomorrow with the marshal's arrival, Hiram would return with broom in hand to a more humble status.

"Doc Curtis," Hiram repeated. "Sure I know where he lives. Been patchin' me up since I was sloppin' hogs on my granpap's farm. And who might you be?"

"Captain Jesse McQueen."

"McQueen, huh?" Hiram scratched a yellow thumbnail along his stubbled jaw and appeared to recognize the name. "What with all you soldier boys in town, hell, I can't tell y'all apart. Don't get me wrong, me and most others are glad for the troops, what with them Confederate devils about."

"I came in on the *Westward Belle* not an hour ago. But news about the Lawrence raid was all the talk in St. Louis."

On the twenty-first, Confederate guerrillas led by the infamous William C. Quantrill, Bloody Bill Anderson, and the Choctaw Kid had looted and burned Lawrence, Kansas, only a long day's ride from the Missouri border. Over a hundred and fifty citizens had been killed during the raid, most of them innocent townspeople, many of them young men approaching military age who had yet to don a blue uniform. The destruction of Lawrence by Confederate guerrillas was the brutal culmination of years of border warfare that had plagued Missouri, Kansas, and the Indian Territory for too long.

"Folks'll be hearin' about it long after we're gone," Hiram added. "Quantrill was there. And the Choctaw Kid. Bloody Bill himself hung the town marshal and his deputy from the mercantile sign." Hiram stared dolefully at the coffee that somehow seemed as black as his prospects for the future. "He'd already hung 'em. Why do you suppose he shot 'em to doll rags? 'Cause that's what he did afterwards. My cousin seen the whole thing while he hid under the walkway." Hiram slapped the gun riding high on his hip and glared out the window at Main Street with its parade of townsfolk and soldiers as if they offered him a personal affront.

Jesse noticed he was losing the deputy once more to reverie and slid the blank side of a wanted poster in front of the man with the badge.

"Huh?" Hiram looked up.

"Doc Curtis. Maybe you could draw me a map?"

"Oh yeah. Surely. Now see here, all you do is follow Main Street plumb out to the edge of town and turn back toward the river." Hiram took a pencil stub and drew a meandering line on the paper, then a fork in the road. A couple of squiggles indicated the river and a rectangle Doc Curtis's house. "But like I said . . . the doc and his wife are over to the marshal's helpin' with that new baby."

"Thanks," Jesse replied. The way looked pretty cut and dried. He started to leave and had his hand on the door when the deputy spoke again.

"McQueen . . . You kin to a Ben McQueen?"

"Yes," Jesse guardedly answered. "Why?"

"He's dead."

Hiram went on to describe the scene of the ambush, the gunfight at the warehouse, and how Ben apparently managed to shoot dead his two attackers before falling into the river, mortally wounded. McQueen's body washed up on the riverbank, Hiram continued. Doc Curtis had confirmed the man's demise. "I still got the newspaper, somewheres, that tells all about it. If you want to wait just a minute . . . " Hiram glanced up and saw the front door ajar. The noise of the street flooded in with the sunlight and the billowing dust. The deputy was alone in the office.

Forty minutes later, Jesse stood in front of a whitewashed frame house on the outskirts of town. Doc Curtis had built his house on a bluff overlooking the Missouri River where the breezes from the river blew cool and steady. A picket fence separated a dusty front lawn from the dusty road. A few wild-flowers graced the front of the house and lined the few steps up to the porch and front door.

Jesse dismounted from a dun gelding he'd purchased in town. He tethered the animal to a hitching post near a weathered gate. A few chickens scratched in the dirt near the stone walk, but they beat a hasty retreat and vanished around the corner of the house as Jesse approached. He had found the doctor's place with little trouble. Walking the streets of the town, Jesse had felt the tension in the air. Federal troops were everywhere, yet their presence did little to quell the anxiety of the local populace.

He did not know how long he stood by the gelding, his hands folded on the saddle, staring at the empty-looking house. His father was dead. The words could be understood easily enough. It was the trip from his mind to his heart that left him numb and weighed down the movements of his hands and feet as he crossed in front of the fence and followed a well-worn path around the house toward the bluffs over-looking the river.

The back of the house had a rectangular wing consisting of three rooms that the doctor kept for those patients requiring his personal supervision. Since both Curtis and his wife were delivering a baby, Jesse figured the hospital rooms were empty. A barn with a small corral attached lay just beyond the house. The grounds in back of the house were dotted with pin oaks, providing shade for a double-wide swing and a haven for a flock of blue jays who protested Jesse's intrusion.

He made his way to the edge of the bluff. A step further and the land swept down to the banks of the Missouri, a hundred and sixty feet below. Sunlight glinted on the muddy surface and, as he watched, a stern-wheeler rounded the bend back toward town and with smoke trailing from its twin stacks churned past the bluffs on its way northwest to Nebraska Territory and the mountains beyond the plains.

Jesse wiped a forearm across his eyes and felt a lump rise in his throat. He coughed and tried to clear the tightness and failed. He found Abbot's dispatch in his pocket, crumbled it up in anger, and tossed the paper over the edge of the bluff.

What had brought Ben McQueen to Kansas City? Jesse's father had been in Washington trying to impress upon the military authorities that there were forces and influences loose in the Indian Territory that threatened to explode into a second western front if the war office wasn't careful. Kansas City was a long way from Washington, D.C. Jesse closed his eyes and pictured his father as he had been, so strong and indomitable. The pain lessened, to be replaced by a smoldering anger toward Major Peter Abbot, who no doubt had a hand in bringing Ben McQueen out from the halls of Congress to be murdered on some seedy riverfront. The more Jesse thought on it, the angrier he became. He turned toward the house and for the first time noticed smoke trailing from the black iron chimney of the hospital wing of Curtis's house. So the place wasn't deserted after all. Jesse's features flushed with barely controlled rage.

"Major Peter Abbot," he muttered beneath his breath, and started toward the low-roofed patients' quarters. The three rooms shared a long common porch in front. Unshuttered windows looked out on a vegetable garden where rows of corn, peas, butter beans, and squash ripened in the morning sun. But Jesse McQueen didn't give a damn about the wholesome, tranquil setting Mrs. Curtis had labored so hard to create. There were three doors to choose from. Jesse picked the one on the end according to the placement of the smokestack. Also, this room's windows were suspiciously shuttered, ensuring the privacy of the occupant within. Perhaps Abbot was fearful for his own safety. Well, if he wasn't before, the major better be now, Jesse thought as he reached the porch and headed straight for the oaken door. He worked the iron latch and struck the door with his shoulder, sending the door swinging inward to crash against the wall with a loud bang like a gunshot. Jesse leaped inside and, sure enough, Major Peter Abbot, a white-haired man dressed in faded blue military coat and trousers, whirled around, his eyes wide with alarm behind the round wire rims of his spectacles.

"Abbot, you son of a—!" As Jesse burst into the room, Peter Abbot was so startled he dropped his coffee cup and kicked it beneath a dresser as he stepped backward and nearly tripped over a chair.

Jesse froze just inside the room as sunlight flooded in behind him to carve a corridor of amber brightness through the shadows and bathe in its golden glow not only Abbot but another man half reclined upon a brass-frame bed and holding a pair of Colt Dragoons, cocked. He'd come a split second from blowing Jesse's head clean off.

Jesse gulped and stared a moment into those twin gun barrels before focusing on the face behind them. The man in bed slowly lowered his guns, then spoke the two most welcome words Jesse had heard all day.

"Howdy, son," said Ben McQueen.

Chapter Four

"Be careful. That stuff will kill you," Abbot warned as Ben uncorked a jug of Doc Curtis's own home brew.

"I'm already dead. Remember?" Ben replied. He took a swallow and followed it with a deep breath of air. The good doctor was fond of dispensing his whiskey for medicinal purposes, calling it his "kill or cure" tonic. And with a bullet lodged against his spine, Ben McQueen was in the mood for the doctor's remedy.

Jesse sat by his father's bed. The young captain was emotionally spent, having lost a father and gained him in the same day. His initial shock had given way to elation, then to the sobering reality that his father was partially paralyzed and might remain so. Doc Curtis was willing to attempt the necessary surgery to remove the slug but only after Ben had recovered his strength. Jesse's father had nearly drowned and he'd lost a lot of blood. Indeed, Peter Abbot had found him on the riverbank more dead than alive and spirited him away to Doc Curtis.

"I put the word out Ben was dead, figuring it

would be safer for him," Abbot said. "No sense in giving some back-shooter a second chance at you."

"Give the bastard his due," Ben said. "To hit me at that distance, he must be a crack shot."

Jesse had been given a brief account of the ambush in the warehouse. It was unnerving to think the identity of the marksman who had shot Ben McQueen was unknown. He might still be in Kansas City, and still a threat. It was impossible to tell.

Ben adjusted the pillows behind his back and grinned at his gloomy-looking son.

"Cheer up, Jesse. I'll be on my feet again." Ben glanced at Peter and added, "Maybe in time to join you down south."

Jesse turned and stared at Abbot. Realization came like a slow dawn. So there was an ulterior motive to the major's dispatch and his intentions were more than reuniting a son with his injured father. Jesse stood and took the jug of Doc's "kill or cure" from Ben's hands.

"Major, I think I'm gonna need a shot of this," he said, "before I hear what you have up your sleeve." He chanced a swallow from the jug. The liquid coursed like fire down his gullet.

"Damn," Jesse gasped with tears in his eyes. "Now I'm ready for anything. You came near to getting me killed behind the lines in Vicksburg, Uncle Peter. What enemy camp do you want me to bluff my way into now? How about Richmond? I could ride in and tweak Jeff Davis on the nose!"

Major Abbot endured in silence the captain's tirade. Another day he might have called Jesse to task for his lack of respect for rank. But the sons of Ben McQueen were like a part of his own family and he understood the stress Jesse had undergone, first learning of Ben's death and being torn by grief, then finding Ben McQueen alive, though seriously wounded.

"You do me a disservice, Jesse. I merely want you to take a trip into the Indian Territory," Peter said. He saw a look of surprise cross Jesse's features.

"That's right, son," Ben interjected. "He wants you to go home."

"I don't understand," Jesse said.

"Indian Territory is a powder keg and the Choctaw Nation the fuse," Ben continued. "Union sentiment seems strongest among the citizens of Chahta Creek."

Jesse nodded. The town of Chahta Creek was the hub of the thriving Choctaw agricultural and cattle-raising community. Jesse's grandfather, Kit McQueen, had married the half-Choctaw Raven O'Keefe, and they were among the first to settle the area. The McQueen ranch was only about ten miles from the town they had helped to build.

"On the other side are the plantation owners, like Tullock Roberts. They're slave holders and will fight to preserve what they have," Ben said.

"And there's plenty of folks in the middle, small farms with families that want no part of the war," Abbot said. "Many of them your neighbors, Jesse, who just want to be left in peace."

"If only the Knights will let them," Ben sighed. He looked at his son. " 'Knights of the Golden Circle,' they call themselves. Hooded raiders who strike at night against Union sympathizers. The Knights have created a reign of terror in the area, trampling crops, burning barns, and driving off livestock. Some families have sold their land and moved to town. There's talk of mounting reprisals against Confederate sympathizers. So far no one's been killed. But it's only a matter of time."

"The Copperheads are already clamoring for a truce with the South," Abbot said, leaning an elbow on the dresser. A breeze through the window ruffled his white hair and blew it back from his forehead. He frowned and brushed his hair forward to conceal his receding hairline. Major Peter Abbot was not without vanity. "Victory is within our grasp, yet President Lincoln is beset on all sides by his detractors. He cannot afford . . . the nation cannot afford a western front in Indian territory."

Jesse walked to the door of the room and looked out at the sun-drenched yard. Crows lazily circled the garden and alighted on the scarecrow to survey what the birds considered to be their personal domain. He stepped out onto the porch and clapped his hands together to frighten the crows away. They merely studied him with disdain.

Peter Abbot retrieved his hat from a row of pegs set in the wall. He glanced at the man in the bed.

"I'd better start back to the hotel. I don't want to make anyone suspicious."

"I wish you'd tell Cap I'm all right. We go back a long ways. He was having dinner with you when I got shot, for heaven's sake. The man loves me like a brother."

"A little knowledge can be dangerous," Peter said. "Cap Featherstone can't hold his liquor. He talks too much when he's drinking." Abbot crossed the room to the door. "I'll be back," he said with a salute, then he patted Ben's shoulder and left the room. A moment later he joined the captain on the porch. "I'm not going to order you to go, Jesse, but just think about it. Talk to your father. And don't worry, nothing is going to happen to him."

Jesse glanced sharply at the major. "Something already has."

"Yes," the major concurred as he stepped off the porch and headed for the barn where he'd kept his horse out of sight.

Jesse watched the officer depart. The shadow of a cloud glided soundlessly over the house and garden as

Peter Abbot proceeded through the shifting sunlight and at last disappeared inside the barn.

"Don't be too hard on him, son," Ben called out.

Drawn by his father's voice, Jesse returned to the room and his father's bedside. The curtains ruffled by Ben's bed and a breeze fanned his cheek. The open door created a refreshing cross-draft.

"It's not right, you being alone and hurt," Jesse said.

"I've Sam Colt for company," Ben said, patting the Dragoons beside him on the bed. "And one of my sons, until it's time for you to hit the trail south."

"How do you know I'll go? I might just stay here and look after you," Jesse said.

"No."

"Why?"

"Because I don't need you. And your country does."

Jesse slumped defeatedly in the chair next to the bed. "I was afraid you'd say that."

"I'm not telling you anything you didn't already know. Uh!" He winced as a white-hot jolt of pain flashed across the small of his back.

Jesse looked on, helpless as his father struggled with the pain. Ben refused to allow it to best him. His eyes closed; his countenance grew pale and chalky. The whole spell lasted no more than fifteen seconds, but it seemed like hours. Ben's color gradually returned, and he sighed and unclenched his fists.

"See. No problem," he weakly chuckled. "Easy as falling off a log, as Cap would say."

"Is that Cap Featherstone, of Andrews' raiders?" Jesse asked. In April of 1862, Abbot had dispatched twenty-one men under the command of James Andrews to travel undercover into Georgia, steal a train and drive it north, tearing up Confederate railroad lines from Atlanta to Chattanooga. Most of the raiders were eventually caught and hanged. A few escaped. Cap Featherstone had been one of the lucky few.

"One and the same," Ben said. "I knew him during the Mexican War. We trailed together. He's a man to ride the river with. Just steer him clear of whiskey and women. Both have been his undoing more than a few times."

"But you trust him?" Jesse asked.

"With my life," said Ben.

Chapter Five

"I paid you to kill Ben McQueen, not hang around town getting into trouble," said Cap Featherstone to the one-eyed gunman he had just paid Deputy Hiram Hays to set free.

Cap was a robust, burly individual standing just under six feet tall and topping the scales at three hundred pounds. His immense girth was firmly encased in a dark green frock coat and trousers, and a bandanna covered his head where streaks of pink scalp showed through his thinning brown hair. In his early forties, Cap Featherstone sported a thick brown beard shot with silver, and he walked with a cane that had a silver grip molded in the shape of an alligator's head and long jaws. His right knee had a touch of arthritis but he had grown accustomed to the nagging discomfort. Some days he limped more than others. It depended on his state of aggravation. This evening he was fuming. Even more so because the man beside him in the deserted alley seemed so all-fired amused.

"Relax, Cap. A man's got a right to celebrate his birthday, eh? Why, I'm thirty-one today," said Featherstone's companion.

A dog had mauled Hud Pardee as a child and left him blind in the left eye. He kept the scarred, sightless orb covered with a black patch. His good right eye was as blue as ice. He was perhaps an inch taller than Featherstone, elegantly attired in a blousy black silk shirt and a waist sash and black woolen trousers and Spanish boots. His gray hair was swept back from his forehead in ashen waves to reveal clean-cut youthful features and a winning smile that most women found irresistible.

But whatever warmth and charm he exhibited lasted only long enough to get what he wanted out of the people he met. Cap understood such behavior. He knew where he stood with a man like Pardee. The two were bound by a mutual desire for power and gold. Greed could be as strong as blood and as dangerous as a rattler, but the profits to be made with a man like Pardee were worth the risks.

"Relax, Cap," Pardee said again. He rested his hands on the walnut grips of the Navy Colts jutting from the sash at his waist. "I didn't kill anyone. It was just a misunderstanding between me and that little waterfront dove. She wasn't worth near what she claimed. Paris Kate has taken on some lame excuses for a whore. I don't take lip from anyone."

"Beating women is hanging offense to some folks. You're lucky the deputy had a price. And you'll by God pay me back," Cap blustered.

"Sure I will," Pardee said. "And right now. With some news I think you'll find interesting." He reached out and grabbed Cap by the arm, halting the big man in his tracks. Cap glanced up and down the alley. They were standing behind a law office and stage line, well out of sight of the street. An abandoned shed stood behind them, its broken, empty windows as blank as a dead man's eyes.

"Well?" Cap said.

"While I was at Kate's, the captain of the

Westward Belle came to pay a visit and try out one of the new ladies. I heard him tell how a Captain Jesse McQueen got the better of a gambler named Enos Clem and beat him at his own game." Pardee stroked his chin, then gestured with his finger as if he were standing in the parlor of the whorehouse. "Not ten feet away, there's a poker game going on with none other than Clem. He slams his cards down, grabs his money, curses the captain, and tells us all that if he ever sees McQueen again there'll be a reckoning."

"Ben's son," Cap muttered. "Abbot told me the lad was in town. We're supposed to meet tonight in the stables behind the Excelsior Hotel."

"You want me to do him? I brought down the curly wolf. His pup ought to be no problem," Pardee said.

"No! Leave his son alone."

"Seems kinda late for you to be developing a conscience," said the marksman.

"Abbot's no fool. Killing Jesse might throw suspicion on me," Cap explained. "Anyway, Ben was the dangerous one. He could have pulled the factions together. But his sons ain't Injun enough."

"Tell that to the Choctaw Kid," Pardee said, and unfolded a handbill he had lifted from a stack on the deputy's desk.

Cap's eyes widened. He took the wanted poster and tucked it in his pocket. "Leave tonight. There's nothing more for you here. You've celebrated enough. But before you go, I want you to find this Enos Clem . . . " Cap lowered his voice and led the way into the abandoned shed. The plans he had in mind were best revealed in the dark of shadows and dust. They could not bear the light.

Chapter Six

Since his first encounter with Captain Jesse McQueen aboard the *Westward Belle,* Enos Clem's life and fortune had gone to hell in a hand basket. Nothing had turned out right. Lady luck had not only abandoned him, she'd thrown him to the wolves. Unable to win honestly, he'd palmed a couple of face cards in hopes of salvaging a disastrous run of bad fortune at the gaming tables and had been caught with a pair of kings up his coat sleeve. The reaction of the men at the poker game came swift and brutal. He'd tried to elude their grasp, and had lunged from the table and scrambled toward the rear of the Stern Wheeler Saloon only to find his escape route blocked by a crowd of swarthy rivermen anxious to mete out punishment to a card thief. Trickery was something no man could abide.

It was fast approaching eleven o'clock, and this warm summer's night was about to become even hotter if Clem's drunken captors had any say in the matter.

More than a dozen of the Stern Wheeler's patrons had formed a circle around the gambler and carried him out of the saloon and down River Street, past other gambling houses, emporiums, and bordellos, attracting revelers from along the boardwalk, men with too much drink and not enough money and looking for something—anything—to take their minds off the hard work of living.

Marched for three blocks, struggling in vain against his captors, Enos Clem was borne away from the glare of the lantern lights to an empty corral where a bucket of black pitch tar was quickly produced from a lean-to shed. A rum-soaked harlot in a sweat-stained scarlet silk dress fought her way through the throng. She carried a feather pillow overhead for all to see and the men cheered her arrival. Now and then a hand groped for her ample bosom. The woman, Penelope by name, didn't seem to mind.

"Now wait!" Enos Clem pleaded to the faces surrounding him. Boston seemed a lifetime away. He drew himself up, his innate sense of superiority giving him the strength to defy his tormentors. "See here. I won't stand for this."

"O'course you won't, ya bone-headed fool." One of the mob's leaders, a muleskinner named Poke Howard, stepped forward. "You'll be ridin' a rail!" Crude laughter sprang up from the rough-looking crowd.

Enos gazed disdainfully across the lot of them, soldiers, freight haulers, trappers, rivermen, and the whores in their warpaint and silks. He hated them all, but none more than the one who soured his luck and brought him to this cruel pass. Enos pictured the dark-haired captain who had faced him down and humiliated him. The faces in the torchlight paled, a mere blur compared to the image in his mind.

The stench of tar filled the air and a few feathers fluttered past like snowflakes in the warm humid night as Enos was lifted up and over a twelve-foot-long oaken rail. Straddling the timber, he continued to lash out at his tormentors, all to no avail. Poke Howard, the harsh-voiced, heavyset muleskinner, caught the gambler's wrists and another man quickly bound Enos's hands. The bucket was passed from man to man until it reached Poke, who made a show of churning the tar with a short heavy paddle. Another cheer rose up when he hoisted the bucket and pillowcase above his head for the crowd to see.

A couple of shots rang out and bullets cut the handle loose. The bucket fell and dumped tar on the muleskinner. A third shot split open the pillow and gave Poke a faceful of feathers. The mob turned toward the gunman.

Hud Pardee, astride a blaze-faced bay gelding, led a second horse through the crowd. Poke struggled to clear his vision and cursed his unseen assailant. His fists lashed out at the men around him, striking at friend and foe alike until Hud rode up alongside the muleskinner and rapped him on the skull with the barrel of his Colt revolver. The tar-covered man dropped to the ground. A few men from the throng surged forward angrily. Hud Pardee dropped the reins he held and filled his left hand with a second Colt.

"Keep clear," he ordered.

"You're only one man," a voice from the crowd shouted out.

"True. But I'll make the ground run red," Pardee replied. "Now, back off." Then he began to chuckle. "Or make your play." He thumbed back the twin hammers of his Colts.

Enos Clem looked up in amazement. He had no idea who his benefactor could possibly be. He had never set eyes on the gray-haired gunman in the blousy black shirt and woolen trousers, his features shaded by a broad, flat-brimmed hat. The eye patch gave the man the look of a pirate, someone not to be trifled with, and if his image did not cool the temper of the hostile crowd, there was something in the gunman's laugh that transformed the whiskey-bravest heart into a cold and sober coward.

"The hell . . . " a man muttered, and turned away and headed back toward River Street. He was the first but not the last. The throng began to grudgingly give way. However, the brassy whore named Penelope was not about to be cowed. She lifted her hem clear of the dirt and hurried forward scolding as she came.

"Now see here, you one-eyed good-for-nothing son of a mule, what gives you the right to interfere?" Her red hair had come undone in back, and strands of carrot-colored curls splayed out from behind her ears. Crimson streaks of rouge dipped down her cheeks the angrier and the more animated she became. "I'm not afraid of you. These others may be, but not me. Why if I were a man . . . "

Pardee's hand shot out and cracked her across the head with the Colt as he had done to Poke. The woman groaned and fell back on her ample derriere, then slumped onto her side in the dirt. A trickle of blood mingled with the rouge.

"If you were a man you'd be dead," Pardee told the unconscious whore. The savagery of his blow impressed the remainder of the crowd, who dispersed as quickly as they had gathered, leaving two of their own lying senseless in the dirt.

Pardee returned his guns to his waist sash. He produced a straight razor from his saddlebag and quickly sliced apart the ropes binding the gambler's wrists.

"I am in your debt, sir," Enos said, more than a little unnerved by the conduct of his benefactor. He climbed down off the rail. To his surprise, the one-eyed man offered him the reins to the brown mare standing alongside the bay. Enos glanced up, a questioning expression on his face.

"The *Westward Belle* left this afternoon," Pardee said.

"Well, no matter. I'll catch on with a wagon train bound for California."

"Too late in the year for that. Better to wait until next spring than risk an early snow in the mountains." Pardee dropped the reins, returned the razor to his saddlebag, and, doffing his flat-crowned hat, ran a hand through his ash-gray hair. "Of course, there's more than one place a smart man like yourself could turn a handsome profit—with the help of a friend."

"I'm new here. I don't have any friends," Enos scowled, gathering up his torn coat and retrieving a string tie from the mud.

"You do now," Pardee said in a silky voice. "The name is Hud Pardee." He gestured to the horse. "Mount up."

Enos Clem considered his options. It didn't take long. The future in Kansas City looked bleak. He swatted at the insects that began to buzz his sweat-streaked face. And besides, he couldn't stand the mosquitos. No doubt Pardee was a very dangerous man. *No matter,* Enos thought, *so am I.*

The gambler swung up astride the mare. The animal shifted its stance and whinnied, as if sensing its rider's uneasiness. Enos was hardly a confident horseman.

"To quit this place, I'd ride with the devil himself," the gambler said.

Hud Pardee merely laughed and led the way out of town.

Chapter Seven

Jesse McQueen's first image of Cap Featherstone was one he would remember all the days of his life. He found his father's friend in the stable of the Excelsior Hotel. A wide, thick-necked individual with a black bandanna covering his skull and clad in dark green trousers and boar-hide boots, Cap Featherstone seemed to dominate whatever space he chose to stand in.

Cap had stripped away his coat and shirt and was loading a wagon with barrels of Kentucky bourbon and burlap sacks of malted barley and hops. He'd been at it for the better part of an hour and his hairy torso was matted with sweat. Though he seemed preoccupied with his work, the big man sensed the arrival of Abbot and McQueen, and after manhandling a keg of bourbon onto the flatbed wagon, Cap grabbed up his alligator-head cane and whirled around, ready to cave in the skull of the nearest intruder. Jesse dropped a hand to his revolver, then relaxed as Cap recognized his late-night visitors and lowered the lethal-looking walking stick.

"Damnation, Major. You give a man a start creep-

ing up on me like that. A man can't be too careful."
Cap squinted at Jesse. "By golly, you must be Jesse."
The big man lumbered forward. His thighs were as big
as some men's waists. His belly jostled with every
step. Yet there was uncommon strength in his sloping
shoulders, as evident in the way he had cavalierly
tossed hundred-pound grain sacks onto the wagon
bed.

"I'm proud to meet you, lad. Ah, your father
spoke highly of you, God rest his soul." Cap held out
a gloved hand, thought himself rude, and stripped off
the glove. The back of his hand was covered with
coarse brown hair. He gripped Jesse's hand in his vise-
like paw and ground the younger man's knuckles
together. The pain was startling. Jesse had the distinct
impression he was being tested. He endured the
handshake in silence and tested himself against
Featherstone's solid grip. At last Cap released Jesse's
numb fingers and stepped back to appraise the officer.
Any ordinary soul would have yelped at the good-
natured punishment Cap had served up. Jesse's silence
had spoken volumes. It appeared young McQueen was
cut from the same cloth as his father. That could
mean trouble.

"An honor, sir," Jesse said, flexing his hand.
"The story of Andrews' raiders and their exploits in
Georgia are legendary."

Cap frowned. "Legend?" He glanced at Abbot.
"The truth is somewhat less dramatic, my young
friend. And eminently more painful to recall."

"Jesse will be accompanying you back to Chahta
Creek in his father's place," said Peter.

Cap glanced at the major. "You really think that's
a good idea?"

"Meaning what?"

"Meaning one dead makes the other a target," Cap
replied. "I'd hate to be responsible for the younker."
Cap shook his head.

"I can take care of myself, Cap," Jesse flatly interjected.

"You think so, eh?" Cap retreated a step to appraise the younger man whose dark eyes seemed to smolder with defiance. After two years of blood and thunder, Jesse felt he didn't have anything to prove.

"I'm riding into Chahta Creek and I don't give a good goddamn whether you approve or not," the captain said.

Cap grunted, squared his shoulders, and looked past McQueen to Major Peter Abbot. "Well, the lad is his father's son, right enough," the big man drawled. "Run along, Major. I'll fill his head with what I've learned over the past few months. Maybe I can keep Jesse here from stopping a bullet."

"See to it," Peter replied. "I have business elsewhere in town." He patted the straw and dust from his sleeve and, hesitating, took the opportunity to confiscate the jug of whiskey Cap had left on a nearby bale of hay.

"Ah, Major . . ." Cap moaned.

"You've greased that throat of yours quite enough," Peter said. "And no telling what mischief your wagging tongue has caused."

"What the devil is that supposed to mean?" Cap blurted out to the major's departing back. Peter disappeared through the doorway and closed the double doors after him. A few seconds later there came a crash, the sound of a jug being hurled against the outside wall of the stable. "Bastard!" Cap raised his fist to the empty stalls, then sighed and, turning, winked at Jesse and crossed the aisle. He stepped inside a stall where he kept one of his matched roan geldings. He returned with a canvas bag stenciled OATS on the side. He opened the bag and retrieved a silver flask, which he promptly unscrewed and tilted to his lips.

He offered a drink to Jesse, who declined. Cap shrugged. "Suit yourself." He took another drink and leaned on the wagon. "Abbot's a hard man. Fair, but hard." Cap looked at McQueen. "But he doesn't see the faces."

"I don't understand," Jesse said. He crooked a thumb in his gunbelt and waited for the explanation.

"Eighteen . . . twenty—I've lost count. Andrews' raiders." Cap glanced up at the rafters. A barn rat scampered across an open beam and vanished into the loft. First came a rustle of straw, followed by a couple of brittle yellow blades of grass drifting down from above. "We ran like frightened rats. We were alone. They told us what to do, wreck the Confederate rail lines. But nobody ever told us how to get back. We thought Andrews and the major had put some kind of plan together. Wasn't until we showed our colors and stole the train that we learned just how expendable we were." Cap tucked the flask into his coat pocket and exchanged the whiskey for a cigar of Virginia tobacco that he had rolled and dried himself. A pair of silver snips suddenly came into his hand and he trimmed the end of the cigar, returned the snips to his trousers, and leaned forward to light the cheroot from a nearby lantern. Cap puffed a cloud of smoke that billowed before his face, obscuring his features. Wisps of tobacco smoke clung to his thick brown beard and curled over his upper lip like tusks. For a moment he resembled some savage beast, half man and half wild boar.

"But you returned," Jesse said, studying the man his father called friend.

"Yes. And I promptly quit this damn war. After all, I wasn't a real soldier. Just one of Abbot's spies. I bought a panel wagon and headed into the Indian Territory where I hoped to escape the fighting. Cap Featherstone's Elixirs and Medicine Show." Cap patted the barrels of bourbon. "Never had a bottle returned yet," he chuckled. "Of course, I don't sell off the pure stuff. I dilute this nectar with a little gunpowder and snake poison." Cap Featherstone grinned. "Yessir. I came to Chahta Creek to look up your pa. Didn't know he was gone. And I seen a little place in town just waiting for me to hang a sign outside and rest my wandering soul. Why not? I got me some mixed blood, part Choctaw, a little Cherokee, and some Cajun."

"What about the Knights of the Golden Circle?" Jesse said.

"Nobody knows who they are for sure. They're always hooded. And they strike under cover of darkness. They sprang up a while back and been plaguing the countryside ever since. Folks are being driven off their homesteads. The major heard about it—somehow—and paid a visit to Chahta Creek. He recognized me and talked me into helping out. He didn't have to twist my arm, not when I learned your pa was involved." Cap Featherstone lowered his head. "I should have never let him go to the warehouse alone, no matter what the note said. But whoever left it for him claimed to have information about your brother and that was all Ben needed to know. 'News of your youngest son. Come alone.' And signed 'A Southern Friend.'" Featherstone tossed the cigar in the dirt and crushed it beneath his boot. "I should have followed him," Cap added in a voice thick with regret. He looked up at Jesse. There were tears in the big man's eyes. "I feel almost to blame." Cap sighed, and his powerful shoulders sagged as if burdened by the weight of his assumed guilt. Then he straightened and stroked a hand across his beard and crossed around to the front of the wagon. He reached beneath the seat and brought out the handbill Pardee had pilfered from the town marshal's office. Jesse watched with curiosity as Cap lumbered toward him.

"Since you're coming along, perhaps you'd better

look at this. You may be riding into more trouble than you can handle."

Jesse turned cold as he read the handbill. Its message was simple and direct and damning.

"Wanted dead or alive for the barbarous raid on Lawrence, Kansas, and the murder of its innocent citizens, these guerrilla leaders are hereby charged.

William Quantrill—Will Anderson alias Bloody Bill—Creole Tom Carrington—and Pacer Wolf McQueen, alias—"

Chapter Eight

"The Choctaw Kid!" exclaimed the guard on the Neosho stage. He brought his shotgun to bear on the lone highwayman blocking the bridge over Waterfall Creek. "I seen a poster on him up in Independence."

Pacer Wolf McQueen snapped off a shot from the gun in his left hand and sent the shotgun spinning out of the guard's grasp. The man sitting next to the guard on the coach, a mean-tempered, whiskey-soaked "four-up drier," cracked his whip in an attempt to blind the Confederate holdup man. The Colt in Pacer's right hand thundered and left the stage driver staring down at the wooden handle of his whip. The "black snake" had been shot clean away. The guard dropped a hand to the pistol tucked in his waistband. Pacer walked his skewbald pinto toward the four-horse team. Behind him, the rain-swollen river was ready to overflow its banks. It pounded the bridge supports and threatened to sweep the structure away.

"That would be a fool play," Pacer softly counseled.

"Givin' up my gun to one of Quantrill's butchers don't make any more sense. I heard all about what happened in Lawrence. You'd as soon shoot us as spit," the guard retorted.

Pacer leaned over the side of his horse and spat pointedly in the dirt, then looked up at the men on the seat box. He waited, allowing the guard to reconsider his actions. He didn't want to kill the man if there was any way around it.

"I've come to take up a collection for the Confederacy, my friends," said Pacer. He fixed his eyes on the guard's fingers already curled around the walnut grip of the revolver. Pacer's features hardened. Indeed, his very appearance was that of a cutthroat. He carried a brace of Colt Dragoons; a D-guard knife with a broad heavy blade rode in a scabbard on his left side. He was garbed in the gray shirt and black trousers of a guerrilla fighter. A gray felt hat shielded him from the onslaught of the hot Missouri sun.

Pacer was as tall as his father, well over six feet, but was built leaner than Ben McQueen. His eyes matched the color of the burnished gold wedding band worn by his grandmother, Raven. His shoulder-length red hair, shaggy as a lion's mane, was unbraided according to Choctaw custom. A beaded medicine pouch dangled from around his throat, a gift from Raven, the medicine woman who had raised him. A beaded leather shot bag hung from his belt. A pair of eagle feathers had been braided into the brown mane of his pinto stallion.

"I don't have the time to dally, mister. Drop your gun or make your play," Pacer called out.

The guard sighed, his expression soured, and though he still expected to be shot dead, the man removed his gun with thumb and forefinger and tossed it aside in the dirt.

"Are you a religious man?" Pacer asked.

The guard licked his lips and gulped. "Why?"

"You just brought two dead men back to life," said the Confederate guerrilla.

Pacer walked his mount forward until he was alongside the coach. The canvas sides were rolled up and it was plain to see there were no passengers. This was strictly a mail run. All the better.

"I believe you're carrying draft funds for the Neosho Bank." He had learned from a Confederate sympathizer that the bank had been authorized to distribute a supplementary payroll for the Yankee troops quartered in and around the town. Indeed, Federal troops had occupied Missouri soil since the outbreak of war. Their presence had been a boon to the economy of several small towns like Neosho. Hundreds of miles from home and hearth, lonely soldiers spent their money on liquor and women and the few pleasures to be had in a frontier town. Fresh meat and farm products from the outlying farms commanded high prices but were considered a necessity by soldiers weary of army fare.

"Payrolls are transported by train. Every jackanapes knows that," the driver growled.

Pacer Wolf cocked his revolvers and centered them on the man with the reins. He didn't bother to repeat his threat. Time was running out and he wanted to make it clear his patience was wearing thin.

"Of course, now and then folks make an exception," the driver added, and reached below his seat for a heavy-looking canvas bag that he handed down to McQueen. Pacer holstered a revolver and then hooked the mailbag's leather handle over his saddle horn.

"The Confederate States of America are in your debt," Pacer said with a flourish of his hat. He bowed to the men he had just robbed. A bullet plowed a furrow in the road, several yards from the pinto. The accompanying gunfire alerted Pacer, who whirled about and spied a troop of Federal cavalry on the crest of a wooded ridge a couple of hundred yards from the bridge.

"Now we'll see who has the last laugh, you goddamn renegade," the driver exclaimed. The Union escort had held back on purpose, hoping to surprise and capture any rebel raiders who might be in the vicinity. Their officer, a fresh-faced lieutenant from Baltimore, had watched the robbery unfold through the lens of his spyglass and thought he recognized McQueen from the poster he had seen. Here was a prize indeed, none other than the notorious Choctaw Kid.

Pacer glared at the men on the coach and raised his revolver. The driver's grin faded as he stared into the black, unblinking eye of the gun barrel. But Pacer held his fire, eased the hammer down, and started back toward the bridge. The road was slick and muddy and the pinto momentarily lost its footing in the mud. Pacer kept a firm hold on the reins, brought the animal's head up, and darted past the coach and its four-horse team and trotted down to the bank of the rain-swollen creek. He seemed almost cavalier in his retreat, as if unwilling to be chased from the battlefield.

Back up the trail, over a dozen troopers in blue, all of them inexperienced soldiers, continued to blast away at the guerrilla though he was hopelessly out of range of their pistols. The driver and the guard glanced at one another, reached the same unspoken decision, and leaped from the coach. They retrieved their weapons from the side of the road and hurried after the guerrilla, each man anxious to be the one who dropped the Choctaw Kid. Made bold by the prospect of a reward, they raced for the bridge, hoping to pick off Pacer while his back was turned.

The horseman reached the sturdy-looking span across the steep-sided creek, the handiwork of years of flooding, and lost no time in crossing over to the opposite bank with the stage driver and the guard in close pursuit. The guard's shotgun boomed in his hands, its report thundering above the noise of rushing water but a few yards away. The stage driver knelt in the mud and leveled a pistol at Pacer, who leaned out of the saddle and fired into the earth.

"I clipped his wings," the guard cried out in triumph.

"Shit," the driver muttered, and opened fire. He wanted to claim part of the kill by putting a few slugs in the Kid. Pacer straightened in the saddle and faced the two men. He held up his hands in surrender.

"We got him," the driver roared. "Drop your guns, you blackleg bastard!"

"We? It was my shotgun that took the fight out of him," the guard protested. "That makes him my prisoner."

"We'll see about that," the driver retorted, and lumbered down the road and on to the bridge with the shotgun-toting guard in hot pursuit. Suddenly Pacer spurred his horse and trotted up the road.

"Hold it right there, Kid. I got another load of shot to send your way," the guard warned.

"Climb off that horse, mister," the driver shouted as he stepped onto the bridge and leveled his pistol. He smiled triumphantly as McQueen complied. But his elation dulled at the first smell of smoke. He searched the timbers and spied a telltale ribbon of smoke. Pacer had not been firing into the ground because of a crippling wound. His gun blast had lit a fuse. And where there was a fuse . . .

"Oh sweet Mother!" the driver exclaimed. *"NO!"* *Yes.*

The stage driver and guard took a flying leap back toward the creekbank. They were aided by a deafening blast and a concussive force that propelled the two men through the air and sent them skidding through the mud in a flash of fire, billowing smoke, and raining timber.

The would-be captors emerged from a puddle with brown faces and wide white eyes. Both men were surprised to find themselves still in one piece, which was a hell of a lot more than could be said for the bridge. No one was crossing Waterfall Creek today. As for the Choctaw Kid, he had vanished among the trees like a gray ghost.

The guard wiped the mud from his features and glanced back up the trail toward the oncoming troops. "What are we gonna tell the lieutenant?"

The driver, his ears still ringing, glared at his companion. "We?" the man growled. "He was *your* prisoner."

Chapter Nine

Brigadier General William Steele of the Confederate Army of the West stared down at the rain-soaked money bag Pacer Wolf McQueen had deposited on his map table by way of introduction. Greenbacks and gold coins could be used to purchase much-needed medical supplies and ammunition. As for the bank drafts, unfortunately, the Rebels were without access to Northern banks, save for the guerrillas and mounted cavalry who periodically conducted raids against Union property and fled back into Arkansas. Ordinarily Steele would have welcomed a man like Pacer with open arms and been deeply grateful for the contribution. And he told the young man as much. Pacer listened and believed the officer was grateful, yet ever since riding into Fort Smith, Arkansas, he felt as alien as if he had entered a Federal encampment. A rumble of thunder filtered through the walls of the cabin Steele had appropriated for his headquarters and was now in the process of abandoning. The smell of rain hung heavy in the air and the sky outside looked threatening and dark.

"So you are the Choctaw Kid," the general

remarked, stroking his silver-streaked chin whiskers. His war-weary gaze took the measure of the man standing across from him. Steele glanced at McQueen's strong, sun-bronzed hands, half expecting them to be covered with blood.

"I am Pacer Wolf McQueen," he replied. Once, he had taken pride in the colorful handle he had acquired over the past year. Since the events of the past couple of weeks it had begun to wear a trifle thin.

"You don't look like an Injun," said one of Steele's aides. He was a somber-faced captain named Reno, a remarkably competent officer who had made no attempt to hide his disregard for McQueen.

"My father is a quarter-blood Choctaw," Pacer said. "He used to tell me I had white skin but a red heart." Pacer's attempt at a friendly interchange fell flat. The captain continued to stare at McQueen as if a wild animal had entered the room.

"Why have you come here?" the general asked. His tone was kind yet sad.

"This is the closest Confederate army I could find," Pacer said, taken aback by the officer's attitude. "I want to join one of your cavalry regiments."

"You cannot buy a commission with blood money," Reno blurted.

The general slapped a hand on the table and his cheeks reddened. "Enough, Captain. See that the orders are given to destroy the river bridges across the Arkansas. If my Union counterpart intends to pursue us, he will have to get his armpits wet."

"Yessir," Reno said, and with a second deprecatory glance in Pacer's direction, he left the cabin. Pacer heard the guards snap to attention as the officer stepped through the doorway and out into the gray afternoon.

Steele returned his attention to the Choctaw Kid. "The truth, sir. Is this part of the plunder taken from Lawrence?"

"A few days ago I stopped a stage outside of Neosho, in Missouri. I heard tell there was an army payroll aboard. This is it."

"Hmmm. Captain Reno would think me a fool, but I believe you," said Steele. He patted the bag. The officer had already begun to calculate the best way to spend its contents. There were plenty of profiteers north of the Mason-Dixon Line eager to sell contraband supplies of medicine and munitions to the Rebels, providing the price was right.

"Then take a chance and believe me again. I took no part in the burning of Lawrence or the slaughter of its citizens. I thought we were there to raid a Union supply depot. I learned the truth too late. I have fought and killed for the cause I believe in. But Quantrill's raid was madness. No. It was plain and simple meanness, murdering unarmed innocent townspeople, some of them mere boys." Pacer turned away. The memory plagued him, haunting his sleep with dreams of fire and death. He had come to join the Arkansas Volunteers, to fight the war as it should be fought, with honor. "I'm not here to buy a commission, General. I rode up from the Indian Territory to find the war. I'll fight as a private if you'll have me."

Steele had no doubt the young man standing before him could fight. That was, in the end, precisely the point. All of the border guerrillas were men who dealt lead for breakfast, slept in the saddle, and rode away to fight again another day. Here was a man with a lit fuse for a backbone and a heart of brimstone. And yet he did not fit the mold.

Candles sputtered on the mantel against the south wall. The table lantern painted the twin shadows of the two men upon the mud-chinked walls. The bed in the corner had not been slept in for a night and a day. Slices of bread on a platter at the corner of the table looked crusty and stale, leftovers from a man preoccupied with death. The austere interior of the cabin had none of the comforts of Steele's headquarters in Little Rock. Giving up the cabin was easy enough. Let the Yankee general have the hard bed and the temperamental chimney with its backdrafts and the rickety ladder-backed chairs that never seemed to sit flush on the floor and groaned and creaked when sat upon.

Brigadier General Steele walked to one of the shuttered windows and opened it against a gusting wind. Six thousand men were encamped along the Arkansas River just outside the town of Fort Smith. Cookfires dotted the riverbank, where smoke curled above the treetops. Horses were led to the river and back again. Men went about their jobs with an air of resignation.

"Tomorrow I withdraw to Little Rock, where I'll combine this force with the troops garrisoned there. In all, I can put about twelve thousand men on the battlefield against an overwhelming two-pronged Union offensive building to the north and west." The general closed the shutters and helped himself to a drink from the makeshift table below the window. He poured a glass of bourbon for himself and his visitor, then handed the glass to Pacer. "One man won't matter much to the good. But he could make matters even worse for a regiment with flagging morale."

"Meaning your men would not wish to fight alongside someone who rode with Quantrill," Pacer said in a hard voice.

"It's easier for me to believe you took no part in that Kansas butchery. But then I know what it's like to struggle for trust." Steele chuckled. "You see, I'm a New Yorker. My wife is from Mississippi. I've put down roots in the South. Still, it has taken almost two years for my own men to trust me. And every time I order a retreat, there are some who will question my loyalties. Morale is dismal enough. I don't wish to make it any worse." The general finished his drink.

"Any ties Quantrill or his men had to the Confederacy were severed at Lawrence. Your innocence or guilt doesn't matter." The general returned to his desk and unfurled a surveyor's map of the fortifications around Little Rock. His rumpled gray uniform had a lived-in look reflecting the man who wore it. The buttons were dull and unpolished. The cuffs were becoming frayed. Steele was only in his mid-thirties, but responsibilities had aged the man and bowed his shoulders beneath the weight of an increasingly difficult task, the defense of Arkansas with too few men and supplies.

Pacer tried to think of something to say but words failed him; they slipped and slid and drifted away. Jesse might have argued and won the general over to his way of thinking. Jesse had the gift. Pacer Wolf could see no use in trying. General Steele lifted the map and slid the canvas money bag to the edge of the table. "You can take the money if you wish. It is yours, after all."

"I'm not a thief," Pacer growled. He had stopped the Neosho stage as an act of war and resented the implication to the contrary. "I took that money for the Confederacy. Keep it." He turned and, without a salute, started toward the cabin door.

"We retreat," Steele said. McQueen paused with his hand on the doorlatch. "We retreat and the Union army advances, and on the heels of a Federal victory will come the plunderers, like carrion birds." The general placed a hand upon the map. "Go home, Pacer McQueen. And don't look for war. It will find you soon enough."

Pacer turned to look at the general. In the glare of the flickering lamplight the Confederate officer's deepset features took on what to Pacer seemed a spectral quality. A gust of wind rattled the shuttered window and moaned through a crack in the log walls. Borne on the breeze came the distant call of a raven.

Pacer turned the latch and stepped outside, ignoring the guards in gray who watched him with a mixture of curiosity and resentment etched on their bearded features. Pacer stepped out from under the porch roof and searched the gunmetal sky and at last spied the dark-winged bird circling above the treetops southwest of the Rebel encampment.

Pacer knew then what he had to do. And where he was going. Without so much as a by-your-leave, he caught up the reins of his pinto and left Brigadier General William Steele to his maps and his plans and his gnawing despair.

Chapter Ten

Dreams . . .

Lawrence, Kansas, was burning and there was nothing Pacer Wolf McQueen could do to stop it. Once more, he rode through the smoke-shrouded streets, a man dazed by the carnage he had unwittingly become part of. He had followed Quantrill's black flag into town expecting to battle the Union troops stationed there. So far the only Federals Pacer had seen were a fat old recruiting officer and a pair of grizzled veterans whose crippling wounds had ended their military service. Pacer had discovered the bullet-riddled bodies of all three soldiers in an alley between a hotel and a seamstress's shop.

"C'mon, Pacer," said Sawyer Truett, who had joined Pacer along with a dozen other riders from Indian Territory to take part in the battle. "We're gonna miss out." Truett was a couple of years older than Pacer. The two had been childhood friends. In fact, Truett had come to the McQueen ranch as an orphan and found a home with the McQueens back in the Kiamichi hills.

Gunfire rattled throughout the town. Smoke

churned skyward. Along the streets, guerrillas kicked in doors and crashed through shop windows in an orgy of looting and destruction. Sawyer Truett was anxious to join in the fun. A half-breed Choctaw, Sawyer was of average height, built broad and strong. A scraggly goatee covered his chin, the wispy strands blown as was the long hair poking out from beneath the brim of his battered gray felt hat. With a wild Rebel yell on his lips, Truett spurred his horse past his friend and charged into town, and the mixed-blood Choctaws behind him raised their own war cries and drowned out Pacer's attempts to stem the tide. They ignored his protests and charged after Truett. Pacer had to wrestle his own mount under control to keep the pinto from racing off with the other horses as they trampled the bodies in the alley and disappeared into the fire and smoke.

Find Quantrill. The men will follow his orders. Pacer knew it was his only chance to put an end to the slaughter. He had glimpsed the black flag on the opposite side of town. Quantrill was never far from his color-bearer. Pacer rode clear of the alley. He was determined to circle the town and find the enigmatic guerrilla leader. A touch of his heels against the pinto's flanks and the animal plunged forward through the smoke and carried its rider away on his mission of mercy, a quality Captain William C. Quantrill kept in short supply. The image itself faded and dissolved into a montage of burning buildings and a confusion of townspeople rushing from one conflagration to another. At one point Pacer saw a handful of older men herded against a wall by a pair of Quantrill's men. The guerrillas leveled their pistols and proceeded to shoot their prisoners. Pacer charged into the gunmen and sent them sprawling, allowing the townsmen to scatter and head for home. Pacer never broke stride. He spied Quantrill sitting like a statue upon a black charger at the west end of Main Street. Half a dozen men in gray waited nearby like an honor guard. Four women stood before his horse, pleading for the lives of their husbands as Pacer approached.

Quantrill was a dashing, fair-haired killer dressed in a blousy gray shirt trimmed with gaudy black stitchery. A black slouch hat was tilted back on his forehead. He kept four Colt revolvers tucked in his belt. When he saw Pacer approach, he shushed the desperate women with a wave of his hand. "Ladies, you've met Bloody Bill Anderson, well, here is another of my lieutenants who doesn't have to dance in any man's shadow. None other than the Choctaw Kid himself, Pacer Wolf McQueen. Best beware, he aims to have your scalps dangling from his belt."

Quantrill and his men laughed aloud as the women fled, screaming. With memories of Quantrill and the Choctaw Kid forever etched in their minds, they ran weeping toward the nearest church. Destruction and death had descended on Lawrence, turning wives into widows and leaving mothers to mourn their butchered sons.

"Damn you, Quantrill!" Pacer shouted above the gunfire. "Call your men off. You lied. I'll wager there never were Union troops quartered here!"

"I've given orders to kill every man big enough to carry a gun," the guerrilla leader calmly replied. "I aim to teach these damn abolitionists a lesson they'll never forget."

"Sound retreat," Pacer snarled, and dropped his hand to the Colt at his side. The men surrounding Quantrill trained their captured Union-issue carbines on the Choctaw Kid. They held their fire out of respect for the color of Pacer's uniform and the fact that he didn't pull his gun. Pacer Wolf searched their faces, hoping to catch a glimmer of conscience among Quantrill's guard, but like their captain, the guerrillas had been hating for too long: their hearts had become empty shells devoid of tenderness. If war indeed could be said to hold a mirror up to hell, then such men were the devil's own reflection to whom the flames of carnage had become a way of life and a source of joy.

"In good time, Kid. Just as soon as we pick this ripe town bare." Quantrill winked at his Spencer-toting ruffians. "Every man here will make a pretty penny this day." He started to laugh. At a touch of his heels Quantrill's black horse started down Main Street. The riflemen filed past Pacer as they fell in behind their captain. The last man to ride past was a dashing young desperado whom Pacer knew as the older of the James brothers, Frank James. James paused astride his horse and said, "You're either with us or agin' us, Pacer. Make your choice." Then he rode off after his heavily armed companions.

He remembered being blinded by the smoke and stumbling God only knew how long. He was a part of the destruction of Lawrence. It was a brand he would wear all his days. A mark he could never wash clean. He couldn't save the town, but as he rode back through Lawrence fate provided him a single small opportunity to help curb the wholesale slaughter of the town's young men.

Pacer found three of his friends behind the flaming remains of a two-story hotel just off Main. Sawyer Truett had cornered two young Lawrence men by the stables in back of the hotel. The stables had miraculously escaped the torch until now. Truett brandished his guns while the other mixed-bloods from the Indian Territory prepared to set the structure afire.

Truett's prisoners could have been no more than thirteen or fourteen years of age, mere lads in dungarees; barefoot and frightened for their lives. Truett cocked his guns and fired in the dirt to stop the two boys from edging along the wall.

"Say your prayers, Yank bastards," Truett exclaimed. The boys held out their hands as if intending to ward off the gunshots to come. Then Pacer appeared in front of them and placed his body in the line of fire. "What the hell are you doing, Pacer?"

"We're murdering children now, is it?"

"They're plenty big enough to carry a gun," Truett snapped at his friend.

"Please, mister, we ain't soldiers," one of the boys pleaded. "Ain't no one to keep up the farm if'n I was to join my brothers in the regiment."

"My pa's the preacher. He takes no side and expects the same for me," the other boy spoke up, a note of desperation in his voice.

"Step aside, I say," Truett warned. He was breathing rapidly and his hair was singed. His wide eyes reflected the burning hotel with the excitement of the moment as Pacer walked his mount alongside Truett's. "We've been like family, Pacer. Don't make me hurt you."

"I won't let you shoot them," Pacer softly said. "It's nothing but cold-blooded murder."

Sawyer Truett could only stare in amazement, unable to believe what he was hearing. Then his features turned ugly and he rose up in his stirrups and leveled his Colt revolver at the farm boy and the parson's son. Pacer drew his D-guard knife. With a flick of the wrist he sliced a crimson streak across the back of Truett's hand, just behind the knuckles. Truett howled in pain and dropped his gun. Pacer lashed out and caught his friend flush on the jaw with the heavy brass hilt. Truett groaned, his eyes rolled back in his head, and he slipped from the saddle and landed on his back in the mud. Pacer glared at the two men with the torches as if daring them to interfere. He knew them to be followers, not leaders. The men with the torches retreated out of harm's way. Then one of them, Darvis Porter, dismounted and cautiously approached the fallen man.

Pacer turned to the youngsters. "Run to the woods. Hide there until things quiet down." The two lads looked at one another as if doubting their good fortune. "Run, damn you!" Pacer added, and the two raced off toward the distant line of trees and never looked back. Pacer didn't expect any thanks.

"When Sawyer comes around, he'll kill you," said Darvis. With the Choctaw Kid, he had ridden up from Indian Territory to join the raid. Darvis was more puzzled than ever at Pacer's behavior. Lawrence was easy pickings. What was the matter with McQueen anyway?

"I don't think so," Pacer coolly replied. If his boyhood chum intended to follow the black flag, so be it. But the Choctaw Kid had business elsewhere. He pointed his pinto stallion toward the Missouri road. The heat from the burning buildings continued to warm the back of McQueen's shirt as a reminder of all he had witnessed and, try as he might, could never fully leave behind.

Dreams . . .

Chapter Eleven

The thunderclap, sounding like a Sharps buffalo gun in the confines of the barn, startled Pacer Wolf from his restless sleep and saved him a cracked skull in the process. The Choctaw lay on his back on a bedding of hay in a stall alongside his pinto. The lightning's lurid blue-white glare streamed through the open stable door and outlined a menacing figure standing over Pacer and about to bludgeon him with an ax handle.

Pacer twisted and one long leg lashed out and caught his attacker on the side and sent the mysterious intruder sprawling into the center aisle. Pacer Wolf scrambled to his feet. He caught up his revolver and lunged for his assailant. He kicked the ax handle aside and dragged its former owner to her feet.

Pacer stepped back in disbelief and then turned up the wick on a nearby lantern to make certain—and yes—a young woman of no more than fifteen years stood glaring at him as she fought to catch her breath. His blow had driven the air from her lungs. At last her breathing became less desperate, and still full of fight, she glanced around for the ax handle.

Don't try it," Pacer said, brushing the hair back from his face and taking a better look at the young woman. She was a beauty despite her homespun attire—nankeen pants, a faded red shirt and mud-spattered flat-heeled boots. A battered carpetbag lay in the aisle a few feet away. Her auburn hair spilled past her shoulders in sodden ringlets and her hazel eyes blazed with defiance.

"I didn't mean you no harm," the girl said, "but I needed me a horse." She glanced around the stable at the horses in the stalls and the empty tack room. "Where's Erman? I thought you were him. Erman would never let me have a horse. He's too afraid of the Shapters, especially Frank."

Pacer recognized the first name. The stable's owner, Erman Tree Hawk, was an old Osage who had finally put down his roots in Fort Smith. Pacer had paid the stable man the price of a bottle of cheap whiskey for the use of a stall for the night. The Osage took the money and left to slake his thirst at the nearest saloon and had yet to return. As for Frank Shapter or the girl, Pacer had no inkling who they were. He didn't want to know. The Choctaw Kid had enough problems without looking for more.

"I got to find me a horse," the girl said. "Anything faster than these old carriage nags. Frank's got a Kentucky mare that'll run me down for sure."

Pacer could feel trouble coming. He almost volunteered his help but caught himself in time. "This isn't the only stable in Fort Smith. Maybe you should try elsewhere," he said.

"Frank's looking for me. I can't chance the street." Her gaze settled once more on the pinto.

"Look here, whatever your name is—"

"Lorelei. That's a pretty name, ain't it?" She smiled.

"Not pretty enough to win you my horse."

Yet this winsome lass with her smudged cheeks

and flirtatious smile seemed confident. Pacer remembered how his Grandpa Kit had warned him of the fairer sex, claiming that a determined woman could be more dangerous than a coiled rattler. Pacer was beginning to understand the wisdom of those words spoken so long ago to a boy trapped between two worlds, one red, one white. Of course, Grandpa Kit had added with a wink, "Yessir, such gals might be dangerous but they can sure be a hell of a lot of fun."

Well, right now Pacer Wolf wasn't looking for fun. He just wanted to be left alone. He wanted people to steer clear of him while he worked things out for himself.

Nothing had happened as planned. He'd spent the past year dashing across Northern lines, disrupting communications, raiding stage lines, and helping himself to the deposits in the border-town banks, all for the good of the Confederacy. The Choctaw Kid's reputation as a daredevil had grown. He had taken pride in his own exploits. Now, thanks to Will Quantrill, Pacer's name was linked to the destruction of Lawrence and the deaths of innocent people. His pride had suffered a grievous blow.

Pacer watched the young woman wander over to the open doorway. She felt his eyes on her. She liked that. Lorelei checked her backtrail and paused a moment to enjoy how the downpour concealed the town behind its silvery veil. Fort Smith was shuttered and dark against the elements, and the streets were empty save for a half-dozen forlorn-looking mounts tethered to a pair of hitching rails in front of the Liberty Saloon. Mules and mares and geldings waited with bowed heads and their rumps to the elements as the late summer shower lashed the rutted street. The downpour had a relaxing, almost hypnotic effect until she spied a familiar figure sloshing through the mud. He materialized out of the gray gloom, leading a horse and heading for the stable. Had she left tracks or was he merely following a hunch? Instantly, the hairs on the back of her neck tingled and her heart began to pump excitedly. She turned and gave Pacer a quick appraisal. He wore the black-legged garments of a Confederate guerrilla, which meant he was no stranger to violence and could handle himself. But could he handle the likes of the big man lumbering toward them through the storm? There was only one way to find out.

"Where you bound for, mister?" she asked.

"I'm called Pacer Wolf. And it's to the Indian Territory I'll be heading as soon as this storm eases up."

"Indian Territory? That ought to be far enough," she muttered. She stepped back and studied him. "I've heard tell the Jayhawkers and Yankees have been chasing a red-haired breed called the Choctaw Kid." She beamed with certainty. "You're him! As I live and breathe." Her expression became thoughtful, as if she were planning something. Pacer did not bother to reply. He rubbed a hand across his stubbled cheeks, brushed his long red hair back from his features, then settled his hat and headed for the stall. The pinto neighed and pawed the straw-littered floor with an iron-shod hoof. The animal sensed the alarm in the man. Pacer could not put it into words, but this brash young woman left him unsettled. Something in her eyes made a man go weak inside.

Pacer had an instinct for danger and, storm or no storm, he had business elsewhere. He opened the stall and tossed his saddle over the pinto. The stallion took a breath and swelled its belly, a trick that never worked on Pacer, who nudged the pinto in the ribs and, when the animal exhaled, tightened the cinch. The bridle came next. The Choctaw Kid worked swiftly and smoothly.

Lorelei gathered up Pacer's bedroll and gunbelt

and stepped out into the aisle. She clutched the blankets to her chest. "Take me with you, mister."

Pacer gave the matter a few moments of consideration, then caught control of himself. "Not hardly," he said, coming out for his bedroll. She backed away. "See here, miss."

"I can be real nice to have on the trail. And I won't be in the way."

"It appears you already are," Pacer told her. "And who the hell is—" He glanced past the young woman at the bearded thick-set man looming in the doorway. He was built broad and solid. He'd been walking a while and steam rose from his rain-soaked frock coat and woolen trousers and gave him the appearance of a man carved from brimstone. "Frank," Pacer said, completing his question and dreading the answer.

Frank Shapter paused to wipe the rain from his close-set eyes, then shifted his attention from Lorelei to Pacer and back to Lorelei, who still clutched McQueen's bedroll to her bosom.

"You little trollop. I take you off that mud farm of your pa's and this is the thanks I get. The minute I turn my back, you run off with some no-account drifter."

"Hold off and let the waters clear, mister. I'm sure we can come to some kind of understanding," Pacer interjected. Although he was in Confederate territory, the Union troops weren't all that far off, and to a man on the run in these days of clashing armies and shifting loyalties, just about any town could be considered enemy country.

"You can go to hell," the man in the doorway growled as he advanced on Pacer. The Choctaw Kid palmed the Colt he had tucked in his waistband and trained it on Shapter. The man halted in his tracks.

"Stand aside. I'll be on my way," Pacer told him.

"So you aim to steal my wife," Shapter exclaimed.

Wife? So that was the reason the big man was so all-fired determined. A jealous husband was as unpredictable as a twister and to be avoided at all possible costs.

Pacer kept the man covered and managed to lead the pinto out of the stall. He reached out and took his bedroll and gunbelt from Lorelei and draped them over his saddle. Then with the gun he waved Shapter out of the way and headed for the open door and freedom.

"What about me?" Lorelei said. "You can't just leave me here." The alarm in her voice was real. She followed after Pacer and inadvertently came within arm's reach of Shapter, who caught her by the wrist and hurled her backward against a wall hung with bridles and blankets and carriage harnesses.

"He ain't got no use for you. But I do. You shamed me, girl. You won't be likely to run off again," Shapter said. He turned his back on McQueen as if dismissing him out of hand. Shapter had an abiding respect for the Colt .36 Pacer kept trained on him. Lorelei had no such protection and became the obvious focus of his rage.

"Don't ever let the sunset catch you in this town again," Shapter added as a menacing afterthought. Pacer eased himself through the doorway and out of the stable. The rain had eased somewhat, but the ground was crisscrossed with tiny creeks and rivulets. Each wheel rut was a flash flood in miniature. A cooling breeze rippled the watery curtain, behind which the streets of Fort Smith appeared to dissolve and reform in ever-shifting patterns. Pacer sensed magic in the phenomenon. He paused alongside the Kentucky mare that Frank Shapter had abandoned to the elements after catching sight of Lorelei and the Choctaw Kid within. Pacer stood against the wall in the deepening night and realized he could not bring himself to leave. And this time it had nothing to do

with the likes of Frank Shapter. No one told Pacer
Wolf McQueen to tuck his tail and run. A smart man
would ride, a sensible man would leave and never
look back. The girl was the worst kind of trouble, and
Shapter was a bully in his own backyard with family
and friends to come to his aid if need be. Pacer stood
with his back to the stable wall running through
every argument in a desperate attempt to convince
himself to leave. It was a brave but hopeless gesture.
He looped the reins in his hand over the doorlatch and
then stepped around and entered the stable once
again.

Shapter stood with his back to Pacer. Droplets of
water sprayed from the man's black coat as he back-
handed Lorelei to the hard-packed floor. She cursed
her assailant, her voice thick with pain. It took all her
willpower to hold back the tears.

"You're my wife. The parson hitched us legal.
Better you learn to accept it."

"I don't care what you paid my pa," she said.
"You ain't ever gonna have any rights over me. You
can't make me stay." Her auburn hair spilled forward to partly conceal her hate-filled features. "I'll
leave even if I have to crawl."

"You'll crawl, all right. Get yourself back in the
hay. I aim to take me a poke right now."

Pacer stood inside the door and searched for the
ax handle. He found it lying near a barrel of nails. He
hefted the club in his strong right hand, and advanced
down the aisle where Frank Shapter stood over the
fallen young woman he had bought for the price of a
pair of hogs. With Shapter blocking the aisle, Lorelei
couldn't see past to the Choctaw Kid as he
approached. She wouldn't have warned her tormentor
anyway.

Pacer walked up behind Shapter, who heard a
straw snap too late and started to turn. Pacer swung
the ax handle and caught the bully behind the thighs.

Shapter howled as his legs buckled, and he dropped to his knees. He dug in his coat pocket for a short-barreled Colt he kept tucked away. Pacer ended that threat with a blow to the big man's belly.

"Gawd damn!" Shapter gasped, and leaned forward on both hands. "You son of a bitch." Pacer was prepared to deliver another blow. But Shapter's movements became clumsy. Slowly he flattened facedown on the stable floor and lay still.

Lorelei looked up in surprise. She scrambled to her feet and Pacer noticed a horseshoe that she had concealed in the loose dirt and straw by her side. It was obvious she would not have yielded to Shapter without a fight.

"I knew you'd come back," Lorelei said. She wiped a trickle of blood from her bruised and swollen lip. Her eyes held a gleam of triumph. She retrieved her carpetbag.

Pacer knelt by the fallen man just to make sure Shapter was still breathing. He was relieved to see the man's chest rise and fall.

"I'll stay here in case Frank comes to. You fetch the town marshal and we'll clap our friend in irons. I never met a constable yet who'd tolerate seeing a woman beaten." Pacer prodded the unconscious lout with the toe of his boot. "Reckon he'll lock our friend up and throw away the key."

"I don't think so," Lorelei said. She rolled Shapter over on his back. The man groaned but remained unconscious. Lorelei folded back the flap of his sodden frock coat to reveal the tin star of Fort Smith's town marshal pinned to Shapter's vest.

Pacer closed his eyes and shook his head. "Oh no," he sighed. After borrowing a pair of bridles from the tack wall, he set to work securing Shapter's ankles and wrists with the long black leather reins. Shapter's own neckerchief made an appropriate gag. Pacer

dragged the big man to the rear of the stable and
deposited him in the dimmest corner available.

Pacer hurried down the aisle with Lorelei coming
along a few paces behind. Through the open doorway
he noticed the rain had lessened to a fragile mist
that seemed to hang suspended in the evening air.
Pacer emerged from the barn and slogged across the
muddy ground to the pinto that had pulled free from
the latch but thankfully had remained nearby. The
Kentucky mare was also close at hand. The mare
recognized Lorelei as she held a hand beneath the animal's nostrils, allowing the mare to catch her scent.
Pacer swung into the saddle and fixed the young
woman in his impassive stare.

"I don't have a place to go. Not in Arkansas.
There's Shapters all through the Ozarks," she said.

Pacer tried to stop himself, but the words spilled
out as if they had a life of their own. "You can come
along with me for a spell."

Lorelei grinned. Was this also something she
had known all along? She leaped astride Frank
Shapter's prized Kentucky mare. From a distance
came a rumble of thunder, one final warning. This was
only a lull. The storms were far from over.

PART TWO

Flames of Folly

Chapter Twelve

Raven O'Keefe McQueen heard the wind call her name. She looked up from the kitchen table where she had been preparing a mixture of dried bull berries and wild turnips to be brewed into a medicine for Libby Whitfield. Gip Whitfield, Libby's husband, continued to pace the cozy confines of the sitting room. He had heard nothing but the sound of his own breath and the floorboards creaking beneath his feet. Since old Doctor Linus Dick had his stroke, Chahta Creek was without a physician. But Raven McQueen had learned her lessons well. Her mother had been a Choctaw medicine woman who taught her to look to nature's own bounty for healing.

Raven shoved clear of the table and headed for the front room. She moved quickly and gracefully despite her sixty-seven years. Her long black hair was streaked with gray, but her eyes were flashing and clear. And the lines that crinkled at the corners of her eyes and mouth were but the telltale tracks of wisdom.

She handed Gip a medicine bag filled with the mixture of roots, leaves, and berries she had prepared. The farmer pacing the front room gratefully accepted her preparations.

"You make Libby a full pot of this tea and make certain she drinks every drop," Raven told the worried man.

Whitfield nodded his thanks. He was average in height, boyish-faced with freckled cheeks and straight brown hair. A year ago, Gip had ridden into Indian Territory attached to the 3rd Texas Cavalry. After contracting measles, he had been left behind when Colonel E. B. Greer rode east to join Nathan Bedford Forrest and his hell-for-leather Confederate cavalry in Alabama. Gip had never planned to be a deserter, but after being nursed back to health by Libby Culver, a sweet-tempered Choctaw widow, Gip had found reason after reason to prolong his stay on his benefactor's farm. The war had grown less important to him as his affection for Libby continued to grow. They had been married only two months ago, and although there had been a certain amount of scandal attributed to their relationship at first, once the wedding vows were exchanged, all sins, real or imagined, were forgiven by most of the surrounding community.

"You reckon this will break her fever?" Gip asked, searching for a little reassurance.

"I wouldn't be sending you off with it," Raven replied, "if I didn't think it would help." The brogue she inherited from her Irish father had a habit of creeping into her speech whenever she tried to make a point.

"Well, I ain't doubting you, Mrs. McQueen," Gip added, thrusting the buckskin bag in his coat pocket. "You been real good to us. Even before me and Libby got hitched. You treated us like . . . well . . . "

"Like the good people you both are," Raven said. She patted the farmer's arm and walked him to the front door. He had a good five-mile ride to the Culver farm. It would be night by the time he reached home.

"I pray you come to no harm for helpin' me. There be some who don't have much use for a deserter or anyone who lends me a hand." Gip lowered his voice. "Call themselves Knights of the Golden Circle. Long riders, I call them. Hooded highwaymen with no allegiance except to mischief. No better than Quantrill's bunch, murderin' and attackin' innocent folks—uh, I'm sorry. I spoke out of turn." Gip suddenly recalled that Raven's grandson, Pacer Wolf McQueen, was reputed to have taken part in the raid on Lawrence. Gip reddened and cleared his throat and turned around to retrieve his hat from a peg by the door. It was a comfortable room; indeed, the entire farmhouse was furnished with hand-hewn chairs and tables, and each bedroom contained a wrought-iron bed whose frame had been fashioned in Kit McQueen's own forge back in '51.

"Tell Libby I will be out to visit her as soon as I can," said Raven. Gip Whitfield nodded, and vanished through the door. He hurried out from under the porch and swung up astride the charger he had brought up from Texas. The animal had grudgingly adapted to its new role as a plow horse. With a wave of his hand, Gip sped away, leaving Raven on the porch, a solitary figure framed by lantern-lit windows in a whitewashed wood-frame ranch house.

Kit and Raven McQueen had built their ranch house and laid claim to over a thousand acres twenty miles from town, nestled against the foothills of the Kiamichi Mountains and along the west bank of Buffalo Creek. The house faced south to catch the warm summer breezes. Raven often took her breakfast out on the porch to watch the birds circle and dip above the buffalo grass carpeting the rolling meadow while clouds, like airy ships, sailed in tranquil and stately grace across an ocean of limitless sky.

But the porch did not hold her now. When the wind called, only the hill behind the house, to the

north, would do. Raven darted back inside the front
room, caught up a shawl draped over a wing-backed
rocking chair near the hearth, and proceeded through
the house and the winter kitchen and left by the
back door, which swung awkwardly on a broken
hinge and banged shut in her wake. She trudged
across the yard, scattering hens in her wake. She
paused in her journey to chase the chickens back
into the coop, then continued up the trail that cut a
straight path to the top of the limestone hill behind the
house.

By the time Raven reached the summit of the hill,
the sun was dipping below the horizon and night
crept across the wooded ridges and engulfed the valley that stretched like a deep gash northwest into
the heart of the Kiamichi wilderness. This was an
ancient landscape.

Eons ago, the earth upthrust a mountainous chain
of peaks and corrugated cliffs. Rains fell, cooling the
tortured crust. Seas formed, teemed with life, evapo-
rated into swamps, then vanished over millions of
years and left behind the Kiamichi Mountains as a
legacy to the timeless act of creation and re-creation.
The elder spirits who walked this wilderness whispered ageless songs of life and death.

The wind called her name yet again. Raven stood
upon the hilltop, her silvery black hair streaming
behind her, her arms outstretched as she waited and
watched. The branches of a white oak halfway up the
slope rustled and stirred, the clattering against one
another like chattering teeth. Night deepened. The last
rosy glow to the west faded to grayish blue then
black. Raven broke from her trancelike state and gathered together a small mound of dry brittle branches
and, using crumbled chunks of bark for tinder, struck
a match. After a few tries she had a small flame she
could nourish into a hearty blaze, her spirit fire.
Embers like desperate souls erupted into the night sky

and winked out, leaving only a brief memory of pulsing light imprinted on the eye to mark their passing. Raven's course cotton dress pressed against her legs as she turned toward the direction of the gusting breezes. Her shawl and linen blouse and the proximity of the spirit fire ensured her warmth. When she shivered, it was because of the unknown, the anticipation, the waiting. Time had no meaning now, it held no importance, there was only the wind and the leaping flames, her prayer song rising on the smoke, and the vastness of the night shrouded mountains.

> *Nothing lives long*
> *except the sky and the*
> *mountains and the mystery*
> *that lies between.*

"It's getting dark," Lorelei complained. "I'm tired. We ought to make camp." She looked wistfully at the redbud-lined banks of Buffalo Creek and even in the dim light located several suitable campsites. They were a good five-days ride from Fort Smith, well out of danger from the likes of Frank Shapter and his kin, and still Pacer would not relax. He seemed a driven man, and that puzzled Lorelei. The very first night on the trail she had opened her blankets and offered herself to her new-found companion only to have Pacer gently refuse her charms. She could tell he was attracted to her. More than once over the past week she had caught him watching her. At those times Pacer would quickly focus his attention elsewhere, a ploy that amused the flirtatious and wily young woman. She was accustomed to men wanting her. Desire was a weapon she had often used to her advantage.

Lorelei had charmed Frank Shapter into rescuing her from a dirt-farm existence with a careworn mother and a brutish father who saw in his children just so many laborers to toil in his fallow fields. The marshal of Fort Smith hadn't been much of an improvement, merely a means to an end. Lorelei envisioned herself garbed in flowing silk dresses and escorted by handsome gentlemen and riding in elegant carriages along the hilly boulevards of San Francisco.

"Won't be much further," Pacer Wolf said with a glance over his shoulder at the weary young woman. Lorelei was a handful, all right. He was aware of her shortcomings, but she was a fighter; she showed tremendous spirit and resiliency. These were good qualities in any man or woman. However hardened life might have made her, underneath he sensed a vulnerability that appealed to him. He didn't know if it had been the right decision to bring her along, but he didn't regret it.

They followed the gentle undulations of the creek for another half hour and rode past a scattered herd of about three hundred head of shorthorn cattle before the steep hills to either side drew back and the broader valley of the Kimishi River opened up in the distance. Between Pacer and the junction of Buffalo Creek and the Kimishi River, a campfire burned like a beacon atop the treeless summit of a solitary hill. Pacer reined in and a smile crept across his face. The sun had dipped below the horizon, the last blush of light had faded from the sky. Yet even in the dark of night, Pacer knew home waited just beyond that blaze.

"There's a fire on the hill," Lorelei warily took notice. Her instinct for survival made her cautious.

"A beacon for us." Pacer motioned for the woman to draw abreast of his pinto. "It's my grandmother's way of welcoming us home."

"But how could she know we were coming?" Lorelei asked, her disbelief obvious in her tone.

"That is Raven's way," Pacer replied. He realized it wasn't much of an explanation, but it was the only one he had. Long ago he had learned not to question his grandmother's actions. She was a medicine woman, a healer, and different from other women. He reached inside his shirt and cupped the buckskin pouch dangling from a leather cord around his throat. Raven McQueen had given him the pouch when Pacer was thirteen. He had never looked inside to examine its contents, for that would have broken its spirit power and destroyed the magic. And as Raven once told him, each life ought to have mystery.

She raised Pacer and Jesse after their mother abandoned them. Ben McQueen had arrived at the ranch with two small boys, aged four and two. Kit and Raven welcomed them and gave them a home and a sense of belonging. Though only an eighth Choctaw, the brothers had run as wild as any of the full-bloods and become versed in the ways of the red man and white. While the world of their father appealed to Jesse, it was among the Choctaw that Pacer felt most comfortable. And despite his long red hair and tawny limbs and towering physique, Pacer was accepted by the Choctaw Nation as one of their own.

Frowning, Pacer wondered if the debacle at Lawrence had changed all that. Sawyer Truett had probably spread the word of Pacer's behavior. Treachery, Sawyer would call it, no doubt. And what of Raven? Had she learned of the raid? Would she accept him home? He studied the beacon and resolved that there was only one way to find out.

"Come on," he said to Lorelei. At a touch of his bootheels, the pinto lifted its head from the sweet grass it had discovered and trotted off toward the hill. Fifteen minutes later at least part of his question was answered. Raven was standing at the base of the hill as Pacer cantered his pinto up from the creekbank. She was wrapped in her shawl, her long silvery black hair streaming behind her as she stood watching him, her dark eyes drifting over the girl on the Kentucky mare and back to her grandson.

Pacer dismounted and walked up to the medicine woman and in a hesitant voice said, "Grandmother. I am home."

Raven studied him a moment. How much like his grandfather he seemed, the eyes and hair, everything but the height. Kit McQueen had been a man built compact and leathery tough, much like Jesse. She smiled. Memories of the two boys whooping and hollering, always underfoot and filling her house with noise, came flooding back.

Some called the Choctaw Kid a renegade and a murderer. Others, like Sawyer Truett, had ridden by and accused Pacer of cowardice and betrayal.

Love would not allow her to believe any such foolish talk. And so by her actions she laid her grandson's worries to rest. Raven opened her arms and her heart. Pacer Wolf McQueen had returned home.

"It is good," she said.

Chapter Thirteen

Raven's medicine fire wasn't the only signal that night. A couple of hours after sundown at a place called Hanging Widow Bluffs overlooking the Kimishi River and a couple of miles south of the town of Chahta Creek, a pyre of oak branches was set ablaze. Flames leaped skyward and illuminated the six-foot-tall figure of Hud Pardee, cloaked in saffron-colored robes and hood. The robes concealed his every feature as he waited in the circle of light cast by the dancing flames. He sat astride his blazed-face bay gelding with his back to the hickory tree from which a grieving widow, as legend had it, ended her life. The fire on the bluff could be seen for miles around. Pardee had built it to summon the night riders from their plantations and farms. Given to impatience, he forced himself to remain on the bluff, begrudging the minutes spent waiting. He straightened the hood, all the better to see through the narrow eye slits. A coiled serpent had been embroidered in gold thread above the eye holes. It was the symbol of his authority. He had to give Cap Featherstone credit. The old fox had sensed the Confederate forays were the means of fanning

the embers of rebellion into open conflagration. All to
Cap's own benefit, and Hud Pardee's.

And so the hooded horsemen gathered, drawn
from trails and roads in every direction until more
than forty men had arrived. They did not greet one
another openly, for this wasn't a social gathering,
rather the Knights had come with a single purpose in
mind—to strike fear into the hearts of Union sympathizers and drive out those families who dared not
swear allegiance to the Confederate flag. A way of life
was at stake here. It had been a good life. Despite losing their ancestral homes during their removal from
Mississippi, many of the Choctaws, full blood and
mixed, had prospered. They had built fine plantations
and cultivated vast fields of cotton upon soil nurtured
and watered with the sweat and blood of the slaves
they had brought with them from the deep south.
Those hooded horsemen who owned no slaves feared
the Union would someday confiscate the Choctaw
lands yet again and move them still further westward. The government in Richmond had ceded the
Choctaws, the Cherokees, and the Creeks their lands in
writing for all time and had revoked any and all
claims to the Indian Territory. The Confederate
President had won the trust of many among the
Civilized Tribes. Why, the rebels even had a Cherokee
general in Stand Watie. Now it was the Choctaws' turn
to rise up and be counted. As they formed a circle
around the flames, firelight played upon the saffron
robes of the horsemen and washed their raiments in its
golden glow.

"Knights of the Golden Circle," Pardee called
out. "We are gathered once more to ride with honor
against our enemies and drive them from our home-
land. Those among our people who wish to be like
dogs and fight over the scraps from Mr. Lincoln's
table, then let them head north. We are Choctaw.
We are warriors. We are Knights of the Golden

Circle—free men gathered in a righteous cause. Will you ride with me?"

"Yes!" came the reply as forty-three voices roared out approval.

"And what shall be the fate of Mr. Lincoln's boot lickers, eh?"

"Drive them from our land!" the Knights answered excitedly.

"And who shall stand against us in our sacred mission!"

"No one!" the Knights shouted in return. Several of the men fired revolvers into the air. The crack of gunfire spooked a few of the horses and their riders had to struggle to bring the skittish animals under control. Tullock Roberts, one of the wealthiest plantation owners in the area, had the most trouble. He had ridden a gelding newly broke to the trail. The barrel-chested horseman tugged savagely on the reins and, despite being nearly thrown, at last brought the animal under control. Sam Roberts, a reed-thin eighteen-year-old copy of his father, laughed aloud. Tullock knew his son even through the younger man's robes and he fixed Sam in a withering glare that silenced his son on the spot.

"Where do we ride?" another of the Knights called out. He brandished a torch that he touched to the council fire and set ablaze. Several of the other horsemen followed suit. Soon the Golden Circle became a ring of flickering flames.

"West to the Texas Road. We've given Hack Warner fair warning to close his station. The man has refused. What say you?" Pardee stood in his stirrups and raised his arms aloft. He resembled more a mysterious prophet than a gunfighter.

"Burn him out! Burn him out!" The outcry became a chant that rose in volume and reverberated along the river bank.

"So be it," said the man in the serpent hood.

"Let men of valor lead the way." Pardee waved a hand in a westerly direction. As the Knights departed for the Texas Road, he slowly and deliberately circled the hanging tree and the crackling fire until the last of the Knights had departed. He wanted to make certain there were no stragglers. Any horseman who held back would immediately be suspect. Satisfied as to the enthusiasm and loyalty of his hooded legion, Hud Pardee guided his steed onto the trail west and vanished into the shadows and the settling dust.

Chapter Fourteen

The last thing Tullock wanted on the morning after the raid on Warner's Station was guilt with his grits. He sat back in his chair and sighed as his mulatto house servant, Willow Reaves, scooped a second helping of buttered grits onto her master's plate and added a couple of thick links of spicy sausage. She had already brought the biscuits and left a tureen of sausage gravy.

Tullock was a large, solid man with close-cropped sandy white hair. He had a neck as thick as a bull's. It was said that Tullock Roberts had never been knocked off his feet and was the match of any man. His blunt, square-jawed face attempted to look contrite as Arbitha Roberts, his good wife, renewed her tirade. Arbitha's coppery complexion was streaked with sweat as she paced the dining room, her wide hips brushing the backs of the chairs every time she changed course.

Willow Reaves, a sweet-natured slip of a girl, finished serving Tullock and hurried around the table to the Roberts' eighteen-year-old son. Sam had relished his part in last night's raid. He had personally driven off the way station's horses and burned Hack Warner's supply of hay. He was a pale young man whose tall, angular frame was from time to time wracked by an intermittent cough. A mustache and goatee the same color as his sandy hair added a few years to his appearance. He was exhausted from the night's endeavors, but he still had the energy to admire Willow's supple physique beneath her home-spun cotton dress. The mulatto could feel the young man's glittery eyes ranging over her form. She shifted uncomfortably and finished filling his plate with food.

Arbitha continued to berate her men. How could Tullock drag his son out on such a foray when the poor boy wasn't well? What was Tullock trying to prove? Their plantation was prospering. The fields were as white as a snowfall with a cotton crop, thigh high and ripe for picking. What did they need with trouble? Tullock and Sam had thrown in with hooligans.

"Riding around with sheets over your heads. I say it's a good way to charge head-on into a tree and break your necks," Arbitha added as she ran out of steam. She slumped into her chair at the opposite end of the table from her husband. She waved Willow away as the mulatto approached with the coffee pot. The servant nodded and hurried from the room.

Willow did not like being in the way of these family confrontations; however, she was thankful for the quarrel. It kept young Sam occupied. His attentions were becoming increasingly overt and she did not know how long she could hold Tullock's son at bay. Fortunately, his chronic illness slowed his movements and often sapped his strength. Willow, despite her diminuitive size, felt confident she could fend off the young man's attentions if he got out of hand. How Master Tullock might react was another matter entirely. The lord of Honey Ridge Plantation was quick to anger, never more so when Si Reaves, Willow's husband and the plantation's overseer, had stolen a horse and escaped to the north and freedom. The memory of that day in March still caused Willow to shudder. Oh, how Tullock Roberts had ranted and raved. Willow was certain had it not been for her reputation as the finest cook in all the territory, she would have borne the brunt of Tullock's wrath. He took his overseer's betrayal as a personal affront. Willow could not think of Si without a mixture of relief and hurt. He had escaped, well and good. Among the other slaves he was considered a hero. But to Willow, the man she loved had left her behind, abandoned her to bondage. Although time had cooled the anger, the hurt remained.

"Now, Mama, there's a war on. This is no time for fence sitters. A man must choose a side and stand there and be counted." Tullock ladled a dipper full of sausage gravy over his biscuits and began to eat, taking a bite of biscuit then a chunk of sausage and following that with a forkful of buttered grits. He had always called her "Mama," even before their only child was born.

"It's not as if we killed anybody," Sam spoke up, hoping to placate his irate mother. "Those who stand against us need to be driven out. Our future lies with the South."

"Exactly," Tullock said with a nod to his son. "Anyone who feels different should leave the territory. The sooner the better."

"Mark my word, this will lead to killing and more killing," Arbitha warned.

"If blood is shed it will not be by our hands, not at first. But if those Federalists in Chahta Creek start something, then we will answer them an eye for an eye and a bullet for a bullet." Tullock wiped a forearm across his mouth, noticed his wife's disapproving glare, and picked up his cloth napkin and dabbed at his lips. He looked at Sam and winked. "Your mother's made a tame breed out of me, son."

"You didn't look tame last night." Sam grinned.

"Neither did you, boy, neither did you." Both men broke into laughter, sharing a joke that Arbitha could never be a part of. "Riding and shooting your gun and chasing those horses to beat the band," Tullock said. Sam's laughter dissolved into a coughing spasm that caused his father to glance worriedly at Arbitha. She rose and crossed around the table and stood by her son, placing an arm around his narrow, bony shoulders.

"I'm all right, Mother," he gasped, at last catching his breath. "It was worse last night, what with all the fire and smoke. Darn near coughed myself plumb out of the saddle." He managed a weak smile. "Maybe I'll take me a rest." He slid back from the table, reassured his mother with a pat on her arm, stood in his dusty clothes, and excused himself and left the dining room. His footsteps reverberated in the hallway, then beat a brisk tattoo on the broad wooden stairway that swept up from the foyer to the bedrooms above.

The downstairs consisted of a front parlor and dining room, a conservatory, and a library. The kitchen and pantry ran along the rear of the house. Tullock Roberts had done well for himself in the territory. He had rebuilt and recovered everything that had been lost when, as quarter-Choctaws, his parents had been forced to leave their plantation in the Mississippi Delta. His mother and father had died during the removal of the Civilized Tribes. Bowed but not broken, Tullock had come to this new land determined to achieve more than his parents had ever dreamed. Honey Ridge was twice the size of their Delta home. He had claimed twice the amount of land and, working alongside his slaves, Tullock had made the land yield its wealth in cotton and crops to be shipped eastward to markets in the South.

Riverboats along the Red River carried bales of his cotton on to Shreveport. Yet there were times when he would give it all up for the health of his only son.

"He'll be fine," Arbitha said. At moments like this, she was the stronger of the two. Her mother's love refused to accept anything less than Sam's complete recovery. With her hands on the back of the chair, she faced the doorway through which he had vanished.

"How can you be so certain?" Tullock said.

"Because he's as stubborn as his father," Arbitha said.

"Hmm," Tullock grunted. His fears for the moment defused, he returned his attention to breakfast. He wolfed down the last of his food.

"Take your time," Arbitha gently chided as she returned to her place. Sunlight was clearing the ridge to the east and transformed the cornfields into stalks of gold. "You've been gone all night. The only place you need to hurry to is bed."

"I want to start some of my blacks on harvesting that corn before the damn crows take it all."

"Sawyer can tell them. You hired him to run things."

"I sent him off into the hills yesterday morning. I told him I didn't want to see his face unless he brought me a deer to hang in the smokehouse. He's a natural-born hunter and a crack shot. I expect he'll be along directly." Tullock belched, and endured his wife's withering look of disapproval.

"Uh—pardon me." He started to wipe his mouth on his sleeve again, then switched and reached for the cloth by his plate. He eased away from the table and gathered up the two robes and hoods he had left in a pile on a chair by the door to the kitchen. "See you put these back in the trunk upstairs." He placed them on the table near his wife.

"Grown men playing like children," Arbitha remarked. Now that the sight of the robes had started her up again, she was determined to make her objections known.

"No. This is not a game," Tullock said. "We aim to strike fear in the hearts of these Federalists. And as long as our identities are concealed, there can be no retribution should the Union troops massed on our northern border ever move across to occupy the territory before we can put together a force to push them back." Tullock saw she wasn't convinced and he shrugged in exasperation. "Just hide the blasted things upstairs." He wagged his head and started from the room. "What do women know about war anyway?" he muttered.

Arbitha sighed, and glared at the robes as if they were the harbingers of her misfortune. No one knew the identity of the leader of the Knights, although many of the night riders knew each other despite their robes and hoods. Still, the disguises kept their enemies from making a positive identification and perhaps there was some safety in that. But such a notion did little to dispel Arbitha's sense of foreboding. What did women know of war? "We do the burying and the mourning," she said. But Tullock was outside and heading for the slaves' quarters and there was no one to hear her reply.

Pacer Wolf McQueen stood on the porch of the ranch house and sipped coffee from a blue enameled tin cup. Steam curled up into his nostrils as he held the cup to his lips, then blew gently to cool the dark bitter liquid before he chanced another mouthful. He peered over the cup and studied the homesite in the light of a new day. The barn sure looked in need of repair. Someone had been fixing the roof and had apparently left without completing the task. A tall ladder still rested against the side of the barn. Pacer took a step off the porch and started to cross the side yard when a large snow white goose came charging out of the barn. With its wings spread, the mean-tempered creature seemed huge and angry as a banshee bearing down on Pacer.

"It's me, Hecuba!" Pacer shouted. He dropped his cup and backpedaled toward the safety of the porch. Raven emerged from the house and had a good laugh at her grandson's expense.

Hecuba flapped her wings and lowered her beak like a knight his lance and drove onward. Pacer leaped back onto the porch, leaving the goose to flap and honk and parade victoriously across the field of battle.

"Hecuba. No!" Raven hissed, and added a command in Choctaw. The great white bird shook its head and then waddled off around the side of the house.

"She wasn't around last night," Raven said. "Every once in a while she wanders off; I suspect to meet her paramour back in the woods."

"Keep that up and she's apt to meet her maker and do a turn on the roasting spit," Pacer grumbled. Hecuba had been the bane of his existence for several years. He tolerated the belligerent bird because it made an excellent "watch goose" and could generally be counted on to sound an alert whenever strangers appeared in the vicinity of the ranch house.

Pacer Wolf had been with Quantrill's raiders for the better part of the summer. In his absence he had hired three men to tend the cattle and see to the crops and general upkeep of the homesite. Not a one of them was anywhere to be seen. Raven seemed to read his thoughts.

"Two of the lads ran off to join the Confederate regiment in Arkansas. They collected a week's wages and left. Noble Pierce stayed on another week and a half. Then he heard of a troop of Creeks heading for Kansas to fight for the North and he left, too." Raven shook her head. "All three boys sat around my table and took their supper and ate together like family. And now they'll be trying to kill each other. It doesn't make any sense."

"A man does what he has to do," Pacer said.

"Oh, my life, I swear, such talk is but an excuse for a body's own foolishness. I'm thinking, maybe it's time men did what they *ought* to and not what they *had* to." Raven walked along the porch and sat in a ladderbacked rocking chair. The floorboards creaked as she began to rock. A blue grosbeak glided past the porch, rode an updraft that carried the bird across the meadow and over the banks of the Kimishi River, where it alighted among the reeds and Christmas ferns whose emerald fans swayed in the morning breeze.

"Do you know about the Lawrence raid?" Pacer asked. While settling in for the night he had only offered an explanation for Lorelei's presence and spoke little of himself. To his dismay, she nodded her head.

"News travels quickly. I have already heard several versions," Raven replied. "Sawyer Truett's was most exuberant. Carmichael Ross also devoted an entire front page of the *Chahta Creek Courier* excoriating those who took part in the slaughter."

"And you know I was there."

"Yes."

"And still you welcomed me home. Why?"

Raven turned and color crept into her cheeks. "Daniel Pacer Wolf McQueen. Do you be thinking that I believe every tidbit of hearsay that comes my way? Yes, I've been told the Choctaw Kid has a price on his head for coming to Lawrence. As for what happened and the role you played, I'll believe what I hear from your own lips." She set her cup of coffee aside and folded her arms across her chest. "I know my grandsons. And I know that both you and Jesse, though you might march to different drummers, you both stand for what you believe is right. And I know that neither you nor Jesse nor your father would ever willingly bring dishonor to our name." She nodded and then with a wave of her hand motioned toward the meadow. "This is a good country. The topsoil is rich and thick. We McQueens are like the land, Pacer. Our pride runs deep." She smiled and the skin crinkled about the mouth and eyes. Pacer thought his grandmother had never seemed prettier, for she was passion and fire and quiet wisdom and indomitable strength and enduring faith. "Tell me what happened if you wish, but do not think to win my trust, for you have never lost it."

Pacer was tempted but the land called to him. He wanted to be about the business of being home. "I would like to. Later tonight. I think I'll pick some snap beans for supper." He climbed down the steps and picked up a bucket that Raven kept at the corner of the porch. The medicine woman watched him, noticing the changes in Pacer a year had wrought. Despite a night's sleep in his own bedroom, his movements were wary and tense. Like a cat poised to spring, he remained constantly on guard, as if expecting an attack at any time from any direction. And he carried a Colt revolver either belted around his hips or tucked into the waistband of his trousers wherever he went, even to the garden. She didn't question his actions, though Lord only knew she wanted to. Evidently the Choctaw Kid had made a number of enemies. And the list was growing.

"Yeow! Ouch!" A woman's outcry followed by a series of antagonistic cackles and a good deal of honking shattered Raven's thoughts. She heard the pad of bare feet upon the dirt, and then with another resounding "Ouch!" and a brisk flapping of wings the door to the outhouse creaked open and slammed shut. There followed a stream of curses and insults blue enough to make a muleskinner blush.

Raven listened and waited, a bemused expression on her face. The young woman's curses eventually subsided and became a plaintive call for someone to please—please—free her from the "necessary."

Hecuba continued to dare "someone" to try.

Just try.

Lorelei managed to dress without sitting down. Her posterior still smarted from Hecuba's attack, but at least she had the satisfaction of seeing the goose take a healthy swat from Raven's broom. Escaping the outhouse, Lorelei had hurried back to the house where she pulled on a gingham dress and slipped into a pair of brushed buckskin moccasins that Raven had left by her bed. With a certain degree of trepidation, the fifteen-year-old descended the stairway and stepped once more into the morning sunlight. As she closed the back door behind her, she noticed Raven over by the chicken coop surrounded by a piping flock of young chicks clamoring for the feed she was scattering over the ground. Several white leghorn hens and plump Rhode Island Reds pecked at the ground corn spilling like a golden shower from Raven's outstretched hand. Lorelei stood on the outside of the coop looking in.

"My ma, first thing every morning, used to feed the chickens. My job was to gather the eggs. Once I tripped and dropped my basket and broke nigh all of them. Pa was furious and whipped me good. He liked his eggs of a morning. Reckon eggs was the food he favored most. Some days he traded the extra for a bottle of corn liquor in town." Lorelei chewed absently on the knuckle of her hand as she remembered the incident, reliving each stinging blow from her father's switch. She frowned and looked at Raven. "After, I broke 'em on purpose. Every chance I got. Sometimes I'd wake up real early and sneak out before sunup. I'd take them eggs and crush 'em or bury 'em out in the field." She seemed very satisfied with herself, a smug set to her lips. "Pa thought it was a fox or a coyote or some other kind of critter breaking into the coop. Drove him plumb crazy. I think Ma knew it was me but she never said nothing. She was afraid he would kill me."

"This frontier's a place of great beauty, but it can be hard and unforgiving. And those who live here can turn out the same way. Your father sounds like just such a hard man." Raven glanced at the steep-sided hills bordering the secluded valley of Buffalo Creek.

"I seen iron with more bend," Lorelei replied. She shrugged. "What the hell, most men are bastards."

Raven flashed the girl a stern look. It was a warning, unmistakable and grim, but Lorelei seemed amused.

"I know, if it wasn't for Pacer I'd still be a prisoner in Fort Smith. But he wants something. Everybody wants something." Lorelei studied the older woman a moment, her gaze full of cynical wisdom belying her young age. "I thought Indians were supposed to hide their feelings but, Miss Raven, you are as easy to read as a book. I've seen lightning tamer than the look you just gave me." Lorelei folded her hands in front of her. An auburn strand of hair curled toward the corner of her mouth.

"I'm half Irish, my darling," Raven said. "The Irish in me often takes offense at the drop of a hat. But it's my Choctaw half that's the more dangerous. My mother's people know a thousand ways to take revenge and exact retribution for an affront. We don't forgive or forget."

"That sounds like a warning," Lorelei replied. Her nonchalance was a trifle forced. It disturbed her that Raven seemed beyond the young girl's power to charm.

"As a boy growing up here, Pacer was always

bringing home a stray pup or a bird with a broken wing or anything wounded. Once he rescued a bobcat from a fox trap Sawyer Truett had set. The cat's leg was sorely injured. Pacer nursed the animal back to health and set it free. He still carries the scars from the bobcat's claws."

"And now, here I am, eh?" Lorelei asked, her eyes twinkling.

Raven nodded. She emptied the last of the feed over the chickens and stepped outside the coop and leaned in close to the girl from Fort Smith. "And here you are." A strained silence passed between them. When it ended, Raven and Lorelei understood one another. Raven picked up a basket she had brought from the kitchen and handed it to Lorelei. The medicine woman had just the chore for this most recent of Pacer's "wounded" guests.

"Why don't you gather the eggs?" Raven suggested pleasantly.

Lorelei nodded and smiled cordially and accepted the task. "My pleasure."

Neither woman was fooled.

Pacer's shirt hung from one of the fence posts near the garden. Gathering snap beans was hot work, but Pacer relished the simplicity of the task. The garden offered peace and freedom from the doubts that had begun to plague his waking hours. He realized his return could only be a temporary visit. Raven's valley was merely a calm port in the storm of conflict dividing the country. The war had already proved costly. His beliefs were diametrically opposed to those held by his father and brother. What would they think when they saw the posters calling for the apprehension of the Choctaw Kid? The raid on Lawrence had caused the Confederacy to scorn his service. And in abandoning Quantrill he had no doubt earned the enmity of his friends and comrades at arms. It was too much for him to think through. So he quit and concentrated on twisting the pale green pods off their stems. The vines grew thick about each wooden pole. Pacer lost track of time.

He had filled the first bucket and started on a second when he heard Hecuba sound her warning from over by the barn. He set the bucket aside and walked down between the rows of snap beans and waited at the edge of the garden. Pacer wished he could see the north trail leading from the headwaters of Buffalo Creek to the house. He thought about crossing over to the barn, where he'd be able to have a full view of the upper reaches of the valley. The damn hill blocking his vision was a perfect windbreak but made a blind spot from his current vantage point. Raven and Lorelei were inside. Smoke curled from the chimney and the aroma of baking cornbread drifted on the air. Raven was safe, Lorelei too. Pacer shoved open the makeshift gate and trotted up from the garden and across the path to the "necessary." The chicks hurried to the henhouse as he passed the coop. He slowed his pace as he neared the corner of the house. About a hundred feet from Pacer, the barn cast its shadow across the side yard. From within the barn, a cow issued a deep, doleful moo as if reminding its human owners that it had not been milked this morning. The horses in the corral off to the side of the barn circled the trampled earth and nervously tossed their manes. They, too, were aware of someone riding onto the homestead. But it was Hecuba who sounded the most frantic alert. Spreading her gray-tipped wings, she paced in front of the smokehouse alongside the barn. The goose extended her neck and issued a raucous challenge. She put on such a show that Sawyer Truett was completely absorbed in watching Hecuba, fearing she might charge his already skittish mount or the pack horse he was leading. Sawyer had dropped the carcass of a white-tailed deer across the back of the

plodding brown mare behind him. He'd also loaded a
second bloody hide and packets of venison, hastily
smoked to keep the meat from spoiling until he
reached Tullock Roberts' plantation.

Sawyer sensed movement to his right, and as
Hecuba ceased her alarm he turned to find Pacer
watching him. Sweat rolled across McQueen's bronze
torso, down his arms, and dripped from the knuckles
of his right hand, which dangled loose by the worn
wooden gun butt jutting from the holster at his side.

Sawyer Truett looked much the same as he had in
Lawrence. He wore the loose-fitting gray blouse and
black trousers of a guerrilla. However, he wasn't
bristling with guns like before. He sported a single Colt
Dragoon thrust in his waistband and cradled a long-
barreled Kentucky rifle in the crook of his arm. The
"Kentuck" was his hunting gun. Its blued-steel barrel
encased in a walnut stock was as long as most men
were tall and fired a .52 caliber bullet. The dead car-
casses bore mute testimony to the hunter's marksmanship. Both animals had been killed with
headshots.

"I figured that fresh trail belonged to you,"
Sawyer said. He scratched his black goatee and started
to shift the rifle in his arms. For the moment it was
aimed toward the barn. "The tracks of two horses had
me wondering, though."

"I wouldn't do that," Pacer warned.

Sawyer froze in midmotion and managed a look
of wounded innocence. "You're a might touchy, Pacer
Wolf." The horseman held up his right hand so that
Pacer could see the livid white scrawl of scar tissue
across Sawyer's knuckles, the legacy of McQueen's
knife. "But maybe you have the right to be." Sawyer
doffed his floppy-brimmed hat and wiped the perspiration from his forehead on the sleeve of his guerrilla shirt. "Any man who turns again' his own ought

to keep on guard. 'Cause he's chosen a lonely road to walk."

"What do you want here, Sawyer?"

"I was reared on this land same as you. Reckon I can come callin' on Raven if I've a mind." He glanced up as the back door opened and Pacer's grandmother descended the few steps to the ground. Lorelei appeared but remained on the top landing, framed in the doorway. One cheek was smudged with cornmeal. A morning breeze ruffled the hem of her gingham dress and revealed the pretty turn of her ankles.

"Good morning, Sawyer, you're just in time for cornbread and molasses."

"That's a tempting offer, Miss Raven, but I'm due back at Honey Ridge before any of this meat spoils. I might could butcher it out right here ... " Sawyer's voice trailed off as he noticed Lorelei at the back door. He lowered his voice so only Pacer could hear. "Looks like you took a real interesting way home after you turned tail and run out on us in Lawrence." He stood in his stirrups and swept his hat across his chest and half bowed. "Good morning, miss. I don't believe we've met."

"You can call me Lorelei," she said, laughing at his attempt at gallantry.

"I most certainly will. Every chance I get," Sawyer replied. He flashed her a smile, then returned his attention to Raven. "I figured with no one to hunt for you, half of this buck ought to come in handy."

"We won't be needing it. I'm here now," Pacer interjected before Raven could accept the gift. "I can see to her smokehouse."

Raven looked puzzled. These two had been close as brothers once. They had ridden off as friends. She began to wonder if Sawyer had left something out of his heroic account of the attack on Lawrence. All he had told her was that he had lost sight of Pacer Wolf during the raid and that Pacer had never returned to

Quantrill's troop. He had attributed the jagged scar on his hand to a Union cavalry officer's saber-wielding charge. The two men continued to stare at one another.

"Maybe you better keep on. That meat won't spoil if you ride straight on to the plantation," Pacer firmly suggested.

Sawyer Truett shrugged and settled his hat on his head and touched the brim in farewell to the ladies. Then he turned toward McQueen.

"I'm glad you're back, Pacer. I was worried about you." He glanced down at his rifle and blew a trace of dust from the sights. "We'll get together later and talk over old times." He touched his heels to his horse and trotted off at a brisk pace, leading the pack horse as he went. The white-tailed deer draped over the mare stared at Pacer with eyes as black as death, its head jostling from side to side as if in sad denial of its own fate and foretelling the same for the Choctaw Kid.

Chapter Fifteen

"My spotted dog's got no spots," Cap Featherstone's voice rang out across the rolling landscape as his wagon climbed the last slow rise between him and the town of Chahta Creek nestled in the shadow of the Kiamichi Mountains. The creek that gave the town its name was a narrow ribbon of sweet spring water that skirted the mountains and flowed southeastward to merge with the Kimishi River a couple of miles east of town. The community's founders, including Jesse's grandparents, had chosen a townsite with access to the bubbling creek yet protected on the north and northeast by a maze of steep gorges and tall stands of old-growth timber and the time-eroded ridges of the Kiamichis.

"He used to have, he had lots," Cap continued, in a booming baritone.

> "He walked under a ladder
> when my pa loosed his bladder
> and bleached him as white as
> my socks."

Jesse, astride a rose gray gelding glanced aside at his companion. Kansas City lay two weeks behind them. It was early September, a time of Indian summer. Cap Featherstone had made an interesting travel companion. He had a yarn for every watering hole, a tall tale or two for every campfire. And when he wasn't lying about his exploits or filling the air with his salty recollections of all the women he'd bedded—from hot-blooded señoritas in Santa Fe and Taos to a Paiute princess he had stolen from the Navajos and later sold to a fur trapper bound for the Wind River range—he was serenading the wilderness with ballads and jigs and tunes whose origins were better left unguessed.

Jesse glanced aside at the heavy-set bearded huckster now a proper saloonkeeper, at least according to Cap's description. He intended to make the Medicine Wagon Saloon the talk of the Indian Territory so that when the war ended and commerce returned to the Texas Road (with herds of cattle and Texas vaqueros passing through on their way north) the lure of Cap Featherstone's gambling parlor, saloon, and palace of pleasure would be impossible to resist.

Cap finished his song and winked at Jesse. "Yessir, my young captain, folks said I never would amount to much more than hawking snake oil in two-bit towns. Wait till you see the Medicine Wagon. I've fixed her up proper. Brought me in some gals from as far away as San Antone. A man can't play Abbot's game forever. A man needs something to call his own."

Jesse listened, but he kept his thoughts to himself. The captain had exchanged his uniform for tan duckins pants, a blue pillowticking striped cotton shirt, and a dark brown broadcloth vest and a wide brimmed hat. A gun belt and Colt Dragoon rode high on his hips. A second "hideout" gun, a .22 caliber Smith & Wesson had been tucked away in his right boot. A Spencer .52 caliber carbine gave Jesse added assurance that he was prepared for whatever trouble came his way. And he was indeed beginning to fear the worst after passing the cold charred remains of Hack Warner's station house an hour's ride behind them.

"I fear I may be too late. The countryside appears to be in open conflict, if Warner's station is any indication." Jesse walked the gray abreast of the wagon as it reached the top of the grade and came to a halt in a cloud of billowing dust that drifted over the two men. "Major Abbot wants me to stop a war, but I might just wind up fighting it."

"These are perilous times, younker. I am well rid of the responsibility of worrying about anyone else's hide but my own." Cap considered how that last remark sounded and attempted to clarify his position. "Of course, if you need any help, you just call on old Cap. Ain't no telling what a judicious man might pick up in the way of gossip. Talk flows as fast as rotgut in a place like the Medicine Wagon. The son of Ben McQueen can always count on me to back his play." Cap uncorked a jug he kept below the wagon seat and tilted it to his lips to drink a toast to Jesse's success. He wiped his mouth on his sleeve and smacked his lips. A trickle of corn liquor had dribbled into his belly where it bulged across his belt and buried the buckle in rolls of fat. "Your pa and I go way back. We're like blood kin. I'd be a sorry bastard if I let anything happen to his eldest boy." He pointed the mouth of the jug toward the town, visible in the distance.

"Here's to dreams," he said, and drank another toast. Cap offered the jug to Jesse, who declined. Ben McQueen had called the situation here a powder keg. Well, if that was the case, the Knights of the Golden Circle had already lit the fuse. Jesse Redbow McQueen wondered how much time he had before the entire situation blew up in his face.

*　　*　　*

Carmichael Ross scrutinized the map of Chahta Creek that overlooked her desk in the reception area of her newspaper office. The *Chahta Creek Courier* had been born beneath the spreading branches of an enormous live oak down by the creek bank. Once a week since that first of May in 1850, Carmichael Ross had supplied a newspaper to the families in town and the surrounding area. Carmichael's parents had been New England–born teachers whose missionary zeal had brought them into the territory more than twenty years ago. Carmichael sighed and looked at the portrait of her father, Jacob Ross, captured in oils, frozen in the full bloom of his youth.

It was Jacob who had dreamed of starting a paper and spent a modest inheritance on the printing press and type set his daughter now used with distinction and courage. She wielded the power of the printed page with force and cleverness, doing battle with the common enemies of mankind: intolerance, gullibility, ignorance, and petty fears.

Carmichael reached up and patted her father's image on the canvas. After her father's death a few years ago, Carmichael assumed the responsibility of publishing the *Courier,* refusing to return home to New Haven with her widowed mother.

Carmichael returned her attention to the map of town and the surrounding area. Main Street ran from northwest to southeast, a broad avenue where a wagon could make a wide turn if need be. Main was flanked by Choctaw Street on the west side and Cherokee on the east. A series of orderly, well-laid-out streets intersected Main and its two companion thoroughfares. First Street was the closest to the Kimishi River on the southernmost edge of town. The other streets were numbered consecutively up to Sixth, which was a meandering dirt track that skirted the forested slope of Turtle Mountain, a towering mound of upthrust limestone seamed with gulleys and sporting an apron of thick foliage along its lower half.

Carmichael studied the artist's rendering and decided that her skills were simply not up to the task of carving a wooden negative of the map. She had wanted to make a wood print of the township surrounded by a veritable army of hooded riders with a banner beneath the sketch that read "Knights of the Golden Circle tighten their grip on the loyal patriots of Chahta Creek." Unwilling to lose the banner, she changed the subject and instead set about depicting a man in a frock coat struggling to free himself from the vicelike grip of another man cloaked in robes and a hood. She smiled as she worked, enjoying a moment of self-congratulation. The drawing would be the centerpiece of a page decrying the nightly forays of the hooded raiders. Another column noted the arrival of Daniel Pacer Wolf McQueen back in the area. He had yet to come to town, but that didn't stop Carmichael from preparing a scathing list of the Choctaw Kid's shameful escapades in Missouri and Kansas culminating in his association with William Quantrill and the looting and burning of Lawrence. Raven McQueen was her friend, but the editor's affection for the half-breed medicine woman of Buffalo Creek would not stop her from speaking her mind. She knew Raven would be furious. She was fiercely protective of her grandchildren whether she agreed with their actions or not.

Carmichael worked quickly. Perspiration tickled her neck as she cut into the wood block. She glanced up from time to time, unnerved by the temporary peace of the newspaper office. By the end of the week, she'd have the type set, the printer inked, and be cranking out the next edition. It was a time-consuming task, though a labor of love, and one to which she was committed despite the fact the Knights had frightened off her help with threats of bodily harm. She was an ardent abolitionist, and championed the cause of freedom as embodied by President Abraham Lincoln. Most of the townspeople supported her views, but not enough to risk broken bones by taking a job on the *Chahta Creek Courier*.

She heard children playing on the wooden sidewalk outside the newspaper office. It was a good town whose populace were well-meaning souls, eager to help, hardworking, and independent. Full-blood Choctaws and mixed lived in harmony. Unlike the tribes of the plains, the Choctaws had long ago adopted the white man's dress and customs. Their homes and plantations were the envy of the Mississippi farmers. Carmichael rose from her seat and looked out the window. Fronting Main she looked directly across the street at the bank. Three boys in flour-sack shirts and dungarees scampered past the window. They fired at one another with wooden guns. A girl, several years their junior and obviously someone's little sister, toddled after the boys, determined to take part in the fun.

There was little difference between Chahta Creek and any other midwestern town. Some folks lived in neatly kept whitewashed frame houses. Others had dug the native red clays from the soil and coated the outside walls of their houses, giving them the appearance of red brick siding. The businesses scattered along Main, Cherokee, and Choctaw were single- and two-story structures with the traditional false fronts. As for the townspeople themselves, there were mostly mixed-bloods in the settlement and in the outlying farms and plantations, where wealthy landowners kept slaves and planted cotton on estates to rival anything found in the Deep South.

She watched the passing parade of townspeople, some of whom turned to wave at the woman in the window. This was a busy section of town. The newspaper office was "smack dab" in the middle of things, along with the Chahta Creek Territorial Bank and the Council House where the Choctaw came together to work out their differences and strengthen their cultural and tribal identity. Albert Teel's mercantile was only a few doors down the street. Teel had a reputation for honesty, and his store supplied food, clothes, and hardware for townsfolk and farmers alike. Next to the mercantile was Gude's Good Eats, where a colorful assortment of Chahta Creek's elders gathered every morning to discuss the weather and the war and solve the world's ills over a cup of Mary Lou Gude's coffee and a platter of her biscuits. Heading upstreet toward the forested slope of Turtle Mountain, a person might visit a lawyer, have a haircut and a bath at Robinson's Bath House and Barber Shop or find a comfortable room at the Choctaw House, a two-story hotel with rooms fronting on Main and Fourth. Further still were stables, a hat shop, a freight office, and the marshal's office and jail. The schoolhouse was over on Choctaw Street. Cherokee Street was a collection of stables, corrals, saloons, and a bordello. Such establishments paled in comparison to the Featherstone Medicine Wagon Saloon and Gambling Emporium, an impressive two-story showhall that was every bit as big as the hotel and festooned with banners and lanterns. Billboards pasted to the side walls of the Emporium offered such boasts as "The Finest Kentucky Sippin' Whiskey" and "Fleshly Delights to Excite the Senses" and yet another with a single word, "FARO," which was all one needed to say to lure a man through the double doors. There were always plenty of dreamers and optimists eager to invest their hard-earned savings with lady luck.

Carmichael Ross did not begrudge the town its bawdier elements. Every frontier community had its vices. But it bothered her how the Medicine Wagon had come to dominate the town, casting Featherstone's shadow across the settlement.

Carmichael Ross noticed a pair of hard-bitten riders dismount in front of the bank. She recognized them as the Tellico brothers. Theotis, the eldest, took a moment to stretch his legs. He was a big man with sloping shoulders and a round solid belly framed by a pair of faded yellow suspenders. Moses Tellico was a couple of years younger and a few inches shorter, with a black scrawl of a mustache that drooped below his chin and a crooked nose that had been the recipient of too many punches thrown in too many brawls.

The war had not been kind to everyone in the territory. The closing of northern markets coupled with an early summer drought had played havoc with the Tellicos' farm. The brothers owned no slaves. Coming from both Cherokee and Choctaw heritage, Theotis and Moses were no threat to the large plantation owners like Tullock Roberts, but what mountain land they held was theirs to jealously guard and protect. They weren't the kind to ride off to war to fight for some detached ideal. The Tellicos had no use for the laws and rules of civilized society. The Kiamichis weren't a "civilized" place.

Theotis turned and from across the street doffed his black battered hat and bowed. His gallant pose seemed wholly out of character for a man in fringed buckskins whose stringy black hair hung forward to obscure his hopelessly homely features. Moses grinned over his shoulder at the editor of the *Courier* then led the way inside the bank.

Carmichael grinned. For all their unkempt appearance, the Tellicos were shrewd horsetraders and not to be taken lightly. She didn't envy Lucius Minley, the president of the Chahta Creek Bank, if the brothers had come to renegotiate last year's loan.

Despite their gruff and intimidating ways, Carmichael liked the Tellicos. Oh, the brothers might not be fit company for socially well-bred ladies such as Rose Minley, the banker's wife. No, Theotis and Moses Tellico would never be welcome at the Minleys' table. And it was probably for the best. Carmichael hoped that the brothers controlled their tempers and handled the banker with at least a smattering of finesse.

She watched the Tellicos disappear through the front door of the bank. Sunlight bathed the street. The heat was settling in now. A dust devil stirred into life by the rising heat darted down the alley alongside the bank, whirlwind dancing from sunlight to shadow in a frantic escapade that led past the rain barrel and some abandoned crates children had turned into a fort.

Jesse McQueen rode across the newspaper-woman's field of vision, followed by burly Cap Featherstone, who bellowed at his mules in a thundering voice that rang out along Main Street and announced to everyone in the immediate vicinity the new proprietor of the Medicine Wagon had returned. Cap waved a hand toward the corner of Fourth and Main and addressed the eldest son of the man he had tried to kill in a warm, good-natured tone of voice.

"I'll swing on over to Cherokee and have my lads unload these barrels at the Medicine Wagon. Follow me over and we'll cut the dust and maybe I'll be able to come up with a lie you ain't heard, eh?"

"You'd be hard-pressed." Jesse grinned, and rubbed the small of his back. He was saddle-weary and ready for a hot bath and a shave. He was anxious to see his grandmother, but a trip out to the homestead would have to wait until he talked with the one person in the town who might really know what was going on. "I'll join you later, Cap. But I've still a ways to go yet and I'm already bone tired. I'd spit but I'm afraid the recoil would break me down."

Cap touched a hand to the brim of his hat and bid Jesse farewell, and then steered his wagon around the corner and headed for Cherokee. A mongrel pup scampered out from the dusty front yard of the house that had once served as both dwelling place and infirmary of Dr. Linus Dick. The place was empty now, and no one had come forward to claim the stray dogs and cats the kindhearted doctor had adopted. The pup barked in defiance at the wagon and the plodding mules. Cap ignored the animal until the dog came too near the heels of the mules, then with a deft crack of his whip laid open the pup's back side and sent the animal dashing to cover. It squirmed beneath the doctor's porch and continued to yip as the freight wagon rolled on.

Jesse heard the commotion but his interests lay elsewhere. Carmichael Ross stepped into the doorway of the newspaper office as McQueen rode across the street. He could sense there were more people watching him than the editor of the *Chahta Creek Courier*. He dismounted and looped the reins of his gray over the hitching rail and stepped onto the boardwalk.

"Afternoon, Miss Ross. Is that your name still or has some lucky fella stolen you away from the type box and hand-crank press?"

Carmichael smiled and held up her hands to reveal the smudge of printer's ink that stained the palms of her hands and the sleeves of her high-necked brown dress.

She made no attempt to hide her astonishment at the captain's return home.

"Jesse Redbow McQueen, you're the last person I expected to see. And I cannot laud the company you chose to ride into town with."

"Cap? He's all right. A bit of a rogue, but then again, maybe the man has earned the right. He was my father's friend."

"Was?" She led him into the shade of the office and offered him a seat.

Jesse gave a quick and utterly false accounting of Ben McQueen's demise. Carmichael took it hard for all of a minute or two. Then her professionalism kicked in and she began planning a story for the next edition of the *Courier*. She was not unmoved, however.

"How are things? Really," Jesse said. He hated to lie to the woman, but he had agreed to continue the ruse until notified by Major Abbot. Only Raven would hear the truth.

"Ah." Carmichael tapped her lips with her forefinger. Her lips were naturally wine red. Jesse realized he had never noticed them before. And he had always thought of her as being long-featured and rather plain. But here he was sitting across from her and all he could think of was how strong-willed and courageous she seemed. And how like flawless gems her emerald eyes held him motionless, despite his fatigue. He wondered whether, if someone were to unpin her brown hair, it would hang past her waist. What was she speaking of? Oh yes. Factions. Devisiveness. Frightened people. And the Knights of the Golden Circle.

"And who are the Knights?" Jesse said.

"No one knows or cares to say. But I fear you'll find out soon enough. Even if you've left the Union army," Carmichael replied. She had sensed his distraction but didn't know she had been the cause.

"I hold the rank of captain. But I saw no reason to advertise that or my loyalties while riding south." He glanced out the door at the sunlit street and noticed the children playing at war with wooden swords and guns. If only men would follow the same example as these little ones and fight their battles with club and staff, then hurry home, bruised but unscathed, to the arms of their loved ones. "I passed Hack Warner's station."

"Burned out last week," Carmichael said. "Old news." A mischievous glint in her eye. "Hack Warner overheard one of the Knights having a coughing fit the likes of which just about toppled him from the saddle. There's only one man so consumptive."

"Sam Roberts," Jesse spoke the name aloud. And the son was only a shadow of the father. Well, it stood to reason. Tullock owned one of the largest plantations in the territory. He had a great deal to lose, or felt he did, if the Union cause prevailed.

He would begin with Tullock and, if possible, persuade the plantation owner to peacefully reconcile his differences with his own people. Men had always followed Tullock's lead. No doubt some men still did, under cover of night and their ghostly hoods. Yes, Tullock might even be the leader of the night riders, but it was worth the risk if he could bring the warring factions of the settlement together and avoid unnecessary bloodshed, the likes of which could only bring disaster to the Choctaw Nation.

"I'll pay a visit to Tullock Roberts," Jesse told the editor. Carmichael opened the bottom drawer of her desk and removed two glasses and a rust-colored bottle of bourbon. She poured a most-unladylike portion for herself and slid an empty glass and the bottle across the desk to Jesse. He grinned, remembering when he was twelve and she a woman in her early twenties how Carmichael Ross had given him a Mexican cigarillo after he had caught her smoking them out in the woods. It had been payment for his silence. She had seemed so much older then. She was younger than that now. Their relationship had changed over the course of time. And with almost two years of war behind him, Jesse had aged in ways the passage of months could not record.

"To the memory of your father," Carmichael said, holding up her glass.

The salute made Jesse uncomfortable, but he

went through with it nevertheless. He poured a measure of bourbon for himself and reached over and touched his glass to hers and brushed Carmichael's hand with his. He didn't mind that. Neither did she.

"To Ben McQueen. To justice for my father." He tilted the glass to his lips. The liquid cut the dust and blazed a path to his stomach. Carmichael nodded.

"Justice . . . I wonder if it exists."

"I'd like to think so," Jesse replied. "Maybe it's not in our power to deliver." Jesse stood and walked around the desk and continued on over to the printing press and the trays of type that Carmichael had already prepared for printing. He noticed his brother's name and read the column she had prepared, decrying Pacer Wolf's participation in the Lawrence raid and labeling him a guerrilla capable of the most reprehensible conduct, an indictment in which she included all those who rode with Quantrill's raiders or the Knights of the Golden Circle.

Jesse glanced up and met Carmichael's frank stare. Emotions rode the warpath of his soul. His brother, his enemy.

"He's out at Buffalo Creek," the editor said. "With Raven."

"Maybe I'll ride out that way."

"What will you do?"

"My duty," the captain replied.

Carmichael downed her drink and had started to refill her glass when she caught Jesse watching her with obvious disapproval. "I have ten years on you, Jesse Redbow McQueen. You're hardly fit to be my father."

"No. That's a role I'd not care to assume with you. There'd be another a sight more satisfying."

Her eyebrows arched. "And what would that be?" she asked, more than passing interested.

Before he could answer, a gunshot sounded from across the street. Jesse turned toward the window as the door to the bank across the street was flung open. Buxom Rose Minley, the wife of the president of the Chahta Creek Territorial Bank, lifted up the hem of her gray woolen skirt to reveal a set of shapely ankles as she dashed out into the middle of the street and screamed for someone to fetch Parson Marshal T. Alan Booth. The banker's lady was a tall attractive woman in her late twenties whose high-pitched voice had a piercing quality that carried for several blocks as she pleaded for assistance. "They're killing him! The Tellicos are killing Lucius and robbing the bank!" The marshal was blocks away. Rose Minley's husband would be dead before Booth ever arrived.

"For the love of heaven, isn't there someone who will help us!"

Of course there was.

Chapter Sixteen

Moses Tellico claimed to be the handsome brother. He was a couple of years younger than Theotis and a couple of inches shorter. His features were dark from a life spent outdoors. A black mustache covered his upper lip, its waxed tips drooping down below his chin. His nose was crooked, flattened along one side, and made his entire face seem slightly askew. His cold blue eyes, like those of his brother, were clouded and blurry from too much drink. Sober, they could be hard as flint, like the Tellicos themselves. Moses, despite his fierce appearance, had an ego as fragile as a thespian's. He kept his short-cropped black hair well oiled, parted in the middle, and combed flat against his skull. The perfume of lilac water clung to his woolen coat and pullover cotton shirt.

Now Theotis had no illusions as to his beauty. He was a burly, heavyset brawler with a black beard as long as a bib and a row of broken crooked teeth behind his smile. Both brothers claimed to be part Cherokee, part Choctaw, with a little Welsh blood thrown in on their father's side of the family. The net result was a pair of backwoods boys who lived by their own rules and saw little need for the civilizing laws of the community, which made it all the more difficult for Lucius Minley to explain why the Chahta Creek Territorial Bank had the right and, yes, even the fiscal obligation to foreclose on the Tellicos' farm.

"Let me get this straight, now," Theotis asked, and blew the curl of smoke from the barrel of his Starr revolver. It was one of a matched set that had belonged to their father. That and the land and a penchant for blood feuds had been Old Man Tellico's legacy to his offspring. "Pa give us that land. He's buried there alongside Ma." Theotis doffed his hat and held it over his heart. "And now you aim to run us off!" He tugged his hat back on his head.

"It's not me." Lucius Minley tried yet again to state his position. He looked like the clerk he used to be, a shy, nervous little man whose most ardent wish in all the world was to kick the dust of Chahta Creek from his bootheels and leave the Indian Territory once and for all—perhaps to settle back East, where ruffians like the Tellicos were kept locked up instead of being allowed the run of the streets.

Though timid, Lucius was no fool and knew that if a man wanted to amount to anything in this world he must be willing to take risks. He was doing that right now, and even frightened nearly out of his wits he was determined to see things through. Lucius Minley, a slender, soft-spoken man, wore wire-rimmed spectacles whose round lenses accentuated his round cheeks. He'd allowed his short brown hair to grow into bushy sideburns that hid his ears. Sweat beaded on his forehead as he tried to make his position understood. "It's not me," he repeated with a glance toward Moses. "My friends, there is nothing I would rather do than extend your note. I would loan you the money from my own pocket if I had it. But as the director of this institution, I am required to exercise certain fiscal responsibility."

"What the devil is he sayin', Theotis?" Moses asked. He reached over and began to twirl the wooden globe set in a mahogany brace that dominated the office and was Lucius Minley's pride and joy.

"He's using a bunch of fancy words to say he aims to steal our land," Theotis said, scratching his beard with the Starr's barrel.

"Please be careful with that," Lucius said.

Moses gave the globe a brief appraisal. "What is it?"

"A map of the earth. The entire planet. I brought it all the way from New York." Lucius spoke to the younger Tellico as if he were speaking to a troublesome child, in an attempt to humor the man. "If you like, I can show you where we are, this very minute."

"I don't need no map to tell me where I am," Moses blurted out. "I'm in this here office listening to you trying to steal our land."

"You borrowed money and used your homestead for collateral. The law is quite clear. If you cannot make payment on your note, the bank has the right to foreclose to protect its depositors."

"But we paid you. We gave you every damn dollar we got for selling our horses down in Texas!" Moses stated. It was plain to see he considered the matter settled.

Lucius slid the leather case containing several hundred Confederate dollars back across the desk toward the brothers. "This currency is barely worth the paper it's printed on. The bank cannot accept it. Now, if you'd been paid in gold or Union greenbacks . . . " The banker shook his head and held up his hands in a gesture of helplessness. "I'm deeply sorry."

"Looks like we ain't worth protecting," Theotis growled. He raised his arm and fired another round into the ceiling. White paint and splintered wood showered down on the men in the office and littered the papers on the president's desk. Lucius jumped in his seat. He gave another start as Moses drew his own pistol, another Starr, and squeezed off another couple of rounds after Theotis's two.

"We aim to leave here with a loan, drawn up and officially signed by you, Lucius. Or by Aunt Helen's mustache, come the next rain your roof will leak like a sieve."

"Maybe we ought to take our land out of this globe and go on about our business." Moses holstered his gun and drew a whittling knife from his belt and touched the point to the globe. "Reckon we're about here." He dug the tip of the knife into the globe.

"No!"

"That's enough, Moses. Put the knife away," Jesse said from the doorway. Behind him, the rest of the bank was empty. No one had yet to follow him inside. There was a natural reluctance to do so. The Tellicos had been drinking—or at least that was the word on the street. Folks had seen them imbibing in the back of their buckboard. Tangling with a drunk Tellico was about as smart as running buck naked into a cactus patch—fast or slow, a man was bound to come out the worse for wear.

Moses glanced around and spied Jesse and blinked in surprise. The last thing the Tellicos had heard, Ben McQueen's eldest son had ridden off to fight for the Union. "Lookee here, Theotis. Jesse's come home. Looks like he's even growed some."

"You Tellicos have had your fun. Time to clean up and put your toys away," Jesse said.

"Thank God," Lucius sighed, grateful that providence had sent him a benefactor.

"This don't concern you, Jesse," Theotis warned. "Don't get in the way. I'd lie down in a den of rattlers for your pa, I swear I would, but you get in our way and we'll put you down."

"Put the knife away," Jesse flatly ordered.

"Not till Minley accepts this Confederate money as payment for our note."

"These graybacks aren't worth twenty dollars in Union script," Lucius said. "You might as well offer to pay the note off in flour sacks."

"Sign the note paid in full," Theotis warned, indicating the contract on the banker's desk.

Jesse had heard enough. The interior of the office reeked of burnt gunpowder and home brew. The Tellicos were desperate. Like cougars with their backs to the walls, they were ready to fight to save what was theirs. But Minley no doubt had the law on his side.

"Lucius, it would be a neighborly thing to extend the bank note and allow Moses and Theotis to come up with the money in a proper way." Jesse moved into the room as he talked. Theotis appeared to be the most dangerous: his gun was drawn. The Starr revolver lacked the balance and precision workmanship of a Colt revolver, but it was still a lethal weapon. The bullet holes in the office ceiling were an excellent example of the revolver's effectiveness, however clumsy its manufacture. Jesse stopped in front of the window overlooking the alley. Theotis was just to his left in the center of the room. Moses remained by the globe, reluctant to discard his knife. Lucius Minley was seated at his desk. His advancement from clerk to director had occurred during Jesse's absence, in the year and a half since the war had broken out in earnest. Minley wore his new position of authority like a king his mantle. He refused to be cowed by these unkempt and illiterate Tellico brothers.

"After today's incident, I wouldn't give them spit if they were dying of thirst," Lucius replied.

Theotis turned livid. "Why, you pompous little jaybird. I ain't gonna shoot you, I'm gonna wring your neck!" He started toward the man behind the desk. Jesse reached out and caught him by the arm. Theotis was not about to be stopped. He swung a haymaker that would have taken Jesse's head off if it had landed. But Jesse ducked under the blow, then stepped down and crunched his bootheels onto Theotis's right foot, mashing the big brute's toes.

"Yeeeoowww!" Theotis howled. "Goddamn it, Jesse, that ain't fair."

Jesse batted the gun from the man's grasp and punched him square in the middle of his face, nearly fracturing his hand while cutting a knuckle on Theotis's tooth. Theotis Tellico roared like a bear and shook off the effect of Jesse's blow and charged him, which was precisely what Jesse hoped he'd do. He stepped aside with all the grace of a matador, allowing Theotis to charge past him and through the window directly behind him. In an explosion of glass and shattering wood, Theotis not only carried the entire window along with him but most of the windowframe as well. Moses grabbed up the globe and prepared to hurl it at Jesse, when reinforcements arrived in the person of Parson Marshall T. Alan Booth. Though physically unimposing, there seemed both an aura of "spiritual" as well as "duly-appointed" authority about the man. His hair was smoke gray and as neatly trimmed as his gray beard, cut close to follow the jawline. His complexion was ruddy and vigorous. He had come running at the first sound of trouble, cradling his Colt revolving shotgun in the crook of his arm. As the marshal of Chahta Creek, Booth's job was to uphold the rule of law and order within the town limits, while as parson of the First Congregationalist Church he saw his responsibilities extending beyond the town limits to the furthest reaches of the human soul.

Parson Marshal Booth wore a black frock coat and light wool black trousers, a black shirt with a white collar, and a short-brimmed hat. A shiny six-pointed star rode the left side of his vest, over his heart. In the left-hand pocket of his coat he carried a Navy Colt .36 with a shortened barrel. The right-hand pocket bulged with the reassuring bulk of a worn, leather-bound Bible. T. Alan Booth rushed the door and fired the shotgun into the air to get the attention of the men in the bank director's office. The explosion was deafening in the confines of such a small place. The buckshot blew a hole in the ceiling the size of a country ham. Sunlight streamed through and painted a patch of amber on the office floor. Booth seemed as surprised as anyone by the blast. He cocked the weapon and readied another chamber.

"Christ Almighty! Will you people quit shooting holes in my roof!" Lucius exclaimed with a look of dismay and frustration. His office, his beautiful "civilized" office . . .

"Sorry, Lucius, my thumb slipped," Booth sheepishly replied. He'd wasted a load, but the shotgun's cylinder held three more. He looked around at the other two men in the room. "By golly, is that you, Jesse? What are you doing back?" He immediately checked the eldest son of Ben McQueen for missing limbs. No, the lad appeared whole. He fixed the remaining Tellico brother in a steely-eyed glare. "Moses, I warned you and that boneheaded brother of yours to finish your liquor on the trail home. Now hand over your knife and gun."

Moses meekly lowered his head, blinked his eyes, wavered unsteadily on his feet, then held his knife and Starr revolver for the parson marshal to confiscate.

"They tried to rob the bank, T. Alan. I want them charged with robbery and attempted murder!" Lucius said, at last feeling safe enough to rise from his desk and lean forward on his knuckles until they turned white.

"Murder?" Booth asked.

"See for yourself," Lucius said, indicating the bullet holes above him.

Booth chuckled. "What the hell were you doing? Hiding on the ceiling?"

"We didn't try to rob nobody," Moses growled. "If anyone's been stole from, it's me and Theotis. We tried to pay off our note but he won't accept them Confederate dollars."

At the mention of Moses' older brother, the parson marshal checked the room again, searching through the drifting ribbons of powdersmoke for some sign of the other Tellico.

Jesse jabbed a thumb toward the gaping opening in the wall that used to contain a window. All that remained was a length of frame jutting out from the jagged timber siding and half a torn curtain. A low lingering groan floated in from the alley.

Jesse shrugged as Booth looked questioningly at the captain. "I just tried to help," Jesse said.

"Oh, Lucius. Thank God you're safe!" Rose Minley burst into the office, her hair in disarray and skirt trailing dust from the street. She unleashed the full force of her fury on Moses, who retreated toward Booth for protection. "You brigand. You disreputable . . . oh." Words failed her, and with a sweep of her skirt she joined her husband.

"I'll take these boys back over to the jail and see they're duly charged with disorderly conduct and public drunkenness," said Booth.

"What? They tried to kill me," Lucius said.

"Oh nonsense, Lucius. If they had wanted to kill you, they most assuredly would have," Jesse spoke up. The Tellicos had behaved badly but he couldn't blame them. Lucius Minley certainly wasn't cutting them any slack. "As for robbing the bank, from the looks of things Moses and Theotis were trying to deposit this money." He grabbed a fistful of Confederate dollars. "That's hardly a crime in the banking business."

"Makes sense to me," Booth said. He motioned for Moses to lead the way through the door and out of the office into the main part of the bank. A clerk had already stationed himself behind the appropriate screen.

"Who's going to pay for these damages?" Lucius seemed aghast.

"You've taken everything the Tellicos have," Jesse said.

"How dare you even suggest we make reparations out of our own accounts," Rose Minley indignantly blurted out.

Jesse glanced up at the bullet holes. "Just call it 'overhead.'"

Shug Jones, a chunky, taciturn man just shy of fifty who could be counted on to tend bar and keep his mouth shut, waited at the rear of the Medicine Wagon Saloon. Dobie Johnson, a slim, freckle-faced eighteen-year-old, rootless as a tumbleweed, and with a temper as quick to flare as dry kindling, kept Shug company. Cap Featherstone had seen something of himself in Dobie and had taken the young man under his wing. Dobie was wild and reckless and a favorite of the perfumed ladies of the evening whose affections could be bought for a silver dollar but whose weary hearts were beyond the reach of any man's moneybelt.

"Unload these casks and roll 'em into the storage room," Cap ordered, climbing down from the wagon seat. He rubbed his posterior in an attempt to get some feeling back into his muscles and climbed the back steps to the back door of his office. The Medicine Wagon Saloon was a spacious two-storied building with an office and storage room in back, a broad, high-ceilinged saloon with bedrooms upstairs for the "doves" of the Medicine Wagon to ply their trade. An

ornate stairway wide enough for a man to ride a
horse up dominated the north wall. A balustrade
overhead topped by a heavy velvet drape formed a
darkened hallway off of which seven doorways beck-
oned with promises of earthy delights. Whether a
customer stayed for an hour or a night depended on
the willingness of the fallen angel, the depth of his
wallet, and the gentleman's own stamina.

Cap Featherstone cut through his office, a sparsely
appointed room with a desk, an iron safe against the
rear wall, a highbacked wooden swivel chair behind a
nicked and cluttered desk, and a cabinet into which
the former Medicine Show huckster quickly unloaded
a wooden case of champagne he had protected along
the trail from Kansas. With his own personal treasure
stashed away, he shrugged off his coat and opened his
shirt to the waist. The arthritis in his right knee was
acting up. Leaning on his gator-head cane, the big man
lumbered out into his own little bit of paradise.

The saloon was large enough to hold a dozen
poker tables, a faro table, a chuck-a-luck table, and,
along the south wall, a massive mahogany bar with a
brass footrail, brass spittoons for the patrons, and a
portrait of a reclining nude across whose ample pro-
portions trailed a gauze veil. She was painted life-size
and had an alluring smile, as if inviting each man to
belly up to the bar and share some special tempestu-
ous secret known only to her.

An immense wooden chandelier like a giant
wheel hung from the ceiling by a thick chain. A
dozen lamps were attached to the chandelier, which
could be raised and lowered as needed. A thick iron
rod jutted from the top of the chandelier, and the
chain passed through a hole in the rod like a thread
through the eye of a needle.

The saloon was nearly empty. With Shug out
back unloading the wagon, there was no one to tend
the bar. Hud Pardee had taken Shug's place behind the

bar, but the only drinks he'd poured were for himself. The girls were upstairs taking an afternoon rest save for China Torrence, a solitary lass in silks and feathers and a worn blue satin gown who sat on the ample lap of a muleskinner, her arms draped around the man's neck. China and half a dozen townfolk were gathered around one of the poker tables where Enos Clem held court with a game of three-card monte. It was a deceptively simple game to while away the afternoon. Clem showed the ace of hearts to the muleskinner, then placed the card face-down on the table and flanked it with a pair of queens, also face-down. Then in a burst of lightninglike dexterity, he passed his hands over the cards, shuffling them over and under one another. The teamster thought himself able to spot the ace and placed his bets accordingly. Enos matched him two for one and invited the others to put their faith and their wagers on the teamster's unerring eye.

"Here you are, my good men. The ace is the eagle bird and will win you two for one. Follow the ace with your eyes as it dances with these two lovely ladies. Red queens you lose, gents. Only the ace will carry you home with money in your pockets. Here is the ace. Now here it is. But you only get one chance to find it. Here it is. Now where has it gone? Do you know, sir? Ah, you have a sharp eye, my friend, will you take a chance? The ace is the winning card. Show me the color of your money, my lads. I take no bets from widows, paupers, cripples, or children. But the rest of you, pay your money and take your chances. Twenty dollars, sir? Now there is a man with grit. I respect it, gents. But forgive me if I don't wish any of you luck."

The teamster made his choice. A chorus of groans followed. The prostitute who had been waiting for him to quit the game suddenly realized her would-be paramour had just lost the last of his wages. He had nothing to pay her. She jumped off his lap.

"Hey. Where are you going?" the teamster bellowed in an ugly mood. He shoved clear of the table. Cap could see trouble coming as clear as a thunderhead on a hot summer's day. Cap made his way across the room and placed his massive form in front of the teamster, who seemed little in comparison to Featherstone.

"She's going upstairs to wait for you," Cap said. "And I warrant she'll take the sting out of your losses." One free visit was worth not having his place torn up by the mean-tempered freight hauler, and no doubt the man would not only return but probably bring some friends. Cap turned to the saloon girl and indicated the stairway with a nod of his head in that direction. China was barely nineteen, with the eyes of a woman three times her age and a sallow complexion expertly hidden beneath layers of rouge and powdery makeup. Cap didn't know her name. He didn't want to. The "Babylon Belles" were merely articles of property, with no more importance than the furniture or the liquor. In truth, all three were essential if he was to appeal to all the vices, but his interest was purely professional. He never wagered with his own money, drank whiskey from the bar, or sampled the sinful pleasures of the *bagnio*. This was his own personal code of conduct and as important to him as the commandments to Parson Marshal Booth. He'd added another over the past year—never murder a friend unless it was absolutely necessary. That notion came to him as he joined Hud Pardee at the bar.

The gunman with the black patch over his left eye poured Featherstone a tall glass of cool milk from a clay pitcher Shug kept below the bar. Hud helped himself to a whiskey. He had no code, but, like the trickster coyote, took advantage of every opportunity that presented itself. Whatever pleased him was fair game.

Hud looked much the same as he had in Kansas City, though he had exchanged his black silk shirt for a flannel one identical in color. He continued to wear a black frock coat and waist sash and sport a brace of Navy Colts. He brushed a hand through his ash-gray hair and then held up a shot glass of tea-colored whiskey in salute to Featherstone, who acknowledged by raising his eyebrows then turned his attention to the gambler dealing three-card monte.

"Is that Clem?" Cap asked.

Hud nodded, and waved a hand toward the gambler, who excused himself from the table. Cap noticed that one of the men, Hack Warner, had already lost a couple of precious dollars and sat at the table glaring at the queens and ace as if they had offered him some personal affront. Since the Knights had burnt him out, he had no money to spare.

Enos Clem believed in playing the odds and running with his luck as long as it held. His creed was "Play it to the bust." And right now he was willing to let things ride. He didn't know what game Hud and Cap Featherstone were up to, but as soon as he figured out the rules, he planned on cutting himself a place at the table.

His pale white skin befit a man who spent much of his life in shadowy, smoke-filled saloons, shielded from sunlight and fresh air. But Clem knew what he was missing and preferred it that way. On his way over to the bar, he tossed a coin to the dark-skinned piano player, a freed slave by the name of Tandy Matlock who had taught himself to play the piano at an early age. Tandy had spent the last ten years traveling from saloon to brothel throughout the Indian Territory, but he was nearing seventy now and the snowy-haired old man, reluctant to move on, had begun to think of Chahta Creek as his home. He caught the coin in midflight and touched the short brim of his hat and headed for the piano set in an alcove beneath the stairs. He took a seat before the keyboard and soon the sweet melodic strains of "Will you wait for me, oh Shenandoah" floated through the saloon.

"Enos, this here is Cap Featherstone," Hud said.

"A pleasure to make your acquaintance, sir." Clem held out a small but respectable stack of his winnings for the morning. He had allowed the men at the table to win just enough to keep them interested, and one man to walk away with a profit which Enos planned to win back at a future date.

"Looks like the pleasure is all mine." Cap grinned. He took the bills, cut a percentage for the gambler, and tucked the rest in his pocket. "We'll try to make your stay with us a profitable one."

"I figured the Indian Territory to be nothing but tipis and savages," Clem replied. Hud slid a bottle over to the gambler. His long tapered fingers curled around a shot glass and tossed down a drink, then he sucked in a cooling breath as his eyes began to water.

Hud winked, and patted a nearby glass jar in which a coiled rattler slept in a nest of sagebrush twigs and decaying leaves. "It's the poison from ol' Stonewall here that gives it character." The snake struck at the side of the bottle and Hud on reflex pulled his hand off the glass.

There was a standing offer of a shiny gold double eagle against a dollar for any man who could keep from jerking his hand back when the snake made its killing lunge, fangs bared. It was a wager no one had been able to collect on, but that didn't stop the saloon's patrons from trying. Cap Featherstone had lived long enough to know a man running on whiskey courage who thinks he has no limitations is an easy man to make a profit off.

"Rattler poison, my ass," Enos Clem skeptically

replied. Still, he didn't like the way the two men at the
bar exchanged those knowing glances. He decided to
pursue another topic. "Mr. Featherstone. Now, don't
get me wrong. I'm grateful to be here. But still I can't
help but wonder why Hud saved my skin, staked
me, and brought me here all the way from Missouri."
He pursed his lips and took a moment to mentally tabulate the towns and settlements he had passed through
on his way to Chahta Creek. They all had their share
of saloons and games of chance. "I'm not the only
gambler in the territory . . . "

"Indeed you are not," Cap concurred. "However
I was looking for a man who can do more than deal
faro." Featherstone motioned for Clem to draw near.
"Pardee and I were looking for someone who wouldn't
mind being wealthy even if it meant a little risk now
and then. Someone smart enough to keep his mouth
shut. In short, we're looking for a partner."

Hud Pardee seemed as surprised as Enos by
Cap's announcement. He was only barely willing to
tolerate a fifty-fifty split in the fortune to be made.
Suddenly his share had shrunk into a third. The
warning look in Cap's eyes kept him from blurting out
his displeasure.

"Partners in what?"

"Let's call it a land venture, split three ways," Cap
said. "In the meantime you deal faro and run the
games and see the house wins its share of the spoils."

"No problem," Clem said. He was intrigued,
there was no denying it. Cap Featherstone also had an
aura of success about him. If Cap was into something good, Clem was more than happy to hold onto
the big man's coattails and allow himself to be swept
along with the flow.

"Are you gonna stand over here and jaw or give
me a chance to win my money back?" Hack Warner
said. Although he had been drinking, it didn't affect

his movements, but the stench of rotgut clung to his clothes.

Cap turned to look at Warner, who advanced on the gambler.

"It appears from your lack of manners that you've had enough to drink," Cap said.

"Sure. Sober up and go on home. Only I ain't got a home. The prettiest stretch along the Texas Road and them damn raiders come and burn me out. I built that place with my own two hands. All gone. All gone to the Knights of the Golden Circle!"

"Take a room upstairs and sleep it off, Hack," Cap said in a conciliatory tone. "On the house."

"I go to Lucius Minley to loan me the money to start over and he says collateral—I got to have collateral before he'll advance me a dime. I told him my goddamn collateral got burnt all to hell." Hack was a tough, leathery individual who had hunted and trapped with the Choctaws in Mississippi in the days before the Trail of Tears brought the civilized tribes west to Indian Territory. He had thick bushy eyebrows hunched forward in a scowl. He wore a linsey-woolsey shirt, fringed buckskin breeches, and high-topped moccasins. His hair was a mass of short brown curls shot with silver and thinning on the top.

He pointed to the table. "If I can track a snowshoe rabbit in the snow or trail a curly wolf to its den, I can by God find that little ace, one in three, and win enough to sit down to a proper game of poker."

"I am at your service, my friend," said Enos Clem, and flashed his undertaker's smile. "And the house will wager three to your one on every pass of the cards, eh?" He left the bar and sauntered across the broad open room to the table where Hack Warner and a couple of his cronies were determined to beat the gambler at his own game.

Once Clem was out of earshot, Hud Pardee leaned forward and spoke softly, his single blue eye boring into the big man on the other side of the long solid-looking bar. Hud's knee touched the wooden stock of a sawed-off shotgun Shug kept hidden in case of trouble.

"What the hell are you doing, Cap?" Hud glanced in Clem's direction. "You start cutting people in without my say so? I don't hold with it. You divvy up your share of the pie any way you want, but leave mine alone." Cap shook his head and good-naturedly gestured for Hud to follow him back to his office. Hud stepped around the bar and followed Cap, who seemed disarmingly ebullient, as if without a care in the world. His steps were spry and his cane tap-tapped upon the floor as if keeping time with the music Tandy Matlock continued to play.

Inside the office, Cap whirled around as Hud closed the door. With surprising speed, Cap changed course and barreled into the gunman, pinning the man to the door. Three hundred plus pounds of gristle and bone held the one-eyed man immobile. With a flick of the wrist, the gator-head cane came apart and freed a slender, fourteen-inch-long razor-sharp blade. Cap held the double-edge blade against Hud's throat. In the blink of an eye, Cap Featherstone had gone from a congenial huckster to a stone-cold killer. With the point of the blade lightly pricking his jugular vein, Hud had no intention of reaching for his guns.

"Listen to me! Pardee, you're the best I've ever seen with a gun. For as long as you been trick shootin' with Cap Featherstone's Linaments and Medicine Show, I always said there ain't no one better than Hud Pardee. But good as you are, I could kill you in my sleep." Cap's knife drew blood. A droplet of crimson formed on the tip of the blade. Hud Pardee winced as cold steel pricked his skin, just above his jugular. Cap withdrew the knife and licked the droplet of blood from the tip of the blade. "Don't forget, I'm running things."

"I'll keep it in mind," Hud replied, hoping to save face. Color returned to his cheeks. And when Cap removed his crushing weight, the one-eyed gunman was able to catch a breath once more. "But I still can't see what's to be gained by dealing the gambler in."

"Because it takes more than table stakes for a man to commit murder," Cap said. "But as a partner, with a chance at wealth and power, I doubt there's anything a man like Enos Clem wouldn't do." Cap Featherstone maneuvered his great bulk over to a rack of clay and wooden pipes. Though Cap had his own back to the door, Hud still had the feeling the big man was watching him or at least keenly aware of Pardee's every move. Cap filled a pipe with tobacco and lit it, then turned to face the trick shooter once again. "I've spent enough time on the trail to know Jesse McQueen is no fool. He's every bit the man his father was. And he could be a lot more trouble than I figured. If we have to kill him, I want Clem around to shoulder the blame."

"But what if the gambler should talk?"

Cap flashed his conciliatory smile, and with a curl of tobacco smoke wreathing his head the big man slowly sheathed the length of steel blade back into his cane. "Dead men don't bite."

Chapter Seventeen

"Ain't right, you locking us up," Moses Tellico called out. His crooked nose poked between the iron bars of the cell at the rear of the marshal's office.

"It were Minley who did the stealing. Only he calls it banking," Theotis spoke up. He scratched at his scruffy black mane a moment and produced another sliver of glass. "Damnation, Jesse, what would your pa say if he were to find out you went and tossed me through a window? Why, we're kinda like family ... I mean, ain't the Tellicos always been around when your grandma Raven needed anything?"

"I have heard quite enough out of both of you," T. Alan Booth replied. He passed a couple of blankets through the bars of the cell. "You boys sleep it off. You're just lucky we got you out of there before one of you red-necked peckerwoods went and killed someone, because then you'd be in here awaiting the hangman's pleasure instead of sleeping off a drunk."

Talk of hanging had a quieting effect on both brothers. Moses even seemed contrite when he spoke again. "How long you aim to keep us, T. Alan?"

"A week ought to satisfy Lucius Minley. Then

we'll have to find some way for you to make restitution for damages."

"Galls me to think of having to pay that little weasel anything after what he did," Moses grumbled. He could sense Marshal Booth was about to explode again with anger. "But we will if you say so," he quickly added. Jesse had to grin.

Booth led the way into the front room of the office. The windows were thrown open, and sunlight washed across a wall of posters, a gun rack, a battered desk and chair, and, on the opposite side of the room, a well-padded cot and an iron stove with a blue-enameled pot riding one of the hot plates. Two cups were set close by. A couple of extra shirts and a pair of brown Levi's hung from wall pegs above the head of the cot. Booth always kept a pot of coffee on the stove, but he took his meals at Mary Lou Gude's on the south end of town; hardly convenient but well worth the walk. He considered his own cooking as deadly as venom, an opinion shared by any of the jail's inmates who had sampled the parson marshal's fare.

Booth scratched at his white beard as he appraised the Union captain standing before him.

"What the hell are you doing here, Jesse? I wrote to your father and asked *him* to come."

"He sent me instead," Jesse replied. He didn't bother to elaborate. There seemed no point to telling the peace officer a lie about Ben's death.

"This town and the whole countryside are coming apart at the seams. Your father might have brought them all together. He might have been a balm to the wounds this damn war has opened up." Booth sighed, and crossed the room to the stove where he filled a cup with coffee. He tasted the contents and made a wry face. "I've swallowed better creek water."

"The washbasin still outside?" Jesse asked.

"Where it's always been."

Jesse walked through the front door and around to

the east side of Booth's office which faced the town, looking directly down Main. The jail marked the northern edge of town. The wooded slope of Turtle Mountain rose sharply from the grassland, and beyond lay the steeper ridges and hidden hollows of the Kiamichi Mountains.

The stand and washbasin were shaded by a lean-to roof. Jesse peeled off his vest and his pullover cotton shirt. His torso was streaked with sweat and trail dust that somehow always worked beneath a man's clothes. A shiny silver coin, an English crown sterling, dangled from a leather string around Jesse's neck. Parson Marshal Booth knew the story behind the McQueen "medal." It had been passed from father to son since the days of the Revolutionary War, when General George Washington had scrawled his initials, "G.W.," across the image of the English monarch and presented the coin to Jesse's great grandfather, Daniel McQueen, for his acts of courage and self-sacrifice in support of the thirteen colonies' noble cause.

"So you wear your father's medal. But can you fill his shoes?"

Jesse McQueen studied the town marshal and considered reeling off his exploits behind the Confederate lines in Vicksburg and Jackson. He'd run a gauntlet of Rebel troops, one step ahead of a firing squad. His neck still bore a scar from a hangman's rope, a parting gift from some of New Orleans's citizens who had tried to lynch him as a spy.

"I reckon we'll just have to find out together."

Booth reached out and touched the livid white scar tissue, the mark of the noose that Jesse would always wear. "By heaven, lad, where have you been?"

"It doesn't matter. I'm here now." Jesse fished in his vest pocket and brought out a shiny silver-plated star set in a circle of silver. The word RANGER was imprinted on the underside of the circle while the initials I.T. were etched in the center of the star. He handed Booth a document issued by the government in Washington appointing McQueen to act as a temporary territorial ranger until such time as the conflict in the southeast quarter of the Indian Territory was satisfactorily resolved. The document empowered Jesse to organize all the Union sympathizers if need be and bring them north into Kansas. However, this was to be a measure of last resort.

Booth tilted his hat back on his head and audibly exhaled as he finished reading McQueen's papers of authority. The marshal frowned and looked away. Several of Chahta Creek's inhabitants had followed Jesse and the marshal as they brought the Tellicos up the street from the bank. Most of the same crowd continued to linger at the end of the street. A half-dozen gossiping ladies buzzed excitedly among themselves about the shameful state of law and order although it didn't seem right that the Tellicos should lose their land and oh doesn't Jesse Redbow McQueen cut a handsome figure, and they giggled and laughed and shushed one another.

Al Teel came forward. He was a round, jovial little man with a kind word for everyone and anyone. He was middle-aged and wore his brown hair long in the manner of the old ones, shoulder-length though unadorned. The stub of a handrolled cigar was clenched firmly between his teeth. The cigar wasn't lit. With the war raging through the South and ravaging the tobacco crop, Teel was determined to make his meager supply of cigars last until the cessation. He tended to chew on them rather than smoke them. The loosely rolled leaves tended to burn rather quickly. It was a waste of his precious supply.

Teel held out his hand, and Jesse dried himself off and shook it.

"By heaven, if you were taller I would have figured it was Ben himself come home from Washington." He winked at the younger man. "From the looks of things, the way you handled Moses and Theotis, you're cut in the same image, my lad. Yessiree, cut in the same image." He clapped Jesse on his naked shoulder.

"I was there, too," Booth said, somewhat miffed.

"Of course you were, T. Alan, of course you were." Teel placed a hand on the marshal's forearm in a conciliatory gesture. Then he noticed the badge Jesse had brought with him from Kansas City. "Well, well, well, what have we here? A territorial ranger?"

"It's a temporary assignment," Jesse said.

"Unless the Knights make it permanent," Booth glumly added.

"What do you plan to do?" Teel asked.

"Keep moving and keep low." Jesse grinned. He found his straight razor and shaving soap and proceeded to lather his face. He noticed a couple of children standing behind him. The boy was probably no more than ten. His little sister was a couple of years younger. Studying their reflection in the mirror, Jesse thought he remembered their names.

"John Medicine Fox, you think you're big enough to bring that gray of mine from in front of the newspaper office up here to the corral in back of the jail?"

The boy flashed a toothy smile and hurried forward to stand alongside McQueen. "Howdy, Jesse. I seen you ride in. Is the war over?"

"No," Jesse told him, a tinge of regret in his voice.

"Good!" the boy enthusiastically said. "Then maybe I'll still be able to jine up and win me some medals. Whoo-eee. I'll bet you've seen just about everything."

How do you tell the young about war? Jesse thought. What words can hold the stench of death, the terrible suffering, watching friends die one after the other, the awful waiting, severed limbs and maimed bodies? Where to begin, and how to make the young understand that which numbs the senses and sickens the soul?

"Maybe not everything," Jesse answered. He handed the boy a quarter and watched him scamper off toward the center of town. He felt a tug on his trouser leg and looked down into the depthless eyes of another child, a little girl called Keila Medicine Fox.

"Do you remember me?" she asked.

"Hmm," Jesse teased, apparently deep in thought and struggling to recall her name. The little girl's eyes widened. She was not about to be fooled.

"Jesse McQueen, you know exactly who I am!" The girl folded her arms across her chest and tried to look her sternest.

"Ah yes, you're the little one who likes sugar sticks." Jesse smiled and, reaching in his saddlebag, brought out a small sack of peppermint sticks he'd kept safely tucked away and out of sight of Cap Featherstone, who had an insatiable sweet tooth. The girl squealed with delight and hugged Jesse around the neck.

"I'm gonna show John," she said. Keila turned to run after her brother, then stopped. "Jesse, I thought you'd come back a general or something."

"No, Keila," he told her. "The world has enough generals. I'm just plain old me."

"I like plain old you just fine, Jesse. Maybe even better," she said, and trotted off down Main.

Several other townsmen came forward to welcome Jesse home. He greeted each man in turn. His presence seemed to buoy their spirits. The tensions dividing those sympathetic to the Union and those who favored the Rebel cause had taken a toll on the citizens of Chahta Creek. Neighbors had grown suspicious of neighbors. And the sound of mounted horsemen at night filled the Federalists and abolitionists whether in town or in the countryside with dread. Al Teel, who could contain gossip about as long as a sieve holds water, had gone off to spread the word that Jesse was in town with the authority to invite the factions to come together and help bring peace to the embattled countryside and perhaps an end to the Knights of the Golden Circle and their reign of terror. By the time Jesse had pulled on a clean shirt and pinned his badge to his vest, the onlookers had dispersed and returned to their shops and homes, anxious to pass along to friends and relatives the news of Jesse's arrival and the reason for his return. John Medicine Fox returned with the gray gelding and placed the animal in the corral behind the jail. The boy and his sister unsaddled the animal, found a pair of brushes, and went to work on the horse.

"Does Henri Medicine Fox still run the hotel?" Jesse asked.

T. Alan Booth nodded. He was struggling with the idea of Jesse McQueen's appointment as territorial ranger. He had been the law in Chahta Creek for a mighty long time. And though what happened beyond the town limits was none of his concern, he frequently made it so. Given time, he was certain he could bring the situation under control. He didn't like to think the years were telling on him. Booth wasn't getting any younger but damned if he'd admit that fact to anyone else.

"I'll see about acquiring lodging at the Choctaw House," Jesse said.

"You still don't understand the way things are, do you?" Booth said. "You show up here with papers and a ranger's star and a captain's rank and you think you know so much." The peace officer scoffed and kicked a dirt clod against the stone wall of the jail. A small spider a shade darker than the sandstone scurried up the wall out of harm's way and proceeded to weave its silken web in the corner of the roof above the washstand. Jesse turned to face the parson marshal. The newly appointed ranger had been caught off guard by his old friend's vituperative behavior. Perhaps, Jesse thought, he sees me as a threat to his authority. Booth had been the marshall in Chahta Creek for more than fifteen years. He was a good man and proud.

Booth wandered back toward the jail, grumbling with every step about how it would take more than a slip of paper to bind together these divided people. Jesse made no move to call him back. The marshal would have to come to terms with the situation all by his lonesome. Nothing Jesse could say or do would roll back the clock for Booth or add the glow of youth to his pulpit. Jesse wondered if the peace officer felt a sense of failure over the deteriorating situation in the territory. His self-recrimination was totally unwarranted. Jesse doubted he could do any better. But he had come to try, and by heaven, he would.

Captain Jesse McQueen was no stranger to the owner of the Choctaw House. Henri Medicine Fox had been friends with the McQueen family for many years, and back when Jesse was barely four, Chief Henri had bounced the boy on his knee and told him the creation stories of the Choctaw people. Henri's father had fought alongside Kit McQueen at Horseshoe Bend, where the Choctaw and Cherokee peoples had defeated their mortal enemy, the Creeks. So it seemed odd to Jesse that the man he considered more an uncle than a friend should greet him with such cool reserve. Henri was a square-jawed, plain-spoken man whose once thick solid frame was getting a little soft in the middle. Henri wore his close-cropped brown hair well-oiled and parted in the middle. A mixed-breed, Henri in many ways reflected the French-Creole who had fathered him. The Creole had never formally given Henri his name or registered him in a church. It didn't matter to Henri. The name Medicine Fox suited him fine.

The lobby of the hotel was empty except for a pair of leather-backed chairs. Wildflowers filled a vase by the door. The arrangement had to be the work of Henri's second wife, Ellie. The comely young woman had filled the void in the proprietor's life after the death of Henri's first wife. She loved John and Keila as if they were her own.

"Afternoon, Jesse. I wondered when you'd get around to me," Henri said, looking up from behind the clerk's desk. Pince-nez spectacles perched on the tip of his nose forced him to peer over the wire rims. He wore a four-button pullover shirt with a gold stud button at the collar. A black sleeve garter circled his left arm. His shirt was tucked into high-waisted woolen trousers. He looked much the same as when Jesse had last seen the man almost two years ago, yet walking through the sunlit foyer Jesse sensed that there were indeed changes beneath the familiar surface of his surroundings.

"Ellie always had a way of keeping this the tidiest room in town," Jesse said.

"I've always suspected Ellie was born with a duster in one hand and a broom in the other," Henri replied, and nervously smiled.

"I've decided to put up at the hotel, seeing as I'll be around for a while."

"Oh? You don't want to stay out at your grandmother's place? Raven will be powerful hurt. You might give it some thought."

"I *have* given it some thought, Henri," Jesse matter-of-factly told him. "Any room will do."

Henri lowered his eyes. He stared at the floor beneath his feet. There was nothing interesting to see, but it beat locking eyes with McQueen. A fly landed on the counter and explored the leather cover of the ledger close at hand.

"We can't take you, Jesse. Me and Ellie ain't got a room to spare."

Jesse turned and his gaze swept across a lobby devoid of any traffic whatsoever. If the two-story hotel was indeed teeming with guests, they must be all out in the street or holed up in their rooms. The lobby was a comfortable place to sit and exchange news. And as Henri and his family occupied the downstairs rooms toward the rear of the building, Ellie could be counted on to set out a pot of coffee and a plate of molasses cakes for the guests. When the high-backed chairs were taken, a couple of wooden bench seats lined two walls, with an end table by each bench. No, in the heat of the day, this was the place to be.

"How can they all be taken, Henri? Who's in town?"

"We're full up," the man repeated with a note of anger in his voice.

Jesse grabbed the ledger. Henri tried to stop him, but McQueen batted his hand away and opened the book to its most current page. According to the signatures in the ledger, of the eight rooms upstairs, only three were currently occupied; one by a drummer and the other two by purchasing agents representing the Confederate States of America who were having a difficult time convincing the farmers in the area to accept Richmond-issued currency for produce and cotton. That left five rooms empty.

"I do not want any trouble," Henri said. "I have worked too hard for all this just to see the Choctaw House wind up a pile of ashes." Henri reached over and closed the ledger. "I have nothing for you."

"No," Jesse said. "I reckon you don't." He looked toward the doorway behind the clerk's station. The door was ajar and anyone in the sitting room could overhear the conversation. Jesse had the distinct impression Ellie waited, quiet and listening, just inside the room. "Give Ellie my best," Jesse said, loud enough to carry to the room beyond. His footsteps rapped upon the wood floor as he crossed the lobby and vanished outside. When McQueen was safely out of sight, Henri sighed and turned toward the doorway as Ellie appeared and hurried to his side. She was a narrow-waisted, slim, diminutive woman whose features were sharp to the point of almost being severe. Her hair was hidden beneath a sun bonnet whose brim shaded already darkly tanned skin. A black mole grew above one cheekbone, and when she spoke, her words seemed punctuated by several unnecessary breaths. Today her expression reflected only tension and fear as she stepped into her husband's sheltering embrace.

Another figure filled the doorway and this was far more menacing. It was a big man, clothed in the saffron hood and cloak of the Knights of the Golden Circle. The embroidered serpent in the center of the hood seemed to glisten with a life of its own. Hud Pardee kept his head lowered so that his eye patch would not be visible through the slit in the hood. The coarse heavy fabric served to muffle his voice. Pardee hadn't liked the idea of paying a call by daylight, but Cap had insisted, and the old bastard had certainly figured right about Jesse attempting to room at the hotel. Pardee kept his Navy Colt pointed at the couple.

"You did well," he said. "I knew you could be a sensible man if you wanted to. Now stay that way and your brats won't grow up orphans. Cross us and they might not grow up at all."

Henri's expression changed. Fury like a prairie fire swept over him. His features grew mottled. Ellie was pale and near tears. Henri's voice trembled as he spoke. "You lay a hand on my children and I'll—"

"—die choking in your own blood. Her, too." The Colt swerved toward Ellie. "Stick to your hotel, Mr. Medicine Fox. Don't be clever. I'll shuck these robes and leave by the back door. If I think you're watching me, I'll come back and see you both planted in the boneyard." Hud Pardee didn't wait for a reply, but turned and left. He could tell by their faces they would do as he said.

Pacer Wolf McQueen emerged from Buffalo Creek and, framed by a ring of bright water, he sprayed the air with a fine mist of droplets shaken from his long red hair. The sun in decline flirted with the long ridge of hills to the west. Soon the shadows would reach out and engulf like a silent tide the secluded valley that Raven and Kit McQueen had settled thirty years ago.

Raven sat next to Lorelei, a bucket between them. The two women were sorting snap beans, tossing aside the few that weren't fit for the pot and breaking the other pods in half and sometimes thirds. At the moment, Lorelei was distracted in her labors. The front porch of the farmhouse provided an unob-structed view of the creek bank and the south road cutting through the grasslands. Raven gave the girl a sideward glance and noted that Lorelei was wholly preoccupied with watching the tall rangy physique of Pacer Wolf as he cooled off from a hard day of rebuild-ing the smokehouse. He'd also begun the arduous task of resupplying the woodpile with fresh-cut timber from a deadfall he had found back in the hills. During the afternoon the air had rung with the sound of his ax as he split and stacked the hard gray brown logs. It had been a demanding task beneath an unforgiving sun in a cloudless sky. When Pacer had reached his limit, he stripped off his shirt, chucked aside his gunbelt, kicked off his boots and socks, took off for the creek wearing only his buckskin breeches for mod-esty's sake. Lorelei appeared unable to take her eyes off Pacer. Her hands resumed working but her focus was on Raven's youngest grandson. She dropped the snap beans aside without looking and continued to miss the bucket. Raven chuckled softly, and at that, the girl realized what she was doing and blushed. She bent over and gathered a handful of green beans from the floor and dropped them into the bucket.

"He works hard, but the place is too much for one man to tend," Raven said. "I'll find him some help."

"That's for him to say," Lorelei replied. She looked at the half-breed medicine woman seated beside her. They had been together for more than a week and yet there was so little she knew about the old woman. Lorelei had learned by the ripened age of fifteen it was dangerous to reveal too much about oneself.

"Where's your husband?" Lorelei asked. Perhaps the question had caught Raven off guard or merely in a reflective mood.

"He is buried, back in the hills, in a private, quiet spot," she said, watching her grandson stroll up from the riverbank and seeing her husband reflected in Pacer Wolf. Oh, physically, it was Jesse who favored Kit McQueen, a man of average height who cast a giant shadow. But Pacer's spirit had been one with his grandfather's. The two were cut from the same cloth, as unpredictable as a summer cloudburst, while Jesse was solid and as indomitable as the mountains.

"It was the time of the muddy-face moon when the snows have melted and new grass sprouts from the soil and out of the tired branches new buds bloom." Raven's voice took on a distant quality; her eyes seemed focused on the past, reliving the event.

"Who killed him?" Lorelei asked.

"Killed?" Raven repeated, puzzled by the girl's question.

"Pacer told me he comes from a line of warriors . . . "

Raven smiled, remembering Kit's tales of his father's exploits, fighting the British back in '76. Kit, too, had crossed swords with the British as well as Creek warriors and bloodthirsty pirates. And Ben, her son, had soldiered with the Texas Rangers during the Mexican War. The McQueen men did have a penchant for riding to the sound of gunfire. The medicine woman sighed.

"Yes, the McQueens are warriors. And like all true men of battle, they have stared into the red face of death and looked upon the horrible wasteland of war. Such men long for peace. They fight because they must, because good men and women must always stand against that which is wrong . . . or evil." Raven studied the girl and wondered if Lorelei was understanding any of this. The girl's desire for Pacer was certainly clear enough. She made no attempt to hide her interest. But whether she was capable of deeper introspection was anyone's guess.

"Kit woke early one morning, kissed me for the last time, took his rifle and rode off into the Kiamichis. He never came home. Ben and I rode out to look for him. We found him a few miles to the north. He was sitting against a shagbark hickory, his rifle across his knees, a look of such happiness on his face." A tear formed in the corner of Raven's eye and spilled down her cheek. She did not bother to wipe it away. The hurt, the sense of loss, the pain, were all honest emotions. The death of Kit McQueen, though a wound that would never heal, was something she had learned to live with. The peace of his passing reassured her. She would never forget the expression on his face, as if at the last moment he had looked into the heart of the great mystery and been filled with awe and wonder and unbearable joy.

"The only men I ever known gone under have died hard. Mean and hard, and they deserved every lick," Lorelei said.

Hecuba waddled in front of the porch and began to complain vigorously with a series of squawks that Raven immediately recognized as a warning. How the bird sensed the horseman in the distance defied explanation. Raven shielded her eyes, searched the road, and spied the rider coming up the valley at a gallop. Pacer saw their visitor at the same instant and hurried over to the porch and retrieved the Spencer carbine he'd leaned against a pole supporting the roof overhang. Hecuba flapped her wings and craned her neck forward until the horseman became recognizable as Gip Whitfield. At a word from Raven the goose reluctantly gave ground and fell silent. Ten minutes later Whitfield rode into the front yard. His boyish face was flushed, his hair windblown from his detour out to McQueen's valley. Somewhere along the trail he'd lost his hat. The former Confederate cavalryman was no stranger to the place or to Pacer, who had always figured a man's loyalty was his own affair. He neither forgave or condemned the deserter.

"I hope Libby hasn't taken ill again," Raven said. She could see no reason for Whitfield's visit save his wife's recurring ailments.

"She's fine, Raven," Gip replied. He walked his lathered mount closer to the porch. Raven kept a clay jug of water and a wood dipper suspended from the ceiling at the corner of the porch. He gulped down a dipper full and poured another over his head. Then with water streaming down his face, he turned toward the others.

"Jesse's back. I was in town, looking to buy Libby a hat for her birthday, and Jesse came riding in with Cap Featherstone." Gip glanced at Pacer, who struggled to remain impassive. Raven was standing. Her cheeks had paled. "Al Teel told me your brother's not only a Union captain, he's been appointed a territorial ranger. Ain't no telling what he aims to do. Some figure he's after the Knights, others say he plans to bring the Unionists together and lead 'em north." Gip mopped his brow with a kerchief. "Lord knows where that leaves me. Libby'll want to head north. I might walk into a Yankee prison if I went along." He scratched the back of his neck and shifted uneasily in the saddle. "Tellico boys are in jail again, but what else is new with them two?"

"Why don't you rest a spell, Gip?" Raven said, struggling to come to terms with the news Whitfield had brought. She was profoundly grateful that her eldest grandson had survived the war, thus far. But she dreaded his return and the way it coincided with Pacer's arrival home from the Lawrence debacle.

"No, thank you, ma'am. I'm anxious to be on my way. Libby hates to be by herself." He waved a hand in her direction. "I owe ya'll more'n I can ever repay. I figured you'd want the news about Jesse." He waved to Pacer. "Be seeing you." He wheeled his horse away from the porch and, holding the animal to a trot, rode alongside the fieldstone walk and out of the yard.

He was still in sight, a plume of dust trailing in the wake of his horse, when Pacer cradled the rifle in the crook of his arm and headed for the barn without so much as a by-your-leave.

"Pacer," Lorelei called out. "Come sit by me and rest a spell." She patted a bench alongside her chair. Her voice was sultry and inviting, but its magic was lost on the tall, rawboned young man.

"Where's he going?" Lorelei asked.

Raven wanted to go after Pacer but he was like Kit, his grandfather, just like that wonderful—impossible man. All the arguing in the world wouldn't change Pacer's mind.

"He's going to town."

"This late in the day? It'll be dark by the time he crosses Chahta Creek."

"No matter," Raven said. The plume of dust was fainter now in the amber distance along the valley road. Soon there'd be another. "He has business that cannot wait."

Chapter Eighteen

Jesse had a rough decision to make. He was fixing to ask for second helpings and couldn't decide between Mary Lou Gude's sweet potato pie or the fried rabbit with cream gravy. At last the proprietress and cook of Gude's Good Eats made the decision for him and placed a wedge of pie on one plate and an open biscuit, a rabbit quarter, and a big stirring-spoon-full of gravy onto his dinner plate.

"You spoil me, Miss Gude," Jesse said. "Linc Graywater better watch out or I'm liable to propose before he gets up the nerve to."

"You're too late, Yankee," a deep voice boomed from the kitchen. He stepped into Mary Lou's dining room. There were only a few customers tonight and he instantly recognized Jesse. Graywater was the best blacksmith in Chahta Creek. He looked big as a barn and solid as the hills. His features were thick and his hands were wide and powerful looking. He walked slightly stooped forward in an attempt to ease the ever-present pain in the small of his back. He was forty-one years old and for the last six of those years had been courting Mary Lou. Evidently during Jesse's absence, the blacksmith had finally found the nerve to ask the proper question. Now it was Mary Lou's turn to string him along and allow him to dangle like a puppet for just a little while. After all, Linc had certainly taken his time. Mary Lou lived alone; she was part German and part Choctaw, the product of an unusual union between a Choctaw maiden and a Prussian mercenary who had served under General Jackson during the war with the Creeks. Both parents were gone now, asleep beneath the prairie sod in a graveyard off Choctaw Street.

Mary Lou, at thirty-nine, was past the prime marrying age for most of the eligible men in the area. Her parents had been ailing for much of her early years, and like a devoted daughter, she had given them the best years of her life, caring for them until the death of her father, nine years ago, and, more recently, the demise of her Choctaw mother. Mary Lou had a strong, kind-looking face. She was soft of voice, but her resolve was as solid as iron, and when she made up her mind, she could be irresistible. It was to Linc Graywater's credit that he had worn Mary Lou down. She was preparing to accept his proposal and allow the blacksmith to escort her down the aisle at the Congregationalist church.

"I retract my proposal," Jesse replied. "However, you may hold it in reserve in case this big ox gets cold feet and changes his mind." Jesse pretended to be oblivious to Linc's frowning stare. "Of course, you need only hand him a wedge of sweet potato pie and I'll warrant he'll dance right up to the parson and say his 'I do's' before Booth can crack a Bible."

"Listen to him. Some Yank general boots Jesse a rank or two and then hands him a badge and he thinks he's cock o' the roost," Linc countered. The other patrons of Gude's Good Eats were a quiet, if suspicious, bunch who made every attempt to appear nonchalant and pointedly oblivious to the interchange between the two men. If it came to blows, no one wanted to be in harm's way. However, the tension in the place eased when Mary Lou Gude stepped between Jesse and the blacksmith and ordered one back to the kitchen and the other to finish his dinner.

"You should be more careful, Jesse," Mary Lou chided. "Linc has a short temper these days. It galls him to sit helplessly by while the Knights of the Golden Circle terrorize the countryside."

"I thought he'd be Jeff Davis's man," Jesse said.

Mary Lou sighed and nodded. "He is. But war is one thing and neighbors another. Hack Warner was a friend. Some of the others, too, that have been burned out and driven off their land. Linc Graywater knows the difference between right and wrong no matter where his loyalties lie." The woman patted the bun of brown hair she kept pinned at the nape of her neck. She blushed, becoming self-conscious. "How I prattle on."

She ambled off to check the other tables and see that everyone was taken care of. It was a simple enough task. Mary Lou's place held a dozen tables, four of which ran the length of one wall. Jesse was seated at one of the four, a table furthest from the front door. He wanted to watch the people come and go and he was loath to have his back to the front window. The room's interior was ablaze with the amber light of several oil lamps hung from wall brackets and a wooden circular chandelier sporting half a dozen lamps, all lit. The walls were festooned with chromolithographs depicting scenes from the Bible, including Joseph and his coat of many colors, Cain slaying Abel, Solomon on his throne, and David holding the severed head of Goliath, which was a special favorite of the children. An infant Moses being rescued from the reeds and rushes along the banks of the Nile was special to the ladies for its depiction of a cherublike child, while the men found the scantily clad Egyptian slave girls of more than passing interest. The bill of fare, like the hand-lettered sign on the false front outside, was simple and to the point and rarely changed. It was posted by the kitchen door for all to see. Beef, greens, potatoes, pork, and available fresh game depending on the luck of local hunters.

The front door opened and Carmichael Ross entered the restaurant. She had changed her ink-smudged brown garb for a light blue dress trimmed with lace at the throat and wrists. Carmichael greeted Mary Lou with the casual familiarity born of a long and friendly relationship. With the amenities completed, the editor of the *Chahta Creek Courier* made her way across the room to Jesse's table. McQueen stood as she lowered herself into the chair opposite him. Her long sandy-colored hair looked shiny and soft, as if she had brushed it for an hour. There was a hint of daring in her emerald eyes and Jesse had the distinct impression he ought to be wary of this woman. What was she up to? The more he tried to understand women the more confused he became. Maybe it was better to proceed blindly and trust to blind fortune. *My God, Jesse, slow down. You haven't even been here a full day yet.*

"Are you eating?" Jesse asked the woman.

"I just came for the coffee. And you."

Jesse nearly choked on a wedge of pie crust. Carmichael laughed at his reaction.

"Word travels quickly. The hotel is filled with guests that no one can see." Carmichael shook her head in disgust. A woman of strong convictions, she had no patience with cowards. "Henri Medicine Fox is no more a supporter of the Confederacy than General Grant or Abe Lincoln."

"I don't think his loyalty is in question. Parson Booth tried to warn me, and now I guess I know what he was talking about." Jesse took a sip of coffee. "Some folks will be glad to see me, others will only see the blue uniform I'm not wearing. Henri Medicine Fox is a good man, but he's worried as to what I have in mind. He has a family to think of."

"You are far more tolerant than I," Carmichael remarked.

"And twice as curious," Jesse said. "You came for the coffee and me?"

Carmichael continued to find him amusing. The fact that Jesse was a good ten years younger than she did not bother her for a minute. "I have a room over the newspaper office. It has a table and washbasin and a comfortable enough bed. Elmo Washburn, my typesetter, used to live there."

"What happened to him?" Jesse asked, although he wasn't sure he wanted to find out.

"The Knights cornered him down by the creekbank and held a mock hanging, with him as the guest of honor. If he didn't quit me they promised to return for him and string him up for real." Carmichael shrugged. "Elmo believed them. And took off for Kansas."

"I cannot say as I blame him."

"You would not have left."

"How can you be so certain?"

Carmichael reached across the table and placed her hand upon the front of his shirt and the "medal" he wore. She pressed the English coin against his chest. He understood what she meant. The talisman of the McQueens would not allow him to flee from the night riders. His was a legacy of courage. Generations of McQueens had defied injustice and tyranny and the forces of fear. Carmichael had been a frequent visitor to the valley of the Buffalo. She had heard the stories from Raven, and there were still some pure-bloods back in the hills who remembered the exploits of Kit McQueen.

"Do you want the room?" Carmichael asked.

"Sold," he said.

"Good," she replied. "I'll straighten things up."

"I left my saddlebags back at the jail," Jesse said. "I reckon the parson will let me in."

"I saw him just a few minutes ago. He was standing out front and peering in the window. He looked like a man trying to decide whether or not to come inside." The editor finished her coffee. "Booth is a funny bird. When he saw me, he seemed to make up his mind right then and there to move along on his rounds. It isn't like him to pass up Mary Lou's. He favors her pies."

"My being here doesn't sit well with him. He's been the law for a good many years in Chahta Creek. Now I've returned with papers of authority and a badge. I'm as welcome as the grippe." Jesse swallowed the last morsel of pie and stared at his empty plate. He wished all his problems could be arranged upon the earthenware surface and handled in turn, neatly and at his own discretion.

"You need him, Jesse. If for no other reason than to watch your back."

"I'm not worried," Jesse lied. He looked up and flashed his most winning smile. Carmichael Ross wasn't fooled for a second.

It was said the ancestors of the Choctaw issued from a cave underneath the sacred mound, Nanih Waya, in the southern hills of the place called Mississippi. Jesse had learned the creation story from his grandmother who taught him the legends along with his Christian upbringing. As the story went, these early Choctaw climbed out from beneath the mound and arranged themselves in a circle about the mound and lay down to finish drying. Afterward, they dispersed to occupy the surrounding countryside, but always Nanih Waya remained, like the hub of a wheel, the ceremonial center of the Choctaw Nation. The cross streets of town, from First to Sixth, were supposed to point the way to the sacred mound, the source of all beginning. Though his own bloodline was pretty well diluted, Jesse still felt a sense of belonging here. The ancient roots went deep but did not govern his actions as they did Pacer Wolf's, Jesse thought as he made his way through the moonlit streets of Chahta Creek. Main Street was for the most part deserted. But Cherokee Street evidently had some traffic, and a glow emanated from the northeast corner of town where the Medicine Wagon Saloon was enjoying a thriving business. There were a couple of other saloons along Cherokee, but they were poor cousins to Cap's place. Jesse stood at the center of Fourth and Main and considered paying Featherstone a visit and seeing first-hand the interior of the saloon. But it had been a long day and Jesse wanted to retrieve his saddlebags from Booth's office. He resisted temptation and resumed his earlier course. The black mass of Turtle Mountain loomed ahead of him. The heavily wooded slope was a place of stygian shadows in which an army of devils could easily hide. A breeze had sprung up and, overhead, clouds like wedding veils, tattered and decayed, drifted past the face of the moon. The office and jail were dark. Booth was no doubt still making his rounds and had forgotten to light a lamp for the prisoners.

Jesse quickened his pace, growing uneasy, alone in the street. He covered the remaining two blocks at a trot. The marshal's office and jail had blended in and become one with the menacing darkness of the mountain against which it nestled.

Jesse had just started up the steps when he sensed movement to his left. He froze and reached for the Colt holstered at his side. The Dragoon filled his hand with a reassuring weight. He changed his course and headed for the corner of the building and eased around only to find an empty patch of ground, a worn path leading to the narrow corral and shed where Booth kept his horses, and Jesse's own gray gelding whinnied and pawed the dust. Something was spooking the horses. No telling what had crept out of the ancient hills. Now there was an unsettling notion. But the fact remained, the Kiamichis were home to panthers and brown bears, razorback hogs and red wolves.

Jesse walked the length of the building and paused again at the rear of the jail. The sound of two snoring men drifted through a barrel window. The Tellicos were sleeping off the effects of their home brew. Jesse started toward the corral, his eyes searching the darkness for whatever had alerted the horses. He hurried across the open ground behind the jail and didn't relax until he reached the split rail fencing that surrounded the horse shed. He crouched low and allowed his vision to adjust to his surroundings. That's when he saw the hat. Someone was crouched low behind the flatbed wagon Booth used for ferrying fresh-cut timber from the mountains to the church he was slowly renovating. The wagon was just outside the corral, between the fence and the outhouse. Jesse sank to his knees and waited. Was it possible the intruder hadn't seen him? Jesse crept along the fencing and began to work his way around the corral in order to come up behind the wagon.

Booth's mares whinnied nervously and began to circle the corral. The gelding was unnerved and joined the other two horses as they tried to avoid Jesse's position as well as the section of fence nearest the wagon. The pen was simply too confining. At last the gray gelding and both of Parson Booth's brown mares chose to bunch by the gate as Jesse continued behind the shed, then followed the fence to the far corner of the corral. He picked his way among dry twigs and brittle grasses. Sweat beaded his forehead and trickled down his cheeks. Another step would bring the man by the wagon under his gun. Jesse took a deep breath, crouched on the balls of his feet, then stepped out and leveled his Colt at the figure he had so laboriously stalked. The hat rested atop an ax handle, the blade of the ax deep in the grainy top of a black stump. Jesse's expression hardened. He'd been tricked, but by whom? A gun barrel pressed against his spine provided the answer.

"You always fell for this trick, Jesse," a familiar voice said.

"Hello, Pacer," Jesse replied. He holstered his Colt and turned to look up at his little brother.

They were a study in contrasts. Pacer had all the size with his long-limbed frame and large hands. His shaggy red hair framed his features, burned dark as a full-blood's. He wore a faded gray Confederate shirt and buckskin breeches and calf-high boots. A Union-issue gunbelt circled his waist. The D-guard knife on his left was stamped CSA on the base of its heavy brass hilt.

"I thought all you Yankees were supposed to be ten feet tall and snort fire," Pacer said as he stepped around his brother to retrieve his hat. He continued to keep his guard up and held his Colt at his side.

"And I thought all of you Quantrill's raiders crawled on your belly and hissed at the shadows," Jesse replied. He was angry for allowing himself to be caught by Pacer. Jesse tilted his hat back on his head and folded his arms across his well-muscled chest. He stood several inches shorter than Pacer. His black hair, while unruly, was trimmed. Even in his civilian clothes, Jesse possessed the aura of command.

"I quit his bunch."

"You were a fool to join. It was bad enough seeing the Choctaw Kid wanted for stealing Federal payrolls or horses or a wagonload of supplies. Now it's murder and looting and attacks on innocent people."

"Why have you come here, Jesse?"

"Father sent me. He hoped I might be able to stop a war from breaking out."

"You've seen Ben? How is he?"

"I left him helpless, with a Rebel bullet in his back, waiting for a Yankee surgeon to cut it out."

"Father's wounded . . . How did it happen?" Pacer slipped his gun into its holster and leaned against the wagon. His pulse quickened, fearing the worst.

"He was backshot by some Rebel sympathizers," Jesse told him. "Might have been one of your friends— or did you boys get your fill of bloodletting in Kansas?"

"You've got no call to talk like that. There's a war on," Pacer retorted.

"I know. I've fought it."

They were like the country itself, divided, separated by a gulf of suspicion and mistrust and more than a little pain.

"I've come here to bring these people together if I can. So you and your Knights of the Golden Circle stay out of my way."

"I am not with them," Pacer said.

"You expect me to believe that."

"I don't give a damn what you believe," Pacer snapped. His brother was already getting under his skin. He was losing control of his temper. But Jesse was so damn calm, even when Pacer had him under the gun.

"I'll do what I can to bring a truce to the people here," Jesse said.

"And when you're done . . . "

"I'll leave."

"Alone?"

Jesse reached into his pocket and unfolded the wanted poster and handed it to Pacer, whose hastily sketched likeness adorned the wrinkled page. "No."

Pacer understood. "I'll be watching for you, Jesse," he ominously promised.

Pacer started toward the wooded slope behind the jail. Jesse heard a horse whinny and shake its mane. The sound came from somewhere not too far off among the trees.

Jesse could have tried to stop his brother then and there, but he wanted to avoid a fight if at all possible. The last thing he wanted was his brother's blood on his hands. No, the last thing he wanted was a bullet from his brother's Colt right between the eyes. Taking Pacer was not going to be easy.

"Daniel!" Jesse called out, using his brother's Christian name. "How can you turn against your own people?"

As his brother paused in the darkness, a swirl of fireflies swarmed up from the ground and gave the impression that the tall man had burst into flames.

"Funny—" said Pacer Wolf McQueen before he vanished without a sound. "I was going to ask the same of you."

Chapter Nineteen

Arbitha Roberts heard her husband scream. She bolted awake and pulled on her dressing gown. Her heart pounding within her breast, she cracked open the door to her bedroom and peered around the doorsill, dreading what she would find and knowing she had to look. She discovered her husband standing in the hallway. He wore a nightshirt and clutched a lantern in his trembling hand. Tullock Roberts did not easily show fear. He was a strong-willed, confident man, generous to his friends, defiant toward his enemies. There was no quit in him and very little give. Arbitha had never seen him this way in all her married life. His thick, rough features were drawn and pale. His eyes were wide as he stumbled out of his doorway and headed for his son's bedroom.

"What happened?" Arbitha asked. She stepped into the hall. They had taken to sleeping apart these days, ever since Tullock had involved his son in the Knights of the Golden Circle. She held a hand to her mouth and hurried down the hall. They reached Sam's room almost at the same instant.

Tullock cracked the door open and, holding the

lamp before him, examined the room, the unslept-in four-poster bed, a pile of work clothes discarded upon a chest at the foot of the bed.

"Tullock . . . please . . . what is it?" Arbitha was pleading now. Something had happened, and if it had unnerved a man like her husband, it must be terrible indeed.

"That's right," Tullock muttered. "He went to town. What time is it? No matter. He went to town with Chris, Buck, and the Teel boy. Yes. They went together . . . "

"Tullock Roberts, if you don't tell me what's going on this very minute I'm going to go downstairs and fetch me the stoutest switch I can find and come back and give you the damndest lashing of your life." Arbitha folded her arms across her chest and tried to block him from leaving the room, but Tullock simply brushed her aside as he walked into the hall again and this time knelt and placed his hand upon the hardwood floor. Arbitha followed him. She was beginning to question his sanity. Had some malady overtaken him in the night and left him bereft of his senses?

"I had a dream," he said at last, his voice as soft as the flickering light illuminating the papered walls and the framed pages of poetry Arbitha had carefully written and decorated with a variety of colored inks. No one stopped to read them. Her husband never had the time. Samuel had shown an interest in his youth, but he had become closer to his father now and distant to Arbitha, and he could see no purpose to poetry.

Tullock stood and returned to his room, his bare feet padding on the floor as he crossed to the end table by his bed and poured some water from a white china pitcher into a washbasin. He bent over and cupped water over the back of his neck and then up to his face and straightened with his hair plastered close to his skull like a white cap. He looked in the mirror and saw his wife standing behind him. He could just make out her figure through the cottony material of her gown; the rounded swell of her breasts and the inviting curves of her hips began to replace terror with desire.

"I thought you wouldn't enter this room again unless I forbade Sam to ride with me when the Knights gather."

"What happened? I heard you cry out. I saw you afraid . . . like I'm afraid when you leave with him. What did you see, Tullock? What was it?"

Tullock slumped onto the side of the bed. "Dreams mean nothing." He stared at his folded hands and then reached over and pulled up his sheet and dried his face. "There was blood by my bed. I thought I was awake, but this was the dream. I sat up and swung, climbed out of bed, and stepped in the blood. It was so real I could feel it, smell it."

"Where did it come from?" Arbitha asked in a soft voice.

"It flowed under my door and right up to the side of my bed. I walked across the room and opened the door. The trail of blood was coming from Sam's room. I ran to his door and found it locked. I knocked but there was no answer, then I kicked it in. He was lying on the bed, his arms outstretched and his cold eyes staring at . . . at nothing. He was dead, a black bullet hole in his side and another in his chest and another . . . and another—" He lowered his face into his hands. He had dreamt the death of his son and wanted to hide. Even though he was awake now and all was seemingly well, the dream had left its mark and he doubted he would ever be the same again, and he hated that.

Arbitha drew near and knelt before him and took his hands in hers. Her own eyes were glistening with tears. She believed in the power of dreams, much like the full-bloods and those who still clung to the old ways in their attitude if not their dress. Her husband's dream was a warning. "Listen to the dream," she whispered. "For the love of heaven, listen to the dream and save our son—our only son. Abandon the Knights, because if you don't something terrible will happen. I know it, Tullock. And now, so do you."

"Stay with me?" he said. It was both a question—and an answer.

Morning began with a sacred fire and a column of prayer smoke and Raven McQueen. On the hill behind the farmhouse, flames danced among the circle of ashes left by former blazes. As she had so often in the past, Raven McQueen, herself a product of two different cultures, swayed to the rhythm of her own voice and chanted the spirit songs taught to her by her Choctaw mother.

Raven owned a Bible, one that belonged to her father, and she might have found a prayer to suit her needs among those venerable pages, but the prayers of the Choctaw enabled her to speak directly from the heart and allowed her to open to the All-Father in a ritual as ancient as the land and the morning light.

A blush on the horizon—faint hints of crimson seeped upward into the gray-blue canopy of heaven like an open wound. The land was hushed, as silent as the ribbon of morning mist that rose like some serpentine spectre above the winding undulations of Buffalo Creek. Only the crackling fire sounded as flames devoured the branches Raven continued to add while softly singing.

> "All-Father, Shaker of mountains,
> Whisper of wind, Spirit of birth and
> Death, my words climb to you on the wings
> Of my prayer smoke.
> I fear for my grandsons. They walk separate

Paths and death is the hunter who
Follows their tracks. Be the rain that hides
Them, the wind that washes away the sign
   of their passing."

Her voice was strong as the woman herself was strong. Time had streaked her long black hair with silver but had left her spirit untouched. The brightness of her light within was undimmed. She had yet to sleep. After waiting up for Pacer she had learned from him of his encounter with Jesse. He made no attempt to hide the fact that Jesse intended to make him a prisoner and take him north. As for Ben, news of his injury and the attempt on his life was more than just cause for concern. Yet she felt deep in her soul that he would heal and be well. It was Jesse and Pacer that had her dreading the future. Jesse was not the kind of man to back down from a fight and Pacer was just the man to give him one. These McQueen men could be as obstinate as they were brave. It was up to their grandmother to shake some sense into their heads before a tragedy occurred. Raven ceased her chanting, sighed, and studied the prayer smoke. She followed its winding trail as it dissipated against the dawn and lifted her gaze to heaven. "I'm knowin' what has to be done," she added, a brogue creeping into her voice. "But I wouldn't mind a little help."

Morning began with a woman alone, a whispering breeze and the fiery dance of the sun.

Carmichael Ross had more than coffee on her mind as she stepped out the back door of her house, crossed the alley, and headed for the newspaper office. Balancing a tray laden with coffeepot, cups, biscuits, and a jar of honey, she started up the stairway that ran alongside the building and led to the room above the office. Morning light illuminated the upper story, and the whitewashed wood walls of the office seemed to glow with an almost biblical radiance. Carmichael had slept fitfully, and after her restless night, she rose from her bed before dawn and started the coffee. She heated water and took a bath, placing a dash of lilac into the copper tub. She chose a modest but handsome Sunday dress from among her sorely diminished wardrobe: workclothes were her mainstay these days. She brushed her waist-length hair a hundred strokes until it glistened and flowed softly over her shoulders, brown tresses against a dark green bodice and pale green woolen skirt.

It was a tricky climb, balancing the tray with one hand and lifting the hem of her skirt with the other. But at last she reached the top landing, and with the sun warming her back and shoulders, she knocked upon the door. It wasn't every day she had a male guest and it didn't hurt to be polite. No—neighborly. She was being neighborly. After all, Jesse had come a long way to risk his life to bring two of the territory's warring factions to the peace table. She admired him for his courage and determination. The fact that his dark brown eyes deepened in hue when he watched her or that his laugh was honest and good-natured and that he moved with the sleek sure grace of a mountain cat certainly didn't hurt either. What harm was there in beginning Jesse's first morning back in Chahta Creek with a little special treatment?

She knocked on the door. The latch clicked and the door creaked open on its hinges. Carmichael checked the street to see if anyone was watching, then stepped inside. Had he left the door unlatched on purpose? She entered the room and paused to allow her eyesight to adjust to the shadowy interior.

"Jesse?"

The bed looked slept in. His carpet bag was unpacked and a Federal uniform had been set aside. Though the territory was neutral ground, the fact remained that the woods were thick with Confederate sympathizers who wouldn't hesitate to ventilate that blue jacket and ask questions later. However, it was common knowledge that Jesse was a Union officer. His life was in danger no matter what he wore.

She would have told him that very thing had the room not been hopelessly empty. She must have missed him by a matter of minutes.

"Carmichael Ross, you are a damn fool," she said. There was a chair by the window overlooking the street. The sunlight drew her to the grainy glass. She glanced down at Main Street, devoid of all but a couple of drifters on their way out of town. They left nothing in their wake but tracks in the dirt that the next rain would wash away. Nature had a habit of reclaiming what men left behind, footsteps or temples, which sooner or later became just so many patches of dust. It was the way of the world, thought the newspaperwoman as she morosely returned her attention to the vacant room. She set the tray on the chair nearest the window. A fly cut a series of hasty spirals over the platter and eventually alit on the biscuits.

"Help yourself," she muttered to the insect, and left the room. The devil take the man, she had a newspaper to publish.

Enos Clem was the last person Jesse expected to see in this part of the world, but the gambler was the first person his eyes settled on as he entered Cap Featherstone's Medicine Wagon Saloon. Enos Clem nodded and continued playing solitaire as Jesse checked the spacious interior of the room for any sign of threat. The smell of coffee, cigar smoke, and spilled whiskey caused him to wrinkle his nose and stifle a sneeze.

"Small world," Clem commented without a trace of animosity, which only further aroused the Union officer's suspicions.

"What brings you here, gambler?"

"A lame horse," said Clem.

"And an ill wind," Jesse commented. He was interrupted before he could further question the gambler.

"We're closed," another voice interjected.

Jesse turned toward the sound and came face to face with Cap Featherstone's one-eyed gunman.

"The name is Hud Pardee. Maybe you've heard of me, if you've ever been down the Natchez Trace."

Indeed, Jesse McQueen knew the name, for it was synonymous with gunplay and a "short fuse" temper. Pardee had the reputation as a duelist and a first-rate pistoleer who had killed seven men on the field of honor before heading west. He'd never seen the man until now.

"I know who you are," Jesse told the ashen-haired gunman. His voice was cool and without a trace of emotion.

"And from the look of you," Pardee said, "you must be Jesse McQueen. I'm Cap's partner in the Medicine Wagon. He spoke of you the other night."

"Partner?"

"Sure," Pardee explained. "Cap has the brains to bring in the money and I've the skill to see we keep it." Pardee crooked a thumb in his sash, parting his frock coat to reveal the guns tucked at his waist. He stood taller than Jesse, but if he hoped to overpower McQueen, he failed. True, Pardee was dangerous. But Jesse had known dangerous men before and had sent under a few of them, himself. Pardee was a man to bear watching but he wasn't about to run from him.

"Jesse, my lad," Cap good-naturedly called from the doorway to his office. He held up a pot of coffee and a cup and motioned for McQueen to join him.

"You and me will have to play another hand or two," Clem said. He gathered his cards, shuffled them, and set the deck face-down on the table. He tilted back in his chair and looked up at the officer. At their last encounter, Jesse had worn the blue woolen coat and trousers befitting a Yankee horse soldier. Returning to Indian Territory had certainly worked a change in the officer, now garbed in Levi's and faded buckskin shirt and scuffed boots. He'd pinned the dull silver star to his brown vest. An army-issued Colt Dragoon and gunbelt circled his waist.

Jesse studied the gambler's chalky features. The man's cordial airs were about as out of place as a grin on a cadaver. So Clem wanted to resume the game that had cost him money and pride aboard the riverboat.

"Reckon your luck has changed?" Jesse asked. Enos cut the deck and held up an ace of clubs in his long fingers. He chuckled and continued balancing on the back legs of his chair.

"What do you think?" he answered.

Jesse left the table, allowing the gambler to have the last word. He heard a woman's laughter ring out from upstairs.

"Young Sam Roberts is having himself a good time," Pardee said aloud, and headed for the bar where Shug Jones was filling an assortment of bottles labeled Whiskey, Aged Bourbon, Rye, and Kentucky Mist from the same keg. Freckle-faced Dobie Johnson stood alongside the bartender. It was Dobie's task to doctor the different "spirits"—putting a dash of bitters in one bottle and a dollop of chili peppers in another. The rattler in the glass bottle on the bar hissed and threatened as Jesse crossed the room.

Cap Featherstone filled the doorway to his office. Black woolen trousers strained to contain his heavy thighs; his solid round belly concealed by a blousy white shirt protruded between the folds of his brocaded brown vest. He scratched at his bearded jaw and stepped back into his office.

"Soon as Tandy shows up with a basket from Gude's you bring me a plate of biscuits, hear?"

Dobie Johnson looked up from the whiskey bottles and waved. "Sure thing, Cap," he replied.

Again laughter drifted down from the rooms above. Jesse paused and glanced up as Sam Roberts appeared at the top of the landing. The planter's son wavered, then gripped the balustrade with his left hand to steady himself. A slim doe-eyed girl in a robe trimmed with faded white lace arrived at his side and began tugging at him and giggling. Her tousled brown hair hung in ringlets and wayward strands, framing her thin oval face. Her lips were smeared with rouge, and a black beauty mark dotted her cheek.

"Hack Warner is looking for you, son," Hud called up to the nineteen-year-old. "Says you helped burn him out."

"Talk's cheap for his kind. Has your colored returned with the food?" Sam called down, seemingly unconcerned.

"Not yet, my young friend," Hud replied. "But when he does, I'll send him to your door."

"See to it." The only son of Tullock Roberts was accustomed to having his breakfast at a certain hour. And after the previous night's activities, he was famished.

The girl at his side whispered in his ear. Sam laughed, coughed a moment, then laughed again and waved the girl back to her room. He noticed Jesse for the first time and halted in midturn.

"Jesse McQueen?"

"Hello, Sam." Jesse touched the brim of his hat. He remembered Sam as a young boy, frail, shivering in a thicket alongside Jesse, Ben McQueen, and Tullock Roberts. Trembling from the cold and the strain of having to measure up to his father's expectations, Sam Roberts, all of eleven years old, tried to bring the single-shot percussion rifle to bear on the white-tailed deer that Ben had successfully stalked. Jesse remembered how his own father had talked soothingly to the boy, calmed his fears, steadied his aim. Sam made his first kill that day. His father had blooded him and beamed with pride as they returned to the plantation, and afterward, over venison steaks, Ben and Tullock had toasted each other's health with Kentucky whiskey before a crimson sunset.

"I'll be out to see your father today," Jesse said.

"You might find the reception uncomfortably warm," Sam warned.

"I won't wear a coat," Jesse quipped, and continued into Cap's office. The owner of the Medicine Wagon stood back and welcomed him with open arms. On Jesse's part, discovering Enos Clem and a man like Hud Pardee in Cap's employ tempered his enthusiasm for the likable rogue. He said as much as Cap filled a coffee cup and set a blue-enameled pot back on the Franklin stove at the rear of the room.

"Clem, huh?" Cap asked, and offered his visitor a cup. Jesse refused. He'd drunk enough of the coal oil that Cap called coffee on the trip south from Kansas City. "Hud said he showed up the other day. He was down on his luck and figured the Medicine Wagon was as good a place as any for it to change. He can run a game of faro better'n any man I ever seen. He plays a proper hand of poker, too. Clem's turned the house a tidy profit. I'd like to keep him around. But if you're set on running him out of town . . . "

Jesse shrugged. "Let him stay." There was no love lost between him and the gambler, but it wasn't for McQueen to drive the man out when he hadn't broken any laws.

"What about Pardee? Trouble clings to him like ticks to a hound. He's a dangerous man."

"And these are dangerous times, what with the damn war and night riders chasing good folk from their homes and property," Cap explained. He sat on the edge of a large black safe set against the back wall, which displayed one of Cap's posters from his wagon. The poster touted Cap Featherstone's Miracle Elixir and the benefits to be derived from consuming the potent tonic on a regular basis. According to Cap, the elixir cured grippe, ague, fatigue, numbness, sore limbs, and all manner of blood disorders. Indeed the tonic could do just about everything except make the blind see and the lame walk, although Cap's prose was quick to remind the would-be customer that benefits derived from the elixir continued to be reported from Texas to Ohio.

"A man would be a fool not to keep the likes of Hud Pardee around. I don't intend to wind up like Hack Warner, burned out and nothing to show for my efforts," Cap concluded. "But speaking of fools, just what kind of play are you up to, lad?" The big man took a moment to sip his coffee, then added, "Tullock Roberts is a hard man to whom you are no better than a traitor for turning against your neighbors and friends. He's liable to shoot you on sight."

"I don't think so. But just in case something happens," Jesse said, "get word to Major Abbot for me."

"Why don't you just forget the whole thing, Jesse? It's not worth it. I found that out, months ago." Cap tasted his coffee and wiped his mouth on his shirtsleeve. "Sheep to the slaughter, that's how men like Abbot see us. I left many a good lad behind in Georgia who knew the truth, mark my words."

"You're wrong, Cap."

"He sent you here alone, didn't he?"

"Abbot's hoping to avert a war here. That's why he sent me and not a regiment. By the time he had one to spare, the territory might already be lost." Jesse noticed a territorial map on the wall behind the desk. Several circles had been drawn on the map, ringing Chahta Creek. He could not imagine their significance. More important to him was the bitterness he sensed in Cap Featherstone. Jesse was beginning to question how much he could count on the man.

"Ride clear of Old Man Roberts," Cap warned. "Now that be sage advice, the kind I'd render to my own flesh and blood."

"Tullock is bound to be one of the Knights of the Golden Circle, or at the least he's someone the Rebels will listen to," Jesse said. "Through Carmichael's paper I've called a meeting, this Sunday evening, for all the people, Confederates or Union Loyalists. If I can get both sides talking instead of shooting, maybe I can hammer out a truce that will put an end to the raids. If Tullock will agree to come, a good many of the Reb sympathizers will follow." Jesse took a moment to consider his options and Cap's warning, then he shook his head and added, "Tullock's the man I must first talk to. After all, there was a time he and my father were friends."

"You're as bullheaded as Ben, God rest his soul." He sighed in resignation and crossed the room to stand behind his desk. He'd noticed how Jesse had briefly studied the map. "This is a good land, Jesse. A shrewd man can make something of himself here." He patted Jesse's shoulder. "The Medicine Wagon is only the beginning for me. I aim to cast a long shadow before I'm through." He took up his gator-head cane and rested his hands, one upon the other, on the silver hilt as he leaned forward, his gaze as sharp as a scalping knife.

"To hell with Major Abbot. When you leave Chahta Creek, keep going. Don't look back."

"I can't just ride away," Jesse said.

"What's stopping you, son?"

Jesse reached inside his shirt and held up the initialed coin, his family's legacy. "This."

Chapter Twenty

Tullock Roberts had blood up to the elbows as he stood amidst a group of children and young men who had waited in respectful silence like acolytes as he slit the hog's throat and hung the poor creature up by its heels to bleed dry. The animal lasted but a few seconds. Then it shuddered and died. As the last of the crimson fluids welled from its ripped flesh, Sawyer Truett and a couple of his friends built a fire beneath a large black kettle. The carcass was suspended by a chain around its hind legs hung over an A-frame Tullock had built for the yearly slaughtering at Honey Ridge. It was a good-size hog and would dress out to about a hundred and twenty pounds of meat, less what the children and Truett and his friends managed to lop off and roast over the open fire. But before any sampling took place, the carcass had to be scalded to remove the bristly hair from the animal's flesh. Sawyer played out a little slack as his companions guided the hog into the kettle which rode a pyre of burning tree limbs alongside the A-frame. A few minutes in the kettle was all the carcass needed. Truett and the others hauled the animal out of its bath and tied the rope off and began scraping the loosened hairs and blanched hide from the remains. As soon as a patch of meat showed, Sawyer or another man would carve a hunk of pork and toss it to one of the black children underfoot or take a piece for themselves and hold the morsel by knifepoint over the flames lapping at the sides of the kettle. Grease dripped and sizzled into the fire. The aroma of freshly roasted pork set every stomach growling despite the fact it was barely midmorning and dinner was several hours away. The only man not affected was Tullock Roberts, who stood aside from the young men and seemed transfixed by the stains on his hands and knife.

Sawyer Truett noticed Tullock's distraction and left his friends to saunter over to the preoccupied man.

"You all right, Mr. Roberts?"

Tullock glanced up. It took him a moment to clear his thoughts. He blinked, looked at Sawyer, then over at Buck Langdon, Chris Foot, and Johnny Teel, who did not share his parents' abolitionist sentiments. Chris Foot was a full-blood Choctaw whose family ran a gristmill a few miles from Honey Ridge. Buck Langdon was a big-boned young ne'er-do-well who had ridden into town the night before but had lacked the funds to remain with Sam Roberts and the girls of the Medicine Wagon Saloon. Buck had fallen victim to "faro fever," as Sawyer called it, and squandered the last of his money on the fickle affections of lady luck. Tullock trusted these four. He had stood with them as Sam and those four young men had sworn their allegiance to the Confederate cause around a golden circle of fire almost a year ago. In the matter of his son, pride had turned to deep misgivings overnight.

"What is it?" Tullock said, flustered. "I'm fine. What were you saying?" He shooed the dark-skinned children away and sent them scampering off to the cotton fields stretching out from the house in a vast snowy expanse. Negro men and women dragged long cumbersome canvas bags from row to row and bent their ragged backs beneath the blind and unforgiving eye of the sun as they picked the cotton plants bare. It might take all day to fill a bag, but these poor souls weren't going anywhere, and when "master" wasn't looking, they saw no need to hurry.

"Sawyer here was telling us how you got friends among the Knights to the north of here, up in Cherokee County," Buck said. Meat juices dribbled down his chin. He wiped his mouth on a bandanna that he kept tucked in the hip pocket of his trousers.

"My sister married a Cherokee named Andrew Wallace. He and his men have just about driven out the Federalists." Tullock knelt and wiped the butcher knife clean in the dirt. He couldn't shake the hold his dream had locked on him. The more he tried to drive it from his thoughts, the more tenaciously the images clung, like burrs to a horse's tail. "They have twice our number," Tullock added, straining to follow the conversation.

"Maybe we ought to bring 'em on down and send packing the likes of Carmichael Ross and them others in town who dance to the tune she plays," Chris Foot suggested. He was the youngest of Truett's crowd and, next to Sawyer, the most headstrong. Like the others, he had followed Pacer to Lawrence and felt betrayed by McQueen's conduct. He had nothing but contempt for the Choctaw Kid, a rebel he had once idolized for his solitary raids into Yankee-held territory.

"That's not a bad idea," Sawyer concurred. He looked at Tullock for a response. Now he knew something was the matter, for the "bull of the woods" failed to respond. However this time, instead of daydreaming, he was studying the dirt road that cut through his fields. He shaded his eyes against the glare of the sun.

"Rider coming."

"Who is it?" Buck Langdon said, cramming another strip of pork in his mouth like a chaw of tobacco.

"Jesse McQueen," Sawyer answered. Chris Foot had brought news from town about Jesse's return to Chahta Creek. Tullock could only guess at the reason for Jesse's presence. Now it appeared he was going to find out.

"McQueen here already?" Buck muttered. "He didn't waste any time."

"His kind never do," Tullock said. They were standing off to the side of the house, near the smokehouse. He turned to Sawyer. "Tell Willow to keep Arbitha inside. Then take Chris and Buck with you and stay clear of things until I've talked with McQueen. Johnny here can work on the hog. At least he won't eat as much as Buck."

"I don't like leaving," Sawyer told the master of Honey Ridge.

"You don't have to like it. But by God you'll do as I say!" Tullock's features seemed etched in stone. Now this was the man that Sawyer remembered. Tullock Roberts seemed his old self again.

"Yes sir," the overseer quickly replied. He gestured to Chris and Buck and headed around behind the house. He was anxious to prepare a personal welcome for the plantation's uninvited guest.

Jesse sensed he was being watched. He didn't know by what or whom, but the tingling along the back of his neck had bothered him for the past couple of miles as he rode among the live oak dotted hills. The feeling lingered even when he reached bottom land and fields of golden corn and cotton, prime for harvesting by Tullock's slaves for whom a war was raging and proclamations issued. Emancipation had yet to reach Indian Territory. Jesse corrected himself.

It had now. As a territorial ranger and a Union officer, he was the personification of Lincoln's decree. He passed unnoticed among the laborers in the fields, and the puff of dust kicked up by the gray mare quickly dissipated in the warm September breeze.

Jesse glanced over his shoulder to check his backtrail for the last time and saw nothing but the woods he'd ridden through and the rolling hills like the swells of some emerald sea, frozen in time.

The two-story plantation house was an imposing structure with a whitewashed front that gleamed bright in midmorning. Jesse could tell at a glance it was hog-killing time by the carcass hanging from the A-frame and the scalding pot and the fresh-roasted chunks of pork clutched in the hands of eager dark-skinned children running past him to join their parents toiling in the fields of Honey Ridge.

A blue jay swooped past and alighted on a nearby fence post and proceeded to scold the horseman as he passed by. A pair of coon hounds scampered through the garden in pursuit of a gray rabbit that bounded over the turned earth, darted to left and right, leaped the pumpkins, and vanished in tall cotton just out of reach of the dogs with their baying and barking and snapping jaws.

He saw Tullock walk across the front yard and climb the low steps to stand in the center of the broad-beamed high-roofed porch that fronted the plantation house. He also spied a trio of riders galloping away from one of the barns behind the plantation house. The distance was too great for him to recognize them. They kept their hats pulled low and faces hidden. The man in the lead on a cream-colored horse led the others in a hurried dash to the timbered hills north of the house. Jesse suspected the three might be circling around to come up behind him and block any attempt at escape. He sighed and suppressed his misgivings. He'd been riding into traps ever since the war began, first as a spy in New Orleans, then Vicksburg. Now he'd returned home, alone, gambling the name of McQueen and his own quick wits could keep the Choctaw Nation from tearing itself asunder as the states had done.

He tugged on the reins and walked his gray the remaining few yards to the porch. Tullock lifted his red-stained hand and motioned for Jesse to halt.

"You don't need to dismount," he called out. The broad-shouldered man hooked his thumbs in his suspenders. His eyes were underlined with shadow, from the restless night he'd spent. The heavy door behind him opened and Arbitha emerged from the foyer and joined her husband.

"Jesse McQueen, as I live and breathe, back from the war. Not wounded, I hope."

"No, ma'am. Thank you," Jesse answered. Once the two families had been friends, but the hostilities had sorely tested such bonds.

"Tullock, invite him in. We can be civil to one another, surely."

"He'll not step foot on my property," Tullock replied, unmoved.

"But . . . "

"Woman, I'll not be argued with." The master of Honey Ridge turned to glare at Jesse. "Hear me out, Arbitha. He comes to bring us all down. The end of everything we hold dear follows in his wake."

"You're wrong, Tullock," Jesse said, relaxing in the saddle. "I'm trying to save what I can for you and everyone else."

"Your colors show through whether you're wearing the uniform or not." Tullock shook his head. "Have you forgotten the Trail of Tears, how we were betrayed by the flag you're fighting under? Ask Raven. Ask your grandmother. We were forced to leave our homes and plantations in Mississippi and come to the Indian Territory."

"It was the farmers and planters of the South who moved onto the land the Choctaw left behind, the same Confederates you've chosen to support," Jesse countered. "If anyone should be taken to task it's you." Jesse was struggling to control his temper. He studied his surroundings. Honey Ridge displayed none of the ravages suffered by the plantations along the Mississippi River. Cotton stood knee high in the fields, tasseled corn was as tall as the laborers. The slave shanties were out of sight and out of mind, beyond the barns. It was ever the way; the plantation owners wanted their Negro slaves but didn't like to have to look at them.

"Why should you speak for the Choctaw? You've little enough of the blood in you."

Tullock had left an opening without realizing it. Jesse wasn't about to let it pass.

"I don't intend to speak for anyone—but myself—this Sunday evening in the Council House. Why don't you join me?" Jesse carefully studied the man on the porch. "There's no call for the Choctaw people to destroy themselves in this war. And that's exactly what will happen if the Knights continue to raid. There'll be killing and more people driven out and suffering on every side. Ruination and wholesale slaughter await us. I've seen the destruction. Fathers and sons lost forever. The dead are beyond embracing. They are lost to us forever."

Hearing his remarks, Arbitha gasped and crossed to her husband's side and placed a hand on his arm as if in warning.

"Why come to me about the Knights? I know nothing of them."

"Many people respect you, Mr. Roberts. With your help I might be able to work out a truce that both sides can abide by. The Knights will listen to you. Together we might be able to avert a catastrophe and save the lives of our friends and families. You've only one son, Tullock. Think of him in harm's way. Join me and save his life and that of all the other sons who won't have to die if we can just reach some kind of accord."

"Mr. Roberts, you just say the word and I'll escort McQueen off your land," Johnny Teel called out as he rounded the corner of the house, a muzzle-loading rifle cradled in his arms.

"What do you say, Mr. Roberts?" Jesse asked, ignoring Teel, which only infuriated the storekeeper's son. He marched forward and nudged the gray with the muzzle of his rifle.

Jesse's eyes hardened as he looked down at the man with the rifle. When he spoke, his voice held all the warmth of a death rattle.

"Touch my horse again, Johnny Teel, and it'll be time to root hog or die a poor pig." Jesse's hands never left the saddle pommel but the menace in his voice was starkly real.

"What the devil is that supposed to mean?" Johnny nervously replied, trying to shrug off his lack of confidence. Most men would have turned pale and nervous staring into a rifle barrel. But Jesse Redbow McQueen was not most men.

"He means you're a dead man if you don't back off," Tullock said from the porch. "Get on back to the hog, Johnny, there's a good lad."

At Tullock's insistence Johnny lowered the rifle and retreated to the corner of the porch. Jesse returned his attention to the man on the porch. Arbitha still stood alongside her husband, ready to support him whatever his decision. Her hand on his powerful forearm served as a silent reminder of the dream that had torn his night's sleep asunder and left him counting the hours till dawn, haunted by premonitions of disaster. When Buck Langdon had arrived at sunrise with news of Jesse McQueen's arrival in Chahta Creek, to Tullock's way of thinking, the spirits were telling him something, perhaps even giving him a warning that only a fool would ignore.

"I'll join you," Tullock muttered. "But I don't know what good will come of it." Arbitha breathed a sigh of relief and gripped her husband's arm to assure him of her approval. Johnny Teel stared in amazement at the master of Honey Ridge. He couldn't believe what he was hearing. Sawyer and the others must be told.

"You won't regret it," Jesse said.

"Maybe," Tullock said. "Where's Ben? I expected him to come home to try and patch things up."

"He sent me," Jesse replied.

"You took a chance in coming here," the plantation owner told him.

"Peace was worth the risk."

"I'll listen to what you have to say, but I'm not promising anything," Tullock cautioned.

"But he'll keep an open mind. I'll see to that," Arbitha added, making her own feelings on the matter quite clear. Her husband's dream had been the final straw and given credence to her own misgivings about her family's involvement in the Knights of the Golden Circle. "Now I shall have Willow prepare us some lunch." She whirled about in a flurry of skirt and lace underdresses and vanished through the front door.

"Well, you've won over my child bride," Tullock glowered. "I won't be so easy. I built Honey Ridge up from nothing but buffalo grass and coyotes. I'll not allow some Northern aggressor to take it all away."

Jesse glanced around at the fine house and the fertile fields and the orderly rows of crops; acres upon acres tended by families in bondage. In contrast, Jesse's grandparents had no stomach for slavery. Those same convictions had been passed down from generation to generation. The McQueen homestead on Buffalo Creek might lack the size and wealth and sense of order of Honey Ridge, but neither had the McQueen fields been watered by the sweat of enforced servitude. The hills had never echoed with the rattle of chains or the crack of some overseer's whip. In the Kiamichis a man was bound to the land by a love of the mountains, not by shackles or hopelessness.

"No one wants to take your land, Mr. Roberts, or your home. But winds of change are coming. They'll blow across the country no matter what you—or I— can say. And a man must either bend with the wind, or break." Jesse touched the brim of his hat, bade good-bye to the master of Honey Ridge, and started back down the wheel-rutted drive. Jesse doubted Tullock Roberts would call him back and repeat Arbitha's invitation to dinner.

He was right.

Chapter Twenty-one

Jesse knew he was in trouble when the three hooded riders rode out from behind a dense thicket and blocked the road along which he was traveling. Honey Ridge lay about two miles back through the winding low hills of oak and hickory forest. Jesse refused to show alarm and continued without breaking stride. He rode straight for the leader of the three, who sat straight on his cream-colored gelding. The men were armed with ax handles, which made for sturdy clubs. Jesse considered freeing his rifle but decided against it. He didn't want to escalate the situation into gunplay. He'd had some success with Tullock; maybe this was another situation he could talk himself out of.

The chop-chop-chop of a pileated woodpecker disturbed the natural quiet of the forest. Jesse checked the trees and spied a flash of its crimson crown as the woodpecker stabbed its beak into the bark. The industrious creature would soon have a respectable hole and be able to feast on the nest of carpenter ants it had discovered.

The same tingling as he had earlier experienced

crept along the back of Jesse's neck, and again he was certain he was being watched by someone other than the three Knights blocking the road. Beams of slanted sunlight intersected the path and lay between the Knights and the Union captain like iridescent rods of gold upholding the patches of cobalt-blue ceiling above the treetops.

"I thought you brave souls only came out at night," Jesse said. He was about ten yards from the hooded horsemen and still he did not try to slow his mount.

"We appear whenever and wherever we are needed," Sawyer Truett said. He shifted uncomfortably in the saddle. He did not like the way that Jesse seemed willing to ride right through them without even slowing his gray. Did he take them that lightly? Sawyer frowned beneath his hood and looked first at Buck Langdon on his right and then at Chris Foot on his left. Both men appeared to be unnerved by Jesse's disregard for the threat they posed. "That's far enough. We aim to see you'll not trouble Tullock Roberts again."

Five yards now and closing, Jesse warily approached. "I came here in peace, lads. Sawyer Truett, I recognize that gelding of yours. I even helped you to saddle-break it, have you forgot?" Jesse appraised the other two men. He could not identify them beneath their hoods; still, he tried to appeal to the three and bluff his way past in the process. "With all the trouble the territory has seen lately, there comes a time when men need to sit down and talk before things get completely out of hand. Surely you can see that, even with your heads covered."

"Get him!" Sawyer shouted.

"Then again I could be wrong," Jesse added, and reached for his gun. Sawyer charged forward and brought his ax handle down across Jesse's right arm as he drew his revolver. Pain shot the length of his arm as the Colt went flying. Jesse touched his spurs to the gray and the animal charged forward. Jesse ducked Sawyer's second blow and rode his horse into Chris Foot, who flailed at his attacker. Buck Langdon connected with a roundhouse swing that caught Jesse in the side and sent him tumbling from horseback. He dragged Chris Foot out of the saddle as well and used him as a shield while he tried to catch his breath. Chris twisted free. Jesse's left fist connected with the Choctaw's jaw and Chris stumbled and fell over on his backside.

Jesse wrenched the ax handle from the fallen man's grasp. He turned and managed to block a swipe from Sawyer that would have fractured his collarbone. In the process Jesse left himself open for Buck Langdon's blow to catch him along the side of the head and send him staggering toward the underbrush. He heard the horses approaching and spun on his heels and charged the two horsemen, a move that caught them unprepared. He darted and dodged and caught Buck on the kneecap with enough force to break the ax handle and set the hooded rider howling. Jesse made a lunge for the Colt he'd dropped. Sawyer maneuvered his horse to block McQueen from reaching the revolver lying in the trampled dirt. Jesse swerved at the last second, glanced off the gelding's muscled flanks, and stumbled off through the brush with Sawyer in pursuit.

Jesse dropped to one knee. His right arm was numb to the fingertips, so with his left he freed the .22 caliber Smith & Wesson revolver from his boot. He snapped off a shot that went wide of the mark but served its purpose. Sawyer Truett, realizing he was under the gun, whirled his horse and headed back to safety. He found Chris Foot on horseback, rubbing a swollen jaw, and Buck Langdon clutching his right knee and groaning in agony.

"Goddamn you and your ideas," Buck wailed.

"I ain't about to face Jesse's gun," Chris added, then turned to Buck. "C'mon." He led the way down the road and back toward the plantation. Buck followed his companion, but at a slower pace so as not to jostle his injured leg. Sawyer peered over his shoulder as Jesse staggered into view. Sawyer had a gun in his belt, but Jesse's was drawn and aimed right at his midriff. Courage failed the last of the hooded riders and he beat a hasty retreat. Jesse let him go.

"They just needed a little persuasion is all," Jesse muttered. His right arm was numb, his side ached like hell and blood was dripping from a goose-egg-sized lump on the side of his head, not to mention from his split lip. "Nothing to it," he added. Then he heard the telltale click of a rifle being cocked. He wiped the sweat and blood from his eyes with his good left arm and located the source of the ominous sound. Studying a grove of hickory on the opposite side of the road, Jesse glimpsed a rifle barrel poking between two gnarled tree trunks and parting a tall thicket of Solomon's seal whose broad emerald leaves trembled at the caress of blued steel.

Jesse tried to steady himself as the earth began to reel. He had one chance—well, no chance really against a big-bore rifle—but he made the attempt. His arm shot up and he tried to bring the hide out gun to bear. The Smith & Wesson slipped from his grasp and went spinning off through the shadows and Jesse was left pointing a curled finger at his unseen assailant. He stared stupidly at his empty fist, then turned his palm upward. "Surely we talk before the . . . hand . . . gets completely . . ." He paused and tried to straighten his words out. The road hit him in the face before he could finish.

Chapter Twenty-two

The front door banged back against the inside wall of the marshal's office with the force of a gunshot and startled Parson Marshal T. Alan Booth as he slept with a Bible open to the judgment of Solomon. Those holy pages had left an imprint in his cheeks above his white chin whiskers. He'd been studying scripture, his legs propped upon his desk, his chair tilted back and balanced at a perfect angle for maximum comfort. Johnny Medicine Fox had shattered the marshal's reverie when he kicked open the door and made his raucous entrance. Booth lost his balance, his legs high-kicking toward the ceiling. He yelled and clutched at his leather-bound Bible and pitched over backward, crashing to the floor. He cursed in a most unpreacherlike fashion and struggled to stand, but his legs were caught between the desk and the chair and then there was the matter of his crumpled hat and the tear in one sleeve of his frock coat where it brushed the wall and caught on a splinter.

"You need help, Parson—uh—Marshal Booth?" Johnny said with his arms full of the lunch basket Mary Lou Gude had stuffed with sandwiches and a sweet potato pie for the law officer and his famished prisoners.

"No, goddamn it, I don't need any gall-blasted help!" the marshall fumed. "And forget everything you heard here today."

"Yessir," John said, staring at the one leg that still flailed the air. "Miss Gude promised me a peppermint stick if I'd bring your lunch up and save you a trip."

"Mighty nice of her," Marshal Booth replied, his disembodied voice drifting up from behind the desk. "Maybe I will take a little help."

"Say, Marshal. Have the boy let us out, and we can give you a hand," Moses Tellico called from his cell. The door leading to the jail cells was ajar and the prisoners could see the law officer's mishap. They were enjoying the situation. "Ain't that right, Theotis?"

Moses' burly, older brother was standing alongside him, his thick forearms curled through the bars. "Sure 'nuff Moses. C'mon over here, Johnny Fox, and fetch that there key from the wall peg outside the door and open our cell."

"You boys keep that up and I'll have you on hard biscuits and cold coffee until you serve off your time," the marshal retorted. Booth, with the boy's help, managed to untangle himself from the chair and desk and clamber to his feet.

"Would you be wrestling with your faith again, T. Alan?" Raven said from the doorway. She had arrived in time to see John Medicine Fox help Booth to his feet and dust off his frock coat.

Booth groaned. "Now see here, Miss Raven, don't you be adding to my troubles. And where did you come from, anyway?" Then a look of realization crossed his features. "Ah—you heard about Jesse."

"I thought he might be here," said Raven. "I checked the hotel and found he hadn't taken a room."

"He's staying over at Carmichael's, I suspect. At least him and Ross were acting mighty friendly when

I saw them last night. And she has a room to let right above the *Courier*." When Raven turned to leave, he stopped her by adding, "Of course he ain't there right now 'cause I saw him ride off, heading east." Booth carried the food basket to his desk and sent Johnny on his way. The ten-year-old boy touched the brim of his hat as he walked past Jesse's grandmother and scampered through the open doorway. His image flitted past the window.

"East?" Raven repeated, wondering what exactly her grandson was up to.

Booth seemed to read her thoughts. "My guess is he's heading out to Honey Ridge. But it won't do him any good. I paid Tullock several visits and never had a bit of luck. He won't use his influence to help ease the tensions, no sir. I practically begged him last time. That's one humble pie I don't relish ever tasting again."

Raven brushed her long silver-streaked black hair away from her face. She wore a buckskin blouse and dark blue wool riding skirt. A braided cord around her throat trailed a flat-brimmed hat that dangled between her shoulder blades. "You sound irritated, T. Alan. If he has come to bring peace to the territory, maybe it is a good thing."

"Sure it is," Booth said. He rummaged through the basket and helped himself to one of the sandwiches. He could feel Raven watching him. Blast her, anyhow; those dark eyes of hers seemed to bore clean through him. "What do you want me to do?" He did not try to hide the affection in his voice. It was difficult—and for him, impossible—to be stern with this woman of Irish and Choctaw heritage. She never failed to melt his resolve.

"I want you to watch out for Jesse. His homecoming could prove fatal." Raven walked across the room and placed her hand on Booth's arm.

"Jesse can take care of himself," Booth replied.

Raven was not about to let him off the hook. "Promise me."

"All right. You win." Booth scratched at his close-cropped white beard. "How do you always manage to do that to me?"

"I appeal to the milk of human kindness that's flowing in your veins, my friend."

"Shoot, that milk curdled long ago."

"There's one thing more I want, if you'll do me the favor."

"Yeah?" Booth bit into a roast-beef sandwich. The meat was as tough as shoe leather and his jaws had to work at it a while. What with the war, most of the decent beef had been shipped off to the Confederacy or driven north into Yankee feed pens up in Missouri. He watched Raven march directly to the doorway that led back to the cells.

"Good morning, boys," she said. Moses and Theotis straightened and made an attempt to look presentable. "I should like to take your prisoners."

"What?"

"Pacer needs help out at the farm. I can pay whatever fines the Tellicos have incurred—"

"It's not all that simple," Booth protested. "I can't just let my prisoners roam about at will."

"They won't be. I'll keep them busy. Al Teel told me there was some damage to Lucius Minley's office." Raven tossed a gold double eagle to the marshal of Chahta Creek. "If that doesn't cover the repairs, let me know." A second double eagle followed the first into Booth's outstretched hand. "And consider this a contribution to the church." The parson marshal positively beamed. This would cover the cost of shutters for the church windows.

"Well—have we a deal?" asked Raven.

"Hmmm. I would like to see them sweating instead of lying around waiting for me to wait on them hand and foot." Booth pretended to struggle with his decision when in reality he had already made up his mind. He did not want to appear too lenient. The peace officer stepped around his desk and walked back to the cells.

"Boys, I'll be remanding you to the custody of Raven McQueen. You'll serve your time working for her. See you do that or I'll come after you myself and drag you back here in chains."

Moses stroked and twirled the ends of his droopy mustache and grinned. His pale blue eyes brightened at the prospect of being released. He had prowled the cage like a trapped animal ever since sunup. Big, heavyset Theotis Tellico, ugly as a beating, shambled forward out of the cell. He had slept through most of his incarceration.

"Much obliged, Miss Raven," Moses said. "We'll work for you."

"Where's my rifle? I ain't leavin' without my Starr revolver and my Hawken rifle," Theotis flatly stated.

"Stacked behind the desk. Both rifles and your pistols," Booth said. "But see you leave by the back way or Lucius Minley will have a fit if he sees you lads turned loose."

"You finish your business at Teel's and we'll meet you on the river road over by the cottonwoods," Moses told the medicine woman.

Raven nodded and, after bidding the town marshal farewell, started to leave. Booth followed her and caught the woman by the arm.

"One thing more, Miss Raven."

She turned and faced him as Booth spoke in all seriousness now, his features grave and his voice low.

"Sooner or later Jesse's bound to show up at your place. When that happens, well, the worst place for you to be is standing between Jesse and Pacer Wolf. Promise me you'll stay clear."

"I cannot," Raven said.

Booth studied her a moment, then shrugged. "You McQueens," he said with a sigh and a wag of his head, "are the most . . . most . . . all fired obstinate, stubborn . . ."

"Don't forget muleheaded," Raven added with a bemused smile.

The parson marshal heartily concurred.

Lorelei Swain perched on the wagon seat in front of Al Teel's mercantile and combed her auburn hair until her tresses shone lustrous and silky in the sunlight. Raven had been gone a while and left her to see that absent-minded but sweetly dispositioned Al Teel loaded everything on the list. Lorelei considered the task somewhat tedious until Hud Pardee, riding past on his big black stallion, noticed the comely young woman and swung his horse around to the hitching rail and dismounted alongside the steepsided wagon.

Cap Featherstone's gunman cut a dashing figure this morning in his gray trousers, black sash at his waist, white ruffled shirt, and gray waistcoat. He swept his hat across his chest and gallantly bowed and introduced himself. Lorelei guardedly told him her first name.

"May I help you down, my pretty?" He toyed for a moment with the patch covering his left eye as he quickly took in the ripe contours of her figure. She wore a plain, pale peach-colored dress buttoned to the neck. She struck a coquettish pose and adjusted the hem of her dress to "inadvertently" reveal the slender curve of her ankles.

"I'm waiting for someone," she replied, seemingly indifferent to him.

"Not a husband, I hope," he said.

"No. I'm staying with Raven McQueen out on her farm."

"Slopping hogs and shucking corn, what a terrible

waste. Beauty like yours should be draped in finery, caressed by silks and satins," he purred. "It transforms these homespun rags into the raiments of a queen."

"My, you are a fountain of empty compliments, dear sir," Lorelei replied, and turned a shoulder away from him.

"Come with me and decide for yourself whether they are empty or not." He stepped back and gestured toward his horse. "You can ride like a queen on my stallion."

"Ride where?"

"Why, to the only palace I know of around here. The Medicine Wagon up on the hill, where there is music and merriment and the nights are never dark."

Short, stocky Al Teel emerged from the front of his store, breathing heavily beneath a fifty-pound sack of oats. He heaved it onto the wagon bed alongside a barrel of nails, another of dried apples, and smaller sacks of flour, cornmeal, horseshoes, and a box of fabric scraps Teel had saved for Raven to use in a quilt.

"I think that's the last of it," Teel said, and glanced up into Pardee's grim features. The gunman's expression left no doubt in Teel's mind that he had intruded on Pardee. The gunman's deadly reputation was common knowledge. The merchant hurriedly excused himself and beat a hasty retreat toward the safety of the mercantile. Pardee chuckled, then spied Raven making her way along the wooden sidewalks from the north end of town.

"Are you coming with me?" Pardee asked the girl. He held the reins of his horse in a loose grip with one hand and reached out to help her down from the wagon.

"I don't think so," Lorelei replied. "No." She couldn't believe her own ears. She had no love for farm work, which only left her all the more puzzled. There was an aura of danger about Pardee that appealed to her. There was no denying it. "Maybe later, I don't know."

"The door I'm opening might well be closed to you—*later*." He turned back and mounted the black stallion. The animal's nostrils flared as it fought the bit. Pardee brought the animal under control with a firm hand. He touched the brim of his hat as Raven approached.

"Good morning, Mrs. McQueen. It appears I underestimated that valley of yours, if this sweet little gal is any indication of the treasures you are hiding out there. I might just have to come calling and see your place first-hand."

"Don't," Raven firmly replied. "We already have enough snakes."

Color drained from Pardee's features, and for a brief moment Lorelei thought the one-eyed man was going to pull a gun on Pacer's grandmother. Pardee's hand trembled and muscles along his jaw twitched as he brought his anger under control and trotted his mount back down the street.

"What did he want?" Raven asked. She gave the wagon bed a brief once-over glance and then climbed up alongside the young girl.

"He wanted me to come with him to the sporting house over on Cherokee. I've heard they drink champagne out of real crystal. And the ladies all wear silk and feathers." Her expression took on a dreamlike quality.

"Why didn't you go?" Raven said, bursting the girl's reverie.

Lorelei blinked and then shrugged. "I—I don't know." She studied Raven with newly won respect. "You shouldn't have got him so angry."

Raven leaned over and unwrapped the reins from the brake. She released the brake and with a flick of her wrist started the team of horses forward.

"We have enough snakes," Lorelei repeated,

chuckling. "I swear, I thought he was going to swell up and bust or go for his gun." Her laughter was infectious and carried to Raven. It released the tension and drew the two women together, forging a bond that hadn't existed until now. "You ought to be more careful," Lorelei added. "Pardee doesn't look like someone to trifle with. He's dangerous."

"So am I," said Raven.

After today, Lorelei tended to believe her.

Lucius Minley lingered over his coffee, taking care to enjoy these few precious moments of solitude. Rose Minley was in a terrible mood this morning. They had argued again. He hated to see her so upset. He was concerned, too, for her outbursts centered on the same grievance—Cap Featherstone was not treating them fairly! She could see no reason why Cap should receive the lion's share of the profits from the venture that involved not only Featherstone but the banker as well. Rose Minley wanted her husband to stand up for what was rightfully theirs, equal shares in Cap's elaborate scheme. Lucius, on the other hand, figured he'd just about used up his good luck in yesterday's confrontation with the Tellicos. He was loath to lock horns with the likes of Cap Featherstone.

Lucius sighed, and sipped his coffee and wondered why wives could never understand that some things were better left alone. After all, this whole scheme had been Cap's idea. Nine months had passed since Cap had met with the banker right here in the parlor at the rear of the Minleys' house on Choctaw Street. He had come at night, unannounced, with a plan to make Lucius and himself two very wealthy men. Cap was a keen judge of character and had spent time studying Lucius and knew of the banker's desire to return to the East and leave the territory forever. Cap was also keenly aware that Rose Minley had expensive tastes and that before the Union blockade much of her wardrobe and finery had come from shops in Boston, New York, and Europe by way of New Orleans.

Cap's proposition was simple. He would see to it that the majority of homesteads, businesses, and farms victimized by the Knights of the Golden Circle would belong either to those families owing money to the bank or to families who would be forced by the raids to borrow money from Minley only to eventually be foreclosed upon by the bank once their notes were in default. Now and then someone came in looking to sell out, even at a substantial loss. All foreclosed-upon properties were immediately purchased by Cap Featherstone for a pittance of their real worth. He already had an interest in several businesses in town. Several choice pieces of property totaling thousands of acres were now owned by Cap Featherstone with Lucius Minley as his silent partner. Eventually the war would end. With peace and prosperity the order of the day, Cap intended to be in control of most of the southeast corner of the territory. With such a base, who knew how far Cap could go?

A handful of pebbles clattered against the window and Lucius looked up to see Cap Featherstone standing in the flower garden Rose had so laboriously coaxed from the soil; green plants whose names Lucius could never remember. He was always surprised that a woman of his wife's breeding would deign to dirty her hands in the soil. But she enjoyed flowers and considered their arrival each spring her own personal triumph.

Cap Featherstone's thinning hair was hidden beneath his black bandanna. He kept his gray woolen trousers tucked inside his boarhide boots. His upper torso strained the buttons on his charcoal frock coat. Lucius frowned, but motioned for Cap to come around through the back door that opened into a well-stocked pantry where glass jars of plum and persimmon jellies

and preserves were arranged in orderly rows along
with a few jars of dark purple jelly made from the
ripened fruit of the black nightshade.

The Minleys employed no houseservant except a
woman hired from town to periodically visit and
clean the house both upstairs and down. Rose had an
innate distrust of permanent employees and felt such
servants tended to intrude on one's privacy.

The banker checked his pocket watch and noted
it was seventeen minutes past noon. Rose entered from
the kitchen, all flustered and obviously displeased.

"Lucius, he's here. Mr. Featherstone in broad
daylight paying a visit."

"Maybe our neighbors will think we've invited
him to share our noonday meal."

"The man thinks he can do whatever he pleases.
Really."

"I suppose Cap has his reasons," Lucius said.
"Now, I can't be ungracious, my love."

"No," Rose said, "but since he's come, you tell
him exactly how we feel. A thirty percent share of
Featherstone's holdings is unfair. Heavens, you're
selling off the bank's properties for practically nothing.
Our part in this is equal to his own. Half the profits are
due us. You mustn't settle for a penny less."

"Yes, dear," Lucius patiently agreed. The kitchen
door opened. Rose beat a hasty retreat out of the parlor, down the hall, and up the stairs to her bedroom.
Cap's bulk filled the doorway.

"Afternoon, ma'am," he called to her departing
figure, and touched the silver gator head of his cane to
the narrow brim of his hat. He stepped into the parlor,
a room well lit by a back wall of windows that ran half
the length of the house. The room contained a settee,
a pair of cushioned chairs, end tables, and a harp that
Rose used to play for her father, but which had
remained silent since his death.

"Afternoon, Lucius," Cap said. "You know, the

only cure for a haughty wife is a good roll in the bushy park, if you catch my drift."

"Mr. Featherstone, with all due regards, my domestic life is my own affair and no one else's," Lucius replied. He stood and set his coffee cup aside. "I must protest the timing of this visit. I thought we agreed—"

"We agreed that the bank would sell me all recovered properties. In return, you're listed as co-owner. Farmland and developed townsites we'll one day sell at a substantial profit. The Texas road is paved with gold for us, Lucius, you wait and see." Cap reached inside his coat and brought out a dark amber bottle of French brandy. "A gift. And it's the real thing, not like the rat piss Shug throws together for the customers," Cap added with a wink. He placed the bottle on the closest shelf.

"You are most kind," Lucius said.

"The hell I am. I never do anything without a reason." Cap chose a cushioned, wide-backed chair and sat down. "Hack Warner told me he sold out to the bank after the Knights burned his way station."

"Yes. He wasn't happy with my offer but took it all the same. See here, Featherstone. We can do this at the bank. I'll be back there at one, sharp."

"And what of the Tellicos?" Cap asked, ignoring the banker's suggestion.

"They tried to pay off their note in Richmond dollars. The bank did not accept their payment. As of tomorrow, the Tellico farm belongs to the bank."

"Good. Draw up a deed then on both places. We'll work it just like all the others."

"Maybe we should hold off, what with Jesse McQueen in town," Lucius said.

"I can handle that young pup," Cap replied.

"What if Ben McQueen should show up? He's far cleverer than his son. He might suspect something. I'm worried, I tell you."

"You are always worried. Fortunately, I have enough courage for us both," Cap said with a bemused expression on his face. "Anyway, all you have to do is scribble a few pages of a transaction. The Knights will do most of the work for us."

"What of those folks who cannot be driven off?"

"They'll leave or be buried where they fall." Cap leaned forward on the hilt of his sword cane. He looked as predatory as the silver likeness of the alligator beneath his folded hands.

"No." Lucius gulped the last of his coffee and wished he'd had something stronger in the cup. "I won't be a party to murder."

Cap stroked his beard in thought. There were more silver hairs than brown. Alas, his youth was a distant memory now. But before Cap went under, he'd vowed, he would make his mark, carve an empire out of the Indian Territory. He stared at Lucius. "You'll be a party to whatever I tell you, Lucius."

"I will not be threatened, Mr. Featherstone."

"Threat? Me? You wound me, Lucius." Cap stood and walked across the room and clapped Lucius on the shoulder. "Cheer up, my friend. You now own a third of everything I own. Cotton fields, cattle, grazing lands, timber—why, after the war ends, we'll be rich."

"If we aren't hung first," Lucius grumbled. "Some of these people are my friends."

"It's all right to steal their homes and property, but don't harm them," Cap cut him off. "Be careful, Lucius. You see, I think of our partnership as sacred, like a marriage. We have a bond, you and I, till death do us part." Cap straightened and headed out of the room, whistling as he left, like a man without a care in the world. Lucius grew flushed. It was humiliating to think that Cap took him so lightly. He'd begun to regret ever becoming involved with the owner of the Medicine Wagon Saloon.

"Oh, by the way," Cap said, returning to the parlor doorway. He had moved quietly. Lucius gave a start and his eyes grew wide with alarm. They grew wider still when he heard Cap Featherstone's departing remark.

"Don't lose any sleep over Ben McQueen. Last month, back in Kansas City, I had him killed."

Lucius never heard the back door shut. He did not see Cap make his way across the garden. He was oblivious to Rose, who entered the parlor from the narrow hallway dividing the sun parlor from the library.

"Lucius? Did you tell him? Did you tell him we insist on equal shares of all the transactions?"

Lucius Minley stood and shuffled somnambulantly toward the brandy, broke the seal, and poured a measure into his coffee cup. He had wanted to be rich. He had wanted to be able to keep Rose, to prove to her she had married a man. Ben McQueen . . . dead. The first blood was the hardest. The next one would be easier. And the one after that easier still. If Jesse or Pacer ever suspected the truth . . . there'd be no place to hide. The McQueens would track him till his dying day and hold him accountable for his silence and indirect involvement.

"Lucius?"

"Shut up!" he snapped. The brandy scorched a path down his gullet and heated his gut. Still the hand holding the cup trembled. "Just shut up," he softly repeated. Lucius carried the bottle back to his chair. Maybe another drink would help.

Chapter Twenty-three

Jesse followed the song and the sound of his grandmother's voice out of the darkness and into the light. He opened his eyes and saw Raven, bathed in the amber glow of a lantern, seated at his side. The song had not been a Choctaw chant of healing but rather an Irish lullaby.

> "Pretty little horses in the sun
> Children go a-riding.
> Play until the evening comes
> and sunlight goes a-hiding."

"I'm not five years old anymore, Grandmother," Jesse managed to say. His side hurt, his head and shoulders throbbed, but his vision seemed unaffected, for which he was grateful. Raven looked the same as ever. Her gray-black hair hung past her shoulders and framed her proud features, a mixture of Irish and Choctaw, that radiated her deep affection and concern for this, her eldest grandson.

"So you finally pay your grandmother a visit."
Jesse could tell it was evening, but of which

day? The last thing he remembered was being ambushed and fighting for his life against three club-wielding ruffians. And the rifle, yes, the rifle pointing at him from the underbrush. He tried to sit up. Pain coursed through him like liquid fire.

"It's a quarter past midnight," Raven said. "You've been here since sundown."

"How?"

Raven shifted in her chair. Jesse realized he was stretched out upon a daybed that had been set up in the front sitting room. He looked past Raven and saw a powerfully muscled black man seated on a three-legged stool near the fireplace. The night had brought a chill that only a cheery blaze could abate. The black man's face seemed chiseled out of obsidian; flared nostrils, a brooding brow, a gnarled lump of meat where his right ear had been. He was dressed in a cotton shirt, woolen dungarees, and boots. His strong hands were firmly clasped around the barrel of his army-issue muzzle loader. A Patterson Colt was holstered on his right hip.

Jesse knew the black man at a glance. This was Si Reaves. Si had been a trusted overseer on Tullock Roberts's plantation. Yet, despite the privileges of his position, freedom had been a lure impossible to resist. One morning while supposedly out hunting, Si pointed his horse north and never looked back—until now. Jesse could guess the reason for the black man's return, however dangerous.

"I been watching the plantation, hopin' Willow might come out to the woods alone. I seen you leave and followed you," Si spoke up in a deep resonant voice. He chuckled. "I figured there'd be trouble a-comin' when I seen Sawyer Truett, Buck Langdon, and Chris Foot climbing into them yella' robes and hidin' out among the trees." Si clambered to his feet. He held up a plate that he'd just sopped clean with a chunk of Raven's crusty bread. "Ma'am . . . you reckon I could get me a little more of that stew? My belly's narrowed some since I been back, what with livin' off'n what I could catch."

"You just help yourself, Si," Raven told him. The runaway slave nodded his thanks and hurried off to the kitchen. She watched him leave and then turned her attention back to Jesse.

"I didn't want to hurt you," Jesse said. "I thought my being under the same roof with Pacer could only cause trouble."

"He told me. You intend to take him back North. Why?"

"You've seen the wanted posters. What happened in Lawrence was no act of war. The slaughter of innocents . . ."

"He was there, but he tried to stop the killing. He took no part in the raid."

"That's his story," Jesse scoffed.

Raven reached out and lifted the medal off his bandaged chest. His shirt hung across the back of a nearby chair. She cupped the coin and held it up to the lamp. George Washington's scrawled initials were plainly visible in the glare.

"This is your father's legacy. He hoped it would remind you of your family's sacrifices, the McQueens' sense of honor and duty. But it was never supposed to make you blind."

"I have eyes," Jesse replied.

"Ah, but the truth is not always as visible as a piece of paper, like some posted warrant. There is a bond between you and Pacer. Let it show you what is true."

"I have talked with Pacer. My brother has chosen to walk a path that has taken him away from me. I see no bond between us now."

"Yet it is there." Raven lifted her gaze. "What is between you and the window?"

Jesse glanced around. The side of the bed was a couple of feet from the windowsill. "There is nothing."

Without warning, Raven clamped a hand over her grandson's nose and mouth, cutting off his air supply. Jesse reached up to claw her hand away but the pain in his side seemed to rob him of his strength. "Now you know the truth," she said. "There is something between you and the window that you cannot live without. You do not see it, yet when I take it away, you struggle and know it is gone." She removed her hand and Jesse sucked in a lungful of air and didn't care how much the action hurt.

Raven reached over and filled a tin cup half full of coffee and handed the cup to Jesse, who sniffed the aroma and gave her a quizzical look. He wondered how she managed to have real coffee when the blockade had cut off such supplies from reaching the South. Even in Indian Territory, the supplies must be scarce. Raven seemed to read his thoughts. She held up the coffeepot and sloshed the contents. "Union supply train."

Jesse nodded. "Another gift from the Choctaw Kid, no doubt," he said dourly.

"Yes," Raven admitted, smiling.

"Hmmm." Jesse glanced around the room. "Where is he?"

"Asleep in his bedroom. Lorelei is using your bedroom, that's why you're down here."

Things were moving a bit too quickly for Jesse to follow. "Who is Lorelei?"

"A friend of Pacer's. She came with him from Arkansas. She is all alone and has no kin. Si asked to sleep in here by the fire. He would have pitched his blanket in the barn but for the Tellicos, who make him nervous."

"Moses and Theotis?"

"I bought their way out of jail. Since they've lost

their farm I've offered them a place here. They can help keep the farm up."

"Always taking in strays," Jesse dryly observed. "There was Sawyer Truett before them. And I can remember two frightened children, long ago. You gave them more than a home, Grandmother. Much more."

"You and Pacer were like my very own. Ben was all grown up, and then one day I had two children to sing to and hold and love. I was sorry you had lost your mother, but I was happy to have you here. Kit felt the same way." Raven patted his arm. "Sleep now." She took the empty cup from him. She examined his bandaged head. The wound had stopped bleeding. No ribs were broken, as far as she could tell. His arm was bruised and already discolored where he'd been clubbed, but that, too, would heal. She watched as Jesse settled back against the pillow and closed his eyes. He'd be sore for several days, but there seemed no permanent damage. He would be fine. All the same, she would stay by her grandson's side throughout the night. It was Raven's way.

Sunlight and hammering woke Jesse at mid-morning. He stirred, wiped the sleep from his eyes, took in his surroundings, then glanced out the window at Pacer, who was struggling to hang Raven's quilting from the porch ceiling. Pacer was oblivious to his older brother's scrutiny, but not to Jesse's presence. Ever since Si Reaves had arrived with Jesse draped across the saddle, Pacer had felt nothing but a dire premonition that fate was toying with them both, bringing them together to instigate a tragic confrontation. He looped a length of rope over a hook in the ceiling and tied the other end through an eyelet in the quilting frame. Raven liked to work out in the fresh autumn air. The porch was deep enough to shield the frame from the elements. Once winter set in she'd move the whole thing inside and commandeer part of a back room, just off the kitchen. Pacer resolved to let one of the Tellicos move her inside.

Bringing Moses and Theotis to Buffalo Creek was a chancy move at best. They were a dangerous breed, fierce mountain folk with peculiar loyalties; slow to anger, but once riled, they'd come fighting with knife and gun, tooth and rock, and keep at it till blood flowed. He'd sent them up the valley to work some of the cattle out of the wooded hillsides and down into the grassy floor. Buffalo Creek wound deep into the Kiamichi Mountains for a few miles to its headwaters, a natural spring flowing out of the side of a humpbacked jumble of rocks where the hills to either side closed in and formed the narrow passage called Buffalo Gap. The gap opened onto a broad pass running north to south along the length of the Kiamichis. If the Tellicos ranged as far as the gap, it would take them most of the morning, depending on how closely they scoured the slopes for stray calves. Si Reaves had gone into the garden to help Raven bring in the sweet corn. The former slave was grateful for Raven's hospitality and had offered to help with whatever work needed to be done.

Hecuba waddled out of the barn and proceeded to chase a grasshopper out into the barnyard. The farm's steadfast and vigilant sentry flapped her snowy wings and hurried off around the far side of the barn in pursuit of the frantically leaping insect. The goose reappeared seconds later and Pacer imagined he could see a self-satisfied gleam in the watchbird's eyes: a morsel of grasshopper protruded from her beak. The bird's head bobbed and dipped and sent the unfortunate grasshopper on a one-way journey down the goose's long neck.

Hecuba scarcely had a moment to enjoy her snack. Suddenly she craned her head forward, flared her wings, and sounded an alert. Pacer watched the bird with amusement that turned to caution. He stepped down from the porch and studied the plume of dust unfurling like a sandy banner at the entrance to the valley.

Inside the house, Jesse also heard Hecuba sound the alert. The tension in Pacer was plainly evident. Jesse watched his younger brother check the loads in his Colt before returning the weapon to its holster as he moved off into the yard.

Jesse swung his legs over the side of the bed, pulled on his trousers, and reached for his gunbelt. A hammer clicked back and he glanced up at a mere slip of a girl, wearing a workshirt and rolled-up trousers. Her cheek was smudged with cornmeal. A length of her auburn hair was dusted as well. Her small hands seemed dwarfed by the flintlock pistols she brandished. The heavy-bore guns were none other than the pair of flintlocks that had belonged to Jesse's great-grandfather, Daniel. Normally they adorned the stone chimney above the mantle, but not now. Jesse froze in midreach. He had no desire to be blown in half by these family keepsakes.

"You must be Lorelei," Jesse said.

"I am."

Jesse nodded toward the window. Hecuba continued to protest the arrival of strangers.

"Maybe I ought to have my gun. Could be trouble on the way."

"It could be already here," Lorelei warily replied, "in this room."

Jesse grinned. He liked her. She had grit and, except for the fact the girl was prepared to shoot him dead, she was mighty nice to look at.

"My great-grandfather used to call his flintlocks 'The Quakers' because they tended to bring peace whenever he drew them from his belt." He rubbed his chin. "I've fired them. They kick like Missouri mules. Darn near broke my wrist once." He looked for some reaction and was rewarded with a glimmer of apprehension in her eyes.

"Maybe a broken arm is a small price to pay," Lorelei told him. "The Choctaw Kid is blue lightning with a gun. But quickness never stopped a bullet in the back."

"My brother is lucky to have you," Jesse replied.

"Nobody *has* me."

"No, ma'am." Jesse could hear the sound of approaching horses. Time was running out. If he wasn't so sore and stiff, he'd have caught up his gun and dove for the floor and taken his chances. The only option open to him was "slow and steady."

"Our visitors may have come looking for me," Jesse said. "I don't aim to face them unarmed." He moved slowly, easing into his boots and then standing upright. "I'll be taking my gun now." He held his breath and braced himself and watched for a flash in the pan that would precede the thunderous explosion in the room. He'd conserve his strength for a last-second burst of speed and a lunge out of harm's way. At this distance, he didn't stand much of a chance. Lorelei held his life in her hands.

Si Reaves wore the look of a hunted man in his sweat-streaked face. Perspiration glistened on his black brow and gleamed against his naked torso. He straightened and stared off toward the mouth of the valley as Hecuba trumpeted her alarm. Raven stepped around the black man and shaded her eyes.

"I can't see from here . . ." she softly said.

"Oh, damn. I'm in a bad way. That cream-colored horse, only one like it I know of. That be Sawyer Truett coming here. And more than likely he got his friends with him." Si looked around the garden as if half expecting some sort of escape route to open up for him just by wishing. It was plain to see he was trapped. The approaching horsemen would cut him down twenty steps past the garden.

"They can't know you're here," Raven said, hoping to calm the frightened man. She noted he had pulled the Patterson Colt from his belt. "Kneel down."

"Ma'am?"

"They won't see you in the corn. You'll look like a patch of shadow," Raven explained with a twinkle in her eye.

"What about Pacer? That ain't exactly a Yankee uniform he's wearing." Si cocked his revolver. The trigger dropped down and pressed into his curled finger. He wasn't going to surrender. No sir. Anybody wanted his hide, they'd have to bleed first.

"Pacer will not give you away," Raven said.

"What makes you so certain? I'm just another runaway nigger to him."

"You came to Buffalo Creek as a friend. *My* friend."

"Miss Raven, you sure got a powerful trust in your own."

"I know my son," Raven replied, and in her thoughts added, *Perhaps better than he knows himself.* War had changed her sons, but only on the surface. They were both good and decent and honorable men who had found their way home. And now they must find each other.

Five men on horseback arranged themselves in a semicircle in the front yard. Pacer had watched them ride up, and made every effort to appear unconcerned. He didn't want to greet his former saddlemates with a rifle in his arms. But the Colt at his side and the D-guard knife riding hilt-forward in a sheath beneath his left arm offered assurance that he could handle his share of any trouble.

Sawyer Truett, the oldest of the lot, sat astride his mount and leaned forward with his forearms crossed on the saddle pommel. Pacer noted Sawyer seemed a little stiff. Chris Foot and Buck Langdon certainly looked worse for wear. Chris had a puffed lip and bruises about the face and neck. Buck was favoring his bandaged right leg. Sam Roberts sat astride his gelding like a warrior prince. He had quarreled with his father earlier in the day and rebuked Tullock for agreeing to attend Jesse McQueen's conciliatory meeting in Chahta Creek. The Knights of the Golden Circle had agreed to meet this night, and nothing in heaven or earth was going to keep Sam from accompanying his friends. Despite his coughing spasms, he was determined to prove himself to the Knights.

Johnny Teel sat in Sam Tullock's shadow, a few paces back from the other four men. Johnny, for all his bravado, was a follower. He would fight for the Confederacy because his friends wore Rebel gray. That reason alone had shaped his decision. He was not the sort of man to break from the pack: he lacked the courage to follow his conscience and walk a lone road. Perhaps that was the reason why he had come to hate a man like Pacer Wolf McQueen.

"Good morning, Pacer," Sawyer said with surprising cordiality. "Appears Raven has kept you busy."

"The place needs working," Pacer admitted. "Thought I'd see to it before heading out."

"I don't blame you. I've come to do a bit of mending myself." Sawyer said, stroking his goatee. He glanced around at the farmhouse and barn. He could see some of the fall garden. Ironically, Sawyer wore a uniform identical to Pacer's: the gray blouse and black trousers and black boots of Quantrill's guerrillas. To Sawyer his garb reflected a cherished ideal. To Pacer they had become merely work clothes. "Pacer," Sawyer continued. "You and me have always been close. Ever since your grandma took me in. Why, I've thought of you as my own flesh-and-blood kin."

Pacer studied the hard-set faces of his visitors. Each man had been a friend, someone he had played with and hunted alongside. Sawyer spoke the truth. On the McQueen farm, it had always been the three boys—Sawyer, Pacer, and Jesse. A quarrel with one was a quarrel with all three.

"My friends are welcome here," Pacer said.

"Good. It ain't right, all of us not being together. We want you to join us," Sawyer said. "Don't we?" he added, turning to his companions.

"Come on, Pacer. Saddle up. We're gathering men for tonight," Buck Langdon blurted out. "The Choctaw Kid has a place in the Golden Circle."

"We even got a hood to cover that ugly face of yours," Chris Foot said with a grin. He held up a saffron-colored hood. The black eyeholes made for a macabre effect in his hands.

Sam Roberts walked his mount forward and handed Pacer a copy of the front page of the *Chahta Creek Courier*. An announcement dominated the page. It called for a gathering of all the Choctaw, both pure-blood and mixed and anyone who made their homes or owned land in this southeast corner of the Indian Territory to come to the Council House in town Sunday evening, three days hence.

"Your brother, Jesse, is trying to start trouble," Sam said.

Pacer read the announcement Carmichael Ross had so enthusiastically placed in the center top half of the page. "It says here folks of either Union or Confederate persuasion are welcome in a spirit of peace. Sounds like he's trying to *stop* something to me." He handed the page back to Sam who crumbled it up and tossed it in the dirt at Pacer's feet.

"He even got my pa to agree to show up at the Council House. And there's plenty of others who will follow my pa's lead."

"The way we see it," Sawyer interjected, "the

time for talk ended at Fort Sumter. What's needed here are men of action."

"Like the Knights of the Golden Circle," Pacer said.

"Exactly," Sawyer said. "We've revealed ourselves to you, Pacer, as a sign of good faith. We want you to ride with us. I can put aside what happened at Lawrence and offer my hand in friendship. What do you say?"

Pacer looked up at Sawyer's outstretched hand. Was this a place then for the Choctaw Kid? Among night riders waging a campaign of wanton destruction and terror against the innocent? He could picture Quantrill standing in the farm yard and laughing. Laughing.

"No," said Pacer. "We disgraced the Confederacy and ourselves at Lawrence. When I join battle again, it will be against soldiers, not defenseless farmers or innocent storekeepers. You wear the hoods not to conceal your identity, but to hide your shame."

Sawyer's hand slowly lowered. His dark eyes grew livid. He scowled, and drew himself erect.

"Nobody talks to me like that," Sam Roberts growled.

"Everybody talks to you like that," Pacer retorted, on the prod, his bronze eyes flashing fire.

"You got no call to insult me," Buck Langdon said. Sunlight glittered off a watch chain stretched across the roll of fat padding his midrift. He'd brushed his coat back and freed access to the gun holstered high on his left hip.

"Buck . . . you gave me call when you joined this bunch."

"Appears to me you're running away and hiding just like you did from the Yankees in Lawrence," Sawyer Truett declared.

"I ran from myself that day and from what I feared to become," Pacer replied in a quiet voice as if he were having a dialogue with himself instead of confronting five armed men.

"You aren't with us, then you be agin' us," Sawyer told him. "The line's drawn."

"So be it," Pacer said.

"Maybe we ought to settle things here and now," Chris Foot, the full-blood, suggested. He dropped a hand to his gunbelt. Sam Roberts and Buck Langdon concurred and lowered their hands to their gun butts. Sawyer made no move and that had the others puzzled. They halted in midaction.

"What the hell's the matter, Sawyer?" Sam asked. "There's five of us and one McQueen."

Pacer was poised, ready to react. His attention was centered on the young men who had been the friends of his childhood. He was devoid of emotion now and prepared to take the lives of as many of his attackers as he could before their bullets cut him down.

"Better make that two." The voice came from off to Pacer's right. He recognized his brother without bothering to turn and see for himself.

Sawyer and the others were taken completely by surprise as Jesse appeared on the porch, his gun drawn and leveled at the Knights. Sawyer gave Pacer a look of betrayal and bitter accusation.

"How's the leg, Buck?" Jesse asked.

"The knee's been swollen since you . . ." Buck realized he should not have been answering. He'd been tricked into confessing his part in the attack on Jesse. ". . . and it hurts like the devil," he finished.

"Good," said Jesse.

"It looks like it's your call," Pacer said to Sawyer.

Tullock Roberts's overseer shook his head. "Another day," Sawyer said. "My time will come."

"Pray it doesn't, old friend," said Pacer. He heard footsteps behind him and saw Sawyer touch the brim of his hat. He sensed his grandmother's presence.

Then Raven was past him and moving through the line of fire, placing herself in danger and wholly unconcerned with the standoff. Tension permeated the air. Like smoke from a brushfire, it made breathing difficult and left the mouth dry.

Raven walked right up to Sawyer and handed him a basket of sweet corn. "Take this to Arbitha for me, she's partial to the sweet corn we grow here." She fumbled with the basket and almost dropped it. Sawyer managed to catch the gift with both hands and eventually tucked it under his left arm. Raven looked around at the other men. "Why, Johnny Teel, how's your sister?"

"Ma'am?" the young man squirmed in the saddle. "Didn't know she's been ailing."

"She took a fall off a ladder at your father's store and hit her head against the counter. It bruised her pretty bad and gave her dizzy spells. I left Albert a poultice to ease the swelling."

"Mighty nice of you, Missus McQueen."

"There's chicken and biscuits if you boys have finished your visit," Raven continued.

"Thank you, Raven, but we aren't hungry," Sawyer spoke up, attempting to humor what seemed to be an oblivious old woman.

"Oh, very well," Raven said, and started toward the house. She turned and smiled beatifically. "Pacer . . . Jesse . . . we'll finish these boys, then eat. We can bury them after dinner." She lifted a Navy Colt and aimed the weapon at Sawyer, who recognized his own gun. Still holding the basket, he glanced down at his empty holster and realized the sweet corn had been a ruse to occupy the man while Raven disarmed him.

"Damn!" he muttered, and threw the basket to the ground, scattering the ears of freshly picked corn as he glowered at the medicine woman who had outsmarted him. The other Knights found the odds had grown increasingly unacceptable. Sam Roberts touched the brim of his hat and backed his horse out of the yard. Christ Foot and Johnny Teel bid farewell to Pacer and their regards to Raven and followed Tullock's son out of the yard. Buck Langdon hesitated. The idea of biscuits and chicken was pretty enticing.

"You're welcome to dinner," Raven said, training the Navy Colt on the chunky young night rider. She cocked the gun. "But you may find the dessert rather difficult to swallow."

"Yeah. I reckon so," Buck said. He looked at Sawyer and then swung his horse around and beat a hasty retreat. Sawyer Truett made a point of being the last to leave. He glanced around at the barnyard and house with its deep porch, the signal-fire hill rising above the homestead, the sun-dappled creek bordered by the heavily wooded hills of the Kiamichis. Kit McQueen had taken Pacer, Jesse, and Sawyer into the mountains and taught them the lore of the woods and the power of silence. Sawyer lowered his gaze to Pacer and Raven. The medicine woman approached Sawyer and returned the gun to its rightful owner. The horseman felt a twinge of remorse, then wrapped his conscience in his own righteous anger.

"You shouldn't have shamed me, Grandmother Raven," he said.

"It is better to lose face than your life," she replied.

"Bold talk won't stop the Knights of the Golden Circle. Ours is a noble cause you once subscribed to, Pacer McQueen, before you cut out on your friends." He turned his smoldering gaze on the youngest of the McQueens. "We're all after you now, Pacer. Confederates and Federals alike. You and me were like brothers once. But a bullet has no kin." Sawyer hauled back on the reins and reared his mount, forcing Pacer to leap out of reach of the horse's flashing hooves as the last of the Knights of the Golden Circle galloped down the winding road that followed the undulations of Buffalo Creek toward the mouth of the valley.

Pacer looked at his brother and grandmother and beyond them caught a glimpse of Lorelei, brandishing a pair of pistols and standing, partly concealed, in the shadow of the doorway. Then he returned his attention to the medicine woman who had single-handedly defused the situation.

"Grandmother?" he began, exasperated. She might have been killed. Raven cut him off with a wave of her hand.

"You boys wash up. Jesse, it's about time you quit your bed and pitched in to help around here." She marched out of the barnyard and headed for the house. "Pacer, you take care to bring in the corn Sawyer dropped. Arbitha's loss shall be our gain."

Pacer nodded and started to obey Raven's instructions. But there was his older brother standing before him, battered but willing to back the Choctaw Kid's play.

"Why'd you come out here, Jesse?"

"Beats the hell out of me," Jesse said.

"Maybe you figure to save me for some Federal hangman."

"Go to the devil!"

"I'm on my way," Pacer replied, and touched the brim of his gray felt hat.

"It's just like you," Jesse growled, "to turn everyone against you."

"Wouldn't have it any other way," Pacer answered.

"You're like the man who trapped a panther," Jesse said. "One day he decided to ride it."

"Yeah? What happened?" Pacer asked, braced for the story's moral, resentful, yet naturally curious.

Jesse didn't keep his brother waiting. "He found out the man who chooses to ride the panther can never dismount."

Chapter Twenty-four

The Medicine Wagon was doing a brisk business. The spacious gambling hall was crowded with townspeople eager to forget, at least for a while, these dark and troubled times. A wagon train of settlers fleeing the war had arrived, bound for Denver. Several of the settlers were enjoying one final night of celebration before pressing on to Colorado Territory. China and the other girls were doing a brisk trade; the staircase was crowded with an assortment of anxious patrons who climbed the mahogany steps that led to the sporting parlors upstairs. The faro table dominated the center of the gambling hall. Enos Clem was handling the crowd around the table and bringing in a fair share of the winnings for the house. Mean-tempered Shug Jones, behind the bar, kept the glasses filled while Hud Pardee and his protégé, young Dobie Johnson, watched over the throng like shepherds guarding their flock. At the first sign of trouble— surly behavior from a drunk, threatened violence between two gamblers, or a quarrel over a girl's favors—and Hud Pardee was there. The gunman's reputation and his menacing presence had a decidedly calming effect. Dobie was always standing off to the side, backing the gunman and adding an extra element to Pardee's considerable threat.

Cap Featherstone was making money tonight and he should have been delighted. But the news Hud Pardee had brought from the gathering of the Knights had left Cap in a dour mood. Only a half hour ago Pardee had returned from the gathering of the Knights with news that Tullock Roberts had agreed to attend the meeting Jesse had called for Sunday evening. Worse still, when several of the older heads among the Knights heard of Tullock's willingness to attend the council, they had quickly voiced their own desire to follow the plantation owner's lead. Only the younger bucks demanded more raids, urged on by Pardee but unsupported by the landowners who were loath to continue the raids without first talking things over with Tullock. Most of the Knights knew one another beneath their robes, while Pardee had purposefully kept his identity a secret. He was not one of their own. Over the course of several weeks, Pardee's authority had begun to slip in the face of Tullock's popularity. The Knights respected Pardee's wish to keep his identity concealed. But the price of secrecy was a shift in allegiance from Pardee to Roberts.

One of Cap's "doves," a red-haired woman in her midtwenties whose pockmarked features were concealed beneath a layer of powder and rouge, stood alongside the piano set in the alcove beneath the stairway and sang a melancholy rendition of "Campfires on the Tennessee." The harlot's clear sweet voice had mercifully escaped the ravages of strong drink and tobacco smoke and the other hazards of her profession: disease and violent abuse.

Tandy Matlock's black bony fingers skimmed over the keys in a trilling finish and then proceeded into a chorus of "Dixie," which the songstress in her faded frills and feathers exuberantly sang. If Tandy minded the song, the wise old freed man kept his opinions to himself. At the Medicine Wagon he had food and a dry place to sleep, and if Cap and the others thought of Tandy as more of a fixture than a person, so much the better. In times of violence and guerrilla warfare it was best to be invisible.

Cap watched as Sam Roberts, Sawyer Truett, and their three companions descended on a nearby table whose occupants, Hack Warner and a friend, glanced up into the sullen young faces surrounding them and grudgingly vacated their chairs. Johnny Teel grinned and waved as Hack unsteadily brushed past them. He stopped and stared at Sam Roberts, standing nose to nose and toes to toes with the younger man. Cap tensed, awaiting the explosion. At the last second Hud Pardee materialized out of a drifting fog bank of tobacco smoke and whispered something in Hack's ear. Hack paled and continued on across the room, shadowed every step of the way by Pardee, who congratulated Warner on his choice of behavior and bought him a drink. Buck Langdon and Chris Foot wasted no time heading upstairs. They cornered China on her way down and took her along, arguing every step of the way as to who would take the first "poke."

Cap caught Pardee's attention and motioned for the gunman to join him in the office. Sam Roberts also left his table and headed for Cap, reaching the barrel-chested owner before Hud.

"Why, it's young Roberts," Cap said, and extended his hand in greeting.

"Evening, Mr. Featherstone," Sam replied. His voice was hoarse from a spasm that had left his reed-thin frame trembling. An hour earlier, as the Knights debated their course of action on the bluffs overlooking the Kimishi River, Sam had been wracked by a brief but exhausting fit of coughing.

"We're always pleased to have you here," Cap continued in a silken tone.

"Pleased enough to extend my credit? I should like to try my hand at the faro table. I believe your new dealer, Enos Clem, is vulnerable tonight."

"Why, certainly," Cap said, and in a magnanimous gesture produced a pad and stub of pencil from his coat pocket, scrawled "$100" on the piece of paper, and initialed the amount.

"Present that to Enos and claim your chips."

"Thanks, Mr. Featherstone. I'm good for it," Sam said, brightening. "I'll pay you back."

"Of course you will," Cap exclaimed, and clapped the younger man on the shoulder and sent him on his way. His gestures were expansive, his smile wide and full of teeth. But his eyes were cold as the double-edge steel blade concealed in his cane as he softly repeated more ominously, "Of course you will."

Pardee had been holding back, allowing Sam Roberts to finish with the owner of the Medicine Wagon. As Sam departed for the faro table in the center of the room, Pardee took his place by the office door. The one-eyed gunman was ominously attired in black coat and trousers, black shirt and sash. As it turned out, for what Cap Featherstone had in mind, Pardee's choice of colors was most appropriate.

The Medicine Wagon Saloon and Gambling House wasn't the only site of celebration. Back at Buffalo Creek the McQueens were having their own humble celebration centered around a ten-foot-long, hand-hewn table flanked by two equally long benches and set outside beneath the spreading branches of a red oak. Raven McQueen looked from her place at the head of the table over her new-found brood and thought how this was one of the strangest assortments of guests she'd entertained in quite some time.

Moses and Theotis Tellico took up one side of the groaning board. What these rough-looking mountain men might lack in the way of manners they made up for with their hearty appetites and good-natured banter. Pacer, Lorelei, and Si Reaves sat across from the Tellicos. A Confederate guerrilla, a headstrong girl, and a runaway slave. And at the other end of the table, Captain Jesse McQueen, Union officer and territorial ranger.

The Tellicos had missed the confrontation with the Knights but had listened in bemused and respectful silence to accounts from Jesse, Lorelei, and Pacer as to the manner in which Raven had disarmed Sawyer Truett and just about single-handedly defused a very dangerous and volatile situation.

Theotis slapped his thigh and loosed a mighty laugh that sprayed the front of his shirt with stew juice. Moses wiped his mustache on the sleeve of his buckskin shirt and wagged his head and sighed.

"Glory be, Miss Raven, you got more grit than a buffalo wallow. I'd have liked to seen you take the measure of them boys and that's for sure, that's for durn sure." He scratched his crooked nose and his pale eyes twinkled merrily.

"I'm with Moses," Theotis added. "You can back me anytime, Miss Raven. Of course, me and my brother usually get the job done on our own." His right hand patted the heavy octagonal barrel of a .52 caliber Hawken rifle leaning against the table. Like the Starr revolvers the brothers shared, Moses had a Hawken rifle identical to his brother's within easy reach of his right hand. Both men were expert marksmen. In the mountains, a poor shot went hungry and either moved into the flatlands or stayed and starved to death.

No one was going to starve to death at Raven's table. She had built a fire in a rock-lined pit, hung a black stew pot over the flames and tossed in chunks of beef, potatoes, corn, and beans and covered the ingre-

dients with water. The stew had simmered all afternoon while Raven and Lorelei made cornbread.

It was a pleasant evening, with a cool, whispery
breeze that set the firelight flickering and caused the
smoke to trail off in a southerly direction. In the
glow of the fire, Raven watched as Lorelei crumbled a
couple of wedges of cornbread into a tin plate, soft-
ened the bread with milk from a clay pitcher, and
ladled meat broth over the mush. Raven had an idea
what the girl was up to. Another change had taken
place in the girl, and this time Moses and Theotis were
to blame.

The Tellicos had returned late in the afternoon.
They were tired from chasing cattle out of the under-
brush-choked hillsides flanking the valley. The brothers had worked their way to the gap, where the hills
closed in and almost choked off the creek. The gap was
at the end of a dogleg and roughly forty yards from hillside to hillside. Ahead of the gap stretched a hundred
yards of clear ground, devoid of cover and carpeted
with buffalo grass and, in the spring, tiny white flowers, red blossoms and Indian paint brush, blue stem
grass and weeds. The Tellico brothers had not returned
from their labors empty-handed. Theotis had found a
litter of week-old pups underneath a deadwood red oak
that time and the elements had toppled into decay. The
elder Tellico, after a brief search, had found the
remains of the bitch down by the creekbank. The carcass had been picked clean by scavengers. Two of the
pups had died as well, but miraculously enough, the
other three were weak but still game.

When Lorelei mumbled an embarrassed thank-
you for the meal, and rose from the table with plate in
hand, she headed straight for the barn. She had taken
charge of the puppies' welfare and had spent most of
the afternoon in the loft where a warm, straw-filled
wooden box served as the puppies' new home. Pacer
watched her depart, then dawdled with the food on

his plate for another minute or two, while trying to think of some appropriate excuse to leave the table. Raven took a moment to accept Moses' compliment concerning her "grit," then leaned toward Pacer.

"It's been my experience pups like those in the barn can be quite a handful. Maybe you ought to go see if Lorelei needs any help."

"I might do just that," Pacer said, and shoved clear of his plate and the congealing remains of his dinner.

Si Reaves appeared to relax when he was no longer sitting beside the Confederate-gray shirt of the notorious Choctaw Kid. Jesse noticed the black man's obvious sense of relief.

"He'd never turn you in, Si," Jesse commented.

"I look at him and I sees a Johnny Reb," the former slave said.

"Neither Pacer or I have any use for slavery. No man has the right to own another."

"Then why ain't he fightin' for Mr. Lincoln like you?"

Jesse glanced over at his grandmother, who merely nodded as if anticipating what he was about to say.

"Pacer may only be an eighth Choctaw, but his heart is one with the full-bloods. The government has a poor record when it comes to treaties with the red man. Pacer cannot bring himself to support the Federals. I've tried to talk sense to him, but he's stubborn, like his grandmother." Jesse smiled at Raven, who brushed her hair back and blushed with amusement. "Pacer has his eyes turned toward yesterday," Jesse continued. "I'm looking toward the future. This nation cannot last divided. The country must come together again if any of us are to survive and live free."

"Dang if you don't talk pretty as one of them politicians me and Theotis seen over in St. Louis once last spring," Moses said. He sopped up the last of the broth on his plate with a wedge of cornbread, then looked over at Raven with an unspoken request for a third helping.

"A hearty appetite is the best compliment to any meal of mine," she said.

"Yes, ma'am. Thankee kindly," he replied, and made another trip to the cookpot.

"You know, when Si here brung you in and I seen you lookin' stove up and swollen," Theotis remarked to Jesse, "I figured it served you right for helpin' Parson Marshal Booth bring us in. Then your grandma showed me as to how you probably kept me from shooting that no-account banker and that would have been some real bona-fide trouble. So then I kinda felt sorry for you." The mountain man speared a chunk of fatty meat with his fork and plopped the morsel in his mouth, then lifted the plate to his lips and began to slurp the remaining juices. Moses, returning to his place, glanced disdainfully at his brother and tapped him on the shoulder.

"Mind your manners, big brother."

Theotis looked around, then continued his noisy practice, although this time he held the plate with the little finger of each hand politely raised.

Moses flashed a condescending smile and attacked his third plateful of stew. He made no attempt to hide the fact he relished every mouthful.

"Well, I'm glad you Tellicos don't hold a grudge," Jesse told them. "Because I'm going to need your help. This council I've called could blow up in my face." He wore a shrewd expression now, and his humus-colored eyes searched the faces of the two mountain men as if judging just how much he could reveal to the brothers. The Tellicos, by their own admission, didn't much care who emerged victorious from the war. Like many mountain folk, they felt removed from the conflict. But Jesse was here to bring their isolation to an end.

"What do you have in mind?" Theotis asked. He set

aside his plate, pulled his napkin from the front of his shirt, and dropped it on the table. He leaned forward, his belly straining the buckskin lacings of his shirt.

"I want you to dig a few holes—well, more than a few—and some of them need to run three or four yards in length and maybe six to eight feet deep. And I want them covered with a woven net of branches and grass."

"Bear traps. That's what you want," Moses said.

"Yes," Jesse told him. He removed a slip of paper from his pocket and placed it on the table. It was a hastily drawn map of Buffalo Creek bordered by the Kiamichis. He traced the terrain to the gap at the northwest end of the valley where the mountains closed in and formed a bottleneck and the spring-fed creek bubbled out of the base of an upthrust limestone cliff. "I want them here," said Jesse, and placed a finger on the gap.

"What do we get out of this?" Moses asked, his gaze narrowing.

"The satisfaction of knowing you've helped your country," Jesse said.

"Horsepiss," said Moses, then he turned to Raven. "Pardon me . . . uh . . ." He couldn't untie his tongue quick enough to think of a proper apology.

"And I'll see you get your farm back."

"You can do that?" Theotis asked in a skeptical tone.

"I am not without authority," Jesse said.

"It'd be a powerful lot of digging," Moses added.

"Pa kept a cache of blasting powder back in the hills. You can use all you want. That ought to save your backs." Jesse held out his hand. "Have we an agreement?"

"I reckon so," Moses said, reaching across his brother to clasp Jesse's outstretched hand before McQueen had second thoughts.

"I'm for it," Theotis said, then rubbed his bristly

chin and sighed. "But it seems you taken leave of your senses, all them bear pits. Why, you're a-wasting your time, Jesse. We ain't seen any bear around these parts for ten year or more. They all been hunted out. So you ain't about to catch one in all them traps no matter how many we dig." He chuckled, and winked at Moses. "No sirree, Captain McQueen. You been gone too long. There just ain't any bear."

"I know."

Moses jabbed his brother with an elbow. "Jesse wants us to dig him some holes in the ground, we'll do it. Seems a better way than most to get us back our farm. What do you want to use for bait in these here pits?"

"Just dig them," Jesse said. He stared out at the night-shrouded hills. "The bait will come later."

The puppies were three satin brown bundles of fur that tugged and ripped and burrowed to safety beneath the straw as Lorelei plucked one after the other from the box and set them on the wooden floor of the hayloft. She placed each pup near a tin plate of crumbled cornbread and milk. The pups recognized the milk smell. The bravest of the three, a mongrel with a diamond-shaped patch of white fur on its face, was the first to venture to the plate, but once he began to greedily devour the contents of the plate the other two joined him and proceeded to lap up their share of dinner. Lorelei continued to stroke the frightened little animals and speak to them in a soft and gentle voice.

"All alone. Mama's gone and left you. Poor babies," she sighed, kneeling. "Poor babies." The adventuresome puppy chewed on her finger with his milk teeth when she picked him up in her hands. The pup's eyes were black slits and its bark defiant but pitifully weak. Lorelei admired the animal's brave gesture and gently lowered the struggling animal to the plate. The puppy lost no time in wedging himself between his siblings and resumed eating.

"I like this side of you. Why do you hide it?" Pacer said from the ladder as he climbed the few remaining rungs to the hayloft. He stood and was careful to duck beneath the roof beams as he approached the young woman and her pups. Dust and tiny dry twigs filtered to the packed earth floor below, a rain that fell with his every step. The floorboards creaked beneath his weight.

Lorelei blushed and turned away. The old anger was quick to return.

"Don't make a mistake and think me soft because I feel sorry for these little ones," Lorelei said.

"I saw you earlier today, in the doorway with my grandfather's guns. Soft? No. Anything but that," Pacer replied.

"You helped me once. I was ready to do the same for you." Lorelei looked up into Pacer's gold-flecked eyes.

"Ah. So you are a woman who pays her debts."

"Now you're making fun of me," Lorelei said, frowning.

"No. Well, yes, maybe I am. But I do not mean to." Pacer lifted a pup in his big right hand. The animal nipped at his fingers and batted his thumb with its velvet brown paw. After a few moments, Pacer gently returned the struggling puppy to the false security of its box. The spotted one continually escaped to freedom and bravely set off across the loft, making a few paces on its own before Lorelei scooped the pup in her arms and deposited it in the box.

"They're like you . . . anxious to be on your way. For them it's the other side of the barn. With you, only California will do."

Lorelei shrugged. "Alike? We'll see. Anyway, I think I may stay on."

"Why?"

"Your mother has asked me to help her with the quilt."

"I think you should leave," Pacer forcefully suggested. "Perhaps you should go to St. Louis and hook up with a wagon train and make your way west." He could tell instantly he had bruised the young woman's feelings, and was tempted to leave things as they were. Her features froze, and she stood and walked away from him.

"Oh, I see," she muttered.

He stood and caught her arm and turned her around.

"No, you don't," he said. "I've enemies on all sides. A man like me is the last person you should be around. What happened in the yard this afternoon is a pale shadow of what's about to come."

Lorelei lowered her gaze to his restraining hand. He released his hold but she did not pull away.

"I'll stay," Lorelei said. "I've never known a man like you, Pacer Wolf McQueen," Lorelei said. "So I'll stay here. I want to see what happens to a man like you."

"I'll try to make it interesting," Pacer said. She was pretty in the lanternlight. The gentleness he glimpsed made her all the more attractive.

"In that case, I'll keep my powder dry. And when the struggle's over, if you're still alive, I might give you one last chance to kiss me." She hurried off then before Pacer could reply and descended to the center aisle of the barn. A few seconds later Pacer was completely alone save for the puppies, the horses in the stalls, and noble Hecuba, scratching in the dust near the tack room.

Lorelei was an enigma, all right, but then weren't all women? He glanced down at the puppies. He couldn't rid himself of a single troubling notion. The defenseless creatures had found a haven smack dab in the middle of a battlefield. He didn't envy them—or himself. When the shooting started, guns were apt to be aimed at him. By rights he ought to be plenty worried.

But then again—there was the matter of that kiss.

Chapter Twenty-five

Jesse had allowed himself an extra couple of days on the family farm. He'd spent the time in the good company of his grandmother and worked as best he could, alongside Si Reaves, the Tellicos, and his own younger brother, in replacing the roof of the barn which had suffered considerable damage from a hailstorm well over four months ago. Taking care not to overextend himself, Jesse hoped to speed the healing process. He wanted to be as well as possible for the council on Sunday night.

Jesse ate heartily and involved himself in the easy camaraderie of the men he worked alongside, and for two days politics and the brutal realities of war seemed far away. He knew the illusion couldn't last. And so did the Choctaw Kid.

Jesse was uncertain how to resolve the matter of his brother. He had come to realize that Pacer was not responsible for the Lawrence massacre. However, the Choctaw Kid was still a notorious guerrilla raider who had plagued the Union troops and settlements of Missouri and Kansas. Daniel Pacer Wolf McQueen gave no indication that he intended to curb his activities. On this Saturday morning Jesse had yet to reach a decision on the matter.

Jesse woke early from a troubled sleep. He'd dreamt of black wings against a crimson dawn and heard the cry of a bird become a howl of agony that reverberated in his skull. He sat up and wiped cold sweat from his brow. He dressed quickly, grabbed his gunbelt and hat, and stepped outside into the cool of morning. The yard was empty, the farm, dark and vacant-looking though he knew the Tellicos had pitched their bedrolls in two of the empty stalls. Jesse looked east and beheld a sky awash with streamers of blood-red clouds encroaching on the purple-black roof of night. He caught his breath, the dream image still fresh in his mind and now become real here before him. He lowered his gaze and spied a solitary shawl-wrapped figure on the wooden bridge Jesse's father and grandfather had built across Buffalo Creek. It was a simple structure, wide enough for a wagon and sturdy enough to bear a heavy load if necessary. Rails of split red oak ran the length of either side.

"Christ almighty, doesn't she ever sleep?" Jesse muttered to himself, and stepped off the porch and strode purposefully across the yard, eyeing the lurid sky and remembering. It was as if he were walking in the dream. Black wings against the blood-red sky. A raven's wings. What else? But why the cries of anguish and the icy creep of fear along his spine?

She waited for him on the bridge, and when her grandson was in earshot she said, "So you also have had the dream."

Jesse drew up sharply and stared at the half-breed medicine woman for several silent moments. "I wish you'd stop doing that."

"What?"

"You tell me what I'm doing before I get to tell

you," Jesse said. He paused to consider his reply and wondered if it made sense. Then with a shrug, he admitted the dream that had awakened him. Raven merely nodded sagely and turned to study the dawn.

"Did you send me the dream?"

"No. It came from the All-Father, the same as mine."

"I don't understand any of this."

"Someone will die today," she said. "But you would know this if you were quiet and listened."

"Who will die?"

Raven shook her head. "It is rare for the spirits to reveal a name. The warning at sunrise is all we can know."

"I've seen the sun come up like this before," Jesse protested. He did not like all this talk of death. Tomorrow he would hold council and try to convince the people in and around Chahta Creek to come together in peace and abandon the course of division and bloodshed. The last thing he needed was some ill omen from his grandmother. "It was a dream, it meant nothing. The clouds are just clouds."

"Sing the song with me, the song for the dying. Sing for the one who will die alone this day," Raven said.

"No. I walk the white road now," Jesse flatly stated. "Let Pacer be here. It is for him to speak the words and make the prayer."

"The dream came to you," Raven told him. She steadied herself against the railing and shivered as a gentle wind picked up out of the north. "The blood of my mother flows in your veins, passed from me to my son and then to you. The power of the Old Ones is real and you cannot deny it."

Jesse reached out and put his arms around Raven and held her close. He whispered in her ear, "I love you, Grandmother." She seemed so little in his arms. The years were slipping away and the time was not far off that he would lose her. Just thinking of it made him miss her already. "I love you," he repeated. "But I follow a path of my own choosing and there is no place for ghosts or whispering spirits." He glanced up as the skyline brightened in hue and the crimson clouds paled to blushing pink. A golden sun crested the hills and pursued the last of the fleeing shadows along the banks of Buffalo Creek.

"See. Here is the sun and no one has died," Jesse said with a wave of his hand. "Tomorrow I'll return to town. Carmichael's probably wondering if I'm ever coming back, and T. Alan Booth hopes I won't." He placed a hand on his grandmother's arm. "Come back to the house. You'll catch a chill."

"In a minute," Raven said. "There is something I must do." She turned her back on her grandson and faced the risen sun and softly began to chant in a melodious voice.

> "Grandfather Spirit.
> Earth shaker. Sky splitter.
> Voice of Thunder and
> Sacred Dreamer.
> You have given me the sight that
> is beyond seeing and I accept it.
> Hear my voice,
> may my words ride the wind to your ears.
> I have seen blood upon the clouds.
> I have heard the dying one.
> Follow his cries. Bind him to you,
> O Grandfather Spirit.
> Earth shaker. Sky splitter.
> Voice of thunder.
> Sacred Dreamer."

Jesse retraced his route back to the farmhouse. The song hounded him every step of the way. It tugged at his heart. *But I walk a different path.* From the porch her voice was faint. *I am a Union captain come here to stop the violence.* Inside the house he could not hear Raven at all. *It is not my way.* He made his way to the kitchen and started coffee and tried to distance himself from Raven's admonitions. He slumped onto a chair and, resting his elbows on the kitchen table, cradled his face in his hands. The song for the dying, why now? And for whom? The old words like ancient spirits clutched at his thoughts and would not set him free.

CAP FEATHERSTONE'S MEDICINE SHOW
POTABLES AND ELIXIRS TO RESTORE
THE HEALTH AND REFRESH THE SPIRIT

Cap lovingly dusted the side panel of his medicine wagon as he walked alongside the four-wheeled coach and peered around the corner of the wagon at the frock-coated figure standing in the doorway of the carriage shed. Parson Marshal Booth had come from Cap's gambling house, where the women were as fiery as the liquor and sin, not Sunday dinner, was the offering of the day.

"Run out of credit, T. Alan?" Cap asked, amused.

Booth stood ramrod-stiff, his sober attire neatly creased and closely fitting the marshal's six-foot frame. Morning sunlight glinted off the star pinned to his vest as his coat parted and Booth hooked his thumbs in the wide gunbelt worn high on his hips.

"More than one grave's been bought for the price of a clever remark," the marshal replied. He had yet to have his coffee at Gude's and was in a foul mood.

"I meant no harm, T. Alan," said Cap. He knew such familiarity bothered Booth. It amused him to goad the lawman.

"A rider came in from Honey Ridge. Tullock sent him to fetch me out of bed so's I could mosey over here and fetch Samuel and either toss him in jail or send him home. Seems the lad's been gone two days. Al Teel told me he saw Sam right here at your saloon just the other night."

"That's correct. I extended his credit and Sam spent the last two days battling his own private demons." Cap shook his head and folded his arms across his great girth. The bandanna he wore to hide his thinning hair was soaked with sweat along his forehead. It was warm in the shed and Cap had already been in here longer than he wanted to be. "Heard he was at odds with his pa. Anyway, he left for home a little after sunup, and I can guarantee he was considerable happier than when he walked through my doors."

"No doubt poorer as well." A bee circled Booth's flat-brim hat, hovered near his stern features, only to be brushed away and then return to plague the Bible-toting lawman like some impish sprite.

"Hell, Marshal, a man has to make a profit. Where's the harm in that?"

Booth saw no point in debating the issue. Cap might be friend to Jesse McQueen, but that didn't warrant anything but suspicion from this lawman. "He's gone, huh?" His lanky arm shot out with suspicious speed and he crushed the bothersome insect against the doorsill.

"Left on his own horse and rode out of town. Said he was going to try and talk his father out of coming to McQueen's council."

"He'll fail there. When Tullock makes up his mind about something, there's no stopping him." Booth shrugged. "Well, I've done what I said I would." He retreated into the sunlight. "If you see Jesse before I do, tell him to stop by my office."

"Sure thing, T. Alan. Always glad to be of help." Cap smiled and propped a foot up on the singletree. He watched the lawman depart and, satisfied the threat of discovery was on its way to Gude's Good

Eats, turned to the small man cowering in the shadows of the carriage shed. "You can come out now."

With a rustle of straw crunching underfoot, Lucius Minley emerged from his hiding place. He checked the open doorway and breathed a sigh of relief.

"That was close," the banker remarked.

"You worry too much," Cap said. He removed the smaller man's wire-rimmed spectacles and cleaned them on a kerchief from his pocket. He handed the eyewear back to Minley, who immediately fitted them over his ears. Time and his association with Cap Featherstone had prematurely aged the former clerk. He had learned of the council and heard the rumor that both factions of Union and Confederate sympathizers had agreed to set their differences aside and face one another across an oaken table in the Council House.

"Maybe you don't worry enough," Lucius testily snapped. "If Jesse succeeds in talking peace, our plans are finished. There'll be no one else eager to sell out. Why, some folks might even want to settle back on the landholdings. When they discover I've sold the notes to you, there'll be the devil to pay." Lucius began to pace the floor alongside the medicine wagon.

"And this is why you wanted to see me?" Cap put a fatherly arm around the banker's narrow shoulders. He leaned down and brought his mouth close to Lucius's right ear. Cap's lips brushed the man's brown sideburns as he spoke in a whisper. "Go back to your ledgers and your afternoon sherry, Lucius. I'll handle things."

"What are you going to do?"

"You don't really want to know," Cap said. It was a flat statement of fact.

"No. I suppose . . ." Lucius lost his train of thought and shook his head. Images came to mind. He remembered a flash flood and a terrible storm. He had been caught out in a downpour and had fought the elements all the way to town. Lucius had just brought his carriage across the Kimishi River bridge two miles from town when a veritable wall of black water came rushing out of the mountains; a terrible onslaught of mud and uprooted trees that crashed into the bridge with enough force to shatter some of the supports. Lucius heard the tortured, almost feeble wail and spied a panther caught in the flood. In vain the great gray cat fought the imprisoning currents that dashed it against the spiked roots and branches of flood-tossed trees. The feline carnivore strove to reach the bank, to find some meager purchase with which to save its life. But the raging river hungered for victims. Five minutes earlier it might have claimed Lucius and knocked his carriage from the bridge, but having allowed the man to escape, the Kimishi would not relinquish its other prey. The floodwaters dashed the panther against the bridge supports and broke the feline's back, then bore the hapless predator away into the black night. Standing in the shadow of the carriage shed with Cap Featherstone's heavy left arm draped across his shoulders, Lucius Minley began to feel like the panther, trapped in something over which he no longer had control and being borne irrevocably to destruction.

Greed had lured Lucius Minley into the flood. No one had forced him. He had only himself to blame. But this realization was a paltry solace at best. There was nothing to do but allow the raging current to sweep him along and hope for the best. For Lucius it was too late to pray.

Chapter Twenty-six

Death came for Samuel Roberts at a quarter past ten. Sam was bound for home and having his troubles. His cough had returned with a vengeance after two days of wanton celebration in the smoke-shrouded interior of the Medicine Wagon Saloon. The daylight hours he'd spent in restless sleep among the arms of more women than he cared to count. Their names and their charms were a blur to him now. Evenings were whiskey-soaked and spent gambling. With Cap extending his credit he had behaved, ironically, as if there were no tomorrow.

The anger toward Tullock Roberts had subsided into a weary sense of betrayal. It wasn't Sunday yet, however, and there was still a chance to change his father's mind about attending the council meeting. The Knights of the Golden Circle had come too far to accept any settlement other than a victory for the Confederacy and the complete independence of the Indian Territory as promised by the government in Richmond. He took pride in belonging to the Knights and recognized he was part of an irregular army of hooded riders ranging throughout the Choctaw and

Creek lands and those of the Cherokee and Osage. One day all the Knights would come together to plague any Federal incursion while ridding the territory of Union sympathizers. By rights, a man like his father should lead such a force. Tullock had many friends and distant relatives among the Creeks and Cherokees, and he was held in high esteem throughout the Choctaw Nation and the Indian Territory.

"Pa must have been listening to Mother," Samuel told the stallion he rode. The animal continued to plod along the winding road that followed the Kimishi River before turning east and striking out across the rolling landscape. Samuel's head was throbbing. He sat unsteadily in the saddle and looked toward the sparkling patch of water glimpsed through a grove of willows and scrub oaks and cottonwoods and decided he'd found the perfect place for a man to take his rest. No doubt Tullock and Arbitha were already distraught over Sam's two-day absence. Maybe if his father worried a little more, Tullock might just learn to accept his son's advice and listen to reason instead of a fretful, though well-meaning, woman.

Sam turned off the road to Honey Ridge and rode down to the riverbank, dismounted, and, as an afterthought, tugged off his boots and socks and eased his sore feet into the nearest eddying pool. He sighed aloud as cool water washed over his callused toes. The wild grasses beneath him cushioned his bony frame. The young man reclined upon the earth and let the peacefulness soothe his soul. He tilted his hat forward to shield his eyes from the slanting sunbeams and, yawning, went to sleep.

He dreamed of willing ladies and laughter, of cards upon a table and Enos Clem, shaking his head and laying down three treys that beat Sam's two pair, kings and tens. Enos Clem grinned and reached across the table to rake in his winnings.

"You lose," he said. The voice sounded as if it

issued from a cavern or sinkhole, reverberating in tone as it echoed Sam's defeat. "You lose . . . lose . . . lose."

A boot in the ribs jolted Sam awake. He gave a start, then sat upright and scrambled to his bare feet.

"Wha—" he sputtered. "What?" He blinked and rubbed a hand over his face, shivered, and peered around at the man who had interrupted his sleep.

Hud Pardee brushed the trail dust from his black frock coat, which parted to reveal his ruffled gray shirt, string tie, and the black satin sash at his waist. One Navy Colt rode butt-forward, tucked inside his waistband. He held a second revolver gripped in his right hand, pointed at the ground.

"Hud . . . What are you doing out here?" Sam asked. His headache had lessened, but his chest muscles were sore from coughing. The fresh air seemed to do him good, however, and his spasms were coming less frequently. He hurriedly dried his feet and pulled on his boots. "Thought I'd take a little rest. China and the others plumb wore me out." He grinned, and finished with his boots and straightened. He wore a butternut-colored short coat, dark brown woolen trousers, and a collarless, cream-colored shirt whose blousy sleeves were held off his wrists by black garters around his biceps. He appeared not to notice the gunman's drawn revolver. "But what *are* you doing here?"

"Looking for you. Lucky, I spotted your horse or I'd have passed by."

"What do you want to see me about? I left my promissory note with Cap Featherstone."

"Indeed you did," Hud said. "But I have more important matters to discuss. I could not help but overhear your remarks about Tullock and how you want to keep him from the council." Hud smiled. "I think I've come up with the perfect idea. What if some of the Yankee sympathizers struck at our men?" He reached behind him and dug his hood from the saddlebag. Sam instantly recognized the emblem and reached out to touch the fabric.

"Hud Pardee, now, that's hard to believe. You've been calling the Knights together all this time . . ."

"Cap would have come along, but he's too tired and too damn fat to sit a horse," Hud chuckled. "But never you mind. Your pa will change his mind when he sees what the abolitionists have done. Yessir, just as soon as he finds the body he'll forget everything else but revenge."

Sam shifted nervously. He still did not understand. "Whose body?"

"Yours," said Hud, and raised his gun and shot Samuel Roberts once, twice to be certain, and a third time just for fun.

Chapter Twenty-seven

Mixed-breed and full-blood came to the Council House at Chahta Creek from as near as next door and as far as three hours' hard ride. They came by horse or buckboard or carriage. Many were hard-scrabble farmers, some were masters of large cotton plantations, while others were ranchers, cattlemen from west of the Texas road. And the citizens of Chahta Creek were not to be left out. More than twenty families were represented at the council. Carmichael Ross had been the first person to arrive at the meeting house, and she had taken it upon herself to fill all the oil lanterns and see they were properly lit. Two large storm lanterns were hung to either side of the front door on the outside wall where they could illuminate the front walk and the oaken door.

Carmichael had been so busy with preparing the Council House, she never noticed Jesse until he walked through the front door, the second person to arrive. His bootheels rapped on the wood floor of the meeting room, announcing his presence, and Carmichael breathed a sigh of relief to see him. She was optimistic about his chances for success. Jesse's father had negotiated many private and personal disputes and had the reputation of a peacemaker. Like his father, Jesse was determined to prevent the Choctaws from becoming embroiled in the civil conflict splitting the nation. Carmichael knew there were men of reason and good conscience on both sides of the fence, and she hoped the peacemaker's son could appeal to their better natures.

For Jesse it had been an arduous ride from Buffalo Creek. He arrived sore and stiff and in a foul mood. But as the townsfolk began to arrive at the Council House, his aches faded and his spirits began to rise. Gip and Libby Whitfield rode up to the meetinghouse in a rough-riding flatbed wagon. Gip took note of Jesse's bruises as he climbed off the bench seat and helped Libby down.

"Evening, Captain McQueen," Gip said. "What happened to you?" Libby patted dust from the hem of her coarsely woven cotton dress. The pale blue material looked gray in the lamplight.

"I fell off my horse," Jesse said.

"Oh? How many times?"

"Only once. But I had help." Jesse grinned. The two men took a moment to size up one another.

Round-cheeked, sweetly disposed Libby Whitfield put her arm in Gip's. "I hope you don't mind us being here, Jesse."

The Union captain had learned of Gip's former involvement with the Texas volunteers from Raven, who had also explained that the Rebel cavalryman had forsaken his regiment to remain with the woman he had come to love more than life, duty, or personal honor.

"I said everyone is welcome and that's what I meant. Everyone," he told her. He offered Gip his hand and Whitfield, no longer expecting the worst, relaxed and shook Jesse's hand. Then the Whitfields went inside and were followed by another group

from town. Linc Graywater had closed down his
forge and ridden up from the north end of town to join
Mary Lou Gude as she left her restaurant for the
meeting. The burly blacksmith was more than happy
to relieve his lady love of the heavy reed basket she
was attempting to carry across the street. Jesse made
no effort to hide his curiosity as she approached.

"Evening, Jesse. Seems to me folks is always a
sight more peaceable when they have something tasty
in their bellies, so I made a mess of corn fritters and
packed a couple of jars of dark honey that Linc robbed
from a hive he keeps back of the livery stable."

"It's fittin' too," Linc said. "I ate me a fritter just
before leaving Mary Lou's."

"That was mighty thoughtful of you, Mary Lou,"
Jesse told her. A gust of wind out of the north chased
a pile of leaves along the street. Linc turned in the
direction of Turtle Mountain. If a storm came, it
would glimmer lightning and outline the black ridge
in shimmering flashes of electric energy. He sniffed
the air.

"Winter's coming. I smell rain." He shook his
shaggy head. "Maybe I should've brought my horses in
from the corral."

"We'll be finished before it hits," Jesse reassured
him.

Linc shrugged. "All right. But if I hear thunder I'm
heading back to the stable." He nodded to Carmichael
as she emerged from the Council House to stand
alongside Jesse. Unable to resist the aroma of freshly
baked bread, the editor dipped a hand into the basket
and snared a fritter.

"Hey!" Linc protested with a twinkle in his eye.

Carmichael broke the fritter. Steam escaped in the
cool night air. She plopped a morsel into her mouth.

"Well?" Mary Lou asked, waiting for her friend's
judgment.

"I have always believed the pen is mightier than

the sword," Carmichael said. "But the skillet may be mightier than them both."

Mary Lou beamed. She loved compliments and turned to slap her suitor on the forearm. "See. Now, why can't you think up nice compliments like that?"

"Ain't nothin' more eloquent to a good cook than a man's hearty appetite. Ain't that right, Jesse?"

McQueen held up his hands in mock surrender. "I'll ride clear of that question, Linc. I've troubles enough." He stood aside and allowed the couple to enter. Jesse walked into the street and looked toward the bridge over the Kimishi River, but there was no sign of Tullock Roberts or any of the riders from Honey Ridge.

"People are beginning to get restless, Jesse," said Carmichael. "T. Alan's managed to quiet them by leading a prayer, but once he's finished . . ."

"I know," Jesse said. He returned to the Council House, stepped inside, and walked down the side aisle toward the table up front. The room was warm from the press of bodies.

"And so, heavenly Father, we ask your blessings on this gathering," Parson Marshal Booth intoned with head bowed and Bible in hand. "We ask that you grant us wisdom in our endeavors and patience for one another. Amen."

Everyone echoed "Amen" whether they meant it or not and then all eyes were fixed on Jesse. He noticed that the abolitionists and those loyal to the Union dominated the benches toward the front of the room, while the townsfolk and planters with Confederate sympathies congregated at the rear of the room.

Booth glanced past Jesse, then leaned forward and whispered, "Where's Tullock?"

"Not arrived yet," Jesse said. He repeated his news aloud for his audience. "I know there are some among you who expected to see Tullock Roberts here and I appreciate your concern. Out of respect for my friend I shall delay what I've come to propose until Tullock arrives."

"I don't see why we need to wait on that slaver," one of the townsmen said from up front.

"Yeah. Tullock acts like he's the Lord Almighty and we're to jump whenever he puts his foot down," another man added.

"You talk mighty bold when he ain't here," one of the men from the back called out.

"It's still a free country," Albert Teel said. "And it will remain so long after the Confederacy lies in ruins."

"Long live Jefferson Davis and Stand Watie. Down with Mr. Lincoln!"

"The devil take Johnny Reb!"

A group of men from either faction stood and glared across the room at one another, their hands curled into fists.

"Go ahead. Don't stop. Grab for your guns. Kill yourselves. If what's what you want to do, then get on with it!" Jesse shouted above the din. Both sides turned to watch him.

"And when the gunsmoke clears, what will you have left? Widows and orphans struggling to make a go of the little they have?"

"You're a Yankee. Why should they listen to you?"

Jesse recognized the voice. It belonged to Hud Pardee. The gunman had slipped unnoticed into the room. He was flanked by Shug Jones and Dobie Johnson. Pardee hooked his thumbs in his waist sash. People shifted in their seats to watch him. Jesse also spied Lucius Minley in the shadows near the door. The banker seemed anxious to keep from calling attention to himself. And there was Enos Clem, a most disconcerting participant.

"It's true I am a captain in the Union army. I've

also been appointed territorial ranger. But I'm here now as Jesse McQueen, the son of Ben McQueen. I am here as one of you." Jesse looked around the room, making eye contact with as many of the townspeople as he could.

"I'll hear what Jesse has to say," Henri Medicine Fox said, rising to his feet. With his wife and children back at the hotel, safe behind locked doors, Henri felt free to stand and make his presence known.

"Ever since Kit McQueen married the daughter of Chief Iron Hand, his family has bound its fortune to the Choctaw Nation. We are brothers here." Henri studied the faces of those around him. "All of us, brothers, sisters—we are one with each other. Let us listen to what one of our own has come to tell us."

The gathering quieted. Henri turned and nodded to Jesse as if to say "I owed you that," and then he returned to his seat.

"My friends—" Jesse said. For all the eloquence that might have been his, he got no further. Once again someone interrupted him, this time a friend. Carmichael Ross stepped inside the meetinghouse, her features pale and eyes wide with alarm.

"Jesse!"

The tone of her voice galvanized him into action. He excused himself and hurried along the side aisle as the rest of his audience stood and began to amble toward the door. They were curious to see what had alarmed the newspaperwoman. The gathering emerged in twos and threes, spilling out into Main Street. Jesse had to shoulder his way through the crowd until at last he reached the boardwalk. He gulped a lungful of cool north breeze and made his way to the front of the throng that was gathering around Carmichael Ross and the three new arrivals. Parson Marshal T. Alan Booth appeared at Jesse's side. His features were pale and serious. Like Jesse, he figured something bad had happened. He was unprepared for just how bad.

Cap Featherstone sat astride a chestnut stallion. His frock coat was dusty and the knees of his trousers were mud-soaked. He spied Jesse and motioned for him to come forward. The other horseman was Sawyer Truett, sitting motionless astride his mount. The overseer's eyes narrowed as he watched Jesse, and his gun hand trembled, not from fear but from his efforts to restrain himself. He wanted to draw his revolver and avenge his earlier humiliations at McQueen's expense. Common sense held his anger in check—not to mention the Colt revolving shotgun cradled in the parson marshal's left arm.

Between the two horsemen, Tullock Roberts was perched on the bench seat of a buckboard. He stared straight ahead, as if focused on that which was beyond the comprehension of the townspeople gathered around him.

"You better see this," Cap said, indicating the wagonbed. Jesse walked up to the wheel and peered over the side and looked down at the remains of Samuel Roberts. He looked like a broken doll, his limbs lifeless and his eyes closed. Three black bulletholes dotted the front of the dead man's shirt, which was caked with dried blood.

"His riderless horse showed up at Honey Ridge," Sawyer Truett solemnly explained. "Mr. Roberts and me checked at the Medicine Wagon and then backtracked looking for him. Cap was kind enough to join us. It was him that found Sam."

"I was sorely grieved to make the discovery," Cap interjected. "He was stretched out by the banks of the Kimishi not far from town." He reached in his coat and brought out a bottle of elixir, uncorked it, and took a long pull. By now, T. Alan Booth had seen the dead man, as had several others, and word was quickly spreading through the crowd of onlookers.

"You'll take me out there," the parson marshal told Cap. "Don't you worry, Mr. Roberts, I'll find whoever did this."

"I already know who killed Samuel," Tullock said in a distant voice as if he were trying to remove himself from this tragedy. His powerful frame shifted on the seat and the metal leaf spring creaked beneath him. He held up a small white sheet of paper, a little larger than a playing card. He saw Carmichael Ross standing close-by and handed her the note.

"You read it. You're a woman of many words. Read these. They were pinned to my boy's chest by his killer." His voice was bleak as gray mist, cold as an open grave. When she wavered he repeated, "Read it!"

Carmichael flinched, glanced at the faces of the people surrounding her. It was obvious they waited to hear. She proceeded, haltingly at first, then in a loud, clear voice.

"Thus shall perish all enemies of the Union. Beware, you Knights, Rebels, and Enslavers, your hour of reckoning is at hand."

Jesse walked along the wagon and took the note from Carmichael, read it to himself, then shook his head.

"Tullock, this note proves nothing."

"It does to me," Tullock retorted, the anger rising in him. "It proves you killed him," he said to Jesse. "And you." He looked at Carmichael. "And any of you that sides with these Federals. All of you killed my boy, the same as if you pulled the trigger!"

"Now see here, Tullock," Booth said, approaching the front of the wagon. Here was dangerous talk that needed to be immediately curtailed.

"No. You see! Take a good look!" Tullock's volume increased and his tone grew harsh, and the hatred that welled in him was all-consuming and as endless as death. "I shall go among my wife's people, the Cherokee and the Creek, and they will gather with those Choctaw I call friend and together we will avenge my son. Chahta Creek, the Kimishi River, Buffalo Creek will flow red with blood before I'm through."

Tullock stood and, with whip in hand, looked over the gathering. Then hauling on the reins he cracked the whip and turned his team of horses, circled his wagon, and headed back the way he came. Sawyer Truett rode proudly at his side.

The crowd of spectators began to disperse. Several men headed for their horses. Tullock Roberts was their man; they shared his outrage and would support his hunger for revenge.

Jesse watched helplessly as the plantation owner departed with more than half the people who had come to the council. They might have held together for Ben McQueen, but his son . . . that was another matter.

"Looks like your luck's played out this time," a voice said.

Jesse turned and faced Enos Clem. The gambler's lip curled in a smug sneer as he stood behind the Union captain. He lifted his coat flaps to show he wasn't armed. Then he walked back up the street and was joined after a few paces by Dobie Johnson and Hud Pardee. The one-eyed gunman from Natchez licked his fingertips, flashed Jesse a contemptuous smile, and joined the others.

"Don't take it so hard, younker," Cap said, leaning down from horseback to clap Jesse on the shoulder. "You tried. I doubt your father could have done any better, God rest his soul." Cap started his horse toward the north end of town. "Stop by and have a drink later, on the house."

Jesse nodded, but he didn't mean it. He looked at the Council House, empty now.

"What will you do?" Carmichael asked.

"My orders were to try and forge a bond of peace between the tribal nations. Failing that, I am to lead these abolitionists north into Union-controlled Kansas where they'll be safe from Confederate harassment."

The north wind gathered the leaves and sent them swarming down Main Street in a sudden gust like an attacking army. They swirled about the legs of the townspeople then rushed onward, given life by the wind, charging blind and dashing themselves against the battlements of night.

It was nature's own foreshadowing of the battle to come.

"So be it," said Jesse McQueen. Despite his efforts, the Choctaw Nation was at war.

PART THREE

Rage at Sundown

Chapter Twenty-eight

Tullock Roberts had been gone for over a week, and Sawyer Truett was anxious for the master of Honey Ridge to return with his promised reinforcements. Sawyer wasn't the kind of man who took lightly to waiting. But he didn't see that he had any choice. Although the Knights were willing to confront the Federal loyalists now that many of the families had gathered for protection out at Buffalo Creek, Sawyer and his compatriots were reticent about attempting any sort of raid. The odds were none too favorable. At the present, the forces were approximately equal. However, Tullock promised to return with forty or fifty men, and with such a force added to the Choctaw Knights, Sawyer could envision them sweeping over McQueen's column of abolitionists. Sawyer had never been close to Jesse, but Pacer Wolf was another matter, and it pained him that the Choctaw Kid had not joined his brothers of the Golden Circle. He continued to hope the youngest McQueen would see the error of his ways.

It was a damp and drizzly night and Sawyer was anxious to be out of the elements. However, as overseer his duty was to make the rounds of the plantation to ensure that everything was properly in order and the men he posted as sentries were awake and at their posts. As far as Sawyer was concerned, this corner of the Indian Territory was at war and he wasn't taking any chances.

He approached the darkened smokehouse to the rear of the manor and called out in a hoarse whisper. "Chris . . . Chris . . . get on to the kitchen and send Buck out here."

A caped figure detached itself from the darkness of the smokehouse. Sawyer nodded, satisfied that Chris could still be trusted to remain alert. Buck Langdon was something else entirely. The hungry rascal couldn't stay out of the kitchen, especially whenever Willow Reaves was about. Buck made no secret of his growing interest in the sweet-natured mulatto, and with Tullock gone from the plantation Buck felt freer than ever to press his advances. Sawyer generally tried to ignore the whole situation. The mulatto was on her own. Sawyer's chief concern was that Buck pulled his share of sentry duty, and that meant the watch from midnight to daybreak.

"You tell Buck to move his fat ass along. I want to get on around to the front to see if Johnny's awake," Sawyer explained as the sentry continued on to him. Chris had yet to make any reply.

"Everything clear along the back road? Did you see anyone?" Sawyer asked as his friend drew close and threw back his cape, tilted the brim of his hat, and poked a gun in the overseer's ribs.

"He didn't see a thing," Jesse said.

"Son of a bitch!" Sawyer reached for his gun, then felt the iron muzzle of Jesse's Dragoon Colt press against his Adam's apple. He froze. Someone grabbed his wrists and bound them at the small of his back, slipped a gag around his head, and then led him over to the smokehouse where he was forced to lie down alongside the bound and gagged form of Chris Foot. Chris was a full-blood. It should have been impossible for anyone to sneak up on the Choctaw and get the drop on him. But Jesse McQueen had done it. Sawyer cursed himself for underestimating his adversary. He stared malevolently at Jesse as someone securely tied his feet together and left him on his belly. Jesse knelt by the overseer's side.

"If you try to escape or cause any commotion, I'll come back and crack your skull. Do you understand?"

Sawyer nodded. Jesse McQueen had the upper hand for now. Sawyer burned with anger and shame and swore that one day . . . one day . . .

"Hey, darlin'," Buck said, elbows on the long wooden kitchen table. He was watching Willow trim a pie. It was foolish to be making apple pies at midnight, but Arbitha had told her to have one prepared by morning because Arbitha was certain, simply certain, that Tullock would be home sometime during the morning. Willow didn't ask the poor woman how she knew. Arbitha Roberts was out of her head with grief over the death of her son. Willow, despite her years of servitude at the hand of this family, could not bring herself to hate Arbitha. In truth, she was moved to pity for the matriarch of Honey Ridge. If Arbitha needed a pie for morning, then so be it.

"Darlin', why don't you come on over here and sit on my lap? It'd be a sight more comfortable than standin'. And my lap is mighty warm. You could shuck that apron and all them clothes and still be plenty warm."

"Mr. Langdon, how you carry on," Willow said, hoping to make light of the situation.

"Girl, I'm serious." Buck finished his coffee, set the cup aside, and patted his lap. "C'mon over here and sit a spell."

"No sir." Willow glanced toward the door to the

dining room, then to the back door which was closer to her.

Buck glanced over his shoulder to see if Mrs. Roberts had entered the dining room. He saw no one. He was between her and the rest of the house.

"Yes, ma'am, I know what you're thinkin'. But Mrs. Roberts is upstairs. She ain't gonna be any help at all. I reckon you could run outside, but it's cold and damp, and why chance catchin' your death of the croup when you got a warm cozy spot right here?" He patted his thighs and tried his most winning smile. When that didn't work, he sighed and his gaze hardened.

"You know, I can take what I want or you can give it."

"Leave me alone," Willow told him. She held up the paring knife with which she had been trimming the pie crust. The weapon looked pitifully small.

Buck shook his head and rose from the table. "Now, that ain't a proper way for a lady to act. Of course, you ain't no lady. Just some nigra's woman and even he run out on you. How long has it been? Me and Sam used to ruminate on just how ripe you were."

She began backing toward the door. "Miss Roberts!" she yelled. "Miss Roberts!"

Buck flinched as if struck. He hadn't expected her to call out. He lunged for Willow. She twisted aside and darted to the back door. Buck leaped an overturned bench and lost his balance, stumbled, glanced off a shelf of preserves, and sent a row of mason jars crashing to the floor. He caught a glimpse of Willow as she dashed through the open doorway. He regained his balance and cleared a spreading puddle of scuppernong jelly, leaped through the doorway and straight into a hard black fist that spun him three-quarters of the way around, knocked two teeth out of his mouth, and dropped him in the dirt.

Willow was half a dozen yards from the back of the house. She lost a shoe but never a stride. Lithe as a doe, she ran flat out until she was stopped by a word spoken by one she had loved and still loved.

"Wife!"

Willow slid in the soft earth and spun around. Her hand fluttered to her mouth as she gasped and stared with amazement at Si Reaves, outlined in the deep glow streaming through the kitchen door. Unable to believe her own eyes, she faltered, then ran to his arms. They held one another for a long silent moment.

"I told you I'd come for you. I said I would," Si whispered in her ear.

"And I waited. And I never gave up watchin'," Willow tearfully replied. She peered over his shoulder and glimpsed someone in the shadows. She stiffened and tightened her hold on her husband, then relaxed as Jesse McQueen stepped into the kitchen's glare.

"Willow . . . what was that crash? Did you call me?" Arbitha Roberts had entered the kitchen and had yet to realize anything was amiss.

"You two go on," Jesse said. "See if any of the others wish to join us."

"Where we going?" Willow asked, keeping her voice low.

"To freedom, gal. To freedom," Si told her. "With Jesse and them families that took a stand against holding our people in chains."

"I'll join you down by the shanties," Jesse said, and walked up the steps to the back door. Si nodded, and tugged Willow's arm and led her off into the night.

Jesse made his way into the kitchen. It was warm here and fragrant with the aroma of pies and bread and the cloying scent of spilled jellies and preserves. Jesse began to sweat inside his heavy blue woolen shirt and buckskin jacket.

Arbitha had wrapped a beige dressing gown

around her ample frame. Her thick black ringlets were tangled as if she had been asleep in bed only moments ago.

"Willow?" she called in a weak voice. "Oh," she said, noticing Jesse at last. "It's you."

"Willow is gone, Arbitha." Jesse eased into the room and cautiously approached the table. His fears of alarming the woman were wholly ungrounded; she did not seem frightened at all. Jesse had come to the plantation often enough as a boy and been warmly received by her. Now, the tragic death of her son had left Arbitha all but living in the past, a fantasy created out of her own desperate denial.

"I heard Willow calling me. Is she all right?"

"Yes, ma'am. But she won't be returning. Si has taken her away."

"Oh my. That is alarming. I shall miss her, but I don't blame the child. Still, what shall I do?"

"You'll get by, Arbitha. I'm sorry about Samuel. Tullock doesn't believe me, but I am."

"Tullock doesn't believe in anything right now but the hurt in his soul," Arbitha said. She patted the wrinkles from her dressing gown and primped her hair. "I look a fright. I've been so tired lately. My boy is dead and my arms feel so empty now. I used to carry him around like a lump on my back when he was little." She shook her head, refusing any more of the memories. The portion she had was already too much. "You're taking folks up north."

"Yes, ma'am," Jesse replied. "But they'll return when this cursed war is ended. Maybe people can learn to live as neighbors again."

"My husband will come after you." Arbitha had no doubt but that Tullock Roberts would exact bloody revenge upon Jesse and the other abolitionists. He was driven by the Old Testament admonition of "an eye for an eye" and a "tooth for a tooth."

And a life for a life—or many lives.

"He'll destroy you," she added with utter certainty.

"He can try." Jesse remained uncowed by Arbitha's dire prediction. He'd struggled for peace with all his might. He waged war the same way.

"Good-bye, Mrs. Roberts. Take care."

"Good-bye, Jesse McQueen," Arbitha said in a frail voice. She sat near the oven and peered in at the flames whose lurid glare played upon her sorrowful features. "Willow, bring me the sherry, that's a good dear. I should like some sherry to help me sleep. Willow—" She looked around and found herself alone in the kitchen. Jesse was gone. Maybe he hadn't really been here at all. So many ghosts had visited her lately. Oh Lord, so many ghosts. What had Jesse said? And where had Willow wandered off to?

"I'll have to speak to that girl," Arbitha mumbled to herself. To her broken . . . hearted . . . self.

Chapter Twenty-nine

That same night, in Chahta Creek, a departure of a different sort was taking place. Lucius Minley sat hunched over his desk in his house on Choctaw Street, his thin face looking sallow in the glow of the lamp. He was hurriedly writing, his pen scratching the surface of the pages on which he scrawled an account, not only of his own actions over the past months but those of Cap Featherstone, those he had personally witnessed and those Cap had alluded to. He paused and a look of alarm came to his face as he heard some commotion in the alley. He listened for a moment. Was that the sound of breaking glass? A dog began to bark, then abruptly quit. He forced the interruption from his mind and continued to outline Cap Featherstone's conspiracy and the manner in which he had used an already volatile situation to his own advantage.

Again Lucius paused and read what he had written so far. It was precise and factual, clear cut, and wholly incriminating of himself and most especially Featherstone and his associates. Missing were the motives Lucius knew had brought him to this impasse.

He had loved a woman who had driven him to *be* more, to *aspire* to more. Yes, his own personal ambition and greed had been part of it, but he would have never acted without his wife's insistence. She had encouraged his involvement with the likes of Featherstone. But the price of power and wealth had begun to weigh heavy on Lucius's soul. Falsifying bank records to show Cap paid considerably more for properties than he actually had was one thing. But to be a part of murder . . .

He stood and walked to the door of his study and was tempted for a moment to return to his bedroom, to lie down by Rose and take her in his arms. No. She was still angry with him for not standing up to Cap Featherstone. She had called him weak. The saloon-keeper was taking advantage of them both, she reiterated, and if Lucius had any backbone he would demand a larger share of the profits to be made after the war. Without the banker's complicity, Cap had no legal way of acquiring the land he sought. Lucius was integral to the scheme. Featherstone certainly did not have enough funds to purchase the notes the bank was carrying.

Lucius frowned and returned to his desk. For a moment he had actually been tempted to confront Cap. Thankfully, common sense took over, fueled by the memory of his latest encounter with him earlier in the day. The saloonkeeper hadn't offered so much as a Yankee dollar for the deed to the Choctaw House Hotel. Lucius had advanced Henri Medicine Fox three hundred dollars and promised to hold ownership of the hotel until the end of hostilities, when Henri intended to return with his family to the business he had built with his own two hands.

"Henri Medicine Fox is a friend," Lucius had protested.

"He isn't *my* friend," Cap had replied, pacing the confines of the banker's office. His massive girth stirred the air and rustled the papers on Minley's desk everytime he crossed in front of the banker. "Sign the transfer of ownership. Mark down I paid the bank four thousand."

"My God. The bank will need some funds to operate with. Why, I've even fired the tellers and am doing everything myself. You agreed to provide me with enough funds to do business. I've barely two hundred dollars in the safe."

"Lucius, you have an annoying habit of arguing with me," Cap had said. He'd stopped pacing and leaned forward using his massive arms for support. His thick ugly features had been inches from the banker's face. Even two hours later, Lucius could still smell the saloonkeeper's breath.

"Do as you're told." Cap had straightened and shoved the documents in front of Lucius. "Let's get this over with. I've wasted enough time here. One day you'll thank me. When this town builds back up, that hotel will be a real money-making venture and you'll have a share of it. That is, if you can keep from talking yourself into an early grave."

Now in the quiet of the midnight hour, amid his home's familiar and comfortable surroundings, Lucius closed his eyes and watched himself do Featherstone's bidding. There had been no other way. Not then. But Lucius had glimpsed something in Cap's eyes; for one brief second he had beheld his own death. There would come a time when Cap would no longer need him and what then? What could Lucius expect from one who had arranged the death of his own friend, Ben McQueen?

So you see, Jesse, my motives in this are not entirely unselfish. As Cap murdered your father so will my life also be forfeit, of that I have no doubt now. My only recourse is to flee and put as much distance as possible between Featherstone and myself. Greed and lust were my undoing. I cannot make amends for my wrongs, but I can at least tell you who your enemy is and in saving your life perhaps save my own.

Lucius signed the letter, placed it inside an oil-skin packet, secured it with a leather string, and weighted the packet with a fist-sized stone. He did not intend to personally deliver his confession to Jesse McQueen out at Buffalo Creek. But Lucius knew someone who would—Carmichael Ross. He scrawled Jesse's name on a slip of paper and tucked it inside the leather string, then hefted the entire thing in his right hand. He saw no problem in pitching the stone through a window in Carmichael's house. He'd be blocks away before she could light a lantern and step outside.

Well on his way. Lucius liked that thought. He stood and tucked the packet in his coat pocket, lifted a black barrister's satchel which contained the few remaining funds taken from the bank's safe. He had robbed his own bank. The very notion made him giggle. He wished he could see Cap's face when the saloonkeeper learned—no—Cap's was the last face he'd ever want to see after tonight.

His horse was saddled and waiting out back. It was time to cut his losses. His gaze drifted to the stairway.

"Bye, Rose," he whispered. Then he crept from the house. Somewhere, back East, away from the war and this uncivilized country, a new life waited. He intended to find it.

In her bedroom, Rose Minley stirred in her sleep, reached out and rested her hand upon the empty pillow beside her, and then began ever so gently to snore.

Chapter Thirty

At a quarter past eight on the morning of October 16, Tullock Roberts led his command of forty-four volunteers across Chahta Creek and into town. They had ridden most of the night to get there by morning. He'd been pushing his men hard for several days now and they deserved a rest. He'd give them the day. Word had reached him that Jesse McQueen had gathered the abolitionists at Buffalo Creek and was preparing to take them north. McQueen was a fool. No matter where the abolitionists attempted to escape, Roberts's Knights could easily overtake a bunch of frightened Yankees in mule-drawn wagons. If they chose to make a stand, so much the better. With the Yankees outnumbered and outgunned, his men would sweep over the column and destroy it.

The patriarch of Honey Ridge rode up Main Street. The men behind him were a hard-looking bunch dressed in a mixture of buckskins and Confederate military attire. Some wore short-brimmed caps, others broad-brimmed gray flannel hats and waist-length coats. There were Creeks with close-cropped hair and Cherokees whose long black locks hung free and trailed in the wind like the manes of the horses they rode. These men rode with Tullock because they shared his allegiance to the Confederacy. Several of the volunteers were related to Arbitha, herself the product of a Cherokee father and a Creek mother. Bloodlines, however strained, were ties impossible to ignore. When word spread of the murder of Arbitha's only son at the hands of abolitionists, that was reason enough to fight at Tullock's side.

The street was empty except for a pair of mongrel hounds that eyed the company of armed men with extreme misgiving and then scampered off toward the nearest alley. At a signal from the man in command, the armed company halted in front of the *Chahta Creek Courier*, one of the few businesses along Main Street that had not been abandoned.

Carmichael Ross was inside. And she was in a bad mood. The editor had been awakened just after midnight by a rock crashing through her bedroom window. She'd picked her way through the glass and reached the windowsill, pistol in hand, in time to catch a glimpse of the culprit responsible as he galloped off in the direction of the river road, south of town.

She'd stepped on the oilskin-wrapped packet on her way back to bed and read by moonlight the hastily scrawled instructions. Carmichael didn't understand why she had been chosen as Jesse's personal mail carrier, but she hoped it was worth the price of her bedroom window.

Now in the office of the *Courier*, she tucked the packet in her saddlebag as Tullock's raiders formed out in front of the newspaper and she heard her name called in a booming voice by Tullock Roberts.

"Carmichael Ross! *Carmichael Ross!*"

The woman glanced toward the window and the horsemen crowding the street. Tendrils of steam drifted up from her tin coffee cup. The grounds had been boiled twice and then mixed with dried berries and wild herbs to make a particularly nasty morning beverage which only a healthy dollop of rye whiskey made palatable.

A second cup clinked as the man seated in the office with her drained his cup. With Gude's Good Eats all boarded up, there had been few places where T. Alan Booth might take his breakfast. In the company of an old friend seemed a natural choice.

"You were right," Booth said. "Tullock came here first thing. Reckon he doesn't appreciate your 'Yankee' bias."

The parson marshal slid his chair back, stood, and started toward the door. He tucked the flap of his frock coat behind the holstered revolver on his right.

"T. Alan, what are you doing?" Carmichael asked.

"Upholding the law," he replied.

"Look through the window. Take a good look. They're the law now."

He hesitated, pondering her words of warning. Booth was not the kind of man to back down from trouble. But he was also a realist. Ordinarily he might have tried to run a bluff on the armed men in the street. But Tullock Roberts had lost a son and was out for revenge and did not care what the cost.

"Only two things in this office can't be replaced. You . . . and me." She rose from her chair and caught him by the arm and shifted her gaze to the door at the rear of the office.

"I've a couple of horses out back," she added, then held up the packet that had so rudely crashed through her window and ruined her morning.

"We can deliver this to Jesse and find out what's

so important that someone had to break my window." Carmichael was tempted to find out for herself if only she hadn't been cursed with a pesky sense of honor. However, once she placed the packet in Jesse's hands, nothing was going to stop her from looking over his shoulder while he read it.

Carmichael reached the back door, eased it open, and saw the alley was clear. Across the alley was a small, rudely constructed barn that needed a coat of paint and some fresh timber to replace patches of rotted siding. She had never gotten around to having the structure repaired. Now it didn't matter.

"C'mon, T. Alan. Now is *not* a good day to die."

The parson marshal wrestled with his pride. At last common sense prevailed. He followed Carmichael into the alley. By the time they rode out of the barn Tullock had loosed half a dozen men inside the newspaper office and they were having themselves a time, overturning trays of type, hammering the press, smashing furniture, and tossing the last of the paper into the street. The *Chahta Creek Courier* might be out of business but, riding a swift horse into the morning sun, Carmichael Ross was already planning her first edition when the day came to print again.

Cap Featherstone appeared nonplussed by the turn of events as he waited on the top step in front of the Medicine Wagon Saloon. Cap had never looked finer in his brown frock coat and gold brocaded vest, his bandanna made from the same material as his vest. He leaned upon his sword cane and studied a circling hawk over Turtle Mountain. He hummed "Sweet Betsy from Pike" and tapped the side of his boot with the cane. The batwing doors behind him creaked on their hinges as Hud Pardee stepped out onto the boardwalk to join his employer. The gunman was not exactly dressed for the trail in dark woolen trousers and ruffled white shirt. His black sash held his guns within easy reach. Excitement gleamed in his cold blue eyes. Enos Clem was the next to appear. His pasty skin seemed even paler today. The gambler had come to realize he'd bought into a game before checking to see how it was played. However, he recognized in the crafty personage of Cap Featherstone a winning hand. He resolved to play along until the turn of the final card.

"Tullock's back . . . and with the men he promised." Enos Clem called over his shoulder into the saloon as Tullock Roberts paraded his command in front of the marshal's office and then turned off Main Street and continued along Sixth toward the imposing, solitary structure of the house that Cap built.

Tullock sensed he and his men were being watched from behind windows and closed doors by townsfolk who professed Confederate sympathies. They were unsure of Roberts's intentions. Not so the father of Samuel Roberts. Tullock knew what needed to be done. And by heaven, he had brought the men to see it through. By the time he reached the Medicine Wagon, a dozen men had filtered out of the saloon and were standing in the middle of Cherokee Street to await the master of Honey Ridge.

"Welcome back, Tullock," Cap said, beaming expansively. "Your boys look thirsty. Hungry, too. There's fixings inside. Help yourself."

"We'll see how welcome," Tullock gruffly remarked. A religious man, he had no use for gamblers and saloon doves. However, the aroma of biscuits and bacon wafting through the doorway was beginning to change his opinion of Featherstone. Cap glanced at Hud, nodded, and faced the vengeful father.

"A man in my profession learns to be a shrewd judge of character. I know what's on your mind," Cap told the plantation owner. "You're wondering just what side of the fence I'm on. You wonder whether my lads and I will ride with you." Cap chuckled, and reached inside his coat and withdrew a saffron-colored hood, a coiled snake stitched above the eyes. "Hell, Mr. Roberts, we've been riding with you all along."

Tullock recognized the hood and relaxed in the saddle. Perhaps he had misjudged Featherstone after all. Suddenly one of the men in the street fidgeted and caught Tullock's attention. The plantation master did a double take, then frowned in recognition.

"Sawyer . . . and Buck Langdon . . . I left you and the other lads at Honey Ridge. What are you doing here?"

Sawyer Truett ran a hand through his oily dark hair, then kicked a dirt clod and scratched at his goatee. It had taken all his courage to come into town and face Tullock Roberts.

"Morning, Mr. Roberts. Me and Buck figured you'd come here first." Sawyer's mouth was dry. A trace of white spittle formed at the corner of his mouth. "We wanted you to hear it from us. Chris and Johnny, they got scared and run off. We stayed to set things aright."

"What the devil are you trying to tell me?" Tullock snapped. "Has something happened to Arbitha?"

"No sir," Sawyer quickly replied. Buck wagged his head behind the overseer. "Jesse would've never done her no harm."

"Jesse McQueen." Tullock spoke the name as one might utter a curse. He had the distinct feeling he wasn't going to like the news Sawyer was so reticent to reveal.

"He and Si Reaves paid a visit. They uh . . . well . . . got the drop on us and took off with the slaves." Once he started, Sawyer spoke quickly to get the worst of it over and be done with it.

"Not everyone took off," Buck Langdon interjected, trying to look on the bright side. "Some of the older coloreds stayed on."

"The older coloreds," Tullock grimly repeated.

"Jesse's probably got them out at Buffalo Creek," Sawyer said. "Reckon they're about ready to push north through Buffalo Gap and follow the Kiamichi trail out of the mountains."

At a signal from Tullock, the men of his command dismounted. Some were assigned to lead the horses to water and hay. The rest crowded through the front of the saloon, where a hot meal and strong drinks were provided on the house. Cap stood aside as the Knights of the Golden Circle jostled past. At last, he and Tullock were face to face once again. Sawyer had remained at Tullock's side.

"What are your plans, Mr. Roberts?" Cap asked.

"To rest my men and their mounts," Tullock replied. He wiped a hand over his square jaw and then rubbed the back of his neck. He was tired, but there'd be time to sleep when the job ahead was finished. "We'll leave in time to bring us to Buffalo Creek by sundown." He spoke plainly, firmly. Though driven by a thirst for revenge, Tullock resolved to take his time. Jesse's column of refugees wasn't going anywhere that Tullock couldn't overtake them. If Jesse and the loyalists tried to run, Tullock would pick them off, wagon by wagon. If they elected to fight, one good charge and the Knights of the Golden Circle would swarm over McQueen and the fools who had followed him to their own destruction. As far as Tullock was concerned, the outcome was inevitable. The ghost of his son cried out from the grave and would not know peace until the blood of his killer soaked the earth. Tullock was not the kind of father to deny his son.

It was simply a matter of time now. Come sundown. Hurry, sundown.

Chapter Thirty-one

After learning from Carmichael Ross of Tullock Roberts's return to Chahta Creek, Jesse McQueen ordered Theotis and Moses Tellico to guide the column of wagons and carts through Buffalo Gap, taking care to keep any stragglers from ending up in the grass-covered traps the brothers had blasted and dug out of the valley floor.

Mixed-blood Choctaws and freed slaves gathered up what belongings they could carry and started up the valley. Si and Willow Reaves and the field hands from Honey Ridge had walked and ridden into the valley with nothing but the ragged homespun clothes on their backs. Another nineteen mouths to feed had put a severe strain on the food rations. Raven, moved to pity the hungry fugitives yearning to be free, had thrown open her larder and the garden she had tended all summer. Peas were gathered, the sweet corn harvested, the smokehouse stripped clean. With the column under way, Jesse took the time to examine the contents of the packet Carmichael had brought him along with Parson Marshal Booth and the news that Tullock

Roberts and the Knights of the Golden Circle were close at hand. Several families had complained that Jesse had delayed departure and invited ruination. Yet such people were reluctant to attempt the journey north on their own despite their outspoken disapproval.

Jesse walked away from the farmhouse and sat on the edge of the oak table where summer dinners had always been held beneath the shading boughs of a red oak. He sat alone, his features rigid, as if etched in stone.

Raven watched him and knew from Jesse's lack of expression that he was upset. She had seen that same look in her husband, Kit, and in her son, Ben, when times were at their worst and desperate measures were in order. Carmichael started past her, but Raven caught her friend by the arm.

"He will tell you what you need to know," she said.

The editor nodded, and waited alongside the older woman. T. Alan Booth paced the ground a few yards behind the women. He was like a stallion chafing at the bit. Nothing had turned out the way he figured. He detested the fact that he had been chased from town, but he could tell he was needed here just by looking at the families hoping to reach the Kansas border. These were storekeepers and merchants and farmers, not soldiers or militiamen. Hack Warner could use a gun. And there went Linc Graywater with Mary Lou Gude. The blacksmith was a capable man and would fight if pushed. Gip Whitfield had been one of the Texas Volunteers and was a fair shot. And the Tellicos were noted for their prowess with knife and gun and had never been known to run from a brawl. Seven seasoned veterans . . . eight if the Choctaw Kid sided with them, which Booth doubted. The rest, especially the freed slaves, even Si

Reaves, were lambs to the slaughter for the likes of Tullock Roberts's night riders unless Captain McQueen had a plan.

Jesse folded the banker's confession, wrapped it in the oilskin and stood, warring with the desire to ride immediately for Chahta Creek and confront Cap Featherstone. He remembered the map of the surrounding territory in Cap's office and the peculiar markings, which Jesse now realized denoted the land Featherstone had surreptitiously acquired. Cap's ambitions had led him to profit on the misery of others and transformed him from Ben McQueen's trusted friend to his would-be assassin.

The air was thick with the dust of the column as wagons, carts, and horses pulled away from the farmhouse and followed Buffalo Creek up between the forested hills that gradually closed in the deeper the trail wound into the mountains. Jesse hesitated and glanced toward his gray gelding, still tethered to the corral fence. It took all his self-control to keep from leaping astride the gray and galloping off toward town and Cap Featherstone.

But the weight of the medal against his chest turned his thoughts from revenge to the duty and responsibility of the column he intended to lead to safety. Cap Featherstone would have to wait. He walked across the yard to Raven and handed the packet to Carmichael Ross.

"You might want to see this," he said to Booth, who moved forward to stand alongside the editor already beginning to read Lucius Minley's incriminating farewell. To Raven he said, "Hack Warner's left with your wagon. You and Lorelei better hurry along in the buggy. I don't want you riding through the gap without one of the Tellicos to show you the way."

"I'm staying here. I won't be driven from my land by Tullock Roberts or anybody else."

"Grandmother . . . do not even start." He caught her by the arm and walked her back toward the house. The buggy had been brought out of the shed by the barn and left in front of the house. Lorelei already sat on the seat with Hecuba planted firmly on her lap. The goose honked and complained at all the commotion and craned its neck to peer around the buggy's black canvas siding. Si Reaves walked his mount, allowing three sweet-faced children to sit astride the animal. Willow walked proudly at his side, and the newly freed slaves behind them began to lift their voices in songs of praise and deliverance that Jesse thought were a trifle premature. He wished he felt as confident. Come sunrise, their songs of thanksgiving might turn to mourning. He was going to need all the help he could get.

Raven was no match for her grandson's strength. She ceased struggling and allowed him to propel her across the yard and right up to the buggy. Without a "by your leave" Jesse lifted Raven in his arms and deposited her alongside Lorelei. He handed the medicine woman the reins and leaned in and kissed her on the cheek.

"Hmmm. It seems you leave me no choice," she sighed.

"None at all," Jesse said. "Don't stop until you reach the gap. One of the Tellicos will lead you through." He looked at Lorelei. "See that she keeps out of mischief."

"I can try," the young woman replied.

"Fair enough." Jesse stepped away from the horse as Raven flicked the reins and guided her spirited dun onto the path left by the advancing column. Carmichael and Parson Marshal Booth rode up to the house. The editor leaned down from horseback and returned the packet to Jesse.

"I never trusted Featherstone," Carmichael said.

"He was a good man once, or so I was told. War changes a man."

"Maybe it just hid what was there all along," Carmichael said.

"I reckon as you'll be heading into Chahta Creek," Booth spoke up. His tone was formal; his sun-darkened visage, framed by a shock of white hair and beard, wore a stern expression.

"After I've dealt with the Knights and Tullock Roberts."

"Yes, of course. I had no doubt but that you'd finish what you started. But afterwards, I should like to ride with you. If you have no objections to a bullheaded lawman tagging along."

"None at all," Jesse said.

The parson marshal pursed his lips a moment, then extended his hand in friendship.

"I'm a little late in this, Jesse, but welcome home." He chuckled as he shook hands with Ben McQueen's eldest son.

Moments later the dust of their departure was settling at Jesse's feet. The Union officer had one final act before he could join the column. He had one final farewell to make, one last reconciliation to attempt.

He shielded his eyes from the glare of the sun and spied the twisting gray tendrils of smoke rising from the top of the knoll behind the house. Pacer knelt by a medicine fire, his long-limbed frame outlined against a brilliant azure sky. His voice drifted on the north wind as he called on the All-Father for guidance. Despite his fair skin and his unbound mane of red hair, he sounded for all the world like a Choctaw warrior praying for guidance, for answers Jesse hoped to supply.

Sunlight dappled the surface of Buffalo Creek. As if strewn with jewels, the watercourse gleamed and sparkled the length of the valley. The wind carried the cool kiss of winter, and formations of geese, ever the precursor of the changing seasons, had begun to appear with regularity over the northern hills. Patches of grass had begun to yellow, and the red oaks trembling in the wind were turning brown and preparing to lose their lustrous foliage.

Jesse climbed the hill behind the house, retracing a well-worn route. How often he had followed this same course to find his grandmother conversing with the spirits. Now he approached his brother, kneeling before a similar prayer smoke. Jesse could not deny that something stirred in his own soul as he took his place alongside his younger brother. Pacer Wolf wore blackleg trousers and cavalry boots, but he had stripped to the waist and his muscular torso bore a single streak of blood where he had slashed his own flesh and added his own blood to the flames.

Jesse picked up a stick and began drawing in the dirt between them. He outlined Buffalo Gap and scrawled in a series of Xs to denote the covered pits.

"I've given the Tellicos instructions to halt the column at the opposite end of the gap. We'll draw the wagons up in a line. The Knights will have to come at us right down the middle. They'll figure we only have time for one volley and then they'll be through our line of defense. The pits will break their charge, confuse them, and allow our gunfire to really do some damage, enough I hope to take the fight out of them. Strung out in a column we'd be at their mercy.

That's why I've been waiting. I'd rather fight Tullock on my own ground. Well, he's coming and I'm going to have to deal with him."

Pacer studied the crude sketch at his side, then looked at his brother. He reached out and cupped the medicine bag that Raven had given him long ago. He had never opened it or examined its contents and he never would.

"My brother, you carry the medal and it is your birthright and your legacy of our family. It is the path you must walk. You have embraced the white truth and I, the red truth."

"You don't know me as well as you think," Jesse said. "Nor do you know yourself. Daniel Pacer Wolf McQueen . . . Jesse Redbow McQueen . . . see it in our names. We hold both truths, my brother. Deny one and you can never be more than half a man. I know that now. I can love my country and fight to preserve it and still hear the spirits whisper in the wind, still be a seeker of visions, still find magic among the bones of the rain." Jesse reached out and placed his hand upon his brother's shoulder. "I need you, little brother. When the Knights of the Golden Circle charge down that valley, I shall need the Choctaw Kid."

"It is not my fight."

"Yes, it is," Jesse retorted. "Because these are women and children, storekeepers and farmers, innocent folk just like at *Lawrence*."

The Choctaw Kid gave a start as if he'd been slapped across the face. The allusion to Quantrill's raid achieved the desired effect. Memories flooded back. The pain of being a part of that debacle and the shame. How many times had he replayed the incident in his mind and tried to stop it from happening, to halt the guerrillas' onslaught? One could never undo past mistakes. But Pacer could stop that past from repeating itself. He'd been looking to the flames for an answer. Maybe it was time he looked to himself.

He studied Jesse, and the haunted expression left his face to be replaced by a hint of a smile. "It will be like old times," Pacer said.

In that moment, Jesse knew he had his brother back. He reached inside his coat and handed Pacer the banker's handwritten confession. The McQueens had a common enemy now. "Old times," said Jesse.

Chapter Thirty-two

In the waning afternoon, the western horizon became awash with scarlet and gold light while high wispy clouds turned to lurid pink like a puckered wound. A man didn't need to talk to spirits to sense the foreboding in the air.

A gunshot reverberated the length of the narrowing passage. It was a signal from Gip Whitfield stationed at the opposite end of the pass and it meant the Knights of the Golden Circle were in the valley.

The men behind the wagon barricade halted in midsentence or straightened where they dozed, and came alert and studied their backtrail as a horseman who could only be Gip Whitfield made his way through the gap, taking care to keep close to the hills and skirting the traps that subtly patched the floor of the pass.

Jesse McQueen froze for a moment, turned to Pacer at his side, and said, "Now it begins." Then he continued along the length of the wagon barricade searching for any weak spots in his makeshift defenses. The fortifications weren't exactly formidable. Success depended on confusion and blunting the night riders' initial charge. On the hillsides well out of the line of battle, families had gathered in groups of a half-dozen or more to share food and the warmth of campfires. The townsfolk were nervous. The freed slaves even more so. Everyone had heard Gip's signal, and a pall of quiet had fallen over the camp.

The McQueen brothers made an incongruous pair to be sure. Pacer wore the gray and black uniform of a Rebel raider, while Jesse had donned his Union tunic and short-brimmed campaign hat, his buckskin trousers, and worn black boots. In a land divided by war, they were on the same side in this fight.

Theotis and Moses Tellico were passing a jug of "corn likker" back and forth in the center of the wagon line. The brothers were itching for a fight. Moses noticed Jesse and held up the jug to offer the Union officer a drink. Jesse politely declined. Anything the Tellicos had a hand in brewing was better left untasted. It was said their coonhound broke into their still one night and after lapping a snootful of home brew went blind the next day. The Tellicos were the stuff of legend, no two ways about it.

"It'll be dark in another hour," Theotis said with an over-the-shoulder nod toward the red sky.

"Go easy on the moonshine, Theotis," Jesse warned. "I want you to be able to use that Hawken rifle."

"Shee-it. I won't even need to aim. Them night riders will be thick as ticks on a hound." Theotis took another pull on the jug, then wiped his mouth on his shirtsleeve and grinned.

"I been thinkin', Jesse," Moses spoke up. "We're the bait, ain't we? Yessir, all of us here is bait for them traps we dug."

"Better we face Tullock here than strung out through the Kiamichis," Jesse said.

Moses poked his crooked nose in a kerchief and

blew. He blinked, and wiped his upper lip and returned the rag to his pocket.

Si Reaves and seven of the field hands filed down from the hillside to join the defenders at the barricade.

"Where do you want us, Mr. Jesse?" McQueen took quick stock of the volunteers. Si Reaves was the only man bearing firearms among them. But his companions were resolved and determined to fight for their freedom with rock, club, or bare fist if need be. Once slaves, now free, they were of a single mind. Not one man, woman, or child was going to be brought back to Honey Ridge in chains. "Anybody get through, we drag 'em down and take their guns," Si added, loud enough for all the townspeople at the barricade to hear. "Abolition" was a fine word, Jesse thought, but now it was time to do something more than talk. He had a Dragoon Colt holstered at his side and a second gun tucked in his belt. He drew this revolver and handed it over to one of the field hands, a wiry young man with a noticeable limp.

"You ever loaded cap and ball before?" he asked.

The black man shook his head. "No, suh. But I reckons I can learn."

"I'll show him, Mr. Jesse," Si added.

Hack Warner left his position along the line carrying an extra rifled musket, and passed the weapon to another of the field hands. Al Teel and Linc Graywater came forward, one with a shotgun and the other, a Navy Colt .36. In a matter of minutes the field hands were armed and offered a place behind the defenses. Gip Whitfield seemed uncomfortable by the proximity of the black men but he kept his complaints to himself.

Jesse and Pacer continued along without incident.

"You know brother, they'll try to take us in one charge. Tullock will throw everything he has at us."

"I'm counting on that," Jesse stated matter-of-factly. The more confusion the merrier, he decided. He looked over at the fires dotting the western hillside. The women and children were camped out of harm's way. He studied the long-haired women and excited children at play. Now where was Grandmother Raven? Well, she had to be somewhere. At least she was safe, he thought with satisfaction.

He noticed Carmichael Ross parting the women and children like the Israelites the Red Sea as she descended the hill at a brisk pace with Lorelei in tow, hurrying through the dying sunlight toward the barricade. Jesse took one look at the editor's demeanor and braced himself for the worst.

"What now?" he muttered as the two women approached.

Lorelei shifted nervously and avoided Jesse's gaze. She tried Pacer, but he was as stern looking as Jesse. Both McQueens suspected something was wrong. Lorelei had come down from the hillside to confirm their fears.

"Raven is gone," Carmichael said, breaking the silence.

"What do you mean?" Jesse asked. He gave Lorelei a sharp look, his features dark with anger. "I told you to stay with her."

"Your grandmother had other ideas," Lorelei defensively replied. She retreated a step as if expecting Jesse to strike her. It took her a few moments to realize she had misjudged him. "She took a horse and rode off through the trees."

"My God, where was she heading?" Pacer Wolf exclaimed. As quickly, the answer came to him. "The farm—she's back at the farm."

Lorelei nodded. "She said no one was going to chase her from her home. She made me promise not to tell either of you until it was too late to bring her back." Lorelei brushed her auburn hair back from her oval face and tried to look innocent. "Raven can be very persuasive." She hooked a thumb in her belt. Lorelei wore brown canvas pants and a coarsely woven work shirt. A gun butt jutted from her waistband. A floppy-brimmed hat rode high on her forehead. "As for me, I've chosen my own place to fight."

"You'll do as I say and go where I tell you," Jesse snapped.

"In a pig's eye," she brusquely told him.

"Better back off, Jesse, and save your breath," Pacer interjected. "I've already been down this same road with her. Miss Lorelei here has a mind of her own." He spied Gip Whitfield riding at a dead gallop toward the barricade. The Texan avoided the floor of the gap and kept close to the treeline, skirting the hills. "Raven will be all right," Pacer added. He appraised Lorelei's garb, noting her revolver and a pouch that contained a couple of loaded cylinders for her Colt.

"I can shoot as well as any man. Better than most," she explained. "You'll need me to watch your back."

Pacer saw no reason to try and talk her out of such a decision. Lorelei had her own way of doing things. "Just try and stay out of trouble."

"Me? Of all the nerve. I'll have you know, Mr. Pacer Wolf McQueen, you're going to be glad I'm here before this game is finished."

Jesse turned from the bickering couple and looked aside at Carmichael. But the editor wasn't about to take sides.

"Raven will be all right," she said. "Tullock won't harm her. Even in his rage." Ross patted the barrel of the shotgun she had slipped from her saddle scabbard. "The women don't need me. And I owe those night riders for the *Courier*."

Jesse peered over the barricade at the opposite

end of the gap where the headwaters of Buffalo Creek bubbled out of the side of a rocky slope and cut a furrow in the valley floor. He resisted the temptation to take his gray and race back to the farm. But his place was here, his responsibility, right here.

"Oh, grandmother," he sighed.

Raven McQueen, by her own choice, was on her own.

Chapter Thirty-three

Big Tullock Roberts held up his hand and motioned for his men to continue on past while he reined his horse off the creek trail and rode up to the farmhouse and the medicine woman who watched him from the front porch. Cap Featherstone, Sawyer Truett, and a Creek cattle rancher accompanied him.

"You want us to burn the place?" asked the pockmarked rancher. He had close-set eyes and a cruel turn to his mouth and a torch that he was eager to light. All he needed was the word from Roberts.

"No," Tullock replied.

"Her medicine is strong. It would not be a good idea," Sawyer Truett cautioned. He was wary of the woman. To bring her harm could openly invite ruin.

Cap Featherstone came along quietly. He liked none of this. Tullock's arrival in town had forced him to choose sides and commit himself. He glanced over his shoulder and spied Hud Pardee several yards away, watching him with a bemused expression. Hud enjoyed seeing Cap trapped into doing his own dirty work. Pardee was flanked by Shug Jones and Dobie Johnson, who was excited about the prospect of a fight. The same could hardly be said for Enos Clem, who hadn't counted on becoming involved in a battle. The gambler wanted no part of this. But he didn't want to rile a man like Cap.

Raven McQueen watched the four men ride into her front yard and missed Hecuba. The place seemed empty without the loyal watchbird. Raven made no sudden motion. Indeed, she seemed the epitome of calm, as if these riders were invited guests and meant her no harm.

"You know why I've come," Tullock called out as he walked his mount in front of the house.

"I know. But do you?" Raven asked. She sat in the chair by the quilting frame and began to pick at a loose thread, then she looked at the men with Roberts. She spied Cap Featherstone.

"Where is your son?" Tullock asked her.

"In the gap," she replied. "Waiting for you, Tullock." She shifted and looked directly at Cap. "And for you." Then Raven turned back to Tullock. "Perhaps you have a common enemy," she added. "My son has a letter from Lucius Minley. If you will give him a chance, he might let you read it. Or Cap can probably give you an idea what the letter says. After all, he and Lucius have been busy lately."

Cap's expression noticeably changed. He turned pale but managed to recover his composure as Tullock glanced around at him.

"What's she talking about?"

"I bought some property from the bank." Cap shrugged. "Other than that, I don't know. I've had no other dealings with the man." Cap mustered all his indignation. "I and my men are riding with you. What more do you want from me? I didn't raid your plantation and steal your slaves. I haven't joined the abolitionists, the same ones who killed your son. If there's any reckoning to be done, I'd suggest you take it up with Jesse and Pacer McQueen."

Cap jerked savagely on the reins of his mount and spun the horse away from the farmhouse and galloped out of the yard. The Creek rancher joined him with a condescending sweep of his hat and a guttural farewell toward the woman on the porch.

"Tell me, woman, did you send me the dream of Samuel's death? I must know the truth. One night I saw him dead. And it came to pass. I sensed your hand in this."

"The dream was of your own creation, Tullock Roberts, as was your son's death."

"God damn you, Raven," Tullock growled, his features mottled with the fury he struggled to contain.

"Don't be here when we come back," Sawyer warned.

"You aren't coming back," Raven said.

"Don't listen to her," Tullock replied. He motioned for Sawyer to follow him, and with a touch of the reins and the rider's knee, the stallion turned its head toward Buffalo Gap.

"Sawyer, let him go alone," Raven said, hoping to change the mind of the boy she had helped to raise. But Sawyer had always had a bitterness in him, an anger she had never been able to reach.

"I've sided with Tullock," he told her.

"Then you are lost," Raven said.

"See here, Raven. A lot of the boys have been drinking. When they finish with Jesse they're apt to come back through and fire the farm just for spite." Sawyer leaned over the pommel of his saddle. "I wouldn't be here when they do."

"No, you wouldn't, Sawyer. And I'm sorry for you."

The overseer frowned and urged his horse first into a trot and then a gallop. A wind began to stir the grasses. Lazy cattle ambled out of the way of the night riders and protested the intrusion in their low mournful-sounding voices.

Raven left the porch and in the fading daylight made her way up the knoll behind the house, carrying a lantern with her. When she reached the summit, the medicine woman added several branches to the glowing ashes and dumped the reservoir of coal oil onto a mound of glowing embers. Flames leaped up to greedily feast on the fresh timber. They danced like spirits caught in a whirlwind of time and space, leaping high in a column of fire and sparks to rage against the dying of the light.

Raven began as her mother taught her, adding from her parfleche the roots and dried wildflowers she had gathered in the mountains. She opened a pouch and removed a pinch of soil which she had brought from the ancestral lands of the Choctaw. This was sacred earth and would purify the fire. She pulled her shawl close about her shoulders as a north wind swept over the hill. She knelt and looked up as sacred smoke dispatched against the deepening purple sky. Then she returned her attention to the prayer flames. She took an obsidian-bladed knife from the parfleche and gouged the palm of her hand and allowed the blood to drip into the fire.

"All-Father I offer myself for the
lives of my grandsons.
Shield them from the weapons
of their enemies.
Be the strength in their
arms.
Come spirit of war. Come slayer
Stand at the side of Redbow and Pacer Wolf.

And strike fear in the heart of those who
would harm them."

She closed her eyes and in her mind's eye saw
the faces of her grandsons. Kit would have been
proud to see them, standing tall and strong. And
Ben to find his boys at last side by side. Raven had
never doubted for an instant they would find each
other. They just got lost for a little while was all. She
opened her eyes. A wind gust seemed to blow right
through her willowy frame as flames like winged
creatures conjured from the burning branches shot
upward through the prayer smoke. Gunfire sounded
in the distance. The battle had been joined. But
when she looked toward the upper end of the valley,
she spied an ominous number of riders already
returning from the gap. There were five men, two of
whom she recognized in the twilight—Cap
Featherstone and Hud Pardee.

"You reckon Tullock saw us leave?" Dobie Johnson
grumbled as he sat astride his mount alongside Shug
Jones, whose cheeks bulged from a chaw of tobacco,
and Enos Clem, the dour-looking gambler who
appeared relieved that Cap had brought them out of the
gap.

"Naw," Shug answered. "Tullock and his boys
was charging them wagons. He weren't about to stop
and look over his shoulder just to see if we was
bringing up the rear."

The five horsemen were in a line at the base of
the knoll behind the McQueen farmhouse. Raven's
medicine fire had drawn them like a beacon. Cap
had led the men to the hill and found that Hud
Pardee was only too anxious to climb to the summit
and force Raven to reveal everything she knew about
Lucius Minley and Cap's schemes.

"Crazy old woman," Dobie muttered, staring up the hill. "Hud will put the fear o' God in her." His youthful features radiated confidence and a firm belief in his own immortality.

Hud was older but no wiser. The one-eyed gunman felt the same way. He reached the summit of the knoll and came face to face with the half-breed medicine woman where she knelt by the fire she had built. Hud tucked the flaps of his frock coat back, ran a hand through his ash-gray hair, and sauntered over to the woman. He stood with his hands resting on the guns in his waist sash.

"We meet again, you harridan. But this time I advise you to keep a civil tongue in your head or I'll cut it out."

Raven continued to watch him through the flames. The wind lifted the strands of her long black hair and whipped them about her face. She made no reply. She saw no profit in trading threats with the gunman.

"What do you know about Cap's arrangement with the banker?"

Raven did not reply.

"I asked you a question." He waited. "No?" He shrugged. "Suits me. I don't give a good goddamn whether you answer or not. I'll just drag you downslope and toss you over the saddle. Cap has plenty of ways of making you talk." Hud chuckled softly. "I just came up for the pleasure of telling you I killed your son, Ben. That was me in Kansas City. And I'm going to kill Jesse, too. Maybe even Pacer, although after what he and his friends did in Lawrence, I kind of think of him as a kindred soul." He waited for her reaction. Hud was disappointed to find his remarks seemed to have no effect on her. "The hell with you," he muttered. Hud started to circle the fire and happened to glance toward the woman as the wind shifted the column of prayer smoke. For the first time he realized she held a big-bore flintlock pistol in her slender hand. The barrel of the pistol, one of the "Quakers," looked as big as a cannon. Hud brought up sharply and started to retreat. Raven stood, but the image was one of a woman rising out of the flames.

"Just you wait a second," Hud said, and dropped a hand to one of the guns in his waist sash. It was said of Hud Pardee that along the Natchez Trace and the length and breadth of the Mississippi he was without equal with a gun. No man was his match. But a life ended and a legend began in Indian Territory, hundreds of miles from the Natchez Trace. The "Quaker" spewed fire and smoke and thundered in Raven's hand. A .50 caliber slug in the chest knocked Hud off his feet and drove him into the ground. He rolled over, crawled to his feet, and staggered half a dozen yards, clawing at the front of his ruffled shirt now matted with a crimson stain that continued to spread. He slowly turned and found himself face to face with Raven. Hud's eye was wide with disbelief. The gunman tried to speak, but words failed him. It was Raven who finally broke her silence.

"Don't look so surprised," she said. "I told you we had enough snakes."

Hud rocked back on his heels as his eye glazed over and he toppled backward and rolled down the knoll, tumbling as limply as a discarded doll until he reached the bottom of the slope and came to rest at the feet of his former companions.

Cap gave Enos the nod. "Go on up there and bring that woman down here."

Enos cleared his throat and spat. "The hell you say."

Cap glared at him, then shifted his attention to

Dobie and Shug. The youth could not tear his eyes from Hud Pardee's crumpled form. Shug wore a look of iron.

"I ain't gettin' near that old woman. I ain't lost nothin' up yonder."

Cap looked up the hill and sighed. "C'mon. Minley's woman ought to be able to tell us what's happened. Anybody wants me, let them come to the Medicine Wagon."

The horsemen turned their mounts away from the hill and the woman who waited indomitable and defiant. Raven McQueen saw them leave, but just to be on the safe side she reloaded her gun. Then she returned to her vigil by the sacred fire, for the violent night was far from over.

The battle that had taken almost two weeks to come about lasted but a few minutes. Like a sudden, lethal storm, it sprang up, claimed its victims, and vanished.

One minute Tullock Roberts was charging hell-bent-for-leather and the next, the ground opened beneath him and dumped the master of Honey Ridge Plantation along with several other riders into an eight-foot-deep trench that had been dug and concealed in the floor of the pass. Tullock was thrown clear on impact and managed to scramble up the side of the trench as another three horsemen followed those in the lead and came crashing down on the men still trapped below and struggling to get out. Riders swept past him and Tullock waved them on and limped forward, his revolver drawn. Pain shot through his left leg. His ankle felt fractured or at least badly sprained.

All about him, pandemonium reigned as men and horses crashed into the hidden pits. Tullock saw a pair of attackers disappear, then further along, Buck

Langdon and half a dozen men nose-dived into a trap amid a flurry of broken bones and screams of agony. Tullock's plan had been so simple—mass a headlong charge against McQueen's barricade, weather a volley or two from the defenders, and sweep them aside by sheer force of numbers. The only danger came if the attack slowed. With horror, Tullock saw his column of men not only slow but even halt about fifty yards from the wagons, uncertain of the ground that lay ahead.

"No!" he shouted, struggling to be heard above the din. But his voice was drowned out by a ripple of gunfire that blossomed all along the barricade. Men toppled from horseback, clutching at their mortal wounds. Some of the Knights tried to continue the attack. Four of the horsemen crashed through the branches and woven grass covering a trench. Again the horsemen hesitated as the winnowing gunfire reaped a harvest of death among them.

Jesse McQueen patrolled the barricade, shouting instructions to the field hands to make every shot count. Whenever he saw men waver, he hurried to support them with his presence and coolness under fire. The covered pits had done the job and halted the attackers. In their confusion, they made perfect targets.

Theotis Tellico loosed a wild Rebel yell and blasted a man from horseback and laid his Hawken rifle aside. "C'mon, Moses! You leavin' all the work to me."

"The devil I am," Moses shouted. His Starr revolver spewed powder smoke. He ducked as a slug fanned his cheek, and he returned fire with deadly accuracy. Libby Whitfield moved among the men, loading revolvers and handing them back for the men to use. She stopped by her husband and admonished him to keep his head down, then passed him a loaded gun. Whatever reticence he might have had about firing on these Confederate sympathizers vanished when they came charging down the pass. Now it was a matter of his life or theirs.

Jesse McQueen returned to the center of the barricade, levered a shell into his Spencer, knocked a man from the saddle, loaded, and fired again. A Creek breached the wagons. Jesse shot him as the man rode past. The Creek yelped and pitched forward over his saddle horn. His horse carried him from the fray. Pacer, at Jesse's side, emptied his revolver with uncanny accuracy. When half a dozen men tried to charge the barricade on foot, Pacer climbed over the barricade and placed himself in front of Albert Teel and two of the fieldhands struggling to reload their rifled muskets. Pacer's second gun boomed in almost a single thunderous roll, and when the smoke cleared two men lay mortally wounded and another cradled his battered arm. The other three veered from the Choctaw Kid only to be dropped by Theotis Tellico and Parson Marshal Booth.

The din was horrible to hear. Horses with broken legs struggled to free themselves from the trenches and pits. Men with shattered arms and legs cried out to be rescued while others lay still, their faces contorted, their necks broken. Pacer's gun clicked on an empty chamber. He broke the revolver apart and began to replace the cylinder with a fresh load. One of the Knights he had assumed was dead suddenly sprang up. It was Sawyer Truett. He locked eyes with his intended target and slowly leveled his Colt at the Choctaw Kid.

Jesse saw Truett and trained his rifle on the man and squeezed the trigger. Nothing happened. Pacer, unarmed, dove for the ground as a revolver blasted close to his right ear. Sawyer Truett groaned, pitched forward, and fired into the sod. Pacer looked up to see Lorelei with a Navy Colt in her hand. She winked at him and blew smoke from the barrel.

A ragged line of attackers loosed a final volley at the barricade. One of the field hands groaned and dropped, clutching his shoulder. Jesse ducked behind the wagon and saw another of the defenders whirl about and sink to his knees. Jesse recognized T. Alan Booth, a neat black bullethole right between his eyes. The man was already dead. He fell over on his side. Jesse cursed, and shouted for the defenders to pour fire into Tullock's men. All along the barricade, guns blazed anew, avenging Booth's death fivefold.

The Knights melted away under the onslaught, leaving the dead and wounded behind. Gunfire trailed off as targets became scarce. Soon there was nothing to shoot at but the darkness. Jesse climbed over the barricade and walked out into the pass. The townspeople began to show themselves, scarcely daring to believe the melee had ended. Si Reaves climbed onto a wagon bed and raised his rifled musket over his head. Battle lust burned in his eyes. He stood tall and proud and free.

"Cap! Cap Featherstone!" Jesse's voice reverberated through the pass. He picked his way through the gap. Wounded men moaned for help. As he pressed on, avoiding the pits, the stench of blood and gunsmoke stung his nostrils and burned his lungs, yet he steeled himself to the carnage he had wrought and continued to challenge Cap Featherstone to show himself.

"Not . . . here," a voice weakly called to him.

Jesse whirled and pointed his gun at the man who had answered in the night. It was Tullock

Roberts. The man was battered and bruised and without a weapon.

"They rode me down. My own men. Knocked my gun somewhere." He had captured a horse and had been attempting to pull himself up in the saddle when he spied Jesse. "I think my ankle's broke. I know my arm is."

Jesse noticed the man's left arm was tucked inside his shirt.

"Where's Cap?"

"He didn't think I saw him, but I did. He drifted back and took off with his men. Maybe he showed good sense." Tullock grimaced and braced himself for the gunshot from Jesse's gun. To his astonishment, Jesse holstered his revolver and helped him into the saddle.

"I don't understand . . ." Tullock said after the first wave of pain subsided. He had to will himself upright in the saddle.

"Go home, Tullock. You're all Arbitha has. And pitiful as you are, I won't be a party to causing her more grief."

Jesse slapped the horse's rump and the animal trotted off into the night. The Union officer heard the plod of horses behind him and glanced over his shoulder to spy Pacer and Lorelei coming toward him. The Choctaw Kid led two horses across the trampled ground. Lorelei held the reins of her own mount. Pacer jabbed a thumb toward the abolitionists. "Carmichael said they'll do what they can for the injured. She was darn near civil to me."

"Miracles never cease," Jesse said with a wag of his head. He swung up astride the gray.

Pacer indicated the girl at his side. "Lorelei wanted to come along and see about Grandmother Raven."

Lorelei blushed and nervously added, "Pacer

said I could stay on with Raven. For as long as I want."

"I think that's a fine idea," Jesse replied.

Lorelei flashed a smile. It came awkwardly to her. Good things in her life had been few and far between. She might even be able to tame the Choctaw Kid. She brushed a lock of auburn hair away from her eyes and gave Pacer a knowing smile. He gulped and avoided meeting her gaze.

"Just see you keep Raven from following me to town," Jesse added.

"You going after Cap?" Pacer asked.

"Yes."

"I'm coming with you."

Jesse studied his determined younger brother. There was no denying him. The McQueens would stand or fall—together.

"I wouldn't have it any other way."

Chapter Thirty-four

The rattlesnake lunged at the hand on the jar and Dobie jerked away as the reptile slapped its fangs against the glass and left a smear of venom on the inside wall of its prison.

Enos Clem, standing behind the bar, glanced up from the cards he was dealing himself and chuckled at the young gunman's expense. Dobie scowled and gave the gambler a warning look. Clem shrugged and returned to his cards. He was playing against himself, five-card stud. Cap Featherstone was seated at a large round table set near the rear of the saloon. Shug Jones was standing in a narrow alcove near the piano.

"Don't take it so hard," Cap told the younger man. "I haven't met the man who could hold his hand to the jar and not pull away." Cap had lit only the lights near the front of the saloon, but the light from the lanterns filtered to the rear of the Medicine Wagon, leaving part of the room in shadow and part bathed in a feeble amber glow. Cap had dispatched the girls and given them the run of the hotel until further notice. That Chahta Creek had been reduced to virtually a ghost town did not bother him in the slightest. There'd be enterprising neutrals and

Southern sympathizers anxious to fill the void left by the departing storekeepers. This was his town and he would see it grow to meet his own specific needs. He would shape it. Nurture it along. One day commerce would return. People would be leaving the embattled South and come looking for a place to begin anew. And Cap would be ready, with land and town property.

He looked over at Dobie. "You're certain it was Jesse and Pacer that came riding out of the valley."

Dobie had remained behind in a grove of red oaks where Buffalo Creek flowed into the Kimishi River. It had been his task to bring word to Cap of what had transpired in Buffalo Gap.

"Seen 'em clear in the moonlight, what with that spyglass you give me," Dobie said. "First there came Tullock's men, riding scared, like they'd seen the devil himself. They looked a sorry sight. Then after a while, Jesse and that turncoat brother of his. The Choctaw Kid, hell. I aim to take his measure. I would have dropped him right there, only you told me to come on." Dobie had worn out his horse, racing to bring word to Cap Featherstone.

The burly man at the table nodded and poured himself a glass of milk. He glared at Tandy Matlock. The white-haired, old piano player stiffened. Cap had the evil eye tonight and Tandy was loath to get in the big man's way.

"I pay you to play," Cap growled.

"What you want to hear?"

Cap thought a minute, then laughed softly. "Play 'Dixie.'"

The former slave turned his back to the saloon and began to dance his fingers upon the keys. The familiar tune of the Confederacy merrily shattered the silence and eased the tensions in the room.

Cap Featherstone tapped his foot while finishing his milk. He'd have Shug fix a plate of eggs and sausage a little later on. Just as soon as he had finished with Ben McQueen's young pups.

Jesse and Pacer dismounted and tethered their mounts to the hitching rail in front of the saloon. Jesse studied the night-shrouded town. Buildings looked as empty as open graves. The Medicine Wagon offered some semblance of life, however ominous. Lantern-light streamed over and around and beneath the batwing doors. Strains of "Dixie" drifted into the street.

"Sounds like Cap's having a party," Pacer said.

"And we're the guests of honor," Jesse replied.

"How do you want to do this?"

"Straight on," Jesse said. He drew his revolver from his holster and held it down at his side.

Pacer Wolf noticed his brother's empty holster. "You've already cleared leather. That's not fair," Pacer was confident of his own quickness with a gun.

Jesse gave his brother a stony look. "I didn't come here to be fair." He started up the steps. Pacer caught him by the arm.

"Jesse?" Pacer struggled to find the words while his older brother waited. How to say what was in his heart? "I just wanted ... uh ... you to know ... ."

Jesse smiled, and clapped his brother on the shoulder.

"Yeah. Me, too."

He heard a flutter of wings and caught a glimpse of movement in the shadows. There in the corner of the roof overhanging the porch, a raven perched on a knob of wood and studied the brothers. The bird left its perch and landed on the back of a chair. The raven preened its obsidian feathers and then cocked its head and studied the men with eyes of fire. In a rush of motion the bird took to the air again, launching itself between the McQueens and sailing off into the night sky. Jesse and Pacer looked at one another, and then as if with a single mind they turned and stepped through the doors.

Tandy Matlock quit playing and turned around

on his stool. His hands were trembling now. There was death in the air and he wanted to be as far from the saloon as possible.

"Please, Mr. Featherstone . . . can I go now?"

"Go on," Cap muttered, and waved his hand toward the back door. The front of the room was occupied by Jesse and Pacer Wolf McQueen.

"Thankee," Tandy said, and scrambled away from the piano and hurried past Cap and Dobie and out through the back door. Enos Clem continued to deal himself cards at the bar. Dobie faced the McQueens, his arm limber and ready to sweep the revolver from his holster. Hud Pardee had left a mighty big void, but Dobie figured he was the man to fill it. He ignored Jesse and rooted his attention on the Choctaw Kid. He was confident Pacer was in for a rude surprise.

"I had an unpleasant visit with Rose Minley," Cap said. "It appears my trust in Lucius was misplaced."

"I'd say so," Jesse said, easing further from the door. He did not want to be too close to Pacer when trouble came. He checked Shug by the piano. The man was dangerous but not an immediate threat. Dobie looked fast and skittish as a colt. He was amazed the young tough hadn't already started the gunplay. Cap and the gambler were the real threats here. "Lucius left a letter with Carmichael. It explained a lot of things."

"I shall have to get that back."

"It won't be easy," Pacer spoke up.

"I wish you lads hadn't pushed this. I've enough of your family's blood on my hands," Cap said, and finished his milk. White droplets clung to his mustache.

"My father is alive," Jesse said. He took pleasure in the startled expression that came to Cap's face. His bushy eyebrows raised and he licked his lips. "Major Abbot hid him outside of town."

"Ah—that sounds like Peter," Cap said. "I'm

hurt that he chose not to confide in me." Cap glanced around at the three men on his side of the wide, long gambling parlor.

"I'm dealing you a hand, McQueen," Enos said, shuffling the cards. He slapped down a pair of cards face-up. "Ace of spades for you. Trey of hearts for me. A nine for you. A king for me. Another ace, for you. Pair of aces. Not bad. A five for me. Here's a ten for your aces and for me a trey of diamonds. Pair of treys aren't good enough. Last card. Six of diamonds to you. And for me . . ." He tossed the last card down. "Trey of clubs. Three of a kind beats your aces. See—what did I tell you? My luck's changed." He lowered his hands below the bar.

"Cap. You were my father's friend," Jesse said. "Why?"

"I have to be grateful to Abbot," Cap replied. "That raid in Georgia with Major Andrews' bunch taught me one thing." The owner of the Medicine Wagon cleared his throat. "You have to look out for yourself. I'm the only cause I'll fight for. That makes things a helluva lot simpler." Cap looked from Shug to Dobie and then to Enos. Jesse caught the motion and tensed. "It was for the money, boy," Cap explained. "And the power. You did well with Tullock Roberts. But you're on my ground now. And I am no goddamn gentleman farmer. Neither of you are leaving here alive."

"Talk-talk-talk," Pacer said. "You aim to bury us in words?"

"You got a smart mouth," Dobie Johnson said to the Choctaw Kid. "But cross me and you've crossed the wrong man." He was handsome and reckless and eager. Dobie was living life in the flash of an instant. He was riding high and heading for a fall.

"Well, Jesse, I suppose you better make your pretty speech, tell me I'm under arrest, and order me to tag along quietly to the jail," Cap said.

Jesse reached up with his left hand and unpinned the ranger's badge from his buckskin shirt. "You've got me all wrong, Cap. I didn't come here for the law." With utter contempt for Featherstone, Jesse tossed the badge onto the floor in front of Cap's table.

"Just who do you think you are?" Cap scowled, the anger in him rising to the boiling point.

"Justice," came the reply. Jesse McQueen snapped up his Colt and fired at Cap. Blood spurted from the big man's shoulder and he fell over backward in his chair. He overturned the table to provide himself some cover.

Dobie reached for his gun. He had never moved faster. But his Navy Colt had just cleared leather when Pacer shot him twice in the chest. The second bullet found his lungs and spun him around. His outstretched arm knocked the snake in the bottle off the bar and sent it crashing to the floor.

"Shotgun!" Pacer shouted as Enos brought up a scattergun from a rack close to his hands. Pacer hurled a chair at the gambler. The twin barrels boomed with deafening volume. The chair exploded as Jesse and Pacer hit the floor. Pacer staggered to the front wall and, bracing himself, fired at Clem, who ducked out of sight.

Dobie tried to cling to the bar. "Oh, sweet Jesus. Cap . . . Cap, it hurts." His voice faded.

"Take it like a man," Cap told him. Dobie slid to the floor and lay facedown on the whiskey-stained wood.

Shug darted from the alcove by the piano and bolted for the stairs. The high ground would give him an advantage. He fired twice at Jesse and then took the steps two at a time. Jesse rose up, sighted on the man, and squeezed off a round, chancing a bullet from Cap or the gambler. Cap's aim was off, though only by a little. Jesse caught a faceful of splinters before he crouched low.

He crouched against the floor and peered through the ribbed wooden back of a chair as Shug turned near the top landing.

"Get 'em, Shug. Drive 'em out into the open!" Cap bellowed. A haze of powdersmoke hung in the air and made the eyes water. Instead of firing on the man below, Shug sagged against the banister. The Dragoon Colt in his hand slipped from his fingers. He turned and Jesse saw a dark patch of crimson spread across the back of his shirt. Shug turned again and hung over the railing. The weight of his body pulled him forward and he rolled over the banister and came crashing down on top of the piano, shattered the wood frame, and thudded to the floor, to die in discord.

"AAAAHHHH!" Enos Clem rose up from concealment and clutched at his neck. He fired down at the floor at his feet. Jesse realized he was shooting at the rattler. Enos turned and staggered down along the bar, his hand at his throat. Blood seeped through his clenched fingers. The rattler had given him a mortal wound and he knew it. But he wasn't going to die alone. The gambler turned and leveled his revolver, thumbed the hammer back. Pacer shot him through the heart. The gambler crashed against the whiskey bottles, a card slipped from his coat sleeve—the three of spades—and then he fell in a rain of shattered glass down behind the bar.

Cap Featherstone sat cross-legged and grabbed a fresh cylinder from his pocket, broke the gun apart, and reloaded, checking to make sure there was a percussion cap over each chamber. His shoulder hurt like hell, but he forced the pain from his thoughts and peered to the side of the table he had chosen to hide behind.

Jesse crawled across the floor to Pacer, who sat with his legs out and his back against the wall. His hat was gone and his left arm had been peppered with shot from the shotgun blast. His face was pale and his lips were drawn into a tight line. Jesse examined his younger brother with cold-eyed scrutiny. Pacer shifted his weight. His pants leg was sticky near the thigh. He'd been hit in the left leg by buckshot ricocheting off the chair he'd thrown. If his wounds were serious, Jesse wasn't letting on.

"Have I been 'elected'?" Pacer asked. Shock was starting to set in. The hurting would come in waves until he lost consciousness.

"No," Jesse told him. He wrapped his bandanna around Pacer's thigh. "But you got 'nominated' real good."

"Your brother needs doctoring," Cap called out. "Looks like we've all taken some losses." He scrambled to his knees. He saw his sword cane broken in half by his fall. Another bad omen, Cap thought. It was time to leave. He could try for the back door. But that would leave Ben's boys alive to hunt him down. No. Better to end it here. "Why don't you drag him out of here, Jesse. Else you'll have his death on your conscience."

"Don't worry about me," Pacer shouted.

Cap wagged his head and sighed. He scratched at his beard and took in the saloon's interior. His dream of an empire had begun with the Medicine Wagon. Was it to end here as well? No, he told himself. No. Damn Lucius Minley, he should have killed him right after Samuel Roberts's murder. That was his mistake. He'd left the wrong man alive. He wouldn't make it again. He'd show no mercy and bury his enemies from now on—starting with Ben McQueen's troublesome whelps. "Time to die," he called out.

Jesse shuddered. Menace flowed toward him from the shadowy reaches of the saloon. Icy talons clawed at his heart and for one brief moment his courage almost failed him. Then Pacer Wolf stirred at his side. He shoved his revolver into his brother's hand. "Stop him," he said in a hoarse whisper. And in that moment, Jesse's fear left him, exultation filled his soul. And his voice rang out in a clear, strong challenge.

"C'mon, Cap. What are you waiting for? Ride the panther!"

Cap rose from the floor. He hauled the table up in his left hand, holding the round oaken shield before him as he lumbered toward the front door, firing his revolver as he charged. An animalistic roar tore from his throat. He was a juggernaut, seeming unstoppable, a massive figure of fire and rage and blasting death.

Jesse stood his ground; the Colt revolvers in his hands fired in rapid succession. Bullet holes appeared in the surface of the table, wood chips exploding into the air. Pain seared his right side, but Jesse refused to yield as bullets heated the air and thudded into the batwing doors behind him. Thirty feet, twenty, then ten. Jesse emptied his guns.

And suddenly, Cap halted and the bullet-riddled table crashed to the floor. He stared in disbelief at Jesse, who was still standing, still blocking his path. The whole of Cap's shirt was matted crimson and puckered with bullet holes where the flattened slugs had ripped his flesh and shattered bone.

"I don't understand," he gasped, and then sank to his knees. Cap stared at his adversary. The world was shimmering out of focus, but he willed himself back from the brink of death because he had to know. "Why—aren't—you—dead?" he gasped. He sank forward, losing his hold, feeling the creep of cold and the bliss of final darkness. Jesse's voice followed him into death with the last words Cap ever heard.

"A McQueen is a hard kill."

Epilogue

Ben McQueen was asleep in his cane-backed wheel chair. He'd fallen asleep on the bluff behind Doc Curtis's hospital that overlooked the Missouri River. It was midmorning on the last day of October. With war going to the east, it had taken a Herculean effort on Major Abbot's part to secure a surgeon capable of the operation Ben required. But a week ago the surgery had finally taken place. Ben was still weak from the ordeal, and the wheelchair, while a temporary conveyance, often came in handy after an exhausting early morning walk. It was with great relief that Ben McQueen received the news that his son had brought a column of abolitionists and staunch Union loyalists out of the embattled Indian Territory and across the border into the comparative safety of Kansas. Free of concern for Jesse's well-being, Ben's healing seemed to accelerate. But Ben had worked hard today and his exertions had taken their toll.

"Don't worry. He rests every morning, in the same place. It's the warmest spot in the yard. You know, he never grows tired of watching the river," Abbot said, standing in the shade of Doc Curtis's back door. The half-dozen soldiers posted out front had halted the carriage and called for the major. Pete

Abbot had instantly identified Raven, Jesse, and to his complete amazement, Pacer Wolf McQueen.

Abbot waved toward the sleeping man. "Doc says he's healing nicely. It won't hurt for you to wake him up."

Raven didn't need any urging. She had come all this way to see her son, and nothing or no one was going to stand in her way. Pacer also excused himself and hurried after his grandmother. He was hoping to avoid an uncomfortable exchange with the major. The Choctaw Kid intended to slip away from the clutches of the Yankees at the first opportunity.

As for Jesse, his side was still stiff and he moved too slowly to completely escape Abbot's grasp.

"You did a splendid job, Captain."

"Thank you, sir," Jesse replied.

"I'd like to know how in the name of heaven you managed to—"

Jesse saluted and brushed past the major and rushed to his father's side, forsaking military protocol out of love for Ben McQueen.

"See here," Abbot indignantly began, shoving his spectacles back on the bridge of his nose. He started to take offense. But when he saw Ben awaken and reach out to enfold first his mother and then his two sons, the major's anger melted away. "I suppose it can wait." Abbot retreated into the doctor's house and closed the door, allowing the family McQueen their moment in the sun.

If you have enjoyed *Ride the Panther*, turn the
page for an exciting preview of the sixth volume in best-selling author Kerry Newcomb's
saga of an American military dynasty.

JACK IRON

This Bantam original will be on sale in 1993.
Look for it wherever Bantam Domain Books are
sold.

December 17, 1814

After sailing his three-masted brig into the harbor of Natividad and unleashing his two hundred and thirteen man crew on the inhabitants of Morgan Town, Captain Orturo "the Cayman" Navarre promptly captured the island's governor—Josiah Morgan—and ate him. Navarre neatly prepared his midday meal, flavoring cuts of the governor with peppers, wild onions, garlic, plantain, and chunks of guava. Then, in front of the subdued people gathered in the public square, the Cayman proceeded to dine.

The product of a Spanish father and a Carib mistress, Navarre had been raised by his mother's people to be strong, to suffer pain without flinching, to be cruel and merciless to his enemies and ruthless in battle. The Caribs were cannibals. However, Orturo took his ritualistic meals of human flesh more for the effect it had on others than to appease his own gruesome appetites.

Orturo Navarre finished off the governor and washed him down with a tankard of rum, then slowly but succinctly explained to a council of the port's stunned inhabitants just exactly what he expected from them in return for his protection. The Cayman made his point, gesturing with a rib bone while he spoke, then afterward offered the Cabilde, the town council, a place at his table. Navarre laughed heartily as the merchants politely refused and hurried off to their houses leaving the pirate and his henchmen a tentative promise of their cooperation. No one wanted to end up as the next day's "sumptuous feast."

Orturo Navarre rose from the table in the middle of the town square and, followed by a dozen of his crewmen, retraced his path up the winding street toward the governor's palace, a walled hacienda that had once belonged to the late Josiah Morgan. The palace was a small fortress with ten-foot-high stone battlements surrounding a two-story stone house. A battery of four twenty-four-pounder cannons were nestled in a redoubt below the hacienda's walls and guarded the bay and harbor. Swivel guns loaded with grapeshot dominated the walls of the governor's palace. The island's steep volcanic mountains swept up from the harbor and formed a natural barrier against any attack except from the sea. The palace's fortifications, though formidable, had been undermanned—still, the defenders might have put up quite a struggle had not Navarre brought his black-rigged ship into port under cover of night and captured the governor enjoying himself at a local tavern. (It had been Morgan, trusting to the mercy of his captors, who had surrendered the meager garrison and talked his men out from behind the palace's limestone walls only to see his guardsmen shot down and thrown to the sharks.)

On reaching the hacienda, Orturo Navarre walked to the edge of the cliff overlooking the harbor. The maw of a cannon peered over his shoulder like some baleful black eye. The wind from the bay swept up to ruffle the hem of his dark green brocade cloth coat. He was aptly nicknamed, for his features were mottled and as leathery looking as an alligator's. And his teeth, like those of a Carib, were filed into points. He stood six feet tall. His head, shaved smooth, was like the rest of his torso, burned dark from the sun by a life spent on the high seas. In contrast to his savage habits, Navarre wore finery befitting a European nobleman. A silk waistcoat, lighter green than his coat, sported mother-of-pearl buttons. He had a fondness for ruffled white shirts with lace cuffs. His skin-tight trousers matched his coat and were tucked into thigh-high boots. A bandolier draped across his chest held a matched set of flintlock pistols with bone-handle grips. A cutlass dangled at his left side. He folded his arms and looked out across the bay, fringed with soft white sand and coconut palms. A hundred yards inland, the steep ridges of volcanic rock swept up toward the azure sky. The only other protected bay lay on the opposite side of the island in a place called Obregon's Cove. But it was dotted by reefs and required repeated tacking to reach the shore, a difficult task even for a brig like *The Scourge*, which was gaffe-rigged and could sail close to the wind. But Navarre had a use for Obregon's Cove, as he did for Morgan Town.

He turned toward the collection of shops and taverns and stone houses comprising the port settlement. The town even boasted a church: a squat, thick-walled structure with a bell tower rising above the entrance. The church faced one side of the town square and seemed solid and impervious to the grog halls with which it shared the center of town. These were his people now; every rumrunner, woodworker, and wharf rat.

His second-in-command, a massive-looking African named NKenai, approached his captain and spoke in a deep, resonant voice.

"Captain Navarre, the priest would speak with you." He gestured with a wave of a broad hand toward a reed-thin, rumsoaked-looking individual in black robes and broad-brimmed straw hat that the breeze kept trying to lift from his head. Tiny red veins were etched on his cheeks and nose. His bony hands betrayed the beginnings of arthritis; his joints were swollen and the knuckles enlarged. Father Albert Bernal nervously awaited permission to approach the fiercesome pirate.

Orturo Navarre nodded to his subordinate. The big African grinned, revealing a row of yellow teeth set in the tattooed ebony mask of his face. Sweat glistened on the black man's cheeks and soaked the edges of the cobalt-blue fez the man wore atop his coarsely braided hair. NKenai kept a scimitar in his belt and throwing knives tucked in sheaths at the small of his back. The priest was ringed by several grim-looking men who took care to block Father Bernal's path should he try to retreat from Captain Navarre and return to the village below.

One of the pirates, a grizzled, wire-haired man with broken teeth and rope burns on his neck, jabbed the muzzle of his rifled musket into the priest's side.

"The name is Quince, Bible Thumper. Malachi Quince be my name and I've sinned from Maine to Hispaniola.

There ain't be nothin' I ain't done. What say you to that?" The swarthy little man spat in the dirt at Bernal's feet.

"Ask for forgiveness and the Lord will grant it, my son," the good priest said.

"Only thing I ask for is another twenty good years o' sinning. I want to earn my place in hell." Quince slapped the basket hilt of the cutlass at his side, tossed back his head, and belly-laughed.

Orturo, the Cayman, turned and gestured for the priest to approach. The pirate captain stood with legs splayed wide and arms folded. Indeed, the man radiated a kind of cruel royalty. He had stolen Natividad right out from under its defenders and hadn't lost a single member of his crew. He could hear the songs already praising his daring feat.

"What is it you want, priest?

Bernal gulped and stared down at his trembling hands, then looked up at the pirate. "The Cabilde has promised the cooperation of the town and you have offered protection from . . . uh . . . others. But we wish to know what you have in mind. Why have you come?"

"Why, to make your people rich, padre. To put coins in their pockets. What say you to that? Maybe even coins in your pocket, too, eh."

"I don't understand."

The Cayman glanced at the men standing a few feet away and grinned. "Men will come to this port to spend their money on women and grog. They will come to buy what we have to sell. Ships will flock to us."

"But the island is mostly mountainous. We have some coconut groves near the water, and inland, there are a few valleys where the sugar cane grows, but not enough to bring so many ships." Bernal knew he was treading dangerous ground, yet he intended to press the matter. The Cayman had come to Natividad for a reason and the priest was determined to learn the truth.

"Slaves . . . the black gold of high commerce. I will bring them from Africa and keep them in Obregon's Cove. They can work themselves to good health harvesting sugar cane until the slavers arrive. Natividad shall be the hub of a wheel, and along the spokes, ships will come eager to buy slaves, but not wishing to voyage all the way to Africa. They will come to me. And their crews will spend their money in the whore cribs and rum houses I will build in Morgan Town.

Father Bernal shuddered and his heart was filled with dismay. True, there were many of his flock who had been freebooters and sailed beneath the black flag. But these poor souls had mended their ways and married and lived, brought families to Natividad and made of it a sanctuary. Perhaps such people weren't as civilized as the inhabitants of the mainland. Indeed, they were a rough lot, but they were honest and loyal to one another, and Albert Bernal, with all his vices, had fit right in. He was one of them. And he had helped them build a community and make something of themselves and it didn't matter who among them was wanted for thievery or piracy or who had escaped the hangman's rope, Natividad was a place for a second chance and the priest wasn't going to see it corrupted by the Cayman.

"Slavers," Bernal muttered with contempt. "You would turn us into slavers! The devil's own!" He summoned all his courage. "Perhaps you have made a wrong choice of island," he said, hoping to reason with the pirate. "The people here are frightened but they are all rebels. They do not give in quite so simply as you may think. And you will have Cesar Obregon to deal with."

"Ah, the Hawk of the Antilles." Navarre said in a mocking tone of voice. "I can handle him—but as for your rebellious flock, you must counsel them to obey me."

"No!" the priest blurted out. "I am not much. But the pulpit is sacred. They have built me a church. I shall not desecrate the holy ground by aiding you to destroy my flock."

NKenai started forward. He did not like the priest's tone of voice. The black robe was being disrespectful. And for the African warrior whose sole allegiance was to the Cayman, disrespect could not be tolerated. He drew a dagger from his belt and started forward. The Cayman read his henchman's intent and shook his head. The simple gesture stopped NKenai in his tracks. Navarre stroked his chin and studied the priest. He leaned against one of the twenty-four-pounder cannons below the walls of the governor's palace and looked out over the bay. Below him, mangle-blanc trees clung to the rugged rocky slope. Among those twisted branches nested a variety of lizards, darting dragonflies, and yellow-throated parakeets. There was a constant breeze here, cool and refreshing in the warm glare of sunlight. Orturo the Cayman might be a cannibal, but he was not without an eye for beauty.

Navarre considered the priest's remarks. The last thing he wanted was to deal with some constant and tedious insurrection. He needed Bernal to use his influence to bend the people to Navarre's will. The death of the governor might not be enough, after all.

Inspiration struck him. Navarre called to one of his men, a gnarled-looking freebooter with thinning hair, a full brown beard, and pockmarked features. He wore a loose-fitting shirt and baggy cotton breeches and carried a musket. A pistol and cutlass were tucked in a wide leather belt circling his waist.

The pirate hurried forward, certain Navarre was no doubt sending him out for something important.

"Aye, Cap'n Navarre," the pirate called. Tom Bragg was eager to take his place among Navarre's inner circle of cutthroats.

"How long have you faithfully served me, old friend?" asked Navarre.

"Ever since you fished me out of the sea, Cap'n, and kept my hide from becoming shark bait. Must be nigh on to six years now since the *Magnus* went down." The pirate scratched at his pitted cheek and tried to tabulate the months that had passed since he'd been accepted into *The Scourge*'s crew.

"No man has been more reliable. No man has shown more courage."

"Thankee, Cap'n Navarre," Bragg said, beaming.

The Cayman drew a pistol and fired. Blood spurted from Bragg's left calf and the pirate howled and crumpled to earth. He groaned and clutched at his wounded leg.

Nkenai moved quickly to disarm his comrade to prevent him from doing anything rash.

"Oh, sweet mother of God," Bragg groaned through clenched teeth. A lizard darted out from under a rock and across a patch of blood on the earth.

Navarre turned and held the smoking gun up to Father Bernal's face. The priest grew pale. He had never in his life confronted such raw evil. It left him speechless. The groaning from poor Tom Bragg punctuated the priest's silence. Finally Father Bernal spoke out in indignation.

"This man is your trusted comrade. How could you treat him in so base a manner? What kind of monster are you?"

"Precisely," Navarre said, drawing close to Bernal and placing his hand on the smaller man's shoulder. "Hear me, priest. This man was like my brother. Look at him and think to yourself what course my wrath might take toward the men, women, and children of Natividad who mean no more to me than what I leave in my chamber pot."

Bernal grew pale and his rail-thin frame shuddered at the thought of the endless possibilities, each one more gruesome than the one before.

"In the name of God . . . " he muttered.

"I leave you your God," said Navarre. "But Natividad is mine." He returned the gun to his belt. The Cayman waved a hand, and NKenai took the priest by the arm and started him back down the shell paved road to town. Bragg was carried away to the ship's surgeon to have his wound staunched and cauterized. Navarre tucked a small pouch of Spanish doubloons into Bragg's shirt as he was carried off. "The gold will ease the pain," Navarre told the African who returned to his captain's side.

NKenai nodded. He could see the brilliance in the Cayman's scheme. "Now the Christian shaman will guide his people in the proper way. He will see they do your bidding. You are a clever man, my captain. The heart of a lion but the crafty mind of the fox has Captain Orturo Navarre. Orturo the Magnificent."

Navarre grinned and looked out across the bay, dominated by his brig and guarded by the shore batteries he now commanded. The first stage of his empire. He was filled with a sense of triumph. "I will make these people my own; Natividad shall be my kingdom." He held out his arms as if to embrace the earth and sea and the limitless horizon. "This is only the beginning, NKenai. Who is there to stand against me?" His chest swelled as the wind pressed against him, and with fists clenched the Cayman shouted in exultation—"Who can stand against me!"

Kit McQueen wasn't laughing as the British marine clubbed him with the butt of his musket and sent the red-headed American sprawling in the dirt alongside the lightning-shattered hickory tree that served as a makeshift redoubt. The fallen timber capped a ridge of earth above Drake's Creek five miles east of the Mississippi River. It was the first day of 1815. "And about to be the last for me," Kit thought as the heavyset Cornishman landed on his chest and drew a dagger from his white canvas belt. Kit could read the name stitched into the marine's leather cartridge box. *Tregoning*.

"Now, you Yankee bastard, I'll lift that red scalp of yours the same as your heathen friends would do to me," Tregoning snarled. White spittle clung to his lower lip. His brown eyes widened, his nostrils flared, and his hands trembled with the bloodlust that was upon him. His breath was heavy with the rum he and his mates had been sampling when the Choctaws surprised them.

Kit worked a hand loose from underneath the man straddling him and grabbed a fistful of Tregoning's genitals and squeezed with all his strength. The marine howled, and thrust his knife, but the pain ruined his aim and the blade sank up to the hilt in the black earth inches from McQueen's throat. The marine grabbed the smaller man by the front of his loose-fitting buckskin shirt and dragged him to his feet, forcing Kit to lose his hold.

"You Brits can sing a pretty note," McQueen taunted. He felt the leather cord tear from around his neck as Tregoning staggered back, clutching a torn patch of shirt and the medal, a silver English crown sterling bearing the crudely scrawled initials of George Washington. The coin was a family keepsake, for General Washington himself had presented the makeshift medal to Kit's father, Daniel McQueen.

The English marine glanced around and saw his companions had abandoned him among his enemies. The English private knew when to cut his losses. He spun around and leaped over the log and started down the creekbank. He spied the rest of the skirmishers fleeing into the trees on the other side of the creek. The cowards had scattered at the first volley from the American and his Choctaw allies.

"No, you don't," Kit shouted, and vaulted the fallen hickory. He landed square on the burly Cornishman's shoulders. The impact tumbled them both down the creekbank and left the men splashing in the muddy shallows. The three remaining Choctaw warriors Kit had brought from General Jackson's camp below New Orleans stared at one another in mute amazement, then watched with alarm as another dozen English marines from General Packenham's formidable invasion force filtered through the trees. The soldiers wore faded red coats and white linen trousers and short-brimmed black hats. Their features were windburned masks of menace.

Kit and Tregoning weren't alone in the creek. They shared the mud with three dead marines and a dead Choctaw brave. The brave lay belly-down in the mud of the creekbank. His tomahawk was buried in the chest of one of the Englishmen. The rest of Tregoning's companions couched among the trees on the other side of the creek and were feverishly reloading their rifled muskets when reinforcements arrived.

Kit counted a dozen marines rise up from the emerald shadows; a dozen muskets were aimed at him. McQueen hauled Tregoning, sputtering, out of the water and placed the half-drowned Cornishman between himself and these lethal-looking newcomers about thirty yards away.

"Kill me and you'll kill your mate." Kit shouted, figuring he had the reinforcements stymied. Tregoning would shield him all the way up the embankment to safety. The sergeant in command stepped forward, ran a hand across his neatly trimmed beard, and scowled as he recognized Tregoning. "Shoot them down!" he shouted.

"Christ!" Kit dove to one side and Tregoning the other as this second wave of marines opened fire. Kit and Tregoning chose different routes as they scrambled up toward the Choctaw defenders. Slugs sent geysers of earth erupting from the steep bank. At five foot eight, Kit McQueen offered a smaller target than Tregoning. Kit was as nimble as a panther as he climbed the embankment. The Choctaws returned the gunfire in an attempt to cover his retreat. McQueen and Tregoning darted and leaped through a gauntlet of lead death. For all McQueen's feline grace and quickness, he reached the redoubt but a few seconds ahead of Tregoning, who lumbered across the hickory log and slumped wearily alongside the man whom moments ago he'd been attempting to kill.

Tregoning's chest rose and fell as he sucked in the cold damp air. His breath clouded before his lips. He'd lost his hat, revealing a bald head ringed by a fringe of black hair. His nose had been flattened by a well-thrown punch sometime in the past and issued a faint whistling sound with each and every breath.

Kit McQueen, with his keen bronze gaze, shrewdly appraised his adversary. McQueen ran a hand through his curly mane of red hair that Tregoning had recently attempted to lift with scalping knife in hand. Slugs gouged the makeshift barricade, showering both men with splinters. One of the Choctaws, a youthful brave named Three Snakes, clutched his throat as he rose up to take aim. The brave slumped onto his side and stared with a weakening gaze at the rivulet of blood showing from his wound. Kit watched the man die and his features grew dark with fury. A waste, a damn waste.

"Your friends have won this day, Tregoning. But there will come another, mark my words."

"Friends, hell," Tregoning said. "Your heathens scattered my mates. Them behind the trees are the Chiltern Rifles. They answer only to Sergeant Tiberius, who has no use for me at all."

"So I noticed," Kit dryly observed.

"He caught me playing at 'bushy park' with his dear Megan and has been trying to center me in his sights ever since. Reckon he figures to kill me and blame it on the likes of you." Tregoning wagged his bald head and scratched at his grizzled jawline. "Megan was his wife and a trollop and he's well off to know the old gal for what she is, mark my words." He glanced across at Kit, who finished reloading a matched pair of short-barreled, heavy-bore pistols he called "The Quakers." One shot from these "hand cannons" made enemies into friends or left them dead. Either result was acceptable to Kit McQueen.

"See here—what the devil?" Tregoning noted as Kit trained the pistols at him.

"You're my prisoner," Kit said. "And I'll take that coin in your hand." Kit tucked one pistol in its buckskin holster and held out a mud-grimed palm.

Tregoning frowned, then shrugged and handed over the coin that had become a McQueen legacy. Surrender to the redheaded American squatting at his side seemed preferable to facing the outraged husband, Tiberius Smollet.

"Tregoning! Harry Tregoning!" the sergeant on the opposite creekbank called out. "Stand up so I can see that ugly face of yours."

Kit peered over the edge of the tree trunk and saw that the Chiltern Rifles were reloading and fixing bayonets. He looked back at the two remaining Choctaws. Nate Russell was a year older than McQueen, a warrior of thirty-one winters. He had long black hair and a solid muscular build and wore a blue infantryman's jacket over his buckskin shirt. Nate, like many of the Choctaw Nation, had converted to Christianity. The other warrior, Strikes With Club was a decade younger and had no use for white man's religion. His long hair hung unbound to his shoulders. He was shivering, for he'd cast aside his blanket to free his arms for fighting. He was a handsome brave and much sought after by the maidens of his village.

"Where's Obregon?" Strikes with Club growled. "You said the others would come when they heard our guns."

Kit had no answer for his red-skinned friend. Cesar Obregon, known throughout the Caribbean as The Hawk of the Antilles and whose black flag depicted a skeleton kneeling in prayer, had taken up a position along McQueen's backtrail about a hundred yards from Drake's Creek. The freebooter and his men should have come running at the sound of gunfire. It had been a cold gray afternoon and an interminable-seeming wait, yet Kit and his Choctaws had remained at their post, hoping to intercept the British soldiers who had been studying the American entrenchments below New Orleans. Kit had the disturbing feeling that Cesar and his men had tired of the wintry discomfort and returned to New Orleans without alerting their companions by the creek.

A ripple of musket fire sounded below and another round of slugs thudded into the hickory log, forcing the men behind the makeshift rampart to crouch down.

"Hey, Yankee, be a good lad and haul up that no-good soldier of the king who's with you. Prepare to meet your maker, Harry."

"Now see here, Tiberius," the Cornishman shouted back. "I didn't do nothin' to your Meg that she didn't want me to do."

"You son of a bitch!" came the reply punctuated by a pistol crack.

Harry Tregoning chuckled as shattered bark showered his chest and head.

Kit scowled. He was caught in the middle of two wars, one major and one private. *And if I live to meet up with Cesar Obregon, I'll start a third,* Kit promised himself. Maybe he ought to force Tregoning over the top and allow the marine to buy them some time as Kit and the Choctaws made good their escape. Tregoning seemed to read McQueen's thoughts.

"Now see here, I surrendered right and proper," the marine protested. He didn't like the look in Kit's hard eyes.

"Surrendered hell, you damn near put a knife in my gullet," Kit said, his bronze eyes flashed with fire.

"Well . . . we weren't friends then." Tregoning tried his most winning smile. It came out a crooked leer.

"This Meg Smollet must be blind," Kit said.

"There's something about us men of Cornwall, the women can't keep their bloody hands off us. 'Tis a cruel lot to bear. Too many women can leech a man of his strength. Suck him dry and wither him before his prime. Mistress Smollet did her part."

"Maybe I'll do Tiberius a favor and shoot you myself," Kit said, rolling his eyes and shaking his head in exasperation. What sort of character was this? Kit thought. A minute ago these two were trying to kill each other and now Harry Tregoning was spinning tall tales of his life history as if he were sharing a campfire with the American. It was an amusing notion, an irony to stop and enjoy sometime when it wouldn't get him killed.

Kit swore the next time he picked a human shield he'd have to be more careful. Tregoning might be more trouble than he was worth.

"You staying?" Nate asked. His pistols were loaded and his rifle cocked and primed. Strikes With Club, standing at the blue-jacketed warrior's side, looked as determined as the older brave. Kit had fought the Creeks at Horse Shoe Bend almost a year ago in the good company of these same warriors and the rest of their tribe. He counted many friends among the Choctaw and found them to be brave and crafty fighters, men not given to suicidal tactics.

"Let them come to us. Then we'll make our break for the woods over yonder," Kit said, indicating a grove of oak and hickory blocking their backtrail.

"We won't have long to wait," Nate said, dusting his flashpan with a trace of black powder from his brass flask.

Kit peered over the log and saw that the Chiltern Rifles had fixed bayonets and were on the move. Sergeant Major Smollet led his men in an uncharacteristic advance. They came at a run, crouched low and howling for blood. Kit turned to Tregoning and said, "Help me." He jammed the butt of his rifle beneath the log and indicated Tregoning should do the same with the musket he had dropped during his struggles with Kit.

"Why?" the Cornishman asked, and then considered the possibilities. He'd been dodging the wrath of Tiberius Smollet ever since leaving London. Enough was enough.

"Very well then," Tregoning said, and threw his weight against the fallen tree. Using the muskets as twin levers the two men dislodged the tree trunk, rocked it forward, and sent it tumbling over the edge of the creekbank. Like some juggernaut it crashed into the midst of the marines as they splashed through the shallows of the creek. The jagged stumps of branches wreaked havoc with British flesh and bone. A ragged fusillade from the Chiltern Rifles filled the air with lead. Kit and Tregoning broke for the trees without waiting to see the results of their handiwork. The crash of timber and the screams from the men below spoke volumes. Nate and Strikes With Club fired as they ran. Kit glanced aside and spied a patch of red uniform and squeezed off a shot from his rifled musket as he dashed for the forest. To his amazement and relief, Kit and the others gained the protection of the thicket without incident and vanished in the gray green gloom of the forest.

Nate took the point followed by Strikes With Club, Tregoning, and Kit McQueen, who reloaded on the move and kept a watchful eye for any telltale sign of their pursuers. The four men had the advantage now. They could move quickly and silently while the Chiltern Rifles would have to carefully pick their way along the trail and guard against ambush. Kit was satisfied to take note that Tregoning was keeping up the pace. The Cornishman did not relish the notion of being captured by Smollet now.

"There'll be a hangman's rope waiting for poor Harry Tregoning should he ever go home again," Kit's prisoner bemoaned.

"You're alive now. No man can ask for more," Kit replied. But his own words sounded hollow to him. He did indeed want more. He wanted retribution. Cesar Obregon was going to pay a dear price for abandoning McQueen and the Choctaws.

The north wind began its banshee howl as the trees thinned and the four men started across the clearing where hours earlier, at midmorning, Kit had ordered Captain Cesar Obregon, the Hawk of the Antilles, and a dozen of his privateers to remain in place. Kit knew the freebooters weren't the kind to follow the commands of one who had not flown the black flag. Kit didn't trust any of them. A man like Cesar Obregon was only as loyal as the depth of the purse paying him. The empty meadow offered testament to Obregon's treachery. Kit called a halt and knelt by a campfire and stirred the cold ashes with his fingertip. The Hawk of the Antilles had "flown the coop" hours ago. But why? He was certainly no coward.

"Looking for your mates, eh?" Tregoning asked. He scrutinized the winter-barren trees, the twisted branches dotted with nests and clumps of mistletoe, branches clacked together like old bones or drooped earthward, bowed beneath a load of moss like widow's weeds. "I don't blame them for leaving." Tregoning shivered.

"The tracks head north to New Orleans," Nate said, kneeling at the perimeter of the clearing. "He's gone on back. But why?"

"Maybe he left something there," Strikes with Club interjected, standing midway between Nate and the remains of the campfire.

"Not 'something'—someone," Kit said, realization slowly dawning. There by the ashes a name had been scrawled in the dirt, left for McQueen to discover as if to taunt him with its implications.

The same soft green eyes, the same coppery features and flirting smile that haunted Kit's heart had caused Cesar Obregon to abandon his inhospitable post for the drawing-room passions and scented boudoirs of New Orleans.

Kit McQueen stood and muttered, "The son of a bitch!" He bolted across the clearing and swept past Nate Russell at a dead run.

"C'mon!" McQueen shouted to the others as he plunged through the underbrush obscuring a deer trail that wound through the timbers. In the wake of his passing, remained Kit's friends, his prisoner, and a name written in the dust.

Raven.

BANTAM DOUBLEDAY DELL
PRESENTS THE
WINNERS CLASSIC SWEEPSTAKES

Dear Bantam Doubleday Dell Reader,

We'd like to say "Thanks" for choosing our books. So we're giving you a chance to enter our Winners Classic Sweepstakes, where you can win a Grand Prize of $25,000.00, or one of over 1,000 other sensational prizes! All prizes are guaranteed to be awarded. Return the Official Entry Form at once! And when you're ready for another great reading experience, we hope you'll keep Bantam Doubleday Dell books at the top of your reading list!

OFFICIAL ENTRY FORM

Yes! Enter me in the Winners Classic Sweepstakes and guarantee my eligibility to be awarded any prize, including the $25,000.00 Grand Prize. Notify me at once if I am declared a winner.

NAME

ADDRESS   APT. #

CITY

STATE   ZIP

REGISTRATION NUMBER   01995A

Please mail to: LL-SBA
BANTAM DOUBLEDAY DELL DIRECT, INC.
WINNERS CLASSIC SWEEPSTAKES
PO Box 985, Hicksville, NY 11802-0985

OFFICIAL PRIZE LIST

GRAND PRIZE: *$25,000.00 CASH!*

FIRST PRIZE: FISHER HOME ENTERTAINMENT CENTER

Including complete integrated audio/video system with 130-watt amplifier, AM/FM stereo tuner, dual cassette deck, CD player, Surround Sound speakers and universal remote control unit.

SECOND PRIZE: TOSHIBA VCR *5 winners!*

Featuring full-function, high-quality 4-Head performance, with 8-event/365-day timer, wireless remote control, and more.

THIRD PRIZE: CONCORD 35MM CAMERA OUTFIT *35 winners!*

Featuring focus-free precision lens, built-in automatic film loading, advance and rewind.

FOURTH PRIZE: BOOK LIGHT *1,000 winners!*

A model of convenience, with a flexible neck that bends in any direction, and a steady clip that holds sure on any surface.

OFFICIAL RULES AND REGULATIONS

No purchase necessary. To enter the sweepstakes follow instructions found elsewhere in this offer. You can also enter the sweepstakes by hand printing your name, address, city, state and zip code on a 3" x 5" piece of paper and mailing it to: Winners Classic Sweepstakes, P.O. Box 785, Gibbstown, NJ 08027. Mail each entry separately. Sweepstakes begins 12/1/91. Entries must be received by 6/1/93. Some presentations of this sweepstakes may feature a deadline for the Early Bird prize. If the offer you receive does, then to be eligible for the Early Bird prize your entry must be received according to the Early Bird date specified. Not responsible for lost, damaged, misdirected, illegible or postage due mail. Mechanically reproduced entries are not eligible. All entries become property of the sponsor and will not be returned.

Prize Selection/Validations: Winners will be selected in random drawings on or about 7/30/93, by Ventura Associates, Inc., an independent judging organization whose decisions are final. Odds of winning are determined by total number of entries received. Circulation of this sweepstakes is estimated not to exceed 200 million. Entrants need not be present to win. All prizes are guaranteed to be awarded and delivered to winners. Winners will be notified by mail and may be required to complete an affidavit of eligibility and release of liability which must be returned within 14 days of date on notification or alternate winners will be selected. Any guest of a trip winner will also be required to execute a release of liability. Any prize notification letter or any prize returned to a participating sponsor, Bantam Doubleday Dell Publishing Group, Inc. its participating divisions or subsidiaries or VENTURA ASSOCIATES, INC. as undeliverable will be awarded to an alternate winner. Prizes are not transferable. No multiple prize winners except for Early Bird Prize, which may be awarded in addition to another prize. No substitution for prizes except as may be necessary due to unavailability in which case a prize of equal or greater value will be awarded. Prizes will be awarded approximately 90 days after the drawing. All taxes, automobile license and registration fees, if applicable, are the sole responsibility of the winners. Entry constitutes permission (except where prohibited) to use winners names and likenesses for publicity purposes without further or other compensation.

Participation: This sweepstakes is open to residents of the United States and Canada, except for the province of Quebec. This sweepstakes is sponsored by Bantam Doubleday Dell Publishing Group, Inc. (BDD), 666 Fifth Avenue, New York, NY 10103. Versions of this sweepstakes with different graphics will be offered in conjunction with various solicitations or promotions by different subsidiaries and divisions of BDD. Employees and their families of BDD, its division, subsidiaries, advertising agencies, and VENTURA ASSOCIATES, INC. are not eligible.

Canadian residents, in order to win, must first correctly answer a time limited arithmetical skill testing question. Void in Quebec and wherever prohibited or restricted by law. Subject to all federal, state, local and provincial laws and regulations.

Prizes: The following values for prizes are determined by the manufacturers' suggested retail prices or by what these items are currently known to be selling for at the time this offer was published. Approximate retail values include handling and delivery of prizes. Estimated maximum retail value of prizes: 1 Grand Prize ($27,500 if merchandise or $25,000 Cash); 1 First Prize ($3,000); 5 Second Prizes ($400 ea); 35 Third Prizes ($100 ea); 1,000 Fourth Prizes ($9.00 ea); 1 Early Bird Prize ($5,000); Total approximate maximum retail value is $50,000. Winners will have the option of selecting any prize offered at level won. Automobile winner must have a valid driver's license at the time the car is awarded. Trips are subject to space and departure availability. Certain black-out dates may apply. Travel must be completed within one year from the time the prize is awarded. Minors must be accompanied by an adult. Prizes won by minors will be awarded in the name of parent or legal guardian.

For a list of Major Prize Winners (available after 7/30/93): send a self-addressed, stamped envelope entirely separate from your entry to Winners Classic Sweepstakes Winners, P.O. Box 825, Gibbstown, NJ 08027. Requests must be received by 6/1/93. DO NOT SEND ANY OTHER CORRESPONDENCE TO THIS P.O. BOX.